TWICE TWENTY-TWO

TWICE TWENTY-TWO

Twice Twenty-two

THE GOLDEN APPLES OF THE SUN

A MEDICINE FOR MELANCHOLY

by Ray Bradbury

DRAWINGS BY JOE MUGNAINI

1966

Doubleday & Company, Inc., Garden City, New York

The book title The Golden Apples of the Sun and the lines from
"The Song of the Wandering Aengus" from THE WIND AMONG THE
REEDS, by W. B. Yeats, are reprinted by permission of
The Macmillan Company.

CONTENTS

THE GOLDEN APPLES OF THE SUN

A MEDICINE FOR MELANCHOLY

The Golden Apples
of the Sun

And this one, with love, is for Neva,
daughter of Glinda
the Good Witch of the South

. . . And pluck till time and times are done
The silver apples of the moon,
The golden apples of the sun.

W. B. YEATS

1

THE FOG HORN

Out there in the cold water, far from land, we waited every night for the coming of the fog, and it came, and we oiled the brass machinery and lit the fog light up in the stone tower. Feeling like two birds in the gray sky, McDunn and I sent the light touching out, red, then white, then red again, to eye the lonely ships. And if they did not see our light, then there was always our Voice, the great deep cry of our Fog Horn shuddering through the rags of mist to startle the gulls away like decks of scattered cards and make the waves turn high and foam.

"It's a lonely life, but you're used to it now, aren't you?" asked McDunn.

"Yes," I said. "You're a good talker, thank the Lord."

"Well, it's your turn on land tomorrow," he said, smiling, "to dance the ladies and drink gin."

"What do you think, McDunn, when I leave you out here alone?"

"On the mysteries of the sea." McDunn lit his pipe. It was a quarter past seven of a cold November evening, the heat on, the light switching its tail in two hundred directions, the Fog Horn bumbling in the high throat of the tower. There wasn't a town

for a hundred miles down the coast, just a road which came lonely through dead country to the sea, with few cars on it, a stretch of two miles of cold water out to our rock, and rare few ships.

"The mysteries of the sea," said McDunn thoughtfully. "You know, the ocean's the biggest damned snowflake ever? It rolls and swells a thousand shapes and colors, no two alike. Strange. One night, years ago, I was here alone, when all of the fish of the sea surfaced out there. Something made them swim in and lie in the bay, sort of trembling and staring up at the tower light going red, white, red, white across them so I could see their funny eyes. I turned cold. They were like a big peacock's tail, moving out there until midnight. Then, without so much as a sound, they slipped away, the million of them was gone. I kind of think maybe, in some sort of way, they came all those miles to worship. Strange. But think how the tower must look to them, standing seventy feet above the water, the God-light flashing out from it, and the tower declaring itself with a monster voice. They never came back, those fish, but don't you think for a while they thought they were in the Presence?"

I shivered. I looked out at the long gray lawn of the sea stretching away into nothing and nowhere.

"Oh, the sea's full." McDunn puffed his pipe nervously, blinking. He had been nervous all day and hadn't said why. "For all our engines and so-called submarines, it'll be ten thousand centuries before we set foot on the real bottom of the sunken lands, in the fairy kingdoms there, and know *real* terror. Think of it, it's still the year 300,000 Before Christ down under there. While we've paraded around with trumpets, lopping off each other's countries and heads, they have been living beneath the sea twelve miles deep and cold in a time as old as the beard of a comet."

"Yes, it's an old world."

"Come on. I got something special I been saving up to tell you."

We ascended the eighty steps, talking and taking our time. At the top, McDunn switched off the room lights so there'd be no

reflection in the plate glass. The great eye of the light was humming, turning easily in its oiled socket. The Fog Horn was blowing steadily, once every fifteen seconds.

"Sounds like an animal, don't it?" McDunn nodded to himself.
"A big lonely animal crying in the night. Sitting here on the edge
of ten billion years calling out to the Deeps, I'm here, I'm here,
I'm here. And the Deeps *do* answer, yes, they do. You been
here now for three months, Johnny, so I better prepare you.
About this time of year," he said, studying the murk and fog,
"something comes to visit the lighthouse."

"The swarms of fish like you said?"

"No, this is something else. I've put off telling you because you
might think I'm daft. But tonight's the latest I can put it off, for if
my calendar's marked right from last year, tonight's the night it
comes. I won't go into detail, you'll have to see it yourself. Just
sit down there. If you want, tomorrow you can pack your duffel
and take the motorboat in to land and get your car parked there
at the dinghy pier on the cape and drive on back to some little
inland town and keep your lights burning nights, I won't question or blame you. It's happened three years now, and this is the
only time anyone's been here with me to verify it. You wait and
watch."

Half an hour passed with only a few whispers between us.
When we grew tired waiting, McDunn began describing some of
his ideas to me. He had some theories about the Fog Horn itself.

"One day many years ago a man walked along and stood in
the sound of the ocean on a cold sunless shore and said, 'We
need a voice to call across the water, to warn ships; I'll make one.
I'll make a voice like all of time and all of the fog that ever was;
I'll make a voice that is like an empty bed beside you all night
long, and like an empty house when you open the door, and like
trees in autumn with no leaves. A sound like the birds flying
south, crying, and a sound like November wind and the sea on
the hard, cold shore. I'll make a sound that's so alone that no
one can miss it, that whoever hears it will weep in their souls,
and hearths will seem warmer, and being inside will seem better

to all who hear it in the distant towns. I'll make me a sound and an apparatus and they'll call it a Fog Horn and whoever hears it will know the sadness of eternity and the briefness of life.'"

The Fog Horn blew.

"I made up that story," said McDunn quietly, "to try to explain why this thing keeps coming back to the lighthouse every year. The Fog Horn calls it, I think, and it comes. . . ."

"But——" I said.

"Sssst!" said McDunn. "There!" He nodded out to the Deeps.

Something was swimming toward the lighthouse tower.

It was a cold night, as I have said; the high tower was cold, the light coming and going, and the Fog Horn calling and calling through the raveling mist. You couldn't see far and you couldn't see plain, but there was the deep sea moving on its way about the night earth, flat and quiet, the color of gray mud, and here were the two of us alone in the high tower, and there, far out at first, was a ripple, followed by a wave, a rising, a bubble, a bit of froth. And then, from the surface of the cold sea came a head, a large head, dark-colored, with immense eyes, and then a neck. And then—not a body—but more neck and more! The head rose a full forty feet above the water on a slender and beautiful dark neck. Only then did the body, like a little island of black coral and shells and crayfish, drip up from the subterranean. There was a flicker of tail. In all, from head to tip of tail, I estimated the monster at ninety or a hundred feet.

I don't know what I said. I said something.

"Steady, boy, steady," whispered McDunn.

"It's impossible!" I said.

"No, Johnny, *we're* impossible. *It's* like it always was ten million years ago. *It* hasn't changed. It's *us* and the land that've changed, become impossible. *Us!*"

It swam slowly and with a great dark majesty out in the icy waters, far away. The fog came and went about it, momentarily erasing its shape. One of the monster eyes caught and held and flashed back our immense light, red, white, red, white, like a disk

held high and sending a message in primeval code. It was as silent as the fog through which it swam.

"It's a dinosaur of some sort!" I crouched down, holding to the stair rail.

"Yes, one of the tribe."

"But they died out!"

"No, only hid away in the Deeps. Deep, deep down in the deepest Deeps. Isn't *that* a word now, Johnny, a real word, it says so much: the Deeps. There's all the coldness and darkness and deepness in the world in a word like that."

"What'll we do?"

"Do? We got our job, we can't leave. Besides, we're safer here than in any boat trying to get to land. That thing's as big as a destroyer and almost as swift."

"But here, why does it come *here?*"

The next moment I had my answer.

The Fog Horn blew.

And the monster answered.

A cry came across a million years of water and mist. A cry so anguished and alone that it shuddered in my head and my body. The monster cried out at the tower. The Fog Horn blew. The monster roared again. The Fog Horn blew. The monster opened its great toothed mouth and the sound that came from it was the sound of the Fog Horn itself. Lonely and vast and far away. The sound of isolation, a viewless sea, a cold night, apartness. That was the sound.

"Now," whispered McDunn, "do you know why it comes here?"

I nodded.

"All year long, Johnny, that poor monster there lying far out, a thousand miles at sea, and twenty miles deep maybe, biding its time, perhaps it's a million years old, this one creature. Think of it, waiting a million years; could *you* wait that long? Maybe it's the last of its kind. I sort of think that's true. Anyway, here come men on land and build this lighthouse, five years ago. And set up their Fog Horn and sound it and sound it out toward the place where you bury yourself in sleep and sea memories of a world

where there were thousands like yourself, but now you're alone, all alone in a world not made for you, a world where you have to hide.

"But the sound of the Fog Horn comes and goes, comes and goes, and you stir from the muddy bottom of the Deeps, and your eyes open like the lenses of two-foot cameras and you move, slow, slow, for you have the ocean sea on your shoulders, heavy. But that Fog Horn comes through a thousand miles of water, faint and familiar, and the furnace in your belly stokes up, and you begin to rise, slow, slow. You feed yourself on great slakes of cod and minnow, on rivers of jellyfish, and you rise slow through the autumn months, through September when the fogs started, through October with more fog and the horn still calling you on, and then, late in November, after pressurizing yourself day by day, a few feet higher every hour, you are near the surface and still alive. You've got to go slow; if you surfaced all at once you'd explode. So it takes you all of three months to surface, and then a number of days to swim through the cold waters to the lighthouse. And there you are, out there, in the night, Johnny, the biggest damn monster in creation. And here's the lighthouse calling to you, with a long neck like your neck sticking way up out of the water, and a body like your body, and, most important of all, a voice like your voice. Do you understand now, Johnny, do you understand?"

The Fog Horn blew.

The monster answered.

I saw it all, I knew it all—the million years of waiting alone, for someone to come back who never came back. The million years of isolation at the bottom of the sea, the insanity of time there, while the skies cleared of reptile-birds, the swamps dried on the continental lands, the sloths and saber-tooths had their day and sank in tar pits, and men ran like white ants upon the hills.

The Fog Horn blew.

"Last year," said McDunn, "that creature swam round and round, round and round, all night. Not coming too near, puzzled,

I'd say. Afraid, maybe. And a bit angry after coming all this way. But the next day, unexpectedly, the fog lifted, the sun came out fresh, the sky was as blue as a painting. And the monster swam off away from the heat and the silence and didn't come back. I suppose it's been brooding on it for a year now, thinking it over from every which way."

The monster was only a hundred yards off now, it and the Fog Horn crying at each other. As the lights hit them, the monster's eyes were fire and ice, fire and ice.

"That's life for you," said McDunn. "Someone always waiting for someone who never comes home. Always someone loving some thing more than that thing loves them. And after a while you want to destroy whatever that thing is, so it can't hurt you no more."

The monster was rushing at the lighthouse.

The Fog Horn blew.

"Let's see what happens," said McDunn.

He switched the Fog Horn off.

The ensuing minute of silence was so intense that we could hear our hearts pounding in the glassed area of the tower, could hear the slow greased turn of the light.

The monster stopped and froze. Its great lantern eyes blinked. Its mouth gaped. It gave a sort of rumble, like a volcano. It twitched its head this way and that, as if to seek the sounds now dwindled off into the fog. It peered at the lighthouse. It rumbled again. Then its eyes caught fire. It reared up, threshed the water, and rushed at the tower, its eyes filled with angry torment.

"McDunn!" I cried. "Switch on the horn!"

McDunn fumbled with the switch. But even as he flicked it on, the monster was rearing up. I had a glimpse of its gigantic paws, fishskin glittering in webs between the fingerlike projections, clawing at the tower. The huge eye on the right side of its anguished head glittered before me like a caldron into which I might drop, screaming. The tower shook. The Fog Horn cried; the monster cried. It seized the tower and gnashed at the glass, which shattered in upon us.

McDunn seized my arm. "Downstairs!"

The tower rocked, trembled, and started to give. The Fog Horn and the monster roared. We stumbled and half fell down the stairs. "Quick!"

We reached the bottom as the tower buckled down toward us. We ducked under the stairs into the small stone cellar. There were a thousand concussions as the rocks rained down; the Fog Horn stopped abruptly. The monster crashed upon the tower. The tower fell. We knelt together, McDunn and I, holding tight, while our world exploded.

Then it was over, and there was nothing but darkness and the wash of the sea on the raw stones.

That and the other sound.

"Listen," said McDunn quietly. "Listen."

We waited a moment. And then I began to hear it. First a great vacuumed sucking of air, and then the lament, the bewilderment, the loneliness of the great monster, folded over and upon us, above us, so that the sickening reek of its body filled the air, a stone's thickness away from our cellar. The monster gasped and cried. The tower was gone. The light was gone. The thing that had called to it across a million years was gone. And the monster was opening its mouth and sending out great sounds. The sounds of a Fog Horn, again and again. And ships far at sea, not finding the light, not seeing anything, but passing and hearing late that night, must've thought: There it is, the lonely sound, the Lonesome Bay horn. All's well. We've rounded the cape.

And so it went for the rest of that night.

The sun was hot and yellow the next afternoon when the rescuers came out to dig us from our stoned-under cellar.

"It fell apart, is all," said Mr. McDunn gravely. "We had a few bad knocks from the waves and it just crumbled." He pinched my arm.

There was nothing to see. The ocean was calm, the sky blue. The only thing was a great algaic stink from the green matter

that covered the fallen tower stones and the shore rocks. Flies buzzed about. The ocean washed empty on the shore.

The next year they built a new lighthouse, but by that time I had a job in the little town and a wife and a good small warm house that glowed yellow on autumn nights, the doors locked, the chimney puffing smoke. As for McDunn, he was master of the new lighthouse, built to his own specifications, out of steel-reinforced concrete. "Just in case," he said.

The new lighthouse was ready in November. I drove down alone one evening late and parked my car and looked across the gray waters and listened to the new horn sounding, once, twice, three, four times a minute far out there, by itself.

The monster?

It never came back.

"It's gone away," said McDunn. "It's gone back to the Deeps. It's learned you can't love anything too much in this world. It's gone into the deepest Deeps to wait another million years. Ah, the poor thing! Waiting out there, and waiting out there, while man comes and goes on this pitiful little planet. Waiting and waiting."

I sat in my car, listening. I couldn't see the lighthouse or the light standing out in Lonesome Bay. I could only hear the Horn, the Horn, the Horn. It sounded like the monster calling.

I sat there wishing there was something I could say.

2

THE PEDESTRIAN

To enter out into that silence that was the city at eight o'clock of a misty evening in November, to put your feet upon that buckling concrete walk, to step over grassy seams and make your way, hands in pockets, through the silences, that was what Mr. Leonard Mead most dearly loved to do. He would stand upon the corner of an intersection and peer down long moonlit avenues of sidewalk in four directions, deciding which way to go, but it really made no difference; he was alone in this world of 2052 A.D., or as good as alone, and with a final decision made, a path selected, he would stride off, sending patterns of frosty air before him like the smoke of a cigar.

Sometimes he would walk for hours and miles and return only at midnight to his house. And on his way he would see the cottages and homes with their dark windows, and it was not unequal to walking through a graveyard where only the faintest glimmers of firefly light appeared in flickers behind the windows. Sudden gray phantoms seemed to manifest upon inner room walls where a curtain was still undrawn against the night, or there were whisperings and murmurs where a window in a tomb-like building was still open.

Mr. Leonard Mead would pause, cock his head, listen, look, and march on, his feet making no noise on the lumpy walk. For long ago he had wisely changed to sneakers when strolling at night, because the dogs in intermittent squads would parallel his journey with barkings if he wore hard heels, and lights might click on and faces appear and an entire street be startled by the passing of a lone figure, himself, in the early November evening.

On this particular evening he began his journey in a westerly direction, toward the hidden sea. There was a good crystal frost in the air; it cut the nose and made the lungs blaze like a Christmas tree inside; you could feel the cold light going on and off, all the branches filled with invisible snow. He listened to the faint push of his soft shoes through autumn leaves with satisfaction, and whistled a cold quiet whistle between his teeth, occasionally picking up a leaf as he passed, examining its skeletal pattern in the infrequent lamplights as he went on, smelling its rusty smell.

"Hello, in there," he whispered to every house on every side as he moved. "What's up tonight on Channel 4, Channel 7, Channel 9? Where are the cowboys rushing, and do I see the United States Cavalry over the next hill to the rescue?"

The street was silent and long and empty, with only his shadow moving like the shadow of a hawk in mid-country. If he closed his eyes and stood very still, frozen, he could imagine himself upon the center of a plain, a wintry, windless Arizona desert with no house in a thousand miles, and only dry river beds, the streets, for company.

"What is it now?" he asked the houses, noticing his wrist watch. "Eight-thirty P.M.? Time for a dozen assorted murders? A quiz? A revue? A comedian falling off the stage?"

Was that a murmur of laughter from within a moon-white house? He hesitated, but went on when nothing more happened. He stumbled over a particularly uneven section of sidewalk. The cement was vanishing under flowers and grass. In ten years of walking by night or day, for thousands of miles, he had never met another person walking, not one in all that time.

He came to a cloverleaf intersection which stood silent where

two main highways crossed the town. During the day it was a thunderous surge of cars, the gas stations open, a great insect rustling and a ceaseless jockeying for position as the scarab-beetles, a faint incense puttering from their exhausts, skimmed homeward to the far directions. But now these highways, too, were like streams in a dry season, all stone and bed and moon radiance.

He turned back on a side street, circling around toward his home. He was within a block of his destination when the lone car turned a corner quite suddenly and flashed a fierce white cone of light upon him. He stood entranced, not unlike a night moth, stunned by the illumination, and then drawn toward it.

A metallic voice called to him:

"Stand still. Stay where you are! Don't move!"

He halted.

"Put up your hands!"

"But——" he said.

"Your hands up! Or we'll shoot!"

The police, of course, but what a rare, incredible thing; in a city of three million, there was only *one* police car left, wasn't that correct? Ever since a year ago, 2052, the election year, the force had been cut down from three cars to one. Crime was ebbing; there was no need now for the police, save for this one lone car wandering and wandering the empty streets.

"Your name?" said the police car in a metallic whisper. He couldn't see the men in it for the bright light in his eyes.

"Leonard Mead," he said.

"Speak up!"

"Leonard Mead!"

"Business or profession?"

"I guess you'd call me a writer."

"No profession," said the police car, as if talking to itself. The light held him fixed, like a museum specimen, needle thrust through chest.

"You might say that," said Mr. Mead. He hadn't written in years. Magazines and books didn't sell any more. Everything went

on in the tomblike houses at night now, he thought, continuing
his fancy. The tombs, ill-lit by television light, where the people
sat like the dead, the gray or multicolored lights touching their
faces, but never really touching *them*.

"No profession," said the phonograph voice, hissing. "What
are you doing out?"

"Walking," said Leonard Mead.

"Walking!"

"Just walking," he said simply, but his face felt cold.

"Walking, just walking, walking?"

"Yes, sir."

"Walking where? For what?"

"Walking for air. Walking to *see*."

"Your address!"

"Eleven South Saint James Street."

"And there is air *in* your house, you have an air *conditioner*,
Mr. Mead?"

"Yes."

"And you have a viewing screen in your house to see with?"

"No."

"No?" There was a crackling quiet that in itself was an
accusation.

"Are you married, Mr. Mead?"

"No."

"Not married," said the police voice behind the fiery beam.
The moon was high and clear among the stars and the houses
were gray and silent.

"Nobody wanted me," said Leonard Mead with a smile.

"Don't speak unless you're spoken to!"

Leonard Mead waited in the cold night.

"Just *walking*, Mr. Mead?"

"Yes."

"But you haven't explained for what purpose."

"I explained; for air, and to see, and just to walk."

"Have you done this often?"

"Every night for years."

The police car sat in the center of the street with its radio throat faintly humming.

"Well, Mr. Mead," it said.

"Is that all?" he asked politely.

"Yes," said the voice. "Here." There was a sigh, a pop. The back door of the police car sprang wide. "Get in."

"Wait a minute, I haven't done anything!"

"Get in."

"I protest!"

"Mr. Mead."

He walked like a man suddenly drunk. As he passed the front window of the car he looked in. As he had expected, there was no one in the front seat, no one in the car at all.

"Get in."

He put his hand to the door and peered into the back seat, which was a little cell, a little black jail with bars. It smelled of riveted steel. It smelled of harsh antiseptic; it smelled too clean and hard and metallic. There was nothing soft there.

"Now if you had a wife to give you an alibi," said the iron voice. "But——"

"Where are you taking me?"

The car hesitated, or rather gave a faint whirring click, as if information, somewhere, was dropping card by punch-slotted card under electric eyes. "To the Psychiatric Center for Research on Regressive Tendencies."

He got in. The door shut with a soft thud. The police car rolled through the night avenues, flashing its dim lights ahead.

They passed one house on one street a moment later, one house in an entire city of houses that were dark, but this one particular house had all of its electric lights brightly lit, every window a loud yellow illumination, square and warm in the cool darkness.

"That's *my* house," said Leonard Mead.

No one answered him.

The car moved down the empty river-bed streets and off away, leaving the empty streets with the empty sidewalks, and no sound and no motion all the rest of the chill November night.

3

THE APRIL WITCH

Into the air, over the valleys, under the stars, above a river, a pond, a road, flew Cecy. Invisible as new spring winds, fresh as the breath of clover rising from twilight fields, she flew. She soared in doves as soft as white ermine, stopped in trees and lived in blossoms, showering away in petals when the breeze blew. She perched in a lime-green frog, cool as mint by a shining pool. She trotted in a brambly dog and barked to hear echoes from the sides of distant barns. She lived in new April grasses, in sweet clear liquids rising from the musky earth.

It's spring, thought Cecy. I'll be in every living thing in the world tonight.

Now she inhabited neat crickets on the tar-pool roads, now prickled in dew on an iron gate. Hers was an adaptably quick mind flowing unseen upon Illinois winds on this one evening of her life when she was just seventeen.

"I want to be in love," she said.

She had said it at supper. And her parents had widened their eyes and stiffened back in their chairs. "Patience," had been their advice. "Remember, you're remarkable. Our whole family is odd and remarkable. We can't mix or marry with ordinary folk. We'd

lose our magical powers if we did. You wouldn't want to lose *your* ability to 'travel' by magic, would you? Then be careful. Be careful!"

But in her high bedroom, Cecy had touched perfume to her throat and stretched out, trembling and apprehensive, on her four-poster, as a moon the color of milk rose over Illinois country, turning rivers to cream and roads to platinum.

"Yes," she sighed. "I'm one of an odd family. We sleep days and fly nights like black kites on the wind. If we want, we can sleep in moles through the winter, in the warm earth. I can live in anything at all—a pebble, a crocus, or a praying mantis. I can leave my plain, bony body behind and send my mind far out for adventure. Now!"

The wind whipped her away over fields and meadows.

She saw the warm spring lights of cottages and farms glowing with twilight colors.

If I can't be in love, myself, because I'm plain and odd, then I'll be in love through someone else, she thought.

Outside a farmhouse in the spring night a dark-haired girl, no more than nineteen, drew up water from a deep stone well. She was singing.

Cecy fell—a green leaf—into the well. She lay in the tender moss of the well, gazing up through dark coolness. Now she quickened in a fluttering, invisible amoeba. Now in a water droplet! At last, within a cold cup, she felt herself lifted to the girl's warm lips. There was a soft night sound of drinking.

Cecy looked out from the girl's eyes.

She entered into the dark head and gazed from the shining eyes at the hands pulling the rough rope. She listened through the shell ears to this girl's world. She smelled a particular universe through these delicate nostrils, felt this special heart beating, beating. Felt this strange tongue move with singing.

Does she know I'm here? thought Cecy.

The girl gasped. She stared into the night meadows.

"Who's there?"

No answer.

"Only the wind," whispered Cecy.

"Only the wind." The girl laughed at herself, but shivered.

It was a good body, this girl's body. It held bones of finest slender ivory hidden and roundly fleshed. This brain was like a pink tea rose, hung in darkness, and there was cider-wine in this mouth. The lips lay firm on the white, white teeth and the brows arched neatly at the world, and the hair blew soft and fine on her milky neck. The pores knit small and close. The nose tilted at the moon and the cheeks glowed like small fires. The body drifted with feather-balances from one motion to another and seemed always singing to itself. Being in this body, this head, was like basking in a hearth fire, living in the purr of a sleeping cat, stirring in warm creek waters that flowed by night to the sea.

I'll like it here, thought Cecy.

"What?" asked the girl, as if she'd heard a voice.

"What's your name?" asked Cecy carefully.

"Ann Leary." The girl twitched. "Now why should I say *that* out loud?"

"Ann, Ann," whispered Cecy. "Ann, you're going to be in love."

As if to answer this, a great roar sprang from the road, a clatter and a ring of wheels on gravel. A tall man drove up in a rig, holding the reins high with his monstrous arms, his smile glowing across the yard.

"Ann!"

"Is that you, Tom?"

"Who else?" Leaping from the rig, he tied the reins to the fence.

"I'm not speaking to you!" Ann whirled, the bucket in her hands slopping.

"No!" cried Cecy.

Ann froze. She looked at the hills and the first spring stars. She stared at the man named Tom. Cecy made her drop the bucket.

"Look what you've done!"

Tom ran up.

"Look what you *made* me do!"

He wiped her shoes with a kerchief, laughing.

"Get away!" She kicked at his hands, but he laughed again, and gazing down on him from miles away, Cecy saw the turn of his head, the size of his skull, the flare of his nose, the shine of his eye, the girth of his shoulder, and the hard strength of his hands doing this delicate thing with the handkerchief. Peering down from the secret attic of this lovely head, Cecy yanked a hidden copper ventriloquist's wire and the pretty mouth popped wide: "Thank you!"

"Oh, so you *have* manners?" The smell of leather on his hands, the smell of the horse rose from his clothes into the tender nostrils, and Cecy, far, far away over night meadows and flowered fields, stirred as with some dream in her bed.

"Not for you, no!" said Ann.

"Hush, speak gently," said Cecy. She moved Ann's fingers out toward Tom's head. Ann snatched them back.

"I've gone mad!"

"You have." He nodded, smiling but bewildered. "Were you going to touch me then?"

"I don't know. Oh, go away!" Her cheeks glowed with pink charcoals.

"Why don't you run? I'm not stopping you." Tom got up. "Have you changed your mind? Will you go to the dance with me tonight? It's special. Tell you why later."

"No," said Ann.

"Yes!" cried Cecy. "I've never danced. I want to dance. I've never worn a long gown, all rustly. I want that. I want to dance all night. I've never known what it's like to be in a woman, dancing; Father and Mother would never permit it. Dogs, cats, locusts, leaves, everything else in the world at one time or another I've known, but never a woman in the spring, never on a night like this. Oh, please—we *must* go to that dance!"

She spread her thought like the fingers of a hand within a new glove.

"Yes," said Ann Leary, "I'll go. I don't know why, but I'll go to the dance with you tonight, Tom."

"Now inside, quick!" cried Cecy. "You must wash, tell your folks, get your gown ready, out with the iron, into your room!"

"Mother," said Ann, "I've changed my mind!"

The rig was galloping off down the pike, the rooms of the farmhouse jumped to life, water was boiling for a bath, the coal stove was heating an iron to press the gown, the mother was rushing about with a fringe of hairpins in her mouth. "What's come over you, Ann? You don't like Tom!"

"That's true." Ann stopped amidst the great fever.

But it's spring! thought Cecy.

"It's spring," said Ann.

And it's a fine night for dancing, thought Cecy.

". . . for dancing," murmured Ann Leary.

Then she was in the tub and the soap creaming on her white seal shoulders, small nests of soap beneath her arms, and the flesh of her warm breasts moving in her hands and Cecy moving the mouth, making the smile, keeping the actions going. There must be no pause, no hesitation, or the entire pantomime might fall in ruins! Ann Leary must be kept moving, doing, acting, wash here, soap there, now out! Rub with a towel! Now perfume and powder!

"You!" Ann caught herself in the mirror, all whiteness and pinkness like lilies and carnations. "Who are you tonight?"

"I'm a girl seventeen." Cecy gazed from her violet eyes. "You can't see me. Do you know I'm here?"

Ann Leary shook her head. "I've rented my body to an April witch, for sure."

"Close, very close!" laughed Cecy. "Now, on with your dressing."

The luxury of feeling good clothes move over an ample body! And then the halloo outside.

"Ann, Tom's back!"

"Tell him to wait." Ann sat down suddenly. "Tell him I'm not going to that dance."

"What?" said her mother, in the door.

Cecy snapped back into attention. It had been a fatal relaxing, a fatal moment of leaving Ann's body for only an instant. She had heard the distant sound of horses' hoofs and the rig rambling through moonlit spring country. For a second she thought, I'll go find Tom and sit in his head and see what it's like to be in a man of twenty-two on a night like this. And so she had started quickly across a heather field, but now, like a bird to a cage, flew back and rustled and beat about in Ann Leary's head.

"Ann!"

"Tell him to go away!"

"Ann!" Cecy settled down and spread her thoughts.

But Ann had the bit in her mouth now. "No, no, I hate him!"

I shouldn't have left—even for a moment. Cecy poured her mind into the hands of the young girl, into the heart, into the head, softly, softly. *Stand up,* she thought.

Ann stood.

Put on your coat!

Ann put on her coat.

Now, march!

No! thought Ann Leary.

March!

"Ann," said her mother, "don't keep Tom waiting another minute. You get on out there now and no nonsense. What's come over you?"

"Nothing, Mother. Good night. We'll be home late."

Ann and Cecy ran together into the spring evening.

A room full of softly dancing pigeons ruffling their quiet, trailing feathers, a room full of peacocks, a room full of rainbow eyes and lights. And in the center of it, around, around, around, danced Ann Leary.

"Oh, it *is* a fine evening," said Cecy.

"Oh, it's a fine evening," said Ann.

"You're odd," said Tom.

The music whirled them in dimness, in rivers of song; they floated, they bobbed, they sank down, they arose for air, they

gasped, they clutched each other like drowning people and whirled on again, in fan motions, in whispers and sighs, to "Beautiful Ohio."

Cecy hummed. Ann's lips parted and the music came out.

"Yes, I'm odd," said Cecy.

"You're not the same," said Tom.

"No, not tonight."

"You're not the Ann Leary I knew."

"No, not at all, at all," whispered Cecy, miles and miles away. "No, not at all," said the moved lips.

"I've the funniest feeling," said Tom.

"About what?"

"About you." He held her back and danced her and looked into her glowing face, watching for something. "Your eyes," he said, "I can't figure it."

"Do you see *me?*" asked Cecy.

"Part of you's here, Ann, and part of you's not." Tom turned her carefully, his face uneasy.

"Yes."

"Why did you come with me?"

"I didn't want to come," said Ann.

"Why, then?"

"Something made me."

"What?"

"I don't know." Ann's voice was faintly hysterical.

"Now, now, hush, hush," whispered Cecy. "Hush, that's it. Around, around."

They whispered and rustled and rose and fell away in the dark room, with the music moving and turning them.

"But you *did* come to the dance," said Tom.

"I did," said Cecy.

"Here." And he danced her lightly out an open door and walked her quietly away from the hall and the music and the people.

They climbed up and sat together in the rig.

"Ann," he said, taking her hands, trembling. "Ann." But the

way he said her name it was as if it wasn't her name. He kept glancing into her pale face, and now her eyes were open again. "I used to love you, you know that," he said.

"I know."

"But you've always been fickle and I didn't want to be hurt."

"It's just as well, we're very young," said Ann.

"No, I mean to say, I'm sorry," said Cecy.

"What *do* you mean?" Tom dropped her hands and stiffened.

The night was warm and the smell of the earth shimmered up all about them where they sat, and the fresh trees breathed one leaf against another in a shaking and rustling.

"I don't know," said Ann.

"Oh, but *I* know," said Cecy. "You're tall and you're the finest-looking man in all the world. This is a good evening; this is an evening I'll always remember, being with you." She put out the alien cold hand to find his reluctant hand again and bring it back, and warm it and hold it very tight.

"But," said Tom, blinking, "tonight you're here, you're there. One minute one way, the next minute another. I wanted to take you to the dance tonight for old times' sake. I meant nothing by it when I first asked you. And then, when we were standing at the well, I knew something had changed, really changed, about you. You were different. There was something new and soft, something . . ." He groped for a word. "I don't know, I can't say. The way you looked. Something about your voice. And I know I'm in love with you again."

"No," said Cecy. "With me, with *me*."

"And I'm afraid of being in love with you," he said. "You'll hurt me again."

"I might," said Ann.

No, no, I'd love you with all my heart! thought Cecy. Ann, say it to him, say it for me. Say you'd love him with all your heart.

Ann said nothing.

Tom moved quietly closer and put his hand up to hold her chin. "I'm going away. I've got a job a hundred miles from here. Will you miss me?"

"Yes," said Ann and Cecy.

"May I kiss you good-by, then?"

"Yes," said Cecy before anyone else could speak.

He placed his lips to the strange mouth. He kissed the strange mouth and he was trembling.

Ann sat like a white statue.

"Ann!" said Cecy. "Move your arms, *hold* him!"

She sat like a carved wooden doll in the moonlight.

Again he kissed her lips.

"I do love you," whispered Cecy. "I'm here, it's me you saw in her eyes, it's me, and I love you if she never will."

He moved away and seemed like a man who had run a long distance. He sat beside her. "I don't know what's happening. For a moment there . . ."

"Yes?" asked Cecy.

"For a moment I thought——" He put his hands to his eyes. "Never mind. Shall I take you home now?"

"Please," said Ann Leary.

He clucked to the horse, snapped the reins tiredly, and drove the rig away. They rode in the rustle and slap and motion of the moonlit rig in the still early, only eleven o'clock spring night, with the shining meadows and sweet fields of clover gliding by.

And Cecy, looking at the fields and meadows, thought, It would be worth it, it would be worth everything to be with him from this night on. And she heard her parents' voices again, faintly, "Be careful. You wouldn't want to lose your magical powers, would you—married to a mere mortal? Be careful. You wouldn't want that."

Yes, yes, thought Cecy, even that I'd give up, here and now, if he would have me. I wouldn't need to roam the spring nights then, I wouldn't need to live in birds and dogs and cats and foxes, I'd need only to be with him. Only him. Only him.

The road passed under, whispering.

"Tom," said Ann at last.

"What?" He stared coldly at the road, the horse, the trees, the sky, the stars.

"If you're ever, in years to come, at any time, in Green Town, Illinois, a few miles from here, will you do me a favor?"

"Perhaps."

"Will you do me the favor of stopping and seeing a friend of mine?" Ann Leary said this haltingly, awkwardly.

"Why?"

"She's a good friend. I've told her of you. I'll give you her address. Just a moment." When the rig stopped at her farm she drew forth a pencil and paper from her small purse and wrote in the moonlight, pressing the paper to her knee. "There it is. Can you read it?"

He glanced at the paper and nodded bewilderedly.

"Cecy Elliott, 12 Willow Street, Green Town, Illinois," he said.

"Will you visit her someday?" asked Ann.

"Someday," he said.

"Promise?"

"What has this to do with us?" he cried savagely. "What do I want with names and papers?" He crumpled the paper into a tight ball and shoved it in his coat.

"Oh, please promise!" begged Cecy.

". . . promise . . ." said Ann.

"All right, all right, now let me be!" he shouted.

I'm tired, thought Cecy. I can't stay. I have to go home. I'm weakening. I've only the power to stay a few hours out like this in the night, traveling, traveling. But before I go . . .

". . . before I go," said Ann.

She kissed Tom on the lips.

"This is *me* kissing you," said Cecy.

Tom held her off and looked at Ann Leary and looked deep, deep inside. He said nothing, but his face began to relax slowly, very slowly, and the lines vanished away, and his mouth softened from its hardness, and he looked deep again into the moonlit face held here before him.

Then he put her off the rig and without so much as good night was driving swiftly down the road.

Cecy let go.

Ann Leary, crying out, released from prison, it seemed, raced up the moonlit path to her house and slammed the door.

Cecy lingered for only a little while. In the eyes of a cricket she saw the spring night world. In the eyes of a frog she sat for a lonely moment by a pool. In the eyes of a night bird she looked down from a tall, moon-haunted elm and saw the lights go out in two farmhouses, one here, one a mile away. She thought of herself and her family, and her strange power, and the fact that no one in the family could ever marry any one of the people in this vast world out here beyond the hills.

"Tom?" Her weakening mind flew in a night bird under the trees and over deep fields of wild mustard. "Have you still got the paper, Tom? Will you come by someday, some year, sometime, to see me? Will you know me then? Will you look in my face and remember then where it was you saw me last and know that you love me as I love you, with all my heart for all time?"

She paused in the cool night air, a million miles from towns and people, above farms and continents and rivers and hills. "Tom?" Softly.

Tom was asleep. It was deep night; his clothes were hung on chairs or folded neatly over the end of the bed. And in one silent, carefully upflung hand upon the white pillow, by his head, was a small piece of paper with writing on it. Slowly, slowly, a fraction of an inch at a time, his fingers closed down upon and held it tightly. And he did not even stir or notice when a blackbird, faintly, wondrously, beat softly for a moment against the clear moon crystals of the windowpane, then, fluttering quietly, stopped and flew away toward the east, over the sleeping earth.

4

THE WILDERNESS

"Oh, the Good Time has come at last——"

It was twilight, and Janice and Leonora packed steadily in their summer house, singing songs, eating little, and holding to each other when necessary. But they never glanced at the window where the night gathered deep and the stars came out bright and cold.

"Listen!" said Janice.

A sound like a steamboat down the river, but it was a rocket in the sky. And beyond that—banjos playing? No, only the summer-night crickets in this year 2003. Ten thousand sounds breathed through the town and the weather. Janice, head bent, listened. Long, long ago, 1849, this very street had breathed the voices of ventriloquists, preachers, fortunetellers, fools, scholars, gamblers, gathered at this selfsame Independence, Missouri. Waiting for the moist earth to bake and the great tidal grasses to come up heavy enough to hold the weight of their carts, their wagons, their indiscriminate destinies, and their dreams.

> *"Oh, the Good Time has come at last,*
> *To Mars we are a-going, sir,*

Five Thousand Women in the sky,
That's quite a springtime sowing, sir!"

"That's an old Wyoming song," said Leonora. "Change the words and it's fine for 2003."

Janice lifted a matchbox of food pills, calculating the totals of things carried in those high-axled, tall-bedded wagons. For each man, each woman, incredible tonnages! Hams, bacon slabs, sugar, salt, flour, dried fruits, "pilot" bread, citric acid, water, ginger, pepper—a list as big as the land! Yet here, today, pills that fit a wrist watch fed you not from Fort Laramie to Hangtown, but all across a wilderness of stars.

Janice threw wide the closet door and almost screamed. Darkness and night and all the spaces between the stars looked out at her.

Long years ago two things had happened. Her sister had locked her, shrieking, in a closet. And, at a party, playing hide-and-seek, she had run through the kitchen and into a long dark hall. But it wasn't a hall. It was an unlit stair well, a swallowing blackness. She had run out upon empty air. She had pedaled her feet, screamed, and fallen! Fallen in midnight blackness. Into the cellar. It took a long while, a heartbeat, to fall. And she had smothered in that closet a long, long time without daylight, without friends, no one to hear her screamings. Away from everything, locked in darkness. Falling in darkness. Shrieking!

The two memories.

Now, with the closet door wide, with darkness like a velvet shroud hung before her to be stroked by a trembling hand, with the darkness like a black panther breathing there, looking at her with unlit eyes, the two memories rushed out. Space and a falling. Space and being locked away, screaming. She and Leonora working steadily, packing, being careful not to glance out the window at the frightening Milky Way and the vast emptiness. Only to have the long-familiar closet, with its private night, remind them at last of their destiny.

This was how it would be, out there, sliding toward the stars,

in the night, in the great hideous black closet, screaming, but no one to hear. Falling forever among meteor clouds and godless comets. Down the elevator shaft. Down the nightmare coal chute into nothingness.

She screamed. None of it came out of her mouth. It collided upon itself in her chest and head. She screamed. She slammed the closet door! She lay against it! She felt the darkness breathe and yammer at the door and she held it tight, eyes watering. She stood there a long time, until the trembling vanished, watching Leonora work. And the hysteria, thus ignored, drained away and away, and at last was gone. A wrist watch ticked, with a clean sound of normality, in the room.

"Sixty *million* miles." She moved at last to the window as if it were a deep well. "I can't believe that men on Mars, tonight, are building towns, waiting for us."

"The only thing to believe is catching our Rocket tomorrow."

Janice raised a white gown like a ghost in the room.

"Strange, strange. To marry—on another world."

"Let's get to bed."

"No! The call comes at midnight. I couldn't sleep, thinking how to tell Will I've decided to take the Mars Rocket. Oh, Leonora, think of it, my voice traveling sixty million miles on the light-phone to him. I changed my mind so quick—I'm scared!"

"Our *last* night on Earth."

Now they really knew and accepted it; now the knowledge had found them out. They were going away, and they might never come back. They were leaving the town of Independence in the state of Missouri on the continent of North America, surrounded by one ocean which was the Atlantic and another the Pacific, none of which could be put in their traveling cases. They had shrunk from this final knowledge. Now it was facing them. And they were struck numb.

"Our children, they won't be Americans, or Earth people at all. We'll all be Martians, the rest of our lives."

"I don't want to go!" cried Janice suddenly.

The panic froze her.

"I'm afraid! The space, the darkness, the Rocket, the meteors! *Everything* gone! Why should I go out there?"

Leonora took hold of her shoulders and held her close, rocking her. "It's a new world. It's like the old days. The men first and the women after."

"Why, why should I go, tell me!"

"Because," said Leonora at last, quietly, seating her on the bed, "Will is up there."

His name was good to hear. Janice quieted.

"These men make it so hard," said Leonora. "Used to be if a woman ran two hundred miles for a man it was something. Then they made it a thousand miles. And now they put a whole universe between us. But that can't stop us, can it?"

"I'm afraid I'll be a fool on the Rocket."

"I'll be a fool with you." Leonora got up. "Now, let's walk around town, let's see everything one last time."

Janice stared out at the town. "Tomorrow night this'll all be here, but we won't. People'll wake up, eat, work, sleep, wake again, but we won't know it, and they'll never miss us."

Leonora and Janice moved around each other as if they couldn't find the door.

"Come on."

They opened the door, switched off the lights, stepped out, and shut the door behind them.

In the sky there was a great coming-in and coming-in. Vast flowering motions, huge whistlings and whirlings, snowstorms falling. Helicopters, white flakes, dropping quietly. From west and east and north and south the women were arriving, arriving. Through all of the night sky you saw helicopters blizzard down. The hotels were full, private homes were making accommodations, tent cities rose in meadows and pastures like strange, ugly flowers, and the town and the country were warm with more than summer tonight. Warm with women's pink faces and the sunburnt faces of new men watching the sky. Beyond the hills rock-

ets tried their fire, and a sound like a giant organ, all its keys pressed upon at once, shuddered every crystal window and every hidden bone. You felt it in your jaw, your toes, your fingers, a shivering.

Leonora and Janice sat in the drugstore among unfamiliar women.

"You ladies look very pretty, but you sure look sad," said the soda-fountain man.

"Two chocolate malteds." Leonora smiled for both of them, as if Janice were mute.

They gazed at the chocolate drink as if it were a rare museum painting. Malts would be scarce for many years on Mars.

Janice fussed in her purse and took out an envelope reluctantly and laid it on the marble counter.

"This is from Will to me. It came in the Rocket mail two days ago. It was this that made up my mind for me, made me decide to go. I didn't tell you. I want you to see it now. Go ahead, read the note."

Leonora shook the note out of the envelope and read it aloud:

"Dear Janice: This is our *house if you decide to come to Mars. Will."*

Leonora tapped the envelope again, and a color photograph dropped out, glistening, on the counter. It was a picture of a house, a dark, mossy, ancient, caramel-brown, comfortable house with red flowers and green cool ferns bordering it, and a disreputably hairy ivy on the porch.

"But, Janice!"

"What?"

"This is a picture of *your* house, here on Earth, here on Elm Street!"

"No. Look close."

And they looked again, together, and on both sides of the comfortable dark house and behind it was scenery that was not Earth scenery. The soil was a strange color of violet, and the grass was the faintest bit red, and the sky glowed like a gray dia-

mond, and a strange crooked tree grew to one side, looking like
an old woman with crystals in her white hair.

"That's the house Will's built for me," said Janice, "on Mars.
It helps to look at it. All yesterday, when I had the chance, alone,
and was most afraid and panicky, I took out this picture and
looked at it."

They both gazed at the dark comfortable house sixty million
miles away, familiar but unfamiliar, old but new, a yellow light
shining in the right front parlor window.

"That man Will," said Leonora, nodding her head, "knows just
what he's doing."

They finished their drinks. Outside, a vast warm crowd of
strangers wandered by and the "snow" fell steadily in the summer sky.

They bought many silly things to take with them, bags of
lemon candy, glossy women's magazines, fragile perfumes; and
then they walked out into the town and rented two belted jackets
that refused to recognize gravity and imitated only the moth,
touched the delicate controls, and felt themselves whispered like
white blossom petals over the town. "Anywhere," said Leonora,
"anywhere at all."

They let the wind blow them where it would; they let the wind
take them through the night of summer apple trees and the night
of warm preparation, over the lovely town, over the houses of
childhood and other days, over schools and avenues, over creeks
and meadows and farms so familiar that each grain of wheat was
a golden coin. They blew as leaves must blow before the threat
of a fire-wind, with warning whispers and summer lightning
crackling among the folded hills. They saw the milk-dust country roads where not so long ago they had drifted in moonlit helicopters in great whorls of sound spiraling down to touch beside
cool night streams with the young men who were now gone.

They floated in an immense sigh above a town already made
remote by the little space between themselves and the earth, a
town receding behind them in a black river and coming up in a

tidal wave of lights and color ahead, untouchable and a dream now, already smeared in their eyes with nostalgia, with a panic of memory that began before the thing itself was gone.

Blown quietly, eddying, they gazed secretly at a hundred faces of dear friends they were leaving behind, the lamplit people held and framed by windows which slid by on the wind, it seemed; all of Time breathing them along. There was no tree they did not examine for old confessions of love carved and whittled there, no sidewalk they did not skim across as over fields of mica-snow. For the first time they knew their town was beautiful and the lonely lights and the ancient bricks beautiful, and they both felt their eyes grow large with the beauty of this feast they were giving themselves. All floated upon an evening carrousel, with fitful drifts of music wafting up here and there, and voices calling and murmuring from houses that were whitely haunted by television.

The two women passed like needles, sewing one tree to the next with their perfume. Their eyes were too full, and yet they kept putting away each detail, each shadow, each solitary oak and elm, each passing car upon the small snaking streets below, until not only their eyes but their heads and then their hearts were too full.

I feel like I'm dead, thought Janice, and in the graveyard on a spring night and everything alive but me and everyone moving and ready to go on with life without me. It's like I felt each spring when I was sixteen, passing the graveyard and weeping for them because they were dead and it didn't seem fair, on nights as soft as that, that I was alive. I was guilty of living. And now, here, tonight, I feel they have taken me from the graveyard and let me go above the town just once more to see what it's like to be living, to be a town and a people, before they slam the black door on me again.

Softly, softly, like two white paper lanterns on a night wind, the women moved over their lifetime and their past, and over the meadows where the tent cities glowed and the highways where supply trucks would be clustered and running until dawn. They hovered above it all for a long time.

The courthouse clock was booming eleven forty-five when they came like spider webs floating from the stars, touching on the moonlit pavement before Janice's old house. The city was asleep, and Janice's house waited for them to come in searching for *their* sleep, which was not there.

"Is this *us,* here?" asked Janice. "Janice Smith and Leonora Holmes, in the year 2003?"

"Yes."

Janice licked her lips and stood straight. "I wish it was some other year."

"1492? 1612?" Leonora sighed, and the wind in the trees sighed with her, moving away. "It's always Columbus Day or Plymouth Rock Day, and I'll be darned if I know what we women can do about it."

"Be old maids."

"Or do just what we're doing."

They opened the door of the warm night house, the sounds of the town dying slowly in their ears. As they shut the door, the phone began to ring.

"The call!" cried Janice, running.

Leonora came into the bedroom after her and already Janice had the receiver up and was saying, "Hello, hello!" And the operator in a far city was readying the immense apparatus which would tie two worlds together, and the two women waited, one sitting and pale, the other standing, but just as pale, bent toward her.

There was a long pause, full of stars and time, a waiting pause not unlike the last three years for all of them. And now the moment had arrived, and it was Janice's turn to phone through millions upon millions of miles of meteors and comets, running away from the yellow sun which might boil or burn her words or scorch the meaning from them. But her voice went like a silver needle through everything, in stitches of talking, across the big night, reverberating from the moons of Mars. And then her voice found its way to a man in a room in a city there on another world, five minutes by radio away. And her message was this:

"Hello, Will. This is Janice!"

She swallowed.

"They say I haven't much time. A minute."

She closed her eyes.

"I want to talk slow, but they say talk fast and get it all in. So I want to say—I've decided. I will come up there. I'll go on the Rocket tomorrow. I *will* come up there to you, after all. And I love you. I hope you can hear me. I love you. It's been so long. . . ."

Her voice motioned on its way to that unseen world. Now, with the message sent, the words said, she wanted to call them back, to censor, to rearrange them, to make a prettier sentence, a fairer explanation of her soul. But already the words were hung between planets and if, by some cosmic radiation, they could have been illuminated, caught fire in vaporous wonder there, her love would have lit a dozen worlds and startled the night side of Earth into a premature dawn, she thought. Now the words were not hers at all, they belonged to space, they belonged to no one until they arrived, and they were traveling at one hundred and eighty-six thousand miles a second to their destination.

What will he say to me? What will he say back in *his* minute of time? she wondered. She fussed with and twisted the watch on her wrist, and the light-phone receiver on her ear crackled and space talked to her with electrical jigs and dances and audible auroras.

"Has he answered?" whispered Leonora.

"Shhh!" said Janice, bending, as if sick.

Then his voice came through space.

"I hear him!" cried Janice.

"What does he say?"

The voice called out from Mars and took itself through the places where there was no sunrise or sunset, but always the night with a sun in the middle of the blackness. And somewhere between Mars and Earth everything of the message was lost, perhaps in a sweep of electrical gravity rushing by on the flood tides of a meteor, or interfered with by a rain of silver meteors. In any

event, the small words and the unimportant words of the message were washed away. And his voice came through saying only one word:

". . . love . . ."

After that there was the huge night again and the sound of stars turning and suns whispering to themselves and the sound of her heart, like another world in space, filling her earphones.

"Did you *hear* him?" asked Leonora.

Janice could only nod.

"What did he say, what did he say?" cried Leonora.

But Janice could not tell anyone; it was much too good to tell. She sat listening to that one word again and again, as her memory played it back. She sat listening, while Leonora took the phone away from her without her knowing it and put it down upon its hook.

Then they were in bed and the lights out and the night wind blowing through the rooms a smell of the long journey in darkness and stars, and their voices talking of tomorrow, and the days after tomorrow which would not be days at all, but day-nights of timeless time; their voices faded away into sleep or wakeful thinking, and Janice lay alone in her bed.

Is this how it was over a century ago, she wondered, when the women, the night before, lay ready for sleep, or not ready, in the small towns of the East, and heard the sound of horses in the night and the creak of the Conestoga wagons ready to go, and the brooding of oxen under the trees, and the cry of children already lonely before their time? All the sounds of arrivals and departures into the deep forests and fields, the blacksmiths working in their own red hells through midnight? And the smell of bacons and hams ready for the journeying, and the heavy feel of the wagons like ships foundering with goods, with water in the wooden kegs to tilt and slop across prairies, and the chickens hysterical in their slung-beneath-the-wagon crates, and the dogs running out to the wilderness ahead and, fearful, running back with a look of empty space in their eyes? Is this, then, how it was

so long ago? On the rim of the precipice, on the edge of the cliff of stars. In their time the smell of buffalo, and in our time the smell of the Rocket. Is this, then, how it was?

And she decided, as sleep assumed the dreaming for her, that yes, yes indeed, very much so, irrevocably, this was as it had always been and would forever continue to be.

5

THE FRUIT AT THE BOTTOM OF THE BOWL

William Acton rose to his feet. The clock on the mantel ticked midnight.

He looked at his fingers and he looked at the large room around him and he looked at the man lying on the floor. William Acton, whose fingers had stroked typewriter keys and made love and fried ham and eggs for early breakfasts, had now accomplished a murder with those same ten whorled fingers.

He had never thought of himself as a sculptor and yet, in this moment, looking down between his hands at the body upon the polished hardwood floor, he realized that by some sculptural clenching and remodeling and twisting of human clay he had taken hold of this man named Donald Huxley and changed his physiognomy, the very frame of his body.

With a twist of his fingers he had wiped away the exacting glitter of Huxley's gray eyes; replaced it with a blind dullness of eye cold in socket. The lips, always pink and sensuous, were gaped to show the equine teeth, the yellow incisors, the nicotined canines, the gold-inlaid molars. The nose, pink also, was now mottled, pale, discolored, as were the ears. Huxley's hands,

upon the floor, were open, pleading for the first time in their lives, instead of demanding.

Yes, it was an artistic conception. On the whole, the change had done Huxley a share of good. Death made him a handsomer man to deal with. You could talk to him now and he'd have to listen.

William Acton looked at his own fingers.

It was done. He could not change it back. Had anyone heard? He listened. Outside, the normal late sounds of street traffic continued. There was no banging of the house door, no shoulder wrecking the portal into kindling, no voices demanding entrance. The murder, the sculpturing of clay from warmth to coldness was done, and nobody knew.

Now what? The clock ticked midnight. His every impulse exploded him in a hysteria toward the door. Rush, get away, run, never come back, board a train, hail a taxi, get, go, run, walk, saunter, but get the blazes *out* of here!

His hands hovered before his eyes, floating, turning.

He twisted them in slow deliberation; they felt airy and featherlight. Why was he staring at them this way? he inquired of himself. Was there something in them of immense interest that he should pause now, after a successful throttling, and examine them whorl by whorl?

They were ordinary hands. Not thick, not thin, not long, not short, not hairy, not naked, not manicured and yet not dirty, not soft and yet not callused, not wrinkled and yet not smooth; not murdering hands at all—and yet not innocent. He seemed to find them miracles to look upon.

It was not the hands as hands he was interested in, nor the fingers as fingers. In the numb timelessness after an accomplished violence he found interest only in the *tips* of his fingers.

The clock ticked upon the mantel.

He knelt by Huxley's body, took a handkerchief from Huxley's pocket, and began methodically to swab Huxley's throat with it. He brushed and massaged the throat and wiped the face and the back of the neck with a fierce energy. Then he stood up.

He looked at the throat. He looked at the polished floor. He bent slowly and gave the floor a few dabs with the handkerchief, then he scowled and swabbed the floor; first, near the head of the corpse; secondly, near the arms. Then he polished the floor all around the body. He polished the floor one yard from the body on all sides. Then he polished the floor two yards from the body on all sides. Then he polished the floor three yards from the body in all directions. Then he——

He stopped.

There was a moment when he saw the entire house, the mirrored halls, the carved doors, the splendid furniture; and, as clearly as if it were being repeated word for word, he heard Huxley talking and himself talking just the way they had talked only an hour ago.

Finger on Huxley's doorbell. Huxley's door opening.

"Oh!" Huxley shocked. "It's *you*, Acton."

"Where's my wife, Huxley?"

"Do you think I'd tell you, really? Don't stand out there, you idiot. If you want to talk business, come in. Through that door. There. Into the library."

Acton had *touched* the library door.

"Drink?"

"I need one. I can't believe Lily is gone, that she——"

"There's a bottle of burgundy, Acton. Mind fetching it from that cabinet?"

Yes, fetch it. *Handle* it. *Touch* it. He did.

"Some interesting first editions there, Acton. Feel this binding. *Feel* of it."

"I didn't come to see books, I——"

He had *touched* the books and the library table and *touched* the burgundy bottle and burgundy glasses.

Now, squatting on the floor beside Huxley's cold body with the polishing handkerchief in his fingers, motionless, he stared at the house, the walls, the furniture about him, his eyes widening, his mouth dropping, stunned by what he realized and what he

saw. He shut his eyes, dropped his head, crushed the handkerchief between his hands, wadding it, biting his lips with his teeth, pulling in on himself.

The fingerprints were everywhere, *everywhere!*

"Mind getting the burgundy, Acton, eh? The burgundy bottle, eh? With your fingers, eh? I'm terribly tired. You understand?"

A pair of gloves.

Before he did one more thing, before he polished another area, he must have a pair of gloves, or he might unintentionally, after cleaning a surface, redistribute his identity.

He put his hands in his pockets. He walked through the house to the hall umbrella stand, the hatrack. Huxley's overcoat. He pulled out the overcoat pockets.

No gloves.

His hands in his pockets again, he walked upstairs, moving with a controlled swiftness, allowing himself nothing frantic, nothing wild. He had made the initial error of not wearing gloves (but, after all, he hadn't *planned* a murder, and his subconscious, which may have known of the crime before its commitment, had not even hinted he might need gloves before the night was finished), so now he had to sweat for his sin of omission. Somewhere in the house there must be at least one pair of gloves. He would have to hurry; there was every chance that someone might visit Huxley, even at this hour. Rich friends drinking themselves in and out the door, laughing, shouting, coming and going without so much as hello-good-by. He would have until six in the morning, at the outside, when Huxley's friends were to pick Huxley up for the trip to the airport and Mexico City. . . .

Acton hurried about upstairs opening drawers, using the handkerchief as blotter. He untidied seventy or eighty drawers in six rooms, left them with their tongues, so to speak, hanging out, ran on to new ones. He felt naked, unable to do anything until he found gloves. He might scour the entire house with the handkerchief, buffing every possible surface where fingerprints might lie, then accidentally bump a wall here or there, thus sealing his

own fate with one microscopic, whorling symbol! It would be putting his stamp of approval on the murder, that's what it would be! Like those waxen seals in the old days when they rattled papyrus, flourished ink, dusted all with sand to dry the ink, and pressed their signet rings in hot crimson tallow at the bottom. So it would be if he left one, mind you, *one* fingerprint upon the scene! His approval of the murder did not extend as far as affixing said seal.

More drawers! Be quiet, be curious, be careful, he told himself.

At the bottom of the eighty-fifth drawer he found gloves.

"Oh, my Lord, my Lord!" He slumped against the bureau, sighing. He tried the gloves on, held them up, proudly flexed them, buttoned them. They were soft, gray, thick, impregnable. He could do all sorts of tricks with hands now and leave no trace. He thumbed his nose in the bedroom mirror, sucking his teeth.

"NO!" cried Huxley.

What a wicked plan it had been.

Huxley had fallen to the floor, *purposely!* Oh, what a wickedly clever man! Down onto the hardwood floor had dropped Huxley, with Acton after him. They had rolled and tussled and clawed at the floor, printing and printing it with their frantic fingertips! Huxley had slipped away a few feet, Acton crawling after to lay hands on his neck and squeeze until the life came out like paste from a tube!

Gloved, William Acton returned to the room and knelt down upon the floor and laboriously began the task of swabbing every wildly infested inch of it. Inch by inch, inch by inch, he polished and polished until he could almost see his intent, sweating face in it. Then he came to a table and polished the leg of it, on up its solid body and along the knobs and over the top. He came to a bowl of wax fruit, burnished the filigree silver, plucked out the wax fruit and wiped them clean, leaving the fruit at the bottom unpolished.

"I'm *sure* I didn't touch *them*," he said.

After rubbing the table he came to a picture frame hung over it.

"I'm certain I didn't touch *that,*" he said.

He stood looking at it.

He glanced at all the doors in the room. Which doors had he used tonight? He couldn't remember. Polish all of them, then. He started on the doorknobs, shined them all up, and then he curried the doors from head to foot, taking no chances. Then he went to all the furniture in the room and wiped the chair arms.

"That chair you're sitting in, Acton, is an old Louis XIV piece. *Feel* that material," said Huxley.

"I didn't come to talk furniture, Huxley! I came about Lily."

"Oh, come off it, you're not that serious about her. She doesn't love you, you know. She's told me she'll go with me to Mexico City tomorrow."

"You and your money and your damned furniture!"

"It's nice furniture, Acton; be a good guest and feel of it."

Fingerprints can be found on fabric.

"Huxley!" William Acton stared at the body. "Did you guess I was going to kill you? Did your subconscious suspect, just as my subconscious suspected? And did your subconscious tell you to make me run about the house handling, touching, *fondling* books, dishes, doors, chairs? Were you *that* clever and *that* mean?"

He washed the chairs dryly with the clenched handkerchief. Then he remembered the body—he hadn't dry-washed *it.* He went to it and turned it now this way, now that, and burnished every surface of it. He even shined the shoes, charging nothing.

While shining the shoes his face took on a little tremor of worry, and after a moment he got up and walked over to that table.

He took out and polished the wax fruit at the bottom of the bowl.

"Better," he whispered, and went back to the body.

But as he crouched over the body his eyelids twitched and his

jaw moved from side to side and he debated, then he got up and walked once more to the table.

He polished the picture frame.

While polishing the picture frame he discovered——

The wall.

"That," he said, "is *silly*."

"Oh!" cried Huxley, fending him off. He gave Acton a shove as they struggled. Acton fell, got up, *touching* the wall, and ran toward Huxley again. He strangled Huxley. Huxley died.

Acton turned steadfastly from the wall, with equilibrium and decision. The harsh words and the action faded in his mind; he hid them away. He glanced at the four walls.

"Ridiculous!" he said.

From the corners of his eyes he saw something on one wall.

"I refuse to pay attention," he said to distract himself. "The next room, now! I'll be methodical. Let's see—altogether we were in the hall, the library, *this* room, and the dining room and the kitchen."

There was a spot on the wall behind him.

Well, *wasn't* there?

He turned angrily. "All right, all right, just to be *sure*," and he went over and couldn't find any spot. Oh, a *little* one, yes, right —*there*. He dabbed it. It wasn't a fingerprint anyhow. He finished with it, and his gloved hand leaned against the wall and he looked at the wall and the way it went over to his right and over to his left and how it went down to his feet and up over his head and he said softly, "No." He looked up and down and over and across and he said quietly, "That would be too much." How many square feet? "I don't give a good damn," he said. But unknown to his eyes, his gloved fingers moved in a little rubbing rhythm on the wall.

He peered at his hand and the wallpaper. He looked over his shoulder at the other room. "I must go in there and polish the essentials," he told himself, but his hand remained, as if to hold the wall, or himself, up. His face hardened.

Without a word he began to scrub the wall, up and down,

back and forth, up and down, as high as he could stretch and as low as he could bend.

"Ridiculous, oh my Lord, ridiculous!"

But you must be certain, his thought said to him.

"Yes, one *must* be certain," he replied.

He got one wall finished, and then . . .

He came to another wall.

"What time *is* it?"

He looked at the mantel clock. An hour gone. It was five after one.

The doorbell rang.

Acton froze, staring at the door, the clock, the door, the clock.

Someone rapped loudly.

A long moment passed. Acton did not breathe. Without new air in his body he began to fail away, to sway; his head roared a silence of cold waves thundering onto heavy rocks.

"Hey, in there!" cried a drunken voice. "I know you're in there, Huxley! Open up, dammit! This is Billy-boy, drunk as an owl, Huxley, old pal, drunker than *two* owls."

"Go away," whispered Acton soundlessly, crushed against the wall.

"Huxley, you're in there, I hear you *breathing!*" cried the drunken voice.

"Yes, I'm in here," whispered Acton, feeling long and sprawled and clumsy on the floor, clumsy and cold and silent. "Yes."

"Hell!" said the voice, fading away into mist. The footsteps shuffled off. "Hell . . ."

Acton stood a long time feeling the red heart beat inside his shut eyes, within his head. When at last he opened his eyes he looked at the new fresh wall straight ahead of him and finally got courage to speak. "Silly," he said. "This wall's flawless. I won't touch it. Got to hurry. Got to hurry. Time, time. Only a few hours before those damn-fool friends blunder in!" He turned away.

From the corners of his eyes he saw the little webs. When his

back was turned the little spiders came out of the woodwork and
delicately spun their fragile little half-invisible webs. Not upon
the wall at his left, which was already washed fresh, but upon
the three walls as yet untouched. Each time he stared directly
at them the spiders dropped back into the woodwork, only to
spindle out as he retreated. "Those walls are all right," he insisted
in a half shout. "I won't *touch* them!"

He went to a writing desk at which Huxley had been seated
earlier. He opened a drawer and took out what he was looking
for. A little magnifying glass Huxley sometimes used for reading.
He took the magnifier and approached the wall uneasily.

Fingerprints.

"But those aren't *mine!*" He laughed unsteadily. "I *didn't* put
them there! I'm *sure* I didn't! A servant, a butler, or a maid perhaps!"

The wall was full of them.

"Look at this one here," he said. "Long and tapered, a
woman's, I'd bet money on it."

"Would you?"

"I would!"

"Are you certain?"

"Yes!"

"Positive?"

"Well—yes."

"Absolutely?"

"Yes, damn it, yes!"

"Wipe it out, anyway, why don't you?"

"There, by God!"

"Out damned spot, eh, Acton?"

"And this one, over here," scoffed Acton. "That's the print of
a fat man."

"Are you sure?"

"Don't start *that* again!" he snapped, and rubbed it out. He
pulled off a glove and held his hand up, trembling, in the glary
light.

"Look at it, you idiot! See how the whorls go? See?"

"That proves nothing!"

"Oh, all right!" Raging, he swept the wall up and down, back and forth, with gloved hands, sweating, grunting, swearing, bending, rising, and getting redder of face.

He took off his coat, put it on a chair.

"Two o'clock," he said, finishing the wall, glaring at the clock.

He walked over to the bowl and took out the wax fruit and polished the ones at the bottom and put them back, and polished the picture frame.

He gazed up at the chandelier.

His fingers twitched at his sides.

His mouth slipped open and the tongue moved along his lips and he looked at the chandelier and looked away and looked back at the chandelier and looked at Huxley's body and then at the crystal chandelier with its long pearls of rainbow glass.

He got a chair and brought it over under the chandelier and put one foot up on it and took it down and threw the chair, violently, laughing, into a corner. Then he ran out of the room, leaving one wall as yet unwashed.

In the dining room he came to a table.

"I want to show you my Gregorian cutlery, Acton," Huxley had said. Oh, that casual, that *hypnotic,* voice!

"I haven't time," Acton said. "I've got to see Lily——"

"Nonsense, look at this silver, this exquisite craftsmanship."

Acton paused over the table where the boxes of cutlery were laid out, hearing once more Huxley's voice, remembering all the touchings and gesturings.

Now Acton wiped the forks and spoons and took down all the plaques and special ceramic dishes from the wall shelf. . . .

"Here's a lovely bit of ceramics by Gertrude and Otto Natzler, Acton. Are you familiar with their work?"

"It *is* lovely."

"Pick it up. Turn it over. See the fine thinness of the bowl, hand-thrown on a turntable, thin as eggshell, incredible. And the amazing volcanic glaze? Handle it, go ahead. *I* don't mind."

HANDLE IT. GO AHEAD. PICK IT UP!

Acton sobbed unevenly. He hurled the pottery against the wall. It shattered and spread, flaking wildly, upon the floor.

An instant later he was on his knees. Every piece, every shard of it, must be found. Fool, fool, fool! he cried to himself, shaking his head and shutting and opening his eyes and bending under the table. Find every piece, idiot, not one fragment of it must be left behind. Fool, fool! He gathered them. Are they all here? He looked at them on the table before him. He looked under the table again and under the chairs and the service bureaus and found one more piece by match light and started to polish each little fragment as if it were a precious stone. He laid them all out neatly upon the shining polished table.

"A lovely bit of ceramics, Acton. Go ahead—*handle* it."

He took out the linen and wiped it and wiped the chairs and tables and doorknobs and windowpanes and ledges and drapes and wiped the floor and found the kitchen, panting, breathing violently, and took off his vest and adjusted his gloves and wiped the glittering chromium. . . . "I want to show you my house, Acton," said Huxley. "Come along. . . ." And he wiped all the utensils and the silver faucets and the mixing bowls, for now he had forgotten what he had touched and what he had not. Huxley and he had lingered here, in the kitchen, Huxley prideful of its array, covering his nervousness at the presence of a potential killer, perhaps wanting to be near the knives if they were needed. They had idled, touched this, that, something else—there was no remembering what or how much or how many—and he finished the kitchen and came through the hall into the room where Huxley lay.

He cried out.

He had forgotten to wash the fourth wall of the room! And while he was gone the little spiders had popped from the fourth unwashed wall and swarmed over the already clean walls, dirtying them again! On the ceilings, from the chandelier, in the corners, on the floor, a million little whorled webs hung billowing at his scream! Tiny, tiny little webs, no bigger than, ironically, your—finger!

As he watched, the webs were woven over the picture frame, the fruit bowl, the body, the floor. Prints wielded the paper knife, pulled out drawers, touched the table top, touched, touched, touched everything everywhere.

He polished the floor wildly, wildly. He rolled the body over and cried on it while he washed it, and got up and walked over and polished the fruit at the bottom of the bowl. Then he put a chair under the chandelier and got up and polished each little hanging fire of it, shaking it like a crystal tambourine until it tilted bellwise in the air. Then he leaped off the chair and gripped the doorknobs and got up on other chairs and swabbed the walls higher and higher and ran to the kitchen and got a broom and wiped the webs down from the ceiling and polished the bottom fruit of the bowl and washed the body and doorknobs and silverware and found the hall banister and followed the banister upstairs.

Three o'clock! Everywhere, with a fierce, mechanical intensity, clocks ticked! There were twelve rooms downstairs and eight above. He figured the yards and yards of space and time needed. One hundred chairs, six sofas, twenty-seven tables, six radios. And under and on top and behind. He yanked furniture out away from walls and, sobbing, wiped them clean of years-old dust, and staggered and followed the banister up, up the stairs, handling, erasing, rubbing, polishing, because if he left one little print it would reproduce and make a million more!—and the job would have to be done all over again and now it was four o'clock! —and his arms ached and his eyes were swollen and staring and he moved sluggishly about, on strange legs, his head down, his arms moving, swabbing and rubbing, bedroom by bedroom, closet by closet. . . .

They found him at six-thirty that morning.

In the attic.

The entire house was polished to a brilliance. Vases shone like glass stars. Chairs were burnished. Bronzes, brasses, and coppers were all aglint. Floors sparkled. Banisters gleamed.

Everything glittered. Everything shone, everything was bright!

They found him in the attic, polishing the old trunks and the old frames and the old chairs and the old carriages and toys and music boxes and vases and cutlery and rocking horses and dusty Civil War coins. He was half through the attic when the police officer walked up behind him with a gun.

"Done!"

On the way out of the house Acton polished the front door-knob with his handkerchief and slammed it in triumph!

They found him in the attic, polishing the old trunks and the old frames and the old chairs and the old carriages and toys and music boxes and vases and cutlery and rocking horse and dusty Civil War coins. He was half through the attic when the police officer walked up behind him with a gun.

"Done!"

On the way out of the house they handcuffed and slammed the front door upon him, with his handcuffed and slammed it the moment.

6

INVISIBLE BOY

She took the great iron spoon and the mummified frog and gave it a bash and made dust of it, and talked to the dust while she ground it in her stony fists quickly. Her beady gray bird-eyes flickered at the cabin. Each time she looked, a head in the small thin window ducked as if she'd fired off a shotgun.

"Charlie!" cried Old Lady. "You come outa there! I'm fixing a lizard magic to unlock that rusty door! You come out now and I won't make the earth shake or the trees go up in fire or the sun set at high noon!"

The only sound was the warm mountain light on the high turpentine trees, a tufted squirrel chittering around and around on a green-furred log, the ants moving in a fine brown line at Old Lady's bare, blue-veined feet.

"You been starving in there two days, darn you!" she panted, chiming the spoon against a flat rock, causing the plump gray miracle bag to swing at her waist. Sweating sour, she rose and marched at the cabin, bearing the pulverized flesh. "Come out, now!" She flicked a pinch of powder inside the lock. "All right, I'll come get you!" she wheezed.

She spun the knob with one walnut-colored hand, first one way, then the other. "O Lord," she intoned, "fling this door wide!"

When nothing flung, she added yet another philter and held her breath. Her long blue untidy skirt rustled as she peered into her bag of darkness to see if she had any scaly monsters there, any charm finer than the frog she'd killed months ago for such a crisis as this.

She heard Charlie breathing against the door. His folks had pranced off into some Ozark town early this week, leaving him, and he'd run almost six miles to Old Lady for company—she was by way of being an aunt or cousin or some such, and he didn't mind her fashions.

But then, two days ago, Old Lady, having gotten used to the boy around, decided to keep him for convenient company. She pricked her thin shoulder bone, drew out three blood pearls, spat wet over her right elbow, tromped on a crunch-cricket, and at the same instant clawed her left hand at Charlie, crying, "My son you are, you are my son, for all eternity!"

Charlie, bounding like a startled hare, had crashed off into the bush, heading for home.

But Old Lady, skittering quick as a gingham lizard, cornered him in a dead end, and Charlie holed up in this old hermit's cabin and wouldn't come out, no matter how she whammed door, window, or knothole with amber-colored fist or trounced her ritual fires, explaining to him that he was certainly her son *now*, all right.

"Charlie, you *there?*" she asked, cutting holes in the door planks with her bright little slippery eyes.

"I'm all of me here," he replied finally, very tired.

Maybe he would fall out on the ground any moment. She wrestled the knob hopefully. Perhaps a pinch too much frog powder had grated the lock wrong. She always overdid or underdid her miracles, she mused angrily, never doing them just *exact*, Devil take it!

"Charlie, I only wants someone to night-prattle to, someone to warm hands with at the fire. Someone to fetch kindling for me

mornings, and fight off the spunks that come creeping of early fogs! I ain't got no fetchings on you for myself, son, just for your company." She smacked her lips. "Tell you what, Charles, you come out and I *teach* you things!"

"What things?" he suspicioned.

"Teach you how to buy cheap, sell high. Catch a snow weasel, cut off its head, carry it warm in your hind pocket. There!"

"Aw," said Charlie.

She made haste. "Teach you to make yourself shotproof. So if anyone bangs at you with a gun, nothing happens."

When Charlie stayed silent, she gave him the secret in a high fluttering whisper. "Dig and stitch mouse-ear roots on Friday during full moon, and wear 'em around your neck in a white silk."

"You're *crazy*," Charlie said.

"Teach you how to stop blood or make animals stand frozen or make blind horses see, all them things I'll teach you! Teach you to cure a swelled-up cow and unbewitch a goat. Show you how to make yourself invisible!"

"Oh," said Charlie.

Old Lady's heart beat like a Salvation tambourine.

The knob turned from the other side.

"You," said Charlie, "are funning me."

"No, I'm not," exclaimed Old Lady. "Oh, Charlie, why, I'll make you like a window, see right through you. Why, child, you'll be surprised!"

"Real invisible?"

"Real invisible!"

"You won't fetch onto me if I walk out?"

"Won't touch a bristle of you, son."

"Well," he drawled reluctantly, "all right."

The door opened. Charlie stood in his bare feet, head down, chin against chest. "Make me invisible," he said.

"First we got to catch us a bat," said Old Lady. "Start lookin'!"

She gave him some jerky beef for his hunger and watched him climb a tree. He went high up and high up and it was nice seeing him there and it was nice having him here and all about after

so many years alone with nothing to say good morning to but bird-droppings and silvery snail tracks.

Pretty soon a bat with a broken wing fluttered down out of the tree. Old Lady snatched it up, beating warm and shrieking between its porcelain white teeth, and Charlie dropped down after it, hand upon clenched hand, yelling.

That night, with the moon nibbling at the spiced pine cones, Old Lady extracted a long silver needle from under her wide blue dress. Gumming her excitement and secret anticipation, she sighted up the dead bat and held the cold needle steady-steady.

She had long ago realized that her miracles, despite all perspirations and salts and sulphurs, failed. But she had always dreamt that one day the miracles might start functioning, might spring up in crimson flowers and silver stars to prove that God had forgiven her for her pink body and her pink thoughts and her warm body and her warm thoughts as a young miss. But so far God had made no sign and said no word, but nobody knew this except Old Lady.

"Ready?" she asked Charlie, who crouched cross-kneed, wrapping his pretty legs in long goose-pimpled arms, his mouth open, making teeth. "Ready," he whispered, shivering.

"There!" She plunged the needle deep in the bat's right eye. "So!"

"Oh!" screamed Charlie, wadding up his face.

"Now I wrap it in gingham, and here, put it in your pocket, keep it there, bat and all. Go on!"

He pocketed the charm.

"Charlie!" she shrieked fearfully. "Charlie, where *are* you? I can't *see* you, child!"

"Here!" He jumped so the light ran in red streaks up his body. "I'm here, Old Lady!" He stared wildly at his arms, legs, chest, and toes. "I'm here!"

Her eyes looked as if they were watching a thousand fireflies crisscrossing each other in the wild night air.

"Charlie, oh, you went *fast!* Quick as a hummingbird! Oh, Charlie, come *back* to me!"

"But I'm *here!*" he wailed.

"Where?"

"By the fire, the fire! And—and I can see myself. I'm not invisible at all!"

Old Lady rocked on her lean flanks. "Course *you* can see *you!* Every invisible person knows himself. Otherwise, how could you eat, walk, or get around places? Charlie, touch me. Touch me so I *know* you."

Uneasily he put out a hand.

She pretended to jerk, startled, at his touch. *"Ah!"*

"You mean to say you can't *find* me?" he asked. "Truly?"

"Not the least half rump of you!"

She found a tree to stare at, and stared at it with shining eyes, careful not to glance at him. "Why, I sure *did* a trick *that* time!" She sighed with wonder. "Whooeee. Quickest invisible I *ever* made! Charlie. Charlie, how you *feel?*"

"Like creek water—all stirred."

"You'll settle."

Then after a pause she added, "Well, what you going to do now, Charlie, since you're invisible?"

All sorts of things shot through his brain, she could tell. Adventures stood up and danced like hell-fire in his eyes, and his mouth, just hanging, told what it meant to be a boy who imagined himself like the mountain winds. In a cold dream he said, "I'll run across wheat fields, climb snow mountains, steal white chickens off'n farms. I'll kick pink pigs when they ain't looking. I'll pinch pretty girls' legs when they sleep, snap their garters in schoolrooms." Charlie looked at Old Lady, and from the shiny tips of her eyes she saw something wicked shape his face. "And other things I'll do, I'll do, I will," he said.

"Don't try nothing on me," warned Old Lady. "I'm brittle as spring ice and I don't take handling." Then: "What about your folks?"

"My folks?"

"You can't fetch yourself home looking like that. Scare the inside ribbons out of them. Your mother'd faint straight back like timber falling. Think they want you about the house to stumble over and your ma have to call you every three minutes, even though you're in the room next her elbow?"

Charlie had not considered it. He sort of simmered down and whispered out a little "Gosh" and felt of his long bones carefully.

"You'll be mighty lonesome. People looking through you like a water glass, people knocking you aside because they didn't reckon you to be underfoot. And women, Charlie, women——"

He swallowed. "What about women?"

"No woman will be giving you a second stare. And no woman wants to be kissed by a boy's mouth they can't even find!"

Charlie dug his bare toe in the soil contemplatively. He pouted. "Well, I'll stay invisible, anyway, for a spell. I'll have me some fun. I'll just be pretty careful, is all. I'll stay out from in front of wagons and horses and Pa. Pa shoots at the nariest sound." Charlie blinked. "Why, with me invisible, someday Pa might just up and fill me with buckshot, thinkin' I was a hill squirrel in the dooryard. Oh . . ."

Old Lady nodded at a tree. "That's likely."

"Well," he decided slowly, "I'll stay invisible for tonight, and tomorrow you can fix me back all whole again, Old Lady."

"Now if that ain't just like a critter, always wanting to be what he can't be," remarked Old Lady to a beetle on a log.

"What you mean?" said Charlie.

"Why," she explained, "it was real hard work, fixing you up. It'll take a little time for it to wear off. Like a coat of paint wears off, boy."

"You!" he cried. "You did this to me! Now you make me back, you make me seeable!"

"Hush," she said. "It'll wear off, a hand or a foot at a time."

"How'll it look, me around the hills with just one hand showing!"

"Like a five-winged bird hopping on the stones and bramble."

"Or a foot showing!"

"Like a small pink rabbit jumping thicket."

"Or my head floating!"

"Like a hairy balloon at the carnival!"

"How long before I'm *whole?*" he asked.

She deliberated that it might pretty well be an entire year.

He groaned. He began to sob and bite his lips and make fists. "You magicked me, you did this, you did this thing to me. Now I won't be able to run home!"

She winked. "But you *can* stay here, child, stay on with me real comfort-like, and I'll keep you fat and saucy."

He flung it out: "You did this on purpose! You mean old hag, you want to keep me here!"

He ran off through the shrubs on the instant.

"Charlie, come back!"

No answer but the pattern of his feet on the soft dark turf, and his wet choking cry which passed swiftly off and away.

She waited and then kindled herself a fire. "He'll be back," she whispered. And thinking inward on herself, she said, "And now I'll have me my company through spring and into late summer. Then, when I'm tired of him and want a silence, I'll send him home."

Charlie returned noiselessly with the first gray of dawn, gliding over the rimed turf to where Old Lady sprawled like a bleached stick before the scattered ashes.

He sat on some creek pebbles and stared at her.

She didn't dare look at him or beyond. He had made no sound, so how could she know he was anywhere about? She couldn't.

He sat there, tear marks on his cheeks.

Pretending to be just waking—but she had found no sleep from one end of the night to the other—Old Lady stood up, grunting and yawning, and turned in a circle to the dawn.

"Charlie?"

Her eyes passed from pines to soil, to sky, to the far hills. She called out his name, over and over again, and she felt like staring

plumb straight at him, but she stopped herself. "Charlie? Oh, Charles!" she called, and heard the echoes say the very same.

He sat, beginning to grin a bit, suddenly, knowing he was close to her, yet she must feel alone. Perhaps he felt the growing of a secret power, perhaps he felt secure from the world, certainly he was *pleased* with his invisibility.

She said aloud, "Now where *can* that boy be? If he only made a noise so I could tell just where he is, maybe I'd fry him a breakfast."

She prepared the morning victuals, irritated at his continuous quiet. She sizzled bacon on a hickory stick. "The smell of it will draw his nose," she muttered.

While her back was turned he swiped all the frying bacon and devoured it tastily.

She whirled, crying out, "Lord!"

She eyed the clearing suspiciously. "Charlie, that *you?*"

Charlie wiped his mouth clean on his wrists.

She trotted about the clearing, making like she was trying to locate him. Finally, with a clever thought, acting blind, she headed straight for him, groping. "Charlie, where *are* you?"

A lightning streak, he evaded her, bobbing, ducking.

It took all her will power not to give chase; but you can't chase invisible boys, so she sat down, scowling, sputtering, and tried to fry more bacon. But every fresh strip she cut he would steal bubbling off the fire and run away far. Finally, cheeks burning, she cried, "I know where you are! Right *there!* I hear you run!" She pointed to one side of him, not too accurate. He ran again. "Now you're there!" she shouted. "There, and there!" pointing to all the places he was in the next five minutes. "I hear you press a grass blade, knock a flower, snap a twig. I got fine shell ears, delicate as roses. They can hear the stars moving!"

Silently he galloped off among the pines, his voice trailing back, "Can't hear me when I'm set on a rock. I'll just *set!*"

All day he sat on an observatory rock in the clear wind, motionless and sucking his tongue.

Old Lady gathered wood in the deep forest, feeling his eyes

weaseling on her spine. She wanted to babble: "Oh, I see you, I see you! I was only fooling about invisible boys! You're right there!" But she swallowed her gall and gummed it tight.

The following morning he did the spiteful things. He began leaping from behind trees. He made toad-faces, frog-faces, spider-faces at her, clenching down his lips with his fingers, popping his raw eyes, pushing up his nostrils so you could peer in and see his brain thinking.

Once she dropped her kindling. She pretended it was a blue jay startled her.

He made a motion as if to strangle her.

She trembled a little.

He made another move as if to bang her shins and spit on her cheek.

These motions she bore without a lid-flicker or a mouth-twitch.

He stuck out his tongue, making strange bad noises. He wiggled his loose ears so she wanted to laugh, and finally she did laugh and explained it away quickly by saying, "Sat on a sala-mander! Whew, how it poked!"

By high noon the whole madness boiled to a terrible peak.

For it was at that exact hour that Charlie came racing down the valley stark boy-naked!

Old Lady nearly fell flat with shock!

"Charlie!" she almost cried.

Charlie raced naked up one side of a hill and naked down the other—naked as day, naked as the moon, raw as the sun and a newborn chick, his feet shimmering and rushing like the wings of a low-skimming hummingbird.

Old Lady's tongue locked in her mouth. What could she say? Charlie, go dress? For *shame? Stop* that? *Could* she? Oh, Char-lie, Charlie, God! Could she say that now? *Well?*

Upon the big rock, she witnessed him dancing up and down, naked as the day of his birth, stomping bare feet, smacking his hands on his knees and sucking in and out his white stomach like blowing and deflating a circus balloon.

She shut her eyes tight and prayed.

After three hours of this she pleaded, "Charlie, Charlie, come here! I got something to *tell* you!"

Like a fallen leaf he came, dressed again, praise the Lord.

"Charlie," she said, looking at the pine trees, "I see your right toe. *There* it is."

"You do?" he said.

"Yes," she said very sadly. "There it is like a horny toad on the grass. And there, up there's your left ear hanging on the air like a pink butterfly."

Charlie danced. "I'm forming in, I'm forming in!"

Old Lady nodded. "Here comes your ankle!"

"Gimme *both* my feet!" ordered Charlie.

"You got 'em."

"How about my hands?"

"I see one crawling on your knee like a daddy longlegs."

"How about the other one?"

"It's crawling too."

"I got a body?"

"Shaping up fine."

"I'll need my head to go home, Old Lady."

To go home, she thought wearily. "No!" she said, stubborn and angry. "No, you ain't got no head. No head at all," she cried. She'd leave that to the very last. "No head, no head," she insisted.

"No head?" he wailed.

"Yes, oh my God, yes, yes, you got your blamed head!" she snapped, giving up. "Now, fetch me back my bat with the needle in his eye!"

He flung it at her. "Haaaa-yoooo!" His yelling went all up the valley, and long after he had run toward home she heard his echoes, racing.

Then she plucked up her kindling with a great dry weariness and started back toward her shack, sighing, talking. And Charlie followed her all the way, *really* invisible now, so she couldn't see him, just hear him, like a pine cone dropping or a deep underground stream trickling, or a squirrel clambering a bough; and over the fire at twilight she and Charlie sat, him so invisible, and

her feeding him bacon he wouldn't take, so she ate it herself, and then she fixed some magic and fell asleep with Charlie, made out of sticks and rags and pebbles, but still warm and her very own son, slumbering and nice in her shaking mother arms . . . and they talked about golden things in drowsy voices until dawn made the fire slowly, slowly wither out. . . .

7

THE FLYING MACHINE

In the year A.D. 400, the Emperor Yuan held his throne by the Great Wall of China, and the land was green with rain, readying itself toward the harvest, at peace, the people in his dominion neither too happy nor too sad.

Early on the morning of the first day of the first week of the second month of the new year, the Emperor Yuan was sipping tea and fanning himself against a warm breeze when a servant ran across the scarlet and blue garden tiles, calling, "Oh, Emperor, Emperor, a miracle!"

"Yes," said the Emperor, "the air *is* sweet this morning."

"No, no, a miracle!" said the servant, bowing quickly.

"And this tea is good in my mouth, surely that is a miracle."

"No, no, Your Excellency."

"Let me guess then—the sun has risen and a new day is upon us. Or the sea is blue. *That* now is the finest of all miracles."

"Excellency, a man is flying!"

"What?" The Emperor stopped his fan.

"I saw him in the air, a man flying with wings. I heard a voice call out of the sky, and when I looked up, there he was, a dragon in the heavens with a man in its mouth, a dragon of paper and bamboo, colored like the sun and the grass."

"It is early," said the Emperor, "and you have just wakened from a dream."

"It is early, but I have seen what I have seen! Come, and you will see it too."

"Sit down with me here," said the Emperor. "Drink some tea. It must be a strange thing, if it is true, to see a man fly. You must have time to think of it, even as I must have time to prepare myself for the sight."

They drank tea.

"Please," said the servant at last, "or he will be gone."

The Emperor rose thoughtfully. "Now you may show me what you have seen."

They walked into a garden, across a meadow of grass, over a small bridge, through a grove of trees, and up a tiny hill.

"There!" said the servant.

The Emperor looked into the sky.

And in the sky, laughing so high that you could hardly hear him laugh, was a man; and the man was clothed in bright papers and reeds to make wings and a beautiful yellow tail, and he was soaring all about like the largest bird in a universe of birds, like a new dragon in a land of ancient dragons.

The man called down to them from high in the cool winds of morning, "I fly, I fly!"

The servant waved to him. "Yes, yes!"

The Emperor Yuan did not move. Instead he looked at the Great Wall of China now taking shape out of the farthest mist in the green hills, that splendid snake of stones which writhed with majesty across the entire land. That wonderful wall which had protected them for a timeless time from enemy hordes and preserved peace for years without number. He saw the town, nestled to itself by a river and a road and a hill, beginning to waken.

"Tell me," he said to his servant, "has anyone else seen this flying man?"

"I am the only one, Excellency," said the servant, smiling at the sky, waving.

The Emperor watched the heavens another minute and then said, "Call him down to me."

"Ho, come down, come down! The Emperor wishes to see you!" called the servant, hands cupped to his shouting mouth.

The Emperor glanced in all directions while the flying man soared down the morning wind. He saw a farmer, early in his fields, watching the sky, and he noted where the farmer stood.

The flying man alit with a rustle of paper and a creak of bamboo reeds. He came proudly to the Emperor, clumsy in his rig, at last bowing before the old man.

"What have you done?" demanded the Emperor.

"I have flown in the sky, Your Excellency," replied the man.

"What *have* you done?" said the Emperor again.

"I have just told you!" cried the flier.

"You have told me nothing at all." The Emperor reached out a thin hand to touch the pretty paper and the birdlike keel of the apparatus. It smelled cool, of the wind.

"Is it not beautiful, Excellency?"

"Yes, too beautiful."

"It is the only one in the world!" smiled the man. "And I am the inventor."

"The *only* one in the world?"

"I swear it!"

"Who else knows of this?"

"No one. Not even my wife, who would think me mad with the sun. She thought I was making a kite. I rose in the night and walked to the cliffs far away. And when the morning breezes blew and the sun rose, I gathered my courage, Excellency, and leaped from the cliff. I flew! But my wife does not know of it."

"Well for her, then," said the Emperor. "Come along."

They walked back to the great house. The sun was full in the sky now, and the smell of the grass was refreshing. The Emperor, the servant, and the flier paused within the huge garden.

The Emperor clapped his hands. "Ho, guards!"

The guards came running.

"Hold this man."

The guards seized the flier.

"Call the executioner," said the Emperor.

"What's this!" cried the flier, bewildered. "What have I done?" He began to weep, so that the beautiful paper apparatus rustled.

"Here is the man who has made a certain machine," said the Emperor, "and yet asks us what he has created. He does not know himself. It is only necessary that he create, without knowing why he has done so, or what this thing will do."

The executioner came running with a sharp silver ax. He stood with his naked, large-muscled arms ready, his face covered with a serene white mask.

"One moment," said the Emperor. He turned to a nearby table upon which sat a machine that he himself had created. The Emperor took a tiny golden key from his own neck. He fitted this key to the tiny, delicate machine and wound it up. Then he set the machine going.

The machine was a garden of metal and jewels. Set in motion, birds sang in tiny metal trees, wolves walked through miniature forests, and tiny people ran in and out of sun and shadow, fanning themselves with miniature fans, listening to the tiny emerald birds, and standing by impossibly small but tinkling fountains.

"Is *it* not beautiful?" said the Emperor. "If you asked me what I have done here, I could answer you well. I have made birds sing, I have made forests murmur, I have set people to walking in this woodland, enjoying the leaves and shadows and songs. That is what I have done."

"But, oh, Emperor!" pleaded the flier, on his knees, the tears pouring down his face. "I have done a similar thing! I have found beauty. I have flown on the morning wind. I have looked down on all the sleeping houses and gardens. I have smelled the sea and even *seen* it, beyond the hills, from my high place. And I have soared like a bird; oh, I cannot say how beautiful it is up there, in the sky, with the wind about me, the wind blowing me here like a feather, there like a fan, the way the sky smells in the

morning! And how free one feels! *That* is beautiful, Emperor, that is beautiful too!"

"Yes," said the Emperor sadly, "I know it must be true. For I felt my heart move with you in the air and I wondered: What is it like? How does it feel? How do the distant pools look from so high? And how my houses and servants? Like ants? And how the distant towns not yet awake?"

"Then spare me!"

"But there are times," said the Emperor, more sadly still, "when one must lose a little beauty if one is to keep what little beauty one already has. I do not fear you, yourself, but I fear another man."

"What man?"

"Some other man who, seeing you, will build a thing of bright papers and bamboo like this. But the other man will have an evil face and an evil heart, and the beauty will be gone. It is this man I fear."

"Why? Why?"

"Who is to say that someday just such a man, in just such an apparatus of paper and reed, might not fly in the sky and drop huge stones upon the Great Wall of China?" said the Emperor.

No one moved or said a word.

"Off with his head," said the Emperor.

The executioner whirled his silver ax.

"Burn the kite and the inventor's body and bury their ashes together," said the Emperor.

The servants retreated to obey.

The Emperor turned to his hand-servant, who had seen the man flying. "Hold your tongue. It was all a dream, a most sorrowful and beautiful dream. And that farmer in the distant field who also saw, tell him it would pay him to consider it only a vision. If ever the word passes around, you and the farmer die within the hour."

"You are merciful, Emperor."

"No, not merciful," said the old man. Beyond the garden wall he saw the guards burning the beautiful machine of paper and

reeds that smelled of the morning wind. He saw the dark smoke climb into the sky. "No, only very much bewildered and afraid." He saw the guards digging a tiny pit wherein to bury the ashes. "What is the life of one man against those of a million others? I must take solace from that thought."

He took the key from its chain about his neck and once more wound up the beautiful miniature garden. He stood looking out across the land at the Great Wall, the peaceful town, the green fields, the rivers and streams. He sighed. The tiny garden whirred its hidden and delicate machinery and set itself in motion; tiny people walked in forests, tiny foxes loped through sun-speckled glades in beautiful shining pelts, and among the tiny trees flew little bits of high song and bright blue and yellow color, flying, flying, flying in that small sky.

"Oh," said the Emperor, closing his eyes, "look at the birds, look at the birds!"

8

THE MURDERER

Music moved with him in the white halls. He passed an office door: "The Merry Widow Waltz." Another door: "Afternoon of a Faun." A third: "Kiss Me Again." He turned into a cross corridor: "The Sword Dance" buried him in cymbals, drums, pots, pans, knives, forks, thunder, and tin lightning. All washed away as he hurried through an anteroom where a secretary sat nicely stunned by Beethoven's Fifth. He moved himself before her eyes like a hand; she didn't see him.

His wrist radio buzzed.

"Yes?"

"This is Lee, Dad. Don't forget about my allowance."

"Yes, son, yes. I'm busy."

"Just didn't want you to forget, Dad," said the wrist radio. Tchaikovsky's "Romeo and Juliet" swarmed about the voice and flushed into the long halls.

The psychiatrist moved in the beehive of offices, in the cross-pollination of themes, Stravinsky mating with Bach, Haydn unsuccessfully repulsing Rachmaninoff, Schubert slain by Duke Ellington. He nodded to the humming secretaries and the whistling doctors fresh to their morning work. At his office he checked a few papers with his stenographer, who sang under her

breath, then phoned the police captain upstairs. A few minutes later a red light blinked, a voice said from the ceiling:

"Prisoner delivered to Interview Chamber Nine."

He unlocked the chamber door, stepped in, heard the door lock behind him.

"Go away," said the prisoner, smiling.

The psychiatrist was shocked by that smile. A very sunny, pleasant warm thing, a thing that shed bright light upon the room. Dawn among the dark hills. High noon at midnight, that smile. The blue eyes sparkled serenely above that display of self-assured dentistry.

"I'm here to help you," said the psychiatrist, frowning. Something was wrong with the room. He had hesitated the moment he entered. He glanced around. The prisoner laughed. "If you're wondering why it's so quiet in here, I just kicked the radio to death."

Violent, thought the doctor.

The prisoner read this thought, smiled, put out a gentle hand. "No, only to machines that yak-yak-yak."

Bits of the wall radio's tubes and wires lay on the gray carpeting. Ignoring these, feeling that smile upon him like a heat lamp, the psychiatrist sat across from his patient in the unusual silence which was like the gathering of a storm.

"You're Mr. Albert Brock, who calls himself The Murderer?"

Brock nodded pleasantly. "Before we start . . ." He moved quietly and quickly to detach the wrist radio from the doctor's arm. He tucked it in his teeth like a walnut, gritted, heard it crack, handed it back to the appalled psychiatrist as if he had done them both a favor. "That's better."

The psychiatrist stared at the ruined machine. "You're running up quite a damage bill."

"I don't care," smiled the patient. "As the old song goes: 'Don't Care What Happens to Me!'" He hummed it.

The psychiatrist said: "Shall we start?"

"Fine. The first victim, or one of the first, was my telephone. Murder most foul. I shoved it in the kitchen Insinkerator!

Stopped the disposal unit in mid-swallow. Poor thing strangled to death. After that I shot the television set!"

The psychiatrist said, "Mmm."

"Fired six shots right through the cathode. Made a beautiful tinkling crash, like a dropped chandelier."

"Nice imagery."

"Thanks, I always dreamt of being a writer."

"Suppose you tell me when you first began to hate the telephone."

"It frightened me as a child. Uncle of mine called it the Ghost Machine. Voices without bodies. Scared the living hell out of me. Later in life I was never comfortable. Seemed to me a phone was an impersonal instrument. If it *felt* like it, it let your personality go through its wires. If it didn't *want* to, it just drained your personality away until what slipped through at the other end was some cold fish of a voice, all steel, copper, plastic, no warmth, no reality. It's easy to say the wrong thing on telephones; the telephone changes your meaning on you. First thing you know, you've made an enemy. Then, of course, the telephone's such a *convenient* thing; it just sits there and *demands* you call someone who doesn't want to be called. Friends were always calling, calling, calling me. Hell, I hadn't any time of my own. When it wasn't the telephone it was the television, the radio, the phonograph. When it wasn't the television or radio or the phonograph it was motion pictures at the corner theater, motion pictures projected, with commercials on low-lying cumulus clouds. It doesn't rain rain any more, it rains soapsuds. When it wasn't High-Fly Cloud advertisements, it was music by Mozzek in every restaurant; music and commercials on the busses I rode to work. When it wasn't music, it was inter-office communications, and my horror chamber of a radio wrist watch on which my friends and my wife phoned every five minutes. What is there about such 'conveniences' that makes them so *temptingly* convenient? The average man thinks, Here I am, time on my hands, and there on my wrist is a wrist telephone, so why not just buzz old Joe up, eh? 'Hello, hel*lo!*' I love my

friends, my wife, humanity, very much, but when one minute my wife calls to say, 'Where are you *now,* dear?' and a friend calls and says, 'Got the best off-color joke to tell you. Seems there was a guy——' And a stranger calls and cries out, 'This is the Find-Fax Poll. What gum are you chewing at this very *instant?*' Well!"

"How did you feel during the week?"

"The fuse lit. On the edge of the cliff. That same afternoon I did what I did at the office."

"Which was?"

"I poured a paper cup of water into the intercommunications system."

The psychiatrist wrote on his pad.

"And the system shorted?"

"Beautifully! The Fourth of July on wheels! My God, stenographers ran around looking *lost!* What an uproar!"

"Felt better temporarily, eh?"

"Fine! Then I got the idea at noon of stomping my wrist radio on the sidewalk. A shrill voice was just yelling out of it at me, 'This is People's Poll Number Nine. What did you eat for lunch?' when I kicked the Jesus out of the wrist radio!"

"Felt even *better,* eh?"

"It *grew* on me!" Brock rubbed his hands together. "Why didn't I start a solitary revolution, deliver man from certain 'conveniences'? 'Convenient for who?' I cried. Convenient for friends: 'Hey, Al, thought I'd call you from the locker room out here at Green Hills. Just made a sockdolager hole in one! A hole in one, Al! A *beautiful* day. Having a shot of whiskey now. Thought you'd want to know, Al!' Convenient for my office, so when I'm in the field with my radio car there's no moment when I'm not in touch. In *touch! There's* a slimy phrase. Touch, hell. *Gripped!* Pawed, rather. Mauled and massaged and pounded by FM voices. You can't leave your car without checking in: 'Have stopped to visit gas-station men's room.' 'Okay, Brock, step on it!' 'Brock, what *took* you so long?' 'Sorry, sir.' 'Watch it next time, Brock.' '*Yes,* sir!' So, do you know

what I did, Doctor? I bought a quart of French chocolate ice cream and spooned it into the car radio transmitter."

"Was there any *special* reason for selecting French chocolate ice cream to spoon into the broadcasting unit?"

Brock thought about it and smiled. "It's my favorite flavor."

"Oh," said the doctor.

"I figured, hell, what's good enough for me is good enough for the radio transmitter."

"What made you think of spooning *ice cream* into the radio?"

"It was a hot day."

The doctor paused.

"And what happened next?"

"Silence happened next. God, it was *beautiful*. That car radio cackling all day, Brock go here, Brock go there, Brock check in, Brock check out, okay Brock, hour lunch, Brock, lunch over, Brock, Brock, Brock. Well, that silence was like putting ice cream in my ears."

"You seem to like ice cream a lot."

"I just rode around feeling of the silence. It's a big bolt of the nicest, softest flannel ever made. Silence. A whole hour of it. I just sat in my car, smiling, feeling of that flannel with my ears. I felt *drunk* with Freedom!"

"Go on."

"Then I got the idea of the portable diathermy machine. I rented one, took it on the bus going home that night. There sat all the tired commuters with their wrist radios, talking to their wives, saying, 'Now I'm at Forty-third, now I'm at Forty-fourth, here I am at Forty-ninth, now turning at Sixty-first.' One husband cursing, 'Well, get *out* of that bar, damn it, and get home and get dinner started, I'm at Seventieth!' And the transit-system radio playing 'Tales from the Vienna Woods,' a canary singing words about a first-rate wheat cereal. Then—I switched on my diathermy! Static! Interference! All wives cut off from husbands grousing about a hard day at the office. All husbands cut off from wives who had just seen their children break a window! The 'Vienna Woods' chopped down, the canary mangled! *Silence!* A

terrible, unexpected silence. The bus inhabitants faced with having to converse with each other. Panic! Sheer, animal panic!"

"The police seized you?"

"The bus *had* to stop. After all, the music *was* being scrambled, husbands and wives *were* out of touch with reality. Pandemonium, riot, and chaos. Squirrels chattering in cages! A trouble unit arrived, triangulated on me instantly, had me reprimanded, fined, and home, minus my diathermy machine, in jig time."

"Mr. Brock, may I suggest that so far your whole pattern here is not very—practical? If you didn't like transit radios or office radios or car business radios, why didn't you join a fraternity of radio haters, start petitions, get legal and constitutional rulings? After all, this *is* a democracy."

"And I," said Brock, "am that thing best called a minority. I *did* join fraternities, picket, pass petitions, take it to court. Year after year I protested. Everyone laughed. Everyone else *loved* bus radios and commercials. *I* was out of step."

"Then you should have taken it like a good soldier, don't you think? The majority rules."

"But they went too far. If a little music and 'keeping in touch' was charming, they figured a lot would be ten times as charming. I went *wild!* I got home to find my wife hysterical. *Why?* Because she had been completely out of touch with me for half a day. Remember, I did a dance on my wrist radio? Well, that night I laid plans to murder my house."

"Are you *sure* that's how you want me to write it down?"

"That's semantically accurate. Kill it dead. It's one of those talking, singing, humming, weather-reporting, poetry-reading, novel-reciting, jingle-jangling, rockaby-crooning-when-you-go-to-bed houses. A house that screams opera to you in the shower and teaches you Spanish in your sleep. One of those blathering caves where all kinds of electronic Oracles make you feel a trifle larger than a thimble, with stoves that say, 'I'm apricot pie, and I'm *done,*' or 'I'm prime roast beef, so *baste* me!' and other nursery gibberish like that. With beds that rock you to sleep and

shake you awake. A house that *barely* tolerates humans, I tell
you. A front door that barks: 'You've mud on your feet, sir!'
And an electronic vacuum hound that snuffles around after you
from room to room, inhaling every fingernail or ash you drop.
Jesus God, *I* say, Jesus God!"

"Quietly," suggested the psychiatrist.

"Remember that Gilbert and Sullivan song—'I've Got It on
My List, It Never Will Be Missed'? All night I listed grievances.
Next morning early I bought a pistol. I *purposely* muddied my
feet. I stood at our front door. The front door shrilled, 'Dirty
feet, muddy feet! Wipe your feet! Please be *neat!*' I shot the
damn thing in its keyhole! I ran to the kitchen, where the stove
was just whining, 'Turn me *over!*' In the middle of a mechanical
omelet I did the stove to death. Oh, how it sizzled and screamed,
'I'm *shorted!*' Then the telephone rang like a spoiled brat. I
shoved it down the Insinkerator. I must state here and now I
have *nothing* whatever against the Insinkerator; it was an innocent bystander. I feel sorry for it now, a practical device indeed, which never said a word, purred like a sleepy lion most of
the time, and digested our leftovers. I'll have it restored. Then I
went in and shot the televisor, that insidious beast, that Medusa,
which freezes a billion people to stone every night, staring
fixedly, that Siren which called and sang and promised so much
and gave, after all, so little, but myself always going back, going
back, hoping and waiting until—bang! Like a headless turkey,
gobbling, my wife whooped out the front door. The police came.
Here I *am!*"

He sat back happily and lit a cigarette.

"And did you realize, in committing these crimes, that the
wrist radio, the broadcasting transmitter, the phone, the bus radio, the office intercoms, all were rented or were someone else's
property?"

"I would do it all over again, so help me God."

The psychiatrist sat there in the sunshine of that beatific
smile.

"You don't want any further help from the Office of Mental Health? You're ready to take the consequences?"

"This is only the beginning," said Mr. Brock. "I'm the vanguard of the small public which is tired of noise and being taken advantage of and pushed around and yelled at, every moment music, every moment in touch with some voice somewhere, do this, do that, quick, quick, now here, now there. You'll *see.* The revolt begins. My name will go down in history!"

"Mmm." The psychiatrist seemed to be thinking.

"It'll take time, of course. It was all so enchanting at first. The very *idea* of these things, the practical uses, was wonderful. They were almost toys, to be played with, but the people got too involved, went too far, and got wrapped up in a pattern of social behavior and couldn't get out, couldn't admit they were *in,* even. So they rationalized their nerves as something else. 'Our modern age,' they said. 'Conditions,' they said. 'High-strung,' they said. But mark my words, the seed has been sown. I got world-wide coverage on TV, radio, films; *there's* an irony for you. That was five days ago. A billion people know about me. Check your financial columns. Any day now. Maybe today. Watch for a sudden spurt, a rise in sales for French chocolate ice cream!"

"I see," said the psychiatrist.

"Can I go back to my nice private cell now, where I can be alone and quiet for six months?"

"Yes," said the psychiatrist quietly.

"Don't worry about me," said Mr. Brock, rising. "I'm just going to sit around for a long time stuffing that nice soft bolt of quiet material in both ears."

"Mmm," said the psychiatrist, going to the door.

"Cheers," said Mr. Brock.

"Yes," said the psychiatrist.

He pressed a code signal on a hidden button, the door opened, he stepped out, the door shut and locked. Alone, he moved in the offices and corridors. The first twenty yards of his walk were accompanied by "Tambourine Chinois." Then it was "Tzigane," Bach's Passacaglia and Fugue in something Minor, "Tiger Rag,"

"Love Is Like a Cigarette." He took his broken wrist radio from his pocket like a dead praying mantis. He turned in at his office. A bell sounded; a voice came out of the ceiling, "Doctor?"

"Just finished with Brock," said the psychiatrist.

"Diagnosis?"

"Seems completely disorientated, but convivial. Refuses to accept the simplest realities of his environment and work *with* them."

"Prognosis?"

"Indefinite. Left him enjoying a piece of invisible material."

Three phones rang. A duplicate wrist radio in his desk drawer buzzed like a wounded grasshopper. The intercom flashed a pink light and click-clicked. Three phones rang. The drawer buzzed. Music blew in through the open door. The psychiatrist, humming quietly, fitted the new wrist radio to his wrist, flipped the intercom, talked a moment, picked up one telephone, talked, picked up another telephone, talked, picked up the third telephone, talked, touched the wrist-radio button, talked calmly and quietly, his face cool and serene, in the middle of the music and the lights flashing, the two phones ringing again, and his hands moving, and his wrist radio buzzing, and the intercoms talking, and voices speaking from the ceiling. And he went on quietly this way through the remainder of a cool, air-conditioned, and long afternoon; telephone, wrist radio, intercom, telephone, wrist radio, intercom, telephone, wrist radio, intercom, telephone, wrist radio, intercom, telephone, wrist radio, intercom, telephone, wrist radio . . .

9

THE GOLDEN KITE, THE SILVER WIND

"In the shape of a *pig?*" cried the Mandarin.

"In the shape of a pig," said the messenger, and departed.

"Oh, what an evil day in an evil year," cried the Mandarin. "The town of Kwan-Si, beyond the hill, was very small in my childhood. Now it has grown so large that at last they are building a wall."

"But why should a wall two miles away make my good father sad and angry all within the hour?" asked his daughter quietly.

"They build their wall," said the Mandarin, "in the shape of a pig! Do you see? Our own city wall is built in the shape of an orange. That pig will devour us, greedily!"

"Ah."

They both sat thinking.

Life was full of symbols and omens. Demons lurked everywhere, Death swam in the wetness of an eye, the turn of a gull's wing meant rain, a fan held *so,* the tilt of a roof, and, yes, even a city wall was of immense importance. Travelers and tourists, caravans, musicians, artists, coming upon these two towns, equally judging the portents, would say, "The city shaped like an

orange? No! I will enter the city shaped like a pig and prosper, eating all, growing fat with good luck and prosperity!"

The Mandarin wept. "All is lost! These symbols and signs terrify. Our city will come on evil days."

"Then," said the daughter, "call in your stonemasons and temple builders. I will whisper from behind the silken screen and you will know the words."

The old man clapped his hands despairingly. "Ho, stonemasons! Ho, builders of towns and palaces!"

The men who knew marble and granite and onyx and quartz came quickly. The Mandarin faced them most uneasily, himself waiting for a whisper from the silken screen behind his throne. At last the whisper came.

"I have called you here," said the whisper.

"I have called you here," said the Mandarin aloud, "because our city is shaped like an orange, and the vile city of Kwan-Si has this day shaped theirs like a ravenous pig——"

Here the stonemasons groaned and wept. Death rattled his cane in the outer courtyard. Poverty made a sound like a wet cough in the shadows of the room.

"And so," said the whisper, said the Mandarin, "you raisers of walls must go bearing trowels and rocks and change the shape of *our* city!"

The architects and masons gasped. The Mandarin himself gasped at what he had said. The whisper whispered. The Mandarin went on: "And you will change our walls into a club which may beat the pig and drive it off!"

The stonemasons rose up, shouting. Even the Mandarin, delighted at the words from his mouth, applauded, stood down from his throne. "Quick!" he cried. "To work!"

When his men had gone, smiling and bustling, the Mandarin turned with great love to the silken screen. "Daughter," he whispered, "I will embrace you." There was no reply. He stepped around the screen, and she was gone.

Such modesty, he thought. She has slipped away and left me with a triumph, as if it were mine.

The news spread through the city; the Mandarin was acclaimed. Everyone carried stone to the walls. Fireworks were set off and the demons of death and poverty did not linger, as all worked together. At the end of the month the wall had been changed. It was now a mighty bludgeon with which to drive pigs, boars, even lions, far away. The Mandarin slept like a happy fox every night.

"I would like to see the Mandarin of Kwan-Si when the news is learned. Such pandemonium and hysteria; he will likely throw himself from a mountain! A little more of that wine, oh Daughter-who-thinks-like-a-son."

But the pleasure was like a winter flower; it died swiftly. That very afternoon the messenger rushed into the courtroom. "Oh, Mandarin, disease, early sorrow, avalanches, grasshopper plagues, and poisoned well water!"

The Mandarin trembled.

"The town of Kwan-Si," said the messenger, "which was built like a pig and which animal we drove away by changing our walls to a mighty stick, has now turned triumph to winter ashes. They have built their city's walls like a great bonfire to burn our stick!"

The Mandarin's heart sickened within him, like an autumn fruit upon the ancient tree. "Oh, gods! Travelers will spurn us. Tradesmen, reading the symbols, will turn from the stick, so easily destroyed, to the fire, which conquers all!"

"No," said a whisper like a snowflake from behind the silken screen.

"No," said the startled Mandarin.

"Tell my stonemasons," said the whisper that was a falling drop of rain, "to build our walls in the shape of a shining lake."

The Mandarin said this aloud, his heart warmed.

"And with this lake of water," said the whisper and the old man, "we will quench the fire and put it out forever!"

The city turned out in joy to learn that once again they had

been saved by the magnificent Emperor of ideas. They ran to the walls and built them nearer to this new vision, singing, not as loudly as before, of course, for they were tired, and not as quickly, for since it had taken a month to rebuild the wall the first time, they had had to neglect business and crops and therefore were somewhat weaker and poorer.

There then followed a succession of horrible and wonderful days, one in another like a nest of frightening boxes.

"Oh, Emperor," cried the messenger, "Kwan-Si has rebuilt their walls to resemble a mouth with which to drink all our lake!"

"Then," said the Emperor, standing very close to his silken screen, "build our walls like a needle to sew up that mouth!"

"Emperor!" screamed the messenger. "They make their walls like a sword to break your needle!"

The Emperor held, trembling, to the silken screen. "Then shift the stones to form a scabbard to sheathe that sword!"

"Mercy," wept the messenger the following morn, "they have worked all night and shaped their walls like lightning which will explode and destroy that sheath!"

Sickness spread in the city like a pack of evil dogs. Shops closed. The population, working now steadily for endless months upon the changing of the walls, resembled Death himself, clattering his white bones like musical instruments in the wind. Funerals began to appear in the streets, though it was the middle of summer, a time when all should be tending and harvesting. The Mandarin fell so ill that he had his bed drawn up by the silken screen and there he lay, miserably giving his architectural orders. The voice behind the screen was weak now, too, and faint, like the wind in the eaves.

"Kwan-Si is an eagle. Then our walls must be a net for that eagle. They are a sun to burn our net. Then we build a moon to eclipse their sun!"

Like a rusted machine, the city ground to a halt.

At last the whisper behind the screen cried out:

"In the name of the gods, send for Kwan-Si!"

Upon the last day of summer the Mandarin Kwan-Si, very

ill and withered away, was carried into our Mandarin's court-room by four starving footmen. The two mandarins were propped up, facing each other. Their breaths fluttered like winter winds in their mouths. A voice said:

"Let us put an end to this."

The old men nodded.

"This cannot go on," said the faint voice. "Our people do nothing but rebuild our cities to a different shape every day, every hour. They have no time to hunt, to fish, to love, to be good to their ancestors and their ancestors' children."

"This I admit," said the mandarins of the towns of the Cage, the Moon, the Spear, the Fire, the Sword and this, that, and other things.

"Carry us into the sunlight," said the voice.

The old men were borne out under the sun and up a little hill. In the late summer breeze a few very thin children were flying dragon kites in all the colors of the sun, and frogs and grass, the color of the sea and the color of coins and wheat.

The first Mandarin's daughter stood by his bed.

"See," she said.

"Those are nothing but kites," said the two old men.

"But what is a kite on the ground?" she said. "It is nothing. What does it need to sustain it and make it beautiful and truly spiritual?"

"The wind, of course!" said the others.

"And what do the sky and the wind need to make *them* beautiful?"

"A kite, of course—many kites, to break the monotony, the sameness of the sky. Colored kites, flying!"

"So," said the Mandarin's daughter. "You, Kwan-Si, will make a last rebuilding of your town to resemble nothing more nor less than the wind. And we shall build like a golden kite. The wind will beautify the kite and carry it to wondrous heights. And the kite will break the sameness of the wind's existence and give it purpose and meaning. One without the other is nothing.

Together, all will be beauty and co-operation and a long and enduring life."

Whereupon the two mandarins were so overjoyed that they took their first nourishment in days, momentarily were given strength, embraced, and lavished praise upon each other, called the Mandarin's daughter a boy, a man, a stone pillar, a warrior, and a true and unforgettable son. Almost immediately they parted and hurried to their towns, calling out and singing, weakly but happily.

And so, in time, the towns became the Town of the Golden Kite and the Town of the Silver Wind. And harvestings were harvested and business tended again, and the flesh returned, and disease ran off like a frightened jackal. And on every night of the year the inhabitants in the Town of the Kite could hear the good clear wind sustaining them. And those in the Town of the Wind could hear the kite singing, whispering, rising, and beautifying them.

"So be it," said the Mandarin in front of his silken screen.

10
I SEE YOU NEVER

The soft knock came at the kitchen door, and when Mrs. O'Brian opened it, there on the back porch were her best tenant, Mr. Ramirez, and two police officers, one on each side of him. Mr. Ramirez just stood there, walled in and small.

"Why, Mr. Ramirez!" said Mrs. O'Brian.

Mr. Ramirez was overcome. He did not seem to have words to explain.

He had arrived at Mrs. O'Brian's rooming house more than two years earlier and had lived there ever since. He had come by bus from Mexico City to San Diego and had then gone up to Los Angeles. There he had found the clean little room, with glossy blue linoleum, and pictures and calendars on the flowered walls, and Mrs. O'Brian as the strict but kindly landlady. During the war he had worked at the airplane factory and made parts for the planes that flew off somewhere, and even now, after the war, he still held his job. From the first he had made big money. He saved some of it, and he got drunk only once a week—a privilege that, to Mrs. O'Brian's way of thinking, every good workingman deserved, unquestioned and unreprimanded.

Inside Mrs. O'Brian's kitchen, pies were baking in the oven. Soon the pies would come out with complexions like Mr. Ramirez'—brown and shiny and crisp, with slits in them for the air almost like the slits of Mr. Ramirez' dark eyes. The kitchen smelled good. The policemen leaned forward, lured by the odor. Mr. Ramirez gazed at his feet, as if they had carried him into all this trouble.

"What happened, Mr. Ramirez?" asked Mrs. O'Brian.

Behind Mrs. O'Brian, as he lifted his eyes, Mr. Ramirez saw the long table laid with clean white linen and set with a platter, cool, shining glasses, a water pitcher with ice cubes floating inside it, a bowl of fresh potato salad and one of bananas and oranges, cubed and sugared. At this table sat Mrs. O'Brian's children—her three grown sons, eating and conversing, and her two younger daughters, who were staring at the policemen as they ate.

"I have been here thirty months," said Mr. Ramirez quietly, looking at Mrs. O'Brian's plump hands.

"That's six months too long," said one policeman. "He only had a temporary visa. We've just got around to looking for him."

Soon after Mr. Ramirez had arrived he bought a radio for his little room; evenings, he turned it up very loud and enjoyed it. And he had bought a wrist watch and enjoyed that too. And on many nights he had walked silent streets and seen the bright clothes in the windows and bought some of them, and he had seen the jewels and bought some of them for his few lady friends. And he had gone to picture shows five nights a week for a while. Then, also, he had ridden the streetcars—all night some nights —smelling the electricity, his dark eyes moving over the advertisements, feeling the wheels rumble under him, watching the little sleeping houses and big hotels slip by. Besides that, he had gone to large restaurants, where he had eaten many-course dinners, and to the opera and the theater. And he had bought a car, which later, when he forgot to pay for it, the dealer had driven off angrily from in front of the rooming house.

"So here I am," said Mr. Ramirez now, "to tell you I must give

up my room, Mrs. O'Brian. I come to get my baggage and clothes and go with these men."

"Back to Mexico?"

"Yes. To Lagos. That is a little town north of Mexico City."

"I'm sorry, Mr. Ramirez."

"I'm packed," said Mr. Ramirez hoarsely, blinking his dark eyes rapidly and moving his hands helplessly before him. The policemen did not touch him. There was no necessity for that.

"Here is the key, Mrs. O'Brian," Mr. Ramirez said. "I have my bag already."

Mrs. O'Brian, for the first time, noticed a suitcase standing behind him on the porch.

Mr. Ramirez looked in again at the huge kitchen, at the bright silver cutlery and the young people eating and the shining waxed floor. He turned and looked for a long moment at the apartment house next door, rising up three stories, high and beautiful. He looked at the balconies and fire escapes and back-porch stairs, at the lines of laundry snapping in the wind.

"You've been a good tenant," said Mrs. O'Brian.

"Thank you, thank you, Mrs. O'Brian," he said softly. He closed his eyes.

Mrs. O'Brian stood holding the door half open. One of her sons, behind her, said that her dinner was getting cold, but she shook her head at him and turned back to Mr. Ramirez. She remembered a visit she had once made to some Mexican border towns—the hot days, the endless crickets leaping and falling or lying dead and brittle like the small cigars in the shopwindows, and the canals taking river water out to the farms, the dirt roads, the scorched scape. She remembered the silent towns, the warm beer, the hot, thick foods each day. She remembered the slow, dragging horses and the parched jack rabbits on the road. She remembered the iron mountains and the dusty valleys and the ocean beaches that spread hundreds of miles with no sound but the waves—no cars, no buildings, nothing.

"I'm sure sorry, Mr. Ramirez," she said.

"I don't want to go back, Mrs. O'Brian," he said weakly. "I

like it here, I want to stay here. I've worked, I've got money. I look all right, don't I? And I don't want to go back!"

"I'm sorry, Mr. Ramirez," she said. "I wish there was something I could do."

"Mrs. O'Brian!" he cried suddenly, tears rolling out from under his eyelids. He reached out his hands and took her hand fervently, shaking it, wringing it, holding to it. "Mrs. O'Brian, I see you never, I see you never!"

The policemen smiled at this, but Mr. Ramirez did not notice it, and they stopped smiling very soon.

"Good-by, Mrs. O'Brian. You have been good to me. Oh, good-by, Mrs. O'Brian. I see you never!"

The policemen waited for Mr. Ramirez to turn, pick up his suitcase, and walk away. Then they followed him, tipping their caps to Mrs. O'Brian. She watched them go down the porch steps. Then she shut the door quietly and went slowly back to her chair at the table. She pulled the chair out and sat down. She picked up the shining knife and fork and started once more upon her steak.

"Hurry up, Mom," said one of the sons. "It'll be cold."

Mrs. O'Brian took one bite and chewed on it for a long, slow time; then she stared at the closed door. She laid down her knife and fork.

"What's wrong, Ma?" asked her son.

"I just realized," said Mrs. O'Brian—she put her hand to her face—"I'll never see Mr. Ramirez again."

11

EMBROIDERY

The dark porch air in the late afternoon was full of needle flashes, like a movement of gathered silver insects in the light. The three women's mouths twitched over their work. Their bodies lay back and then imperceptibly forward, so that the rocking chairs tilted and murmured. Each woman looked to her own hands, as if quite suddenly she had found her heart beating there.

"What time is it?"

"Ten minutes to five."

"Got to get up in a minute and shell those peas for dinner."

"But——" said one of them.

"Oh yes, I forgot. How foolish of me. . . ." The first woman paused, put down her embroidery and needle, and looked through the open porch door, through the warm interior of the quiet house, to the silent kitchen. There upon the table, seeming more like symbols of domesticity than anything she had ever seen in her life, lay the mound of fresh-washed peas in their neat, resilient jackets, waiting for her fingers to bring them into the world.

"Go hull them if it'll make you feel good," said the second woman.

"No," said the first. "I won't. I just won't."

The third woman sighed. She embroidered a rose, a leaf, a daisy on a green field. The embroidery needle rose and vanished.

The second woman was working on the finest, most delicate piece of embroidery of them all, deftly poking, finding, and returning the quick needle upon innumerable journeys. Her quick black glance was on each motion. A flower, a man, a road, a sun, a house; the scene grew under hand, a miniature beauty, perfect in every threaded detail.

"It seems at times like this that it's always your hands you turn to," she said, and the others nodded enough to make the rockers rock again.

"I believe," said the first lady, "that our souls are in our hands. For we do *everything* to the world with our hands. Sometimes I think we don't use our hands half enough; it's certain we don't use our heads."

They all peered more intently at what their hands were doing. "Yes," said the third lady, "when you look back on a whole lifetime, it seems you don't remember faces so much as hands and what they did."

They recounted to themselves the lids they had lifted, the doors they had opened and shut, the flowers they had picked, the dinners they had made, all with slow or quick fingers, as was their manner or custom. Looking back, you saw a flurry of hands, like a magician's dream, doors popping wide, taps turned, brooms wielded, children spanked. The flutter of pink hands was the only sound; the rest was a dream without voices.

"No supper to fix tonight or tomorrow night or the next night after that," said the third lady.

"No windows to open or shut."

"No coal to shovel in the basement furnace next winter."

"No papers to clip cooking articles out of."

And suddenly they were crying. The tears rolled softly down

their faces and fell into the material upon which their fingers twitched.

"This won't help things," said the first lady at last, putting the back of her thumb to each under-eyelid. She looked at her thumb and it was wet.

"Now look what I've done!" cried the second lady, exasperated. The others stopped and peered over. The second lady held out her embroidery. There was the scene, perfect except that while the embroidered yellow sun shone down upon the embroidered green field, and the embroidered brown road curved toward an embroidered pink house, the man standing on the road had something wrong with his face.

"I'll just have to rip out the whole pattern, practically, to fix it right," said the second lady.

"What a shame." They all stared intently at the beautiful scene with the flaw in it.

The second lady began to pick away at the thread with her little deft scissors flashing. The pattern came out thread by thread. She pulled and yanked, almost viciously. The man's face was gone. She continued to seize at the threads.

"What are you *doing?*" asked the other woman.

They leaned and saw what she had done.

The man was gone from the road. She had taken him out entirely.

They said nothing but returned to their own tasks.

"What time is it?" asked someone.

"Five minutes to five."

"Is it supposed to happen at five o'clock?"

"Yes."

"And they're not sure what it'll do to anything, really, when it happens?"

"No, not sure."

"Why didn't we stop them before it got this far and this big?"

"It's twice as big as ever before. No, ten times, maybe a thousand."

"This isn't like the first one or the dozen later ones. This is different. Nobody knows what it might do when it comes."

They waited on the porch in the smell of roses and cut grass. "What time is it now?"

"One minute to five."

The needles flashed silver fire. They swam like a tiny school of metal fish in the darkening summer air.

Far away a mosquito sound. Then something like a tremor of drums. The three women cocked their heads, listening.

"We won't hear anything, will we?"

"They say not."

"Perhaps we're foolish. Perhaps we'll go right on, after five o'clock, shelling peas, opening doors, stirring soups, washing dishes, making lunches, peeling oranges . . ."

"My, how we'll laugh to think we were frightened by an old experiment!" They smiled a moment at each other.

"It's five o'clock."

At these words, hushed, they all busied themselves. Their fingers darted. Their faces were turned down to the motions they made. They made frantic patterns. They made lilacs and grass and trees and houses and rivers in the embroidered cloth. They said nothing, but you could hear their breath in the silent porch air.

Thirty seconds passed.

The second woman sighed finally and began to relax.

"I think I just *will* go shell those peas for supper," she said. "I——"

But she hadn't time even to lift her head. Somewhere, at the side of her vision, she saw the world brighten and catch fire. She kept her head down, for she knew what it was. She didn't look up, nor did the others, and in the last instant their fingers were flying; they didn't glance about to see what was happening to the country, the town, this house, or even this porch. They were only staring down at the design in their flickering hands.

The second woman watched an embroidered flower go. She tried to embroider it back in, but it went, and then the road

vanished, and the blades of grass. She watched a fire, in slow motion almost, catch upon the embroidered house and unshingle it, and pull each threaded leaf from the small green tree in the hoop, and she saw the sun itself pulled apart in the design. Then the fire caught upon the moving point of the needle while still it flashed; she watched the fire come along her fingers and arms and body, untwisting the yarn of her being so painstakingly that she could see it in all its devilish beauty, yanking out the pattern from the material at hand. What it was doing to the other women or the furniture or the elm tree in the yard, she never knew. For now, yes, now! it was plucking at the white embroidery of her flesh, the pink thread of her cheeks, and at last it found her heart, a soft red rose sewn with fire, and it burned the fresh, embroidered petals away, one by delicate one. . . .

12

THE BIG BLACK AND WHITE GAME

The people filled the stands behind the wire screen, waiting. Us kids, dripping from the lake, ran between the white cottages, past the resort hotel, screaming, and sat on the bleachers, making wet bottom marks. The hot sun beat down through the tall oak trees around the baseball diamond. Our fathers and mothers, in golf pants and light summer dresses, scolded us and made us sit still.

We looked toward the hotel and the back door of the vast kitchen, expectantly. A few colored women began walking across the shade-freckled area between, and in ten minutes the far left section of the bleachers was mellow with the color of their fresh-washed faces and arms. After all these years, whenever I think back on it, I can still hear the sounds they made. The sound on the warm air was like a soft moving of dove voices each time they talked among themselves.

Everybody quickened into amusement, laughter rose right up into the clear blue Wisconsin sky, as the kitchen door flung wide and out ran the big and little, the dark and high-yellar uniformed Negro waiters, janitors, bus boys, boatmen, cooks, bottle washers, soda jerks, gardeners, and golf-links tenders. They

came capering, showing their fine white teeth, proud of their
new red-striped uniforms, their shiny shoes rising and coming
down on the green grass as they skirted the bleachers and drifted
with lazy speed out on the field, calling to everybody and everything.

Us kids squealed. There was Long Johnson, the lawn-cutting
man, and Cavanaugh, the soda-fountain man, and Shorty Smith
and Pete Brown and Jiff Miller!

And *there* was Big Poe! Us kids shouted, applauded!

Big Poe was the one who stood so tall by the popcorn
machine every night in the million-dollar dance pavilion farther
down beyond the hotel on the lake rim. Every night I bought
popcorn from Big Poe and he poured lots of butter all over it
for me.

I stomped and yelled, "Big Poe! Big Poe!"

And he looked over at me and stretched his lips to bring out
his teeth, waved, and shouted a laugh.

And Mama looked to the right, to the left, and back of us with
worried eyes and nudged my elbow. "Hush," she said. "Hush."

"Land, land," said the lady next to my mother, fanning herself with a folded paper. "This is quite a day for the colored servants, ain't it? Only time of year they break loose. They look
forward all summer to the big Black and White game. But this
ain't nothing. You seen their Cakewalk Jamboree?"

"We got tickets for it," said Mother. "For tonight at the pavilion. Cost us a dollar each. That's pretty expensive, I'd say."

"But I always figure," said the woman, "once a year you got to
spend. And it's really something to watch them dance. They just
naturally got . . ."

"Rhythm," said Mother.

"That's the word," said the lady. "Rhythm. That's what they
got. Land, you should see the colored maids up at the hotel. They
been buying satin yardage in at the big store in Madison for a
month now. And every spare minute they sit sewing and laughing. And I seen some of the feathers they bought for their hats.

Mustard and wine ones and blue ones and violet ones. Oh, it'll be a sight!"

"They been airing out their tuxedos," I said. "I saw them hanging on lines behind the hotel all last week!"

"Look at them prance," said Mother. "You'd think they thought they were going to win the game from our men."

The colored men ran back and forth and yelled with their high, fluting voices and their low, lazy, interminable voices. Way out in center field you could see the flash of teeth, their upraised naked black arms swinging and beating their sides as they hopped up and down and ran like rabbits, exuberantly.

Big Poe took a double fistful of bats, bundled them on his huge bull shoulder, and strutted along the first-base line, head back, mouth smiling wide open, his tongue moving, singing:

"—gonna dance out both of my shoes,
When they play those Jelly Roll Blues;
Tomorrow night at the Dark Town Strutters' Ball!"

Up went his knees and down and out, swinging the bats like musical batons. A burst of applause and soft laughter came from the left-hand grandstands, where all the young, ripply colored girls with shiny brown eyes sat eager and easy. They made quick motions that were graceful and mellow because, maybe, of their rich coloring. Their laughter was like shy birds; they waved at Big Poe, and one of them with a high voice cried, "Oh, Big Poe! Oh, Big Poe!"

The white section joined politely in the applause as Big Poe finished his cakewalk. "Hey, Big Poe!" I yelled again.

"Stop that, Douglas!" said Mother, straight at me.

Now the white men came running between the trees with their uniforms on. There was a great thunder and shouting and rising up in our grandstand. The white men ran across the green diamond, flashing white.

"Oh, there's Uncle George!" said Mother. "My, doesn't he look nice?" And there was my uncle George toddling along in his outfit which didn't quite fit because Uncle has a potbelly, and

jowls that sit out over any collar he puts on. He was hurrying along, trying to breathe and smile at the same time, lifting up his pudgy little legs. "My, they look *so* nice," enthused Mother.

I sat there, watching their movements. Mother sat beside me, and I think she was comparing and thinking, too, and what she saw amazed and disconcerted her. How easily the dark people had come running first, like those slow-motion deer and buck antelopes in those African moving pictures, like things in dreams. They came like beautiful brown, shiny animals that didn't know they were alive, but lived. And when they ran and put their easy, lazy, timeless legs out and followed them with their big, sprawling arms and loose fingers and smiled in the blowing wind, their expressions didn't say, "Look at *me* run, look at *me* run!" No, not at all. Their faces dreamily said, "Lord, but it's sure nice to run. See the ground swell soft under me? Gosh, I feel good. My muscles are moving like oil on my bones and it's the best pleasure in the world to run." And they ran. There was no purpose to their running but exhilaration and living.

The white men worked at their running as they worked at everything. You felt embarrassed for them because they were alive too much in the wrong way. Always looking from the corners of their eyes to see if you were watching. The Negroes didn't care if you watched or not; they went on living, moving. They were so sure of playing that they didn't have to think about it any more.

"My, but our men look so nice," said my mother, repeating herself rather flatly. She had seen, compared the teams. Inside, she realized how laxly the colored men hung swaying in their uniforms, and how tensely, nervously, the white men were crammed, shoved, and belted into *their* outfits.

I guess the tenseness began then.

I guess everybody saw what was happening. They saw how the white men looked like senators in sun suits. And they admired the graceful unawareness of the colored men. And, as is always the case, that admiration turned to envy, to jealousy, to irritation. It turned to conversation like:

"That's my husband, Tom, on third base. Why doesn't he pick up his feet? He just *stands* there."

"Never you mind, never you mind. He'll pick 'em up when the time comes!"

"That's what *I* say! Now, take my Henry, for instance. Henry mightn't be active all the time, but when there's a crisis—just you *watch* him. Uh—I do wish he'd wave or something, though. Oh, *there!* Hello, Henry!"

"Look at that Jimmie Cosner playing around out there!"

I looked. A medium-sized white man with a freckled face and red hair was clowning on the diamond. He was balancing a bat on his forehead. There was laughter from the white grandstand. But it sounded like the kind of laughter you laugh when you're embarrassed for someone.

"Play ball!" said the umpire.

A coin was flipped. The colored men batted first.

"Darn it," said my mother.

The colored men ran in from the field happily.

Big Poe was first to bat. I cheered. He picked up the bat in one hand like a toothpick and idled over to the plate and laid the bat on his thick shoulder, smiling along its polished surface toward the stands where the colored women sat with their fresh flowery cream dresses stirring over their legs, which hung down between the seat intervals like crisp new sticks of ginger; their hair was all fancily spun and hung over their ears. Big Poe looked in particular at the little, dainty-as-a-chicken-bone shape of his girl friend Katherine. She was the one who made the beds at the hotel and cottages every morning, who tapped on your door like a bird and politely asked if you was done dreaming, 'cause if you was she'd clean away all them old nightmares and bring in a fresh batch—please use them *one* at a time, thank yoah. Big Poe shook his head, looking at her, as if he couldn't believe she was there. Then he turned, one hand balancing the bat, his left hand dangling free at his side, to await the trial pitches. They hissed past, spatted into the open mouth of the

catcher's mitt, were hurled back. The umpire grunted. The next pitch was the starter.

Big Poe let the first ball go by him.

"Stee-rike!" announced the umpire. Big Poe winked good-naturedly at the white folks. Bang! "Stee-rike two!" cried the umpire.

The ball came for the third time.

Big Poe was suddenly a greased machine pivoting; the dangling hand swept up to the butt end of the bat, the bat swiveled, connected with the ball—— *Whack!* The ball shot up into the sky, away down toward the wavering line of oak trees, down toward the lake, where a white sailboat slid silently by. The crowd yelled, me loudest! There went Uncle George, running on his stubby, wool-stockinged legs, getting smaller with distance.

Big Poe stood for a moment watching the ball go. Then he began to run. He went around the bases, loping, and on the way home from third base he waved to the colored girls naturally and happily and they waved back, standing on their seats and shrilling.

Ten minutes later, with the bases loaded and run after run being driven in, and Big Poe coming to bat again, my mother turned to me. "They're the most inconsiderate people," she said.

"But that's the game," I said. "They've only got two outs."

"But the score's seven to nothing," my mother protested.

"Well, just you wait until *our* men come to bat," said the lady next to my mother, waving away a fly with a pale blue-veined hand. "Those Negroes are too big for their britches."

"Stee-rike two!" said the umpire as Big Poe swung.

"All the past week at the hotel," said the woman next to my mother, staring out at Big Poe steadily, "the hotel service has been simply terrible. Those maids don't talk about a thing save the Cakewalk Jamboree, and whenever you want ice water it takes them half an hour to fetch it, they're so busy sewing."

"Ball one!" said the umpire.

The woman fussed. "I'll be glad when this week's over, that's what I got to say," she said.

"Ball two!" said the umpire to Big Poe.

"Are they going to *walk* him?" asked my mother of me. "Are they *crazy?*" To the woman next to her: "That's right. They been acting funny all week. Last night I had to tell Big Poe twice to put extra butter on my popcorn. I guess he was trying to save money or something."

"Ball three!" said the umpire.

The lady next to my mother cried out suddenly and fanned herself furiously with her newspaper. "Land, I just *thought!* Wouldn't it be awful if they *won* the game? They *might,* you know. They might do it."

My mother looked at the lake, at the trees, at her hands. "I don't know why Uncle George had to play. Make a fool of himself. Douglas, you run tell him to quit right now. It's bad on his heart."

"You're out!" cried the umpire to Big Poe.

"Ah," sighed the grandstand.

The side was retired. Big Poe laid down his bat gently and walked along the base line. The white men pattered in from the field looking red and irritable, with big islands of sweat under their armpits. Big Poe looked over at me. I winked at him. He winked back. Then I knew he wasn't so dumb.

He'd struck out on purpose.

Long Johnson was going to pitch for the colored team.

He ambled out to the rubber, worked his fingers around in his fists to limber them up.

First white man to bat was a man named Kodimer, who sold suits in Chicago all year round.

Long Johnson fed them over the plate with tired, unassuming, controlled accuracy.

Mr. Kodimer chopped. Mr. Kodimer swatted. Finally Mr. Kodimer bunted the ball down the third-base line.

"Out at first base," said the umpire, an Irishman named Mahoney.

Second man up was a young Swede named Moberg. He hit a high fly to center field which was taken by a little plump Negro

who didn't look fat because he moved around like a smooth, round glob of mercury.

Third man up was a Milwaukee truck driver. He whammed a line drive to center field. It was good. Except that he tried to stretch it into a two-bagger. When he pulled up at second base, there was Emancipated Smith with a white pellet in his dark, dark hand, waiting.

My mother sank back in her seat, exhaling. "Well, I *never!*"

"It's getting hotter," said the lady elbow-next. "Think I'll go for a stroll by the lake soon. It's too hot to sit and watch a silly game today. Mightn't you come along with me, missus?" she asked Mother.

It went on that way for five innings.

It was eleven to nothing and Big Poe had struck out three times on purpose, and in the last half of the fifth was when Jimmie Cosner came to bat for our side again. He'd been trying all afternoon, clowning, giving directions, telling everybody just where he was going to blast that pill once he got hold of it. He swaggered up toward the plate now, confident and bugle-voiced. He swung six bats in his thin hands, eying them critically with his shiny green little eyes. He chose one, dropped the others, ran to the plate, chopping out little islands of green fresh lawn with his cleated heels. He pushed his cap back on his dusty red hair. "Watch this!" he called out loud to the ladies. "You watch me show these dark boys! Ya-hah!"

Long Johnson on the mound did a slow serpentine windup. It was like a snake on a limb of a tree, uncoiling, suddenly darting at you. Instantly Johnson's hand was in front of him, open, like black fangs, empty. And the white pill slashed across the plate with a sound like a razor.

"Stee-rike!"

Jimmie Cosner put his bat down and stood glaring at the umpire. He said nothing for a long time. Then he spat deliberately near the catcher's foot, took up the yellow maple bat again, and swung it so the sun glinted the rim of it in a nervous halo. He

twitched and sidled it on his thin-boned shoulder, and his mouth opened and shut over his long nicotined teeth.

Clap! went the catcher's mitt.

Cosner turned, stared.

The catcher, like a black magician, his white teeth gleaming, opened up his oily glove. There, like a white flower growing, was the baseball.

"Stee-rike two!" said the umpire, far away in the heat.

Jimmie Cosner laid his bat across the plate and hunched his freckled hands on his hips. "You mean to tell me that was a strike?"

"That's what I said," said the umpire. "Pick up the bat."

"To hit you on the head with," said Cosner sharply.

"Play ball or hit the showers!"

Jimmie Cosner worked his mouth to collect enough saliva to spit, then angrily swallowed it, swore a bitter oath instead. Reaching down, he raised the bat, poised it like a musket on his shoulder.

And here came the ball! It started out small and wound up big in front of him. Powie! An explosion off the yellow bat. The ball spiraled up and up. Jimmie lit out for first base. The ball paused, as if thinking about gravity up there in the sky. A wave came in on the shore of the lake and fell down. The crowd yelled. Jimmie ran. The ball made its decision, came down. A lithe high-yellar was under it, fumbled it. The ball spilled to the turf, was plucked up, hurled to first base.

Jimmie saw he was going to be out. So he jumped feet-first at the base.

Everyone saw his cleats go into Big Poe's ankle. Everybody saw the red blood. Everybody heard the shout, the shriek, saw the heavy clouds of dust rising.

"I'm safe!" protested Jimmie two minutes later.

Big Poe sat on the ground. The entire dark team stood around him. The doctor bent down, probed Big Poe's ankle, saying, "Mmmm," and "Pretty bad. Here." And he swabbed medicine on it and put a white bandage on it.

The umpire gave Cosner the cold-water eye. "Hit the showers!"

"Like hell!" said Cosner. And he stood on that first base, blowing his cheeks out and in, his freckled hands swaying at his sides. "I'm safe. I'm stayin' right here, by God! No nigger put *me* out!"

"No," said the umpire. "A white man did. *Me. Get!*"

"He dropped the ball! Look up the rules! I'm safe!"

The umpire and Cosner stood glaring at each other.

Big Poe looked up from having his swollen ankle tended. His voice was thick and gentle and his eyes examined Jimmie Cosner gently.

"Yes, he's safe, Mr. Umpire. Leave him stay. He's safe."

I was standing right there. I heard the whole thing. Me and some other kids had run out on the field to see. My mother kept calling me to come back to the stands.

"Yes, he's safe," said Big Poe again.

All the colored men let out a yell.

"What'sa matter with you, black boy? You get hit in the head?"

"You heard me," replied Big Poe quietly. He looked at the doctor bandaging him. "He's safe. Leave him stay."

The umpire swore.

"Okay, okay. So he's safe!"

The umpire stalked off, his back stiff, his neck red.

Big Poe was helped up. "Better not walk on that," cautioned the doctor.

"I can walk," whispered Big Poe carefully.

"Better not play."

"I can play," said Big Poe gently, certainly, shaking his head, wet streaks drying under his white eyes. "I'll play *good*." He looked no place at all. "I'll play plenty good."

"Oh," said the second-base colored man. It was a funny sound.

All the colored men looked at each other, at Big Poe, then at Jimmie Cosner, at the sky, at the lake, the crowd. They walked off quietly to take their places. Big Poe stood with his bad foot hardly touching the ground, balanced. The doctor argued. But Big Poe waved him away.

"Batter up!" cried the umpire.

We got settled in the stands again. My mother pinched my leg and asked me why I couldn't sit still. It got warmer. Three or four more waves fell on the shore line. Behind the wire screen the ladies fanned their wet faces and the men inched their rumps forward on the wooden planks, held papers over their scowling brows to see Big Poe standing like a redwood tree out there on first base, Jimmie Cosner standing in the immense shade of that dark tree.

Young Moberg came up to bat for our side.

"Come on, Swede, come on, Swede!" was the cry, a lonely cry, like a dry bird, from out on the blazing green turf. It was Jimmie Cosner calling. The grandstand stared at him. The dark heads turned on their moist pivots in the outfield; the black faces came in his direction, looking him over, seeing his thin, nervously arched back. He was the center of the universe.

"Come on, Swede! Let's show these black boys!" laughed Cosner.

He trailed off. There was a complete silence. Only the wind came through the high, glittering trees.

"Come on, Swede, hang one on that old pill. . . ."

Long Johnson, on the pitcher's mound, cocked his head. Slowly, deliberately, he eyed Cosner. A look passed between him and Big Poe, and Jimmie Cosner saw the look and shut up and swallowed, hard.

Long Johnson took his time with his windup.

Cosner took a lead off base.

Long Johnson stopped loading his pitch.

Cosner skipped back to the bag, kissed his hand, and patted the kiss dead center on the plate. Then he looked up and smiled around.

Again the pitcher coiled up his long, hinged arm, curled loving dark fingers on the leather pellet, drew it back and—— Cosner danced off first base. Cosner jumped up and down like a monkey. The pitcher did not look at him. The pitcher's eyes watched secretively, slyly, amusedly, sidewise. Then, snapping

his head, the pitcher scared Cosner back to the plate. Cosner stood and jeered.

The third time Long Johnson made as if to pitch, Cosner was far off the plate and running toward second.

Snap went the pitcher's hand. *Bom* went the ball in Big Poe's glove at first base.

Everything was sort of frozen. Just for a second.

There was the sun in the sky, the lake and the boats on it, the grandstands, the pitcher on his mound standing with his hand out and down after tossing the ball; there was Big Poe with the ball in his mighty black hand; there was the infield staring, crouching in at the scene, and there was Jimmie Cosner running, kicking up dirt, the only moving thing in the entire summer world.

Big Poe leaned forward, sighted toward second base, drew back his mighty right hand, and hurled that white baseball straight down along the line until it reached Jimmie Cosner's head.

Next instant, the spell was broken.

Jimmie Cosner lay flat on the burning grass. People boiled out of the grandstands. There was swearing, and women screaming, a clattering of wood as the men rushed down the wooden boards of the bleachers. The colored team ran in from the field. Jimmie Cosner lay there. Big Poe, no expression on his face, limped off the field, pushing white men away from him like clothespins when they tried stopping him. He just picked them up and threw them away.

"Come on, Douglas!" shrieked Mother, grabbing me. "Let's get home! They might have razors! Oh!"

That night, after the near riot of the afternoon, my folks stayed home reading magazines. All the cottages around us were lighted. Everybody was home. Distantly I heard music. I slipped out the back door into the ripe summer-night darkness and ran toward the dance pavilion. All the lights were on, and music played.

But there were no white people at the tables. Nobody had come to the Jamboree.

There were only colored folks. Women in bright red and blue satin gowns and net stockings and soft gloves, with wine-plume hats, and men in glossy tuxedos. The music crashed out, up, down, and around the floor. And laughing and stepping high, flinging their polished shoes out and up in the cakewalk, were Long Johnson and Cavanaugh and Jiff Miller and Pete Brown, and—limping—Big Poe and Katherine, his girl, and all the other lawn-cutters and boatmen and janitors and chambermaids, all on the floor at one time.

It was so dark all around the pavilion; the stars shone in the black sky, and I stood outside, my nose against the window, looking in for a long, long time, silently.

I went to bed without telling anyone what I'd seen.

I just lay in the dark smelling the ripe apples in the dimness and hearing the lake at night and listening to that distant, faint and wonderful music. Just before I slept I heard those last strains again:

> "—gonna dance out both of my shoes,
> When they play those Jelly Roll Blues;
> Tomorrow night at the Dark Town Strutters' Ball!"

A SOUND OF THUNDER

The sign on the wall seemed to quaver under a film of sliding warm water. Eckels felt his eyelids blink over his stare, and the sign burned in this momentary darkness:

TIME SAFARI, INC.
SAFARIS TO ANY YEAR IN THE PAST.
YOU NAME THE ANIMAL.
WE TAKE YOU THERE.
YOU SHOOT IT.

A warm phlegm gathered in Eckels' throat; he swallowed and pushed it down. The muscles around his mouth formed a smile as he put his hand slowly out upon the air, and in that hand waved a check for ten thousand dollars to the man behind the desk.

"Does this safari guarantee I come back alive?"

"We guarantee nothing," said the official, "except the dinosaurs." He turned. "This is Mr. Travis, your Safari Guide in the Past. He'll tell you what and where to shoot. If he says no shooting, no shooting. If you disobey instructions, there's a stiff

penalty of another ten thousand dollars, plus possible government action, on your return."

Eckels glanced across the vast office at a mass and tangle, a
snaking and humming of wires and steel boxes, at an aurora
that flickered now orange, now silver, now blue. There was a
sound like a gigantic bonfire burning all of Time, all the years
and all the parchment calendars, all the hours piled high and
set aflame.

A touch of the hand and this burning would, on the instant,
beautifully reverse itself. Eckels remembered the wording in the
advertisements to the letter. Out of chars and ashes, out of dust
and coals, like golden salamanders, the old years, the green
years, might leap; roses sweeten the air, white hair turn Irish-
black, wrinkles vanish; all, everything fly back to seed, flee death,
rush down to their beginnings, suns rise in western skies and set
in glorious easts, moons eat themselves opposite to the custom, all
and everything cupping one in another like Chinese boxes, rabbits into hats, all and everything returning to the fresh death,
the seed death, the green death, to the time before the beginning.
A touch of a hand might do it, the merest touch of a hand.

"Hell and damn," Eckels breathed, the light of the Machine
on his thin face. "A real Time Machine." He shook his head.
"Makes you think. If the election had gone badly yesterday, I
might be here now running away from the results. Thank God
Keith won. He'll make a fine President of the United States."

"Yes," said the man behind the desk. "We're lucky. If
Deutscher had gotten in, we'd have the worst kind of dictator-
ship. There's an anti-everything man for you, a militarist, anti-
Christ, anti-human, anti-intellectual. People called us up, you
know, joking but not joking. Said if Deutscher became President
they wanted to go live in 1492. Of course it's not our business to conduct Escapes, but to form Safaris. Anyway, Keith's
President now. All you got to worry about is——"

"Shooting my dinosaur," Eckels finished it for him.

"A *Tyrannosaurus rex*. The Thunder Lizard, the damnedest

monster in history. Sign this release. Anything happens to you, we're not responsible. Those dinosaurs are hungry."

Eckels flushed angrily. "Trying to scare me!"

"Frankly, yes. We don't want anyone going who'll panic at the first shot. Six Safari leaders were killed last year, and a dozen hunters. We're here to give you the damnedest thrill a *real* hunter ever asked for. Traveling you back sixty million years to bag the biggest damned game in all Time. Your personal check's still there. Tear it up."

Mr. Eckels looked at the check for a long time. His fingers twitched.

"Good luck," said the man behind the desk. "Mr. Travis, he's all yours."

They moved silently across the room, taking their guns with them, toward the Machine, toward the silver metal and the roaring light.

First a day and then a night and then a day and then a night, then it was day-night-day-night-day. A week, a month, a year, a decade! A.D. 2055. A.D. 2019. 1999! 1957! Gone! The Machine roared.

They put on their oxygen helmets and tested the intercoms.

Eckels swayed on the padded seat, his face pale, his jaw stiff. He felt the trembling in his arms and he looked down and found his hands tight on the new rifle. There were four other men in the Machine. Travis, the Safari Leader, his assistant, Lesperance, and two other hunters, Billings and Kramer. They sat looking at each other, and the years blazed around them.

"Can these guns get a dinosaur cold?" Eckels felt his mouth saying.

"If you hit them right," said Travis on the helmet radio. "Some dinosaurs have two brains, one in the head, another far down the spinal column. We stay away from those. That's stretching luck. Put your first two shots into the eyes, if you can, blind them, and go back into the brain."

The Machine howled. Time was a film run backward. Suns

fled and ten million moons fled after them. "Good God," said Eckels. "Every hunter that ever lived would envy us today. This makes Africa seem like Illinois."

The Machine slowed; its scream fell to a murmur. The Machine stopped.

The sun stopped in the sky.

The fog that had enveloped the Machine blew away and they were in an old time, a very old time indeed, three hunters and two Safari Heads with their blue metal guns across their knees.

"Christ isn't born yet," said Travis. "Moses has not gone to the mountain to talk with God. The Pyramids are still in the earth, waiting to be cut out and put up. *Remember* that. Alexander, Caesar, Napoleon, Hitler—none of them exists."

The men nodded.

"That"—Mr. Travis pointed—"is the jungle of sixty million two thousand and fifty-five years before President Keith."

He indicated a metal path that struck off into green wilderness, over steaming swamp, among giant ferns and palms.

"And that," he said, "is the Path, laid by Time Safari for your use. It floats six inches above the earth. Doesn't touch so much as one grass blade, flower, or tree. It's an anti-gravity metal. Its purpose is to keep you from touching this world of the past in any way. Stay on the Path. Don't go off it. I repeat. *Don't go off.* For *any* reason! If you fall off, there's a penalty. And don't shoot any animal we don't okay."

"Why?" asked Eckels.

They sat in the ancient wilderness. Far birds' cries blew on a wind, and the smell of tar and an old salt sea, moist grasses, and flowers the color of blood.

"We don't want to change the Future. We don't belong here in the Past. The government doesn't *like* us here. We have to pay big graft to keep our franchise. A Time Machine is damn finicky business. Not knowing it, we might kill an important animal, a small bird, a roach, a flower even, thus destroying an important link in a growing species."

"That's not clear," said Eckels.

"All right," Travis continued, "say we accidentally kill one mouse here. That means all the future families of this one particular mouse are destroyed, right?"

"Right."

"And all the families of the families of the families of that one mouse! With a stamp of your foot, you annihilate first one, then a dozen, then a thousand, a million, a *billion* possible mice!"

"So they're dead," said Eckels. "So what?"

"So what?" Travis snorted quietly. "Well, what about the foxes that'll need those mice to survive? For want of ten mice, a fox dies. For want of ten foxes, a lion starves. For want of a lion, all manner of insects, vultures, infinite billions of life forms are thrown into chaos and destruction. Eventually it all boils down to this: fifty-nine million years later, a cave man, one of a dozen on the *entire world,* goes hunting wild boar or saber-tooth tiger for food. But you, friend, have *stepped* on all the tigers in that region. By stepping on *one* single mouse. So the cave man starves. And the cave man, please note, is not just *any* expendable man, no! He is an *entire future nation.* From his loins would have sprung ten sons. From *their* loins one hundred sons, and thus onward to a civilization. Destroy this one man, and you destroy a race, a people, an entire history of life. It is comparable to slaying some of Adam's grandchildren. The stomp of your foot, on one mouse, could start an earthquake, the effects of which could shake our earth and destinies down through Time, to their very foundations. With the death of that one cave man, a billion others yet unborn are throttled in the womb. Perhaps Rome never rises on its seven hills. Perhaps Europe is forever a dark forest, and only Asia waxes healthy and teeming. Step on a mouse and you crush the Pyramids. Step on a mouse and you leave your print, like a Grand Canyon, across Eternity. Queen Elizabeth might never be born, Washington might not cross the Delaware, there might never be a United States at all. So be careful. Stay on the Path. *Never* step off!"

"I see," said Eckels. "Then it wouldn't pay for us even to touch the *grass?"*

"Correct. Crushing certain plants could add up infinitesimally. A little error here would multiply in sixty million years, all out of proportion. Of course maybe our theory is wrong. Maybe Time *can't* be changed by us. Or maybe it can be changed only in little subtle ways. A dead mouse here makes an insect imbalance there, a population disproportion later, a bad harvest further on, a depression, mass starvation, and, finally, a change in *social* temperament in far-flung countries. Something much more subtle, like that. Perhaps only a soft breath, a whisper, a hair, pollen on the air, such a slight, slight change that unless you looked close you wouldn't see it. Who knows? Who really can say he knows? We don't know. We're guessing. But until we do know for certain whether our messing around in Time *can* make a big roar or a little rustle in history, we're being damned careful. This Machine, this Path, your clothing and bodies, were sterilized, as you know, before the journey. We wear these oxygen helmets so we can't introduce our bacteria into an ancient atmosphere."

"How do we know which animals to shoot?"

"They're marked with red paint," said Travis. "Today, before our journey, we sent Lesperance here back with the Machine. He came to this particular era and followed certain animals."

"Studying them?"

"Right," said Lesperance. "I track them through their entire existence, noting which of them lives longest. Very few. How many times they mate. Not often. Life's short. When I find one that's going to die when a tree falls on him, or one that drowns in a tar pit, I note the exact hour, minute, and second. I shoot a paint bomb. It leaves a red patch on his hide. We can't miss it. Then I correlate our arrival in the Past so that we meet the Monster not more than two minutes before he would have died anyway. This way, we kill only animals with no future, that are never going to mate again. You see how *careful* we are?"

"But if you came back this morning in Time," said Eckels eagerly, "you must've bumped into *us,* our Safari! How did it turn out? Was it successful? Did all of us get through—alive?"

Travis and Lesperance gave each other a look.

"That'd be a paradox," said the latter. "Time doesn't permit that sort of mess—a man meeting himself. When such occasions threaten, Time steps aside. Like an airplane hitting an air pocket. You felt the Machine jump just before we stopped? That was us passing ourselves on the way back to the Future. We saw nothing. There's no way of telling *if* this expedition was a success, *if* we got our monster, or whether all of us—meaning *you*, Mr. Eckels—got out alive."

Eckels smiled palely.

"Cut that," said Travis sharply. "Everyone on his feet!"

They were ready to leave the Machine.

The jungle was high and the jungle was broad and the jungle was the entire world forever and forever. Sounds like music and sounds like flying tents filled the sky, and those were pterodactyls soaring with cavernous gray wings, gigantic bats out of a delirium and a night fever. Eckels, balanced on the narrow Path, aimed his rifle playfully.

"Stop that!" said Travis. "Don't even aim for fun, damn it! If your gun should go off——"

Eckels flushed. "Where's our *Tyrannosaurus?*"

Lesperance checked his wrist watch. "Up ahead. We'll bisect his trail in sixty seconds. Look for the red paint, for Christ's sake. Don't shoot till we give the word. Stay on the Path. *Stay on the Path!*"

They moved forward in the wind of morning.

"Strange," murmured Eckels. "Up ahead, sixty million years, Election Day over. Keith made President. Everyone celebrating. And here we are, a million years lost, and they don't exist. The things we worried about for months, a lifetime, not even born or thought about yet."

"Safety catches off, everyone!" ordered Travis. "You, first shot, Eckels. Second, Billings. Third, Kramer."

"I've hunted tiger, wild boar, buffalo, elephant, but Jesus, this is *it*," said Eckels. "I'm shaking like a kid."

"Ah," said Travis.

Everyone stopped.

Travis raised his hand. "Ahead," he whispered. "In the mist. There he is. There's His Royal Majesty now."

The jungle was wide and full of twitterings, rustlings, murmurs, and sighs.

Suddenly it all ceased, as if someone had shut a door.

Silence.

A sound of thunder.

Out of the mist, one hundred yards away, came *Tyrannosaurus rex*.

"Jesus God," whispered Eckels.

"Sh!"

It came on great oiled, resilient, striding legs. It towered thirty feet above half of the trees, a great evil god, folding its delicate watchmaker's claws close to its oily reptilian chest. Each lower leg was a piston, a thousand pounds of white bone, sunk in thick ropes of muscle, sheathed over in a gleam of pebbled skin like the mail of a terrible warrior. Each thigh was a ton of meat, ivory, and steel mesh. And from the great breathing cage of the upper body those two delicate arms dangled out front, arms with hands which might pick up and examine men like toys, while the snake neck coiled. And the head itself, a ton of sculptured stone, lifted easily upon the sky. Its mouth gaped, exposing a fence of teeth like daggers. Its eyes rolled, ostrich eggs, empty of all expression save hunger. It closed its mouth in a death grin. It ran, its pelvic bones crushing aside trees and bushes, its taloned feet clawing damp earth, leaving prints six inches deep wherever it settled its weight. It ran with a gliding ballet step, far too poised and balanced for its ten tons. It moved into a sunlit arena warily, its beautifully reptile hands feeling the air.

"My God!" Eckels twitched his mouth. "It could reach up and grab the moon."

"Sh!" Travis jerked angrily. "He hasn't seen us yet."

"It can't be killed." Eckels pronounced this verdict quietly, as if there could be no argument. He had weighed the evidence and

this was his considered opinion. The rifle in his hands seemed a cap gun. "We were fools to come. This is impossible."

"Shut up!" hissed Travis.

"Nightmare."

"Turn around," commanded Travis. "Walk quietly to the Machine. We'll remit one half your fee."

"I didn't realize it would be this *big*," said Eckels. "I miscalculated, that's all. And now I want out."

"It *sees* us!"

"There's the red paint on its chest!"

The Thunder Lizard raised itself. Its armored flesh glittered like a thousand green coins. The coins, crusted with slime, steamed. In the slime, tiny insects wriggled, so that the entire body seemed to twitch and undulate, even while the monster itself did not move. It exhaled. The stink of raw flesh blew down the wilderness.

"Get me out of here," said Eckels. "It was never like this before. I was always sure I'd come through alive. I had good guides, good safaris, and safety. This time, I figured wrong. I've met my match and admit it. This is too much for me to get hold of."

"Don't run," said Lesperance. "Turn around. Hide in the Machine."

"Yes." Eckels seemed to be numb. He looked at his feet as if trying to make them move. He gave a grunt of helplessness.

"Eckels!"

He took a few steps, blinking, shuffling.

"Not *that* way!"

The Monster, at the first motion, lunged forward with a terrible scream. It covered one hundred yards in four seconds. The rifles jerked up and blazed fire. A windstorm from the beast's mouth engulfed them in the stench of slime and old blood. The Monster roared, teeth glittering with sun.

Eckels, not looking back, walked blindly to the edge of the Path, his gun limp in his arms, stepped off the Path, and walked, not knowing it, in the jungle. His feet sank into green moss. His

legs moved him, and he felt alone and remote from the events behind.

The rifles cracked again. Their sound was lost in shriek and lizard thunder. The great lever of the reptile's tail swung up, lashed sideways. Trees exploded in clouds of leaf and branch. The Monster twitched its jeweler's hands down to fondle at the men, to twist them in half, to crush them like berries, to cram them into its teeth and its screaming throat. Its boulder-stone eyes leveled with the men. They saw themselves mirrored. They fired at the metallic eyelids and the blazing black iris.

Like a stone idol, like a mountain avalanche, *Tyrannosaurus* fell. Thundering, it clutched trees, pulled them with it. It wrenched and tore the metal Path. The men flung themselves back and away. The body hit, ten tons of cold flesh and stone. The guns fired. The Monster lashed its armored tail, twitched its snake jaws, and lay still. A fount of blood spurted from its throat. Somewhere inside, a sac of fluids burst. Sickening gushes drenched the hunters. They stood, red and glistening.

The thunder faded.

The jungle was silent. After the avalanche, a green peace. After the nightmare, morning.

Billings and Kramer sat on the pathway and threw up. Travis and Lesperance stood with smoking rifles, cursing steadily.

In the Time Machine, on his face, Eckels lay shivering. He had found his way back to the Path, climbed into the Machine.

Travis came walking, glanced at Eckels, took cotton gauze from a metal box, and returned to the others, who were sitting on the Path.

"Clean up."

They wiped the blood from their helmets. They began to curse too. The Monster lay, a hill of solid flesh. Within, you could hear the sighs and murmurs as the furthest chambers of it died, the organs malfunctioning, liquids running a final instant from pocket to sac to spleen, everything shutting off, closing up forever. It was like standing by a wrecked locomotive or a steam shovel at quitting time, all valves being released or levered tight.

Bones cracked; the tonnage of its own flesh, off balance, dead weight, snapped the delicate forearms, caught underneath. The meat settled, quivering.

Another cracking sound. Overhead, a gigantic tree branch broke from its heavy mooring, fell. It crashed upon the dead beast with finality.

"There." Lesperance checked his watch. "Right on time. That's the giant tree that was scheduled to fall and kill this animal originally." He glanced at the two hunters. "You want the trophy picture?"

"What?"

"We can't take a trophy back to the Future. The body has to stay right here where it would have died originally, so the insects, birds, and bacteria can get at it, as they were intended to. Everything in balance. The body stays. But we *can* take a picture of you standing near it."

The two men tried to think, but gave up, shaking their heads.

They let themselves be led along the metal Path. They sank wearily into the Machine cushions. They gazed back at the ruined Monster, the stagnating mound, where already strange reptilian birds and golden insects were busy at the steaming armor.

A sound on the floor of the Time Machine stiffened them. Eckels sat there, shivering.

"I'm sorry," he said at last.

"Get up!" cried Travis.

Eckels got up.

"Go out on that Path alone," said Travis. He had his rifle pointed. "You're not coming back in the Machine. We're leaving you here!"

Lesperance seized Travis' arm. "Wait——"

"Stay out of this!" Travis shook his hand away. "This son of a bitch nearly killed us. But it isn't *that* so much. Hell, no. It's his *shoes!* Look at them! He ran off the Path. My God, that *ruins* us! Christ knows how much we'll forfeit! Tens of thousands of dollars of insurance! We guarantee no one leaves the Path. He left

it. Oh, the damn fool! I'll have to report to the government. They might revoke our license to travel. God knows *what* he's done to Time, to History!"

"Take it easy, all he did was kick up some dirt."

"How do we *know?*" cried Travis. "We don't know anything! It's all a damn mystery! Get out there, Eckels!"

Eckels fumbled his shirt. "I'll pay anything. A hundred thousand dollars!"

Travis glared at Eckels' checkbook and spat. "Go out there. The Monster's next to the Path. Stick your arms up to your elbows in his mouth. Then you can come back with us."

"That's unreasonable!"

"The Monster's dead, you yellow bastard. The bullets! The bullets can't be left behind. They don't belong in the Past; they might change something. Here's my knife. Dig them out!"

The jungle was alive again, full of the old tremorings and bird cries. Eckels turned slowly to regard that primeval garbage dump, that hill of nightmares and terror. After a long time, like a sleepwalker, he shuffled out along the Path.

He returned, shuddering, five minutes later, his arms soaked and red to the elbows. He held out his hands. Each held a number of steel bullets. Then he fell. He lay where he fell, not moving.

"You didn't have to make him do that," said Lesperance.

"Didn't I? It's too early to tell." Travis nudged the still body. "He'll live. Next time he won't go hunting game like this. Okay." He jerked his thumb wearily at Lesperance. "Switch on. Let's go home."

1492.   1776.   1812.

They cleaned their hands and faces. They changed their caking shirts and pants. Eckels was up and around again, not speaking. Travis glared at him for a full ten minutes.

"Don't look at me," cried Eckels. "I haven't done anything."

"Who can tell?"

"Just ran off the Path, that's all, a little mud on my shoes—what do you want me to do—get down and pray?"

"We might need it. I'm warning you, Eckels, I might kill you yet. I've got my gun ready."

"I'm innocent. I've done nothing!"

1999.   2000.   2055.

The Machine stopped.

"Get out," said Travis.

The room was there as they had left it. But not the same as they had left it. The same man sat behind the same desk. But the same man did not quite sit behind the same desk.

Travis looked around swiftly. "Everything okay here?" he snapped.

"Fine. Welcome home!"

Travis did not relax. He seemed to be looking at the very atoms of the air itself, at the way the sun poured through the one high window.

"Okay, Eckels, get out. Don't ever come back."

Eckels could not move.

"You heard me," said Travis. "What're you *staring* at?"

Eckels stood smelling of the air, and there was a thing to the air, a chemical taint so subtle, so slight, that only a faint cry of his subliminal senses warned him it was there. The colors, white, gray, blue, orange, in the wall, in the furniture, in the sky beyond the window, were . . . were . . . And there was a *feel*. His flesh twitched. His hands twitched. He stood drinking the oddness with the pores of his body. Somewhere, someone must have been screaming one of those whistles that only a dog can hear. His body screamed silence in return. Beyond this room, beyond this wall, beyond this man who was not quite the same man seated at this desk that was not quite the same desk . . . lay an entire world of streets and people. What sort of world it was now, there was no telling. He could feel them moving there, beyond the walls, almost, like so many chess pieces blown in a dry wind. . . .

But the immediate thing was the sign painted on the office wall, the same sign he had read earlier today on first entering.

Somehow, the sign had changed:

TYME SEFARI INC.
SEFARIS TU ANY YEER EN THE PAST.
YU NAIM THE ANIMALL.
WEE TAEK YU THAIR.
YU SHOOT ITT.

Eckels felt himself fall into a chair. He fumbled crazily at the thick slime on his boots. He held up a clod of dirt, trembling. "No, it *can't* be. Not a *little* thing like that. No!"

Embedded in the mud, glistening green and gold and black, was a butterfly, very beautiful, and very dead.

"Not a little thing like *that!* Not a butterfly!" cried Eckels.

It fell to the floor, an exquisite thing, a small thing that could upset balances and knock down a line of small dominoes and then big dominoes and then gigantic dominoes, all down the years across Time. Eckels' mind whirled. It *couldn't* change things. Killing one butterfly couldn't be *that* important! Could it?

His face was cold. His mouth trembled, asking: "Who—who won the presidential election yesterday?"

The man behind the desk laughed. "You joking? You know damn well. Deutscher, of course! Who else? Not that damn weakling Keith. We got an iron man now, a man with guts, by God!" The official stopped. "What's wrong?"

Eckels moaned. He dropped to his knees. He scrabbled at the golden butterfly with shaking fingers. "Can't we," he pleaded to the world, to himself, to the officials, to the Machine, "can't we take it *back,* can't we *make* it alive again? Can't we start over? Can't we——"

He did not move. Eyes shut, he waited, shivering. He heard Travis breathe loud in the room; he heard Travis shift his rifle, click the safety catch, and raise the weapon.

There was a sound of thunder.

14

THE GREAT WIDE WORLD OVER THERE

It was a day to be out of bed, to pull curtains and fling open windows. It was a day to make your heart bigger with warm mountain air.

Cora, feeling like a young girl in a wrinkled old dress, sat up in bed.

It was early, the sun barely on the horizon, but already the birds were stirring from the pines and ten billion red ants milled free from their bronze hills by the cabin door. Cora's husband Tom slept like a bear in a snowy hibernation of bedclothes beside her. Will my heart wake him up? she wondered.

And then she knew why this seemed a special day.

"Benjy's coming!"

She imagined him far off, leaping green meadows, fording streams where spring was pushing itself in cool colors of moss and clear water toward the sea. She saw his great shoes dusting and flicking the stony roads and paths. She saw his freckled face high in the sun looking giddily down his long body at his distant hands flying out and back behind him.

Benjy, come on! she thought, opening a window swiftly. Wind blew her hair like a gray spider web about her cold ears. Now

Benjy's at Iron Bridge, now at Meadow Pike, now up Creek Path, over Chesley's Field . . .

Somewhere in those Missouri mountains was Benjy. Cora blinked. Those strange high hills beyond which twice a year she and Tom drove their horse and wagon to town, and through which, thirty years ago, she had wanted to run forever, saying, "Oh, Tom, let's just drive and drive until we reach the sea." But Tom had looked at her as if she had slapped his face, and he had turned the wagon around and driven on home, talking to the mare. And if people lived by shores where the sea came like a storm, now louder, now softer, every day, she did not know it. And if there were cities where neons were like pink ice and green mint and red fireworks each evening, she didn't know that either. Her horizon, north, south, east, west, was this valley, and had never been anything else.

But now, today, she thought, Benjy's coming from that world out there; he's seen it, heard it, smelt it; he'll tell me about it. And he can write. She looked at her hands. He'll be here a whole month and teach me. Then I can write out into that world and bring it here to the mailbox I'll make Tom build today. "Get up, Tom! You *hear?*"

She put her hand out to push the bank of sleeping snow.

By nine o'clock the valley was full of grasshoppers flinging themselves through the blue, piney air, while smoke curled into the sky.

Cora, singing into her pots and pans as she polished them, saw her wrinkled face bronzed and freshened in the copper bottoms. Tom was grumbling the sounds of a sleepy bear at his mush breakfast, while her singing moved all about him, like a bird in a cage.

"*Someone's* mighty happy," said a voice.

Cora made herself into a statue. From the corners of her eyes she saw a shadow cross the room.

"Mrs. Brabbam?" asked Cora of her scouring cloth.

"That's who it is!" And there stood the Widow Lady, her

gingham dress dragging the warm dust, her letters in her chickeny hand. "Morning! I just been to my mailbox. Got me a real beauty of a letter from my uncle George in Springfield." Mrs. Brabbam fixed Cora with a gaze like a silver needle. "How long since you got a letter from *your* uncle, missus?"

"My uncles are all dead." It was not Cora herself, but her tongue, that lied. When the time came, she knew, it would be her tongue alone that must take communion and confess earthly sinning.

"It's certainly *nice,* getting mail." Mrs. Brabbam waved her letters in a straight flush on the morning air.

Always twisting the knife in the flesh. How many years, thought Cora, had this run on, Mrs. Brabbam and her smily eyes, talking loud of how she got mail; implying that nobody else for miles around could read? Cora bit her lip and almost threw the pot, but set it down, laughing. "I forgot to tell you. My nephew Benjy's coming; his folks are poorly, and he's here for the summer today. He'll teach me to write. And Tom's building us a postal box, aren't you, Tom?"

Mrs. Brabbam clutched her letters. "Well, isn't that fine! You *lucky* lady." And suddenly the door was empty. Mrs. Brabbam was gone.

But Cora was after her. For in that instant she had seen something like a scarecrow, something like a flicker of pure sunlight, something like a brook trout jumping upstream, leap a fence in the yard below. She saw a huge hand wave and birds flush in terror from a crab-apple tree.

Cora was rushing, the world rushing back of her, down the path. "Benjy!"

They ran at each other like partners in a Saturday dance, linked arms, collided, and waltzed, jabbering. "Benjy!"

She glanced swiftly behind his ear.

Yes, *there* was the yellow pencil.

"Benjy, welcome!"

"Why, ma'am!" He held her off at arm's length. "Why, ma'am, you're *crying.*"

"Here's my nephew," said Cora.

Tom scowled up from spooning his corn-meal mush.

"Mighty glad," smiled Benjy.

Cora held his arm tight so he couldn't vanish. She felt faint, wanting to sit, stand, run, but she only beat her heart fast and laughed at strange times. Now, in an instant, the far countries were brought near; here was this tall boy, lighting up the room like a pine torch, this boy who had seen cities and seas and been places when things had been better for his parents.

"Benjy, I got peas, corn, bacon, mush, soup, and beans for breakfast."

"Hold on!" said Tom.

"Hush, Tom, the boy's down to the bone with walking." She turned to the boy. "Benjy, tell me all about yourself. You *did* go to school?"

Benjy kicked off his shoes. With one bare foot he traced a word in the hearth ashes.

Tom scowled. "What's it say?"

"It says," said Benjy, "C and O and R and A. *Cora.*"

"*My* name, Tom, see it! Oh, Benjy, it's good you really write, child. We had one cousin here, long ago, claimed he could spell upside down and backwards. So we fattened him up and he wrote letters and we never got answers. Come to find out he knew just enough spelling to mail letters to the dead-letter office. Lord, Tom knocked two months' worth of vittles out of that boy, batting him up the road with a piece of fence."

They laughed anxiously.

"I write fine," said the serious boy.

"That's all we want to know." She shoved a cut of berry pie at him. "Eat."

By ten-thirty, with the sun riding higher, after watching Benjy devour heaped platters of food, Tom thundered from the cabin, jamming his cap on. "I'm going out, by God, and cut down half the forest!" he said angrily.

But no one heard. Cora was seated in a breathless spell. She

was watching the pencil behind Benjy's peach-fuzz ear. She saw him finger it casually, lazily, indifferently. Oh, not so casual, Benjy, she thought. Handle it like a spring robin's egg. She wanted to touch the pencil, but hadn't touched one in years because it made her feel foolish and then angry and then sad. Her hand twitched in her lap.

"You got some paper?" asked Benjy.

"Oh, land, I never thought," she wailed, and the room walls darkened. "What'll we do?"

"Just happens I brought some." He fetched a tablet from his little bag. "You want to write a letter somewhere?"

She smiled outrageously. "I want to write a letter to . . . to . . ." Her face fell apart. She looked around for someone in the distance. She looked at the mountains in the morning sunshine. She heard the sea rolling off on yellow shores a thousand miles away. The birds were coming north over the valley, on their way to multitudes of cities indifferent to her need at this instant.

"Benjy, why, I never thought until this moment. I don't know anybody in all that world out there. Nobody but my aunt. And if I wrote her it'd make her feel bad, a hundred miles from here, to have to find someone else to read the letter to her. She's got a whale-boned-corset sort of pride. Make her nervous the next ten years, that letter setting in her house on the mantel. No, no letter to her." Cora's eyes moved from the hills and the unseen ocean. "Who then? Where? Someone. I just've got to get me some letters."

"Hold on." Benjy fished a dime magazine from his coat. It had a red cover of an undressed lady screaming away from a green monster. "All sorts of addresses in here."

They leafed the pages together. "What's *this?*" Cora tapped an ad.

"'HERE'S YOUR *Power Plus* FREE MUSCLE CHART. Send name, address,'" read Benjy, "'to Dept. M-3 for Free Health Map!'"

"And what about *this* one?"

"'DETECTIVES MAKE SECRET INVESTIGATIONS. PARTICULARS FREE. WRITE: G.D.M. DETECTIVE SCHOOL——'"

"Everything's free. Well, Benjy." She looked at the pencil in his hand. He drew up his chair. She watched him turn the pencil in his fingers, making minor adjustments. She saw him bite his tongue softly. She saw him squint his eyes. She held her breath. She bent forward. She squinted her own eyes and clamped her tongue.

Now, now Benjy raised his pencil, licked it, and set it down to the paper.

There it is, thought Cora.

The first words. They formed themselves slowly on the incredible paper.

Dear Power Plus Muscle Company
Sirs, [he wrote].

The morning blew away on a wind, the morning flowed down the creek, the morning flew off with some ravens, and the sun burned on the cabin roof. Cora didn't turn when she heard a shuffle at the blazing, sun-filled door. Tom was there, but not there; nothing was before her but a series of filled pages, a whispering pencil, and Benjy's careful Palmer Penmanship hand. Cora moved her head around, around, with each *o,* each *l,* with each small hill of an *m;* each tiny dot made her head peck like a chicken; each crossed *t* made her tongue lick across her upper lip.

"It's noon and I'm hungry!" said Tom almost behind her.

But Cora was a statue now, watching the pencil as one watches a snail leaving an exceptional trail across a flat stone in the early morning.

"It's noon!" cried Tom again.

Cora glanced up, stunned.

"Why, it seems only a moment ago we wrote to that Philadelphia Coin Collecting Company, ain't that right, Benjy?" Cora smiled a smile much too dazzling for a woman fifty-five years old. "While you wait for your vittles, Tom, just can't you build that mailbox? Bigger than Mrs. Brabbam's, please?"

"I'll nail up a shoe box."

"Tom Gibbs." She rose pleasantly. Her smile said, Better run,

better work, better *do!* "I want a big, pretty mailbox. All white, for Benjy to paint our name on in black spelling. I won't have any shoe box for my very first real letter."

And it was done.

Benjy lettered the finished mailbox: MRS. CORA GIBBS, while Tom stood grumbling behind him.

"What's it say?"

"'MR. TOM GIBBS,'" said Benjy quietly, painting.

Tom blinked at it for a minute, quietly, and then said, "I'm *still* hungry. Someone light the fire."

There were no stamps. Cora turned white. Tom was made to hitch up the horse and drive to Green Fork to buy some red ones, a green, and ten pink stamps with dignified gentlemen printed on them. But Cora rode along to be certain Tom didn't hurl these first letters in the creek. When they rode home, the first thing Cora did, face glowing, was poke in the new mailbox.

"You crazy?" said Tom.

"No harm looking."

That afternoon she visited the mailbox six times. On the seventh, a woodchuck jumped out. Tom stood laughing in the door, pounding his knees. Cora chased him out of the house, still laughing.

Then she stood in the window looking down at her mailbox right across from Mrs. Brabbam's. Ten years ago the Widow Lady had plunked her letter box right under Cora's nose, almost, when she could as easily have built it up nearer her own cabin. But it gave Mrs. Brabbam an excuse to float like a flower on a river down the hill path, flip the box wide with a great coughing and rustling, from time to time spying up to see if Cora was watching. Cora always was. When caught, she pretended to sprinkle flowers with an empty watering can, or pick mushrooms in the wrong season.

Next morning Cora was up before the sun had warmed the strawberry patch or the wind had stirred the pines.

Benjy was sitting up in his cot when Cora returned from the mailbox. "Too early," he said. "Postman won't drive by yet."

"*Drive* by?"

"They come in cars this far out."

"Oh." Cora sat down.

"You sick, Aunt Cora?"

"No, no." She blinked. "It's just, I don't recall in twenty years *seeing* no mail truck whistle by here. It just came to me. All this time, I never seen no mailman at all."

"Maybe he comes when you're not around."

"I'm up with the fog spunks, down with the chickens. I never really gave it a thought, of course, but——" She turned to look out the window, up at Mrs. Brabbam's house. "Benjy, I got a kind of sneaking hunch." She stood up and walked straight out of the cabin, down the dust path, Benjy following, across the thin road to Mrs. Brabbam's mailbox. A hush was on the fields and hills. It was so early it made you whisper.

"Don't break the law, Aunt Cora!"

"Shh! Here." She opened the box, put her hand in like someone fumbling in a gopher hole. "And here, and here." She rattled some letters into his cupped hands.

"Why, these been opened already! You open these, Aunt Cora?"

"Child, I never touched them." Her face was stunned. "This is the first time in my life I ever even let my shadow touch this box."

Benjy turned the letters around and around, cocking his head. "Why, Aunt Cora, these letters, they're ten years old!"

"What!" Cora grabbed at them.

"Aunt Cora, that lady's been getting the same mail every day for years. And they're not even addressed to Mrs. Brabbam, they're to some woman named Ortega in Green Fork."

"Ortega, the Mexican grocery woman! All these years," whispered Cora, staring at the worn mail in her hands. "All these years."

They gazed up at Mrs. Brabbam's sleeping house in the cool quiet morning.

"Oh, that sly woman, making a commotion with her letters, making me feel small. All puffed out she was, swishing along, reading her mail."

Mrs. Brabbam's front door opened.

"Put them back, Aunt Cora!"

Cora slammed the mailbox shut with time to spare.

Mrs. Brabbam drifted down the path, stopping here or there, quietly, to peer at the opening wild flowers.

"Morning," she said sweetly.

"Mrs. Brabbam, this is my nephew Benjy."

"How nice." Mrs. Brabbam, with a great swivel of her body, a flourish of her flour-white hands, rapped the mailbox as if to shake the letters loose inside, flipped the lid, and extracted the mail, covering her actions with her back. She made motions, and spun about merrily, winking. "Wonderful! Why, just look at this letter from dear Uncle George!"

"Well, ain't that *nice!*" said Cora.

Then the breathless summer days of waiting. The butterflies jumping orange and blue on the air, the flowers nodding about the cabin, and the hard, constant sound of Benjy's pencil scribbling through the afternoons. Benjy's mouth was always packed with food, and Tom was always stomping in, to find lunch or supper late, cold, or both, or none at all.

Benjy handled the pencil with a delicious spread of his bony hands, lovingly inscribing each vowel and consonant as Cora hovered about him, making up words, rolling them on her tongue, delighted each time she saw them roll out on the paper. But she wasn't learning to write. "It's so much fun watching you write, Benjy. Tomorrow I'll start learning. Now take another letter!"

They worked their way through ads about Asthma, Trusses, and Magic, they joined the Rosicrucians, or at least sent for a free Sealed Book all about the Knowledge that had been damned to oblivion, Secrets from Hidden ancient temples and buried sanctuaries. Then there were free packets of Giant Sunflower

seeds, and something about HEARTBURN. They had worked back to page 127 of *Quarter Murder Magazine* on a bright summer morning when . . .

"Listen!" said Cora.

They listened.

"A car," said Benjy.

And up the blue hills and through the tall fiery green pines and along the dusty road, mile by mile, came the sound of a car riding along and along, until finally, at the bend, it came full thundering, and in an instant Cora was out the door running, and as she ran she heard and saw and felt many things. First, from the corner of her eye, she saw Mrs. Brabbam gliding down the road from the other direction. Mrs. Brabbam froze when she saw the bright green car boiling on the grade, and there was the whistle of a silver whistle and the old man in the car leaned out just before Cora arrived and said, "Mrs. Gibbs?" "Yes!" she cried. "Mail for you, ma'am," he said, and held it toward her. She put out her hand, then drew it back, remembering. "Oh," she said, "please, would you mind, would you put it, please . . . in my mailbox?" The old man squinted at her, at the mailbox, back at her, and laughed. "Don't mind," he said, and did just that, put the mail in the box.

Mrs. Brabbam stood where she was, not moving, eyes wild. "Any mail for Mrs. Brabbam?" asked Cora.

"That's all." And the car dusted away down the road.

Mrs. Brabbam stood with her hands clenched together. Then, without looking in her own letter box, turned and rustled swiftly up her path, out of sight.

Cora walked around her mailbox twice, not touching it for a long time. "Benjy, I've got me some letters!" She reached in delicately and took them out and turned them over. She put them quietly in his hand. "Read them to me. Is my name on the front?"

"Yes'm." He opened the first letter with due carefulness and read it aloud in the summer morning:

" 'Dear Mrs. Gibbs . . .' "

He stopped and let her savor it, her eyes half shut, her mouth

moving the words. He repeated it for artistic emphasis and then
went on: "'We are sending you our free folder, enclosed, from
the Intercontinental Mailing Schools concerning full particulars
on how you, too, can take our Correspondence Course in Sani-
tary Engineering——'"

"Benjy, Benjy, I'm so happy! Start over again!"

"'Dear Mrs. Gibbs,'" he read.

After that the mailbox was never empty. The world came rushing and crowding in, all the places she had never seen or heard
about or been to. Travel folders, spicecake recipes, and even a
letter from an elderly gentleman who wished for a lady "—fifty
years old, gentle disposition, money; object matrimony." Benjy
wrote back, "I am already married, but thank you for your kind
and thoughtful consideration. Yours truly, Cora Gibbs."

And the letters continued to pour across the hills, coin col-
lectors' catalogues, Dime Novelty books, Magic List Numbers,
Arthritis Charts, Flea Killer Samples. The world filled up her
letter box, and suddenly she was not alone or remote from people. If a man wrote a form letter to Cora about the Mysteries of
Ancient Maya Revealed, he was likely as not to receive three letters from Cora in the next week, budding out their formal meeting into a warm friendship. After one particularly hard day of
writing, Benjy was forced to soak his hand in Epsom salts.

By the end of the third week Mrs. Brabbam no longer came
down to her mailbox. She didn't even come out the front door of
her cabin to get the air, for Cora was always down at the road,
leaning out, smiling for the mailman.

All too quickly the summer was at an end, or, at least, that
part of the summer that counted most, anyway; Benjy's visit.
There was his red bandanna handkerchief on the cabin table,
sandwiches folded fresh and oniony in it, tied with a mint sprig
to keep it clean to the smell; there on the floor, freshly polished,
were his shoes to get into, and there on the chair, with his pencil
which had once been long and yellow but was now stubby and
chewed, sat Benjy. Cora took hold of his chin and tilted his head,

as if she were testing a summer squash of an unfamiliar variety.

"Benjy, I owe you an apology. I don't think I looked at your face once in all this time. Seems I know every wart on your hand, every hangnail, every bump and every crinkle, but I might pass your face in a crowd and miss you."

"It's no face to look at," said Benjy shyly.

"But I'd know that hand in a million hands," Cora said. "Let anyone shake my hand in a dark room, a thousand people, and out of all those I'd say, 'Well, *this* one's Benjy.'" She smiled quietly and walked away to the open door. "I been thinking." She looked up at a distant cabin. "Ain't seen Mrs. Brabbam in weeks. Stays in all the time now. I've got a guilty feeling. I've done a prideful thing, a thing more sinful than she ever done me. I took the bottom out of her life. It was a mean and spiteful thing and I'm ashamed." She gazed up the hill toward that silent, locked place. "Benjy, would you do me one last favor?"

"Yes'm."

"Write a letter for Mrs. Brabbam."

"Ma'am?"

"Yes, write one of those companies for a free chart, a sample, something, and sign Mrs. Brabbam's name."

"All right," said Benjy.

"That way, in a week or a month the postman'll come by and whistle, and I'll tell him to go up to her door, special, and deliver it. And I'll be sure and be out in my front yard where I can see and Mrs. Brabbam can see I see. And I'll wave my letters to her and she'll wave her letters to me, and everybody'll smile."

"Yes'm," said Benjy.

He wrote three letters, licked the envelopes carefully, stuck them in his pocket. "I'll mail them when I get to St. Louis."

"It's been a fine summer," she said.

"It sure has."

"But, Benjy, I didn't learn to write, did I? I was after the letters and made you write late nights, and we were so busy sending labels and getting samples, land, it seemed there wasn't time to learn. And that means . . ."

He knew what it meant. He shook her hand. They stood in the cabin door. "Thanks," she said, "for everything."

Then he was running off. He ran as far as the meadow fence, leaped it easily, and the last she saw of him he was still running, waving the special letters, off into the great world over the hills.

The letters kept coming for some six months after Benjy went away. There would be the postman's little green car and the sharp ice-rimed shout of good morning, or the whistle, as he clapped two or three pink or blue envelopes into that fine mailbox.

And there was that special day when Mrs. Brabbam received her first real letter.

After that the letters were spaced a week apart, then a month, and finally the postman didn't say hello at all, there was no sound of a car coming up that lonely mountain road. First a spider moved into the mailbox, then a sparrow.

And Cora, while the letters still lasted, would clutch them in her bewildered hands, staring at them quietly until the pressure of her face muscles squeezed clear round shiny drops of water from her eyes. She'd hold up one blue envelope. "Who's this from?"

"Don't know," said Tom.

"What's it say?" she wailed.

"Don't know," said Tom.

"What's going on in that world out there, oh, I'll never know, I'll never know now," she said. "And this letter, and this one, and *this!*" She tumbled the stacks and stacks of letters that had come since Benjy ran off. "All the world and all the people and all the happenings, and me not knowing. All that world and people waiting to hear from us, and us not writing, and them not ever writing back!"

And at last the day came when the wind blew the mailbox over. In the mornings again, Cora would stand at the open door of her cabin, brushing her gray hair with a slow brush, not speaking, looking at the hills. And in all the years that followed she never passed the fallen mailbox without stooping aimlessly to fumble inside and take her hand out with nothing in it before she wandered on again into the fields.

15

POWERHOUSE

The horses moved gently to a stop, and the man and his wife gazed down into a dry, sandy valley. The woman sat lost in her saddle; she hadn't spoken for hours, didn't know a good word *to* speak. She was trapped somewhere between the hot, dark pressure of the storm-clouded Arizona sky and the hard, granite pressure of the wind-blasted mountains. A few drops of cool rain fell on her trembling hands.

She looked over at her husband wearily. He sat his dusty horse easily, with a firm quietness. She closed her eyes and thought of how she had been all of these mild years until today. She wanted to laugh at the mirror she was holding up to herself, but there was no way of doing even that; it would be somewhat insane. After all, it might just be the pushing of this dark weather, or the telegram they had taken from the messenger on horseback this morning, or the long journey now to town.

There was still an empty world to cross, and she was cold.

"I'm the lady who was never going to need religion," she said quietly, her eyes shut.

"What?" Berty, her husband, glanced over at her.

"Nothing," she whispered, shaking her head. In all the years, how *certain* she had been. Never, never would she have need of a

church. She had heard fine people talk on and on of religion and waxed pews and calla lilies in great bronze buckets and vast bells of churches in which the preacher rang like a clapper. She had heard the shouting kind and the fervent, whispery kind, and they were all the same. Hers was simply not a pew-shaped spine.

"I just never had a reason ever to sit in a church," she had told people. She wasn't vehement about it. She just walked around and lived and moved her hands that were pebble-smooth and pebble-small. Work had polished the nails of those hands with a polish you could never buy in a bottle. The touching of children had made them soft, and the raising of children had made them temperately stern, and the loving of a husband had made them gentle.

And now, death made them tremble.

"Here," said her husband. And the horses dusted down the trail to where an odd brick building stood beside a dry wash. The building was all glazed green windows, blue machinery, red tile, and wires. The wires ran off on high-tension towers to the farthest directions of the desert. She watched them go, silently, and, still held by her thoughts, turned her gaze back to the strange storm-green windows and the burning-colored bricks.

She had never slipped a ribbon in a Bible at a certain significant verse, because though her life in this desert was a life of granite, sun, and the steaming away of the waters of her flesh, there had never been a threat in it to her. Always things had worked out before the necessity had come for sleepless dawns and wrinkles in the forehead. Somehow, the very poisonous things of life had passed her by. Death was a remote storm rumor beyond the farthest range.

Twenty years had blown in tumbleweeds, away, since she'd come West, worn this lonely trapping man's gold ring, and taken the desert as a third, and constant, partner to their living. None of their four children had ever been fearfully sick or near death. She had never had to get down on her knees except for the scrubbing of an already well-scrubbed floor.

Now all that was ended. Here they were riding toward a remote

town because a simple piece of yellow paper had come and said very plainly that her mother was dying.

And she could not imagine it—no matter how she turned her head to see or turned her mind to look in on itself. There were no rungs anywhere to hold to, going either up *or* down, and her mind, like a compass left out in a sudden storm of sand, was suddenly blown free of all its once-clear directions, all points of reference worn away, the needle spinning without purpose, around, around. Even with Berty's arms on her back it wasn't enough. It was like the end of a good play and the beginning of an evil one. Someone she loved was actually going to die. This was impossible!

"I've got to stop," she said, not trusting her voice at all, so she made it sound irritated to cover her fear.

Berty knew her as no irritated woman, so the irritation did not carry over and fill him up. He was a capped jug; the contents there for sure. Rain on the outside didn't stir the brew. He side-ran his horse to her and took her hand gently. "Sure," he said. He squinted at the eastern sky. "Some clouds piling up black there. We'll wait a bit. It might rain. I wouldn't want to get caught in it."

Now she was irritated at her own irritation, one fed upon the other, and she was helpless. But rather than speak and risk the cycle's commencing again, she slumped forward and began to sob, allowing her horse to be led until it stood and tramped its feet softly beside the red brick building.

She slid down like a parcel into his arms, and he held her as she turned in on his shoulder; then he set her down and said, "Don't look like there's people here." He called, "Hey, there!" and looked at the sign on the door: *Danger. Bureau of Electric Power*.

There was a great insect humming all through the air. It sang in a ceaseless, bumbling tone, rising a bit, perhaps falling just a bit, but keeping the same pitch. Like a woman humming between pressed lips as she makes a meal in the warm twilight over a hot stove. They could see no movement within the building; there was only the gigantic humming. It was the sort of noise you would expect the sun-shimmer to make rising from hot railroad

ties on a blazing summer day, when there is that flurried silence and you see the air eddy and whorl and ribbon, and expect a sound from the process but get nothing but an arched tautness of the eardrums and the tense quiet.

The humming came up through her heels, into her medium-slim legs, and thence to her body. It moved to her heart and touched it, as the sight of Berty just sitting on a top rail of the corral often did. And then it moved on to her head and the slenderest niches in the skull and set up a singing, as love songs and good books had done once on a time.

The humming was everywhere. It was as much a part of the soil as the cactus. It was as much a part of the air as the heat.

"What is it?" she asked, vaguely perplexed, looking at the building.

"I don't know much about it except it's a powerhouse," said Berty. He tried the door. "It's open," he said, surprised. "I wish someone was around." The door swung wide and the pulsing hum came out like a breath of air over them, louder.

They entered together into the solemn, singing place. She held him tightly, arm in arm.

It was a dim undersea place, smooth and clean and polished, as if something or other was always coming through and coming through and nothing ever stayed, but always there was motion and motion, invisible and stirring and never settling. On each side of them as they advanced were what first appeared to be people standing quietly, one after the other, in a double line. But these resolved into round, shell-like machines from which the humming sprang. Each black and gray and green machine gave forth golden cables and lime-colored wires, and there were silver metal pouches with crimson tabs and white lettering, and a pit like a washtub in which something whirled as if rinsing unseen materials at invisible speeds. The centrifuge raced so fast it stood still. Immense snakes of copper looped down from the twilight ceiling, and vertical pipes webbed up from cement floor to fiery brick wall. And the whole of it was as clean as a bolt of green lightning and smelled similarly. There was a crackling,

eating sound, a dry rustling as of paper; flickers of blue fire shuttled, snapped, sparked, hissed where wires joined porcelain bobbins and green glass insulation.

Outside, in the real world, it began to rain.

She didn't want to stay in this place; it was no place to stay, with its people that were not people but dim machines and its music like an organ caught and pressed on a low note and a high note. But the rain washed every window and Berty said, "Looks like it'll last. Might have to stay the night here. It's late, anyhow. I'd better get the stuff in."

She said nothing. She wanted to be getting on. Getting on to what thing in what place, there was really no way of knowing. But at least in town she would hold onto the money and buy the tickets and hold them tight in her hand and hold onto a train which would rush and make a great noise, and get off the train, and get on another horse, or get into a car hundreds of miles away and ride again, and stand at last by her dead or alive mother. It all depended on time and breath. There were many places she would pass through, but none of them would offer a thing to her except ground for her feet, air for her nostrils, food for her numb mouth. And these were worse than nothing. Why go to her mother at all, say words, and make gestures? she wondered. What would be the use?

The floor was clean as a solid river under her. When she moved forward on it, it sent echoes cracking back and forth like small, faint gunshots through the room. Any word that was spoken came back as from a granite cavern.

Behind her, she heard Berty setting down the equipment. He spread two gray blankets and put out a little collection of tinned foods.

It was night. The rain still streamed on the high green-glazed windows, rinsing and making patterns of silk that flowed and intermingled in soft clear curtains. There were occasional thunderclaps which fell and broke upon themselves in avalanches of cold rain and wind hitting sand and stone.

Her head lay upon a folded cloth, and no matter how she turned it, the humming of the immense powerhouse worked up through the cloth into her head. She shifted, shut her eyes, and adjusted herself, but it went on and on. She sat up, patted the cloth, lay back down.

But the humming was there.

She knew without looking, by some sense deep in herself, that her husband was awake. There was no year she could remember when she hadn't known. It was some subtle difference in his breathing. It was the absence of sound, rather; no sound of breathing at all, save at long, carefully thought-out intervals. She knew then that he was looking at her in the rainy darkness, concerned with her, taking great care of his breath.

She turned in the darkness. "Berty?"

"Yes?"

"I'm awake too," she said.

"I know," he said.

They lay, she very straight, very rigid, he in a half curl, like a hand relaxed, half bent inward. She traced this dark, easy curve and was filled with incomprehensible wonder.

"Berty," she asked, and paused a long while, "how . . . how are you like you are?"

He waited a moment. "How do you mean?" he said.

"How do you *rest?*" She stopped. It sounded very bad. It sounded so much like an accusation, but it was not, really. She knew him to be a man concerned with all things, a man who could see in darknesses and who was not conceited because of his ability. He was worried for her now, and for her mother's life or death, but he had a way of worrying that seemed indifferent and irresponsible. It was neither of the two. His concern was all in him, deep; but it lay side by side with some faith, some belief that accepted it, made it welcome, and did not fight it. Something in him took hold of the sorrow first, got acquainted with it, knew each of its traceries before passing the message on to all of his waiting body. His body held a faith like a maze, and the sorrow that struck into him was lost and gone before it finally reached

where it wanted to hurt him. Sometimes this faith drove her into a senseless anger, from which she recovered quickly, knowing how useless it was to criticize something as contained as a stone in a peach.

"Why didn't I ever catch it from you?" she said at last.

He laughed a little bit, softly. "Catch what?"

"I caught everything else. You shook me up and down in other ways. I didn't know anything but what you taught me." She stopped. It was hard to explain. Their life had been like the warm blood in a person passing through tissues quietly, both ways.

"Everything but religion," she said. "I never caught that from you."

"It's not a catching thing," he said. "Someday you just relax. And there it is."

Relax, she thought. Relax what? The body. But how to relax the mind? Her fingers twitched beside her. Her eyes wandered idly about the vast interior of the powerhouse. The machines stood over her in dark silhouettes with little sparkles crawling on them. The humming-humming-humming crept along her limbs.

Sleepy. Tired. She drowsed. Her eyes lidded and opened and lidded and opened. The humming-humming filled her marrow as if small hummingbirds were suspended in her body and in her head.

She traced the half-seen tubing up and up into the ceiling, and she saw the machines and heard the invisible whirlings. She suddenly became very alert in her drowsiness. Her eyes moved swiftly up and up and then down and across, and the humming-singing of the machines grew louder and louder, and her eyes moved, and her body relaxed; and on the tall, green windows she saw the shadows of the high-tension wires rushing off into the raining night.

Now the humming was in her, her eyes jerked, she felt herself yanked violently upright. She felt seized by a whirling dynamo, around, around in a whirl, out, out, into the heart of whirling invisibilities, fed into, accepted by a thousand copper wires, and shot, in an instant, over the earth!

She was everywhere at once!

Streaking along high monster towers in instants, sizzling between high poles where small glass knobs sat like crystal-green birds holding the wires in their non-conductive beaks, branching in four directions, eight secondary directions, finding towns, hamlets, cities, racing on to farms, ranches, haciendas, she descended gently like a widely filamented spider web upon a thousand square miles of desert!

The earth was suddenly more than many separate things, more than houses, rocks, concrete roads, a horse here or there, a human in a shallow, boulder-topped grave, a prickling of cactus, a town invested with its own light surrounded by night, a million apart things. Suddenly it all had one pattern encompassed and held by the pulsing electric web.

She spilled out swiftly into rooms where life was rising from a slap on a naked child's back, into rooms where life was leaving bodies like the light fading from an electric bulb—the filament glowing, fading, finally colorless. She was in every town, every house, every room, making light-patterns over hundreds of miles of land; seeing, hearing everything, not alone any more, but one of thousands of people, each with his ideas and his faiths.

Her body lay, a lifeless reed, pale and trembling. Her mind, in all its electric tensity, was flung about this way, that, down vast networks of powerhouse tributary.

Everything balanced. In one room she saw life wither; in another, a mile away, she saw wineglasses lifted to the newborn, cigars passed, smiles, handshakes, laughter. She saw the pale, drawn faces of people at white deathbeds, heard how they understood and accepted death, saw their gestures, felt their feelings, and saw that they, too, were lonely in themselves, with no way to get to the world to see the balance, see it as she was seeing it now.

She swallowed. Her eyelids flickered and her throat burned under her upraised fingers.

She was not alone.

The dynamo had whirled and flung her with centrifugal force

out along a thousand lines into a million glass capsules screwed into ceilings, plucked into light by a pull of a cord or a twist of a knob or a flick of a switch.

The light could be in *any* room; all that was needed was to touch the switch. All rooms were dark until light came. And here she was, in all of them at once. And she was not alone. Her grief was but one part of a vast grief, her fear only one of countless others. And this grief was only a half thing. There was the other half; of things born, of comfort in the shape of a new child, of food in the warmed body, of colors for the eye and sounds in the awakened ear, and spring wild flowers for the smelling.

Whenever a light blinked out, life threw another switch; rooms were illumined afresh.

She was with those named Clark and those named Gray and the Shaws and Martins and Hanfords, the Fentons, the Drakes, the Shattucks, the Hubbells, and the Smiths. Being alone was not alone, except in the mind. You had all sorts of peekholes in your head. A silly, strange way to put it, perhaps, but there were the holes; the ones to see through and see that the world was there and people in it, as hard put to and uneasy as yourself; and there were the holes for hearing, and the one for speaking out your grief and getting rid of it, and the holes for knowing the changes of season through the scents of summer grain or winter ice or autumn fires. They were there to be used so that one was not alone. Loneliness was a shutting of the eyes. Faith was a simple opening.

The light-net fell upon all the world she had known for twenty years, herself blended with every line. She glowed and pulsed and was gentled in the great easy fabric. It lay across the land, covering each mile like a gentle, warm, and humming blanket. She was everywhere.

In the powerhouse the turbines whirled and hummed and the electric sparks, like little votive candles, jumped and clustered upon bent elbows of electric piping and glass. And the machines stood like saints and choruses, haloed now yellow, now red, now green, and a massed singing beat along the roof hollows and ech-

oed down in endless hymns and chants. Outside, the wind clamored at the brick walls and drenched the glazed windows with rain; inside, she lay upon her small pillow and suddenly began to cry.

Whether it was with understanding, acceptance, joy, resignation, she couldn't know. The singing went on, higher and higher, and she was everywhere. She put out her hand, caught hold of her husband, who was still awake, his eyes fixed at the ceiling. Perhaps he had run everywhere, too, in this instant, through the network of light and power. But then, he had always been everywhere at once. He felt himself a unit of a whole and therefore he was stable; to her, unity was new and shaking. She felt his arms suddenly around her and she pressed her face into his shoulder for a long while, hard, while the humming and the humming climbed higher, and she cried freely, achingly, against him. . . .

In the morning the desert sky was very clear. They walked from the powerhouse quietly, saddled their horses, cinched on all of the equipment, and mounted.

She settled herself and sat there under the blue sky. And slowly she was aware of her back, and her back was straight, and she looked at her alien hands on the reins, and they had ceased trembling. And she could see the far mountains; there was no blur nor a running-of-color to things. All was solid stone touching stone, and stone touching sand, and sand touching wild flower, and wild flower touching the sky in one continuous clear flow, everything definite and of a piece.

"Wope!" cried Berty, and the horses walked slowly off, away from the brick building, through the cool sweet morning air.

She rode handsomely and she rode well, and in her, like a stone in a peach, was a peacefulness. She called to her husband as they slowed on a rise, "Berty!"

"Yes?"

"Can we . . ." she asked.

"Can we what?" he said, not hearing the first time.

"Can we come here again sometime?" she asked, nodding back toward the powerhouse. "Once in a while? Some Sunday?"

He looked at her and nodded slowly. "I reckon. Yes. Sure. I reckon so."

And as they rode on into town she was humming, humming a strange soft tune, and he glanced over and listened to it, and it was the sound you would expect to hear from sun-warmed railroad ties on a hot summer day when the air rises in a shimmer, flurried and whorling; a sound in one key, one pitch, rising a little, falling a little, humming, humming, but constant, peaceful, and wondrous to hear.

16

EN LA NOCHE

All night Mrs. Navarrez moaned, and these moans filled the tenement like a light turned on in every room so no one could sleep. All night she gnashed her white pillow and wrung her thin hands and cried, "My Joe!" The tenement people, at 3 A.M., finally discouraged that she would *never* shut her painted red mouth, arose, feeling warm and gritty, and dressed to take the trolley downtown to an all-night movie. There Roy Rogers chased bad men through veils of stale smoke and spoke dialogue above the soft snorings in the dark night theater.

By dawn Mrs. Navarrez was still sobbing and screaming.

During the day it was not so bad. Then the massed choir of babies crying here or there in the house added the saving grace of what was almost a harmony. There was also the chugging thunder of the washing machines on the tenement porch, and chenille-robed women standing on the flooded, soggy boards of the porch, talking their Mexican gossip rapidly. But now and again, above the shrill talk, the washing, the babies, one could hear Mrs. Navarrez like a radio tuned high. "My Joe, oh, my poor Joe!" she screamed.

Now, at twilight, the men arrived with the sweat of their work

under their arms. Lolling in cool bathtubs all through the cooking tenement, they cursed and held their hands to their ears.

"Is she *still* at it!" they raged helplessly. One man even kicked her door. "Shut *up*, woman!" But this only made Mrs. Navarrez shriek louder. "Oh, ah! Joe, Joe!"

"Tonight we eat out!" said the men to their wives. All through the house, kitchen utensils were shelved and doors locked as men hurried their perfumed wives down the halls by their pale elbows.

Mr. Villanazul, unlocking his ancient, flaking door at midnight, closed his brown eyes and stood for a moment, swaying. His wife Tina stood beside him with their three sons and two daughters, one in arms.

"Oh God," whispered Mr. Villanazul. "Sweet Jesus, come down off the cross and silence that woman." They entered their dim little room and looked at the blue candlelight flickering under a lonely crucifix. Mr. Villanazul shook his head philosophically. "He is still on the cross."

They lay in their beds like burning barbecues, the summer night basting them with their own liquors. The house flamed with that ill woman's cry.

"I am stifled!" Mr. Villanazul fled through the tenement, downstairs to the front porch with his wife, leaving the children, who had the great and miraculous talent of sleeping through all things.

Dim figures occupied the front porch, a dozen quiet men crouched with cigarettes fuming and glowing in their brown fingers, women in chenille wrappers taking what there was of the summer-night wind. They moved like dream figures, like clothes dummies worked stiffly on wires and rollers. Their eyes were puffed and their tongues thick.

"Let us go to her room and strangle her," said one of the men.

"No, that would not be right," said a woman. "Let us throw her from the window."

Everyone laughed tiredly.

Mr. Villanazul stood blinking bewilderedly at all the people. His wife moved sluggishly beside him.

"You would think Joe was the only man in the world to join the Army," someone said irritably. "Mrs. Navarrez, *pah!* This Joe-husband of hers will peel potatoes; the safest man in the infantry!"

"Something *must* be done." Mr. Villanazul had spoken. He was startled at the hard firmness of his own voice. Everyone glanced at him.

"We can't go on another night," Mr. Villanazul continued bluntly.

"The more we pound her door, the more she cries," explained Mr. Gomez.

"The priest came this afternoon," said Mrs. Gutierrez. "We sent for him in desperation. But Mrs. Navarrez would not even let him in the door, no matter how he pleaded. The priest went away. We had Officer Gilvie yell at her, too, but do you think she listened?"

"We must try some other way, then," mused Mr. Villanazul. "Someone must be—sympathetic—with her."

"What other way is there?" asked Mr. Gomez.

"If only," figured Mr. Villanazul after a moment's thought, "if only there was a *single* man among us."

He dropped that like a cold stone into a deep well. He let the splash occur and the ripples move gently out.

Everybody sighed.

It was like a little summer-night wind arisen. The men straightened up a bit; the women quickened.

"But," replied Mr. Gomez, sinking back, "we are all married. There is no single man."

"Oh," said everyone, and settled down into the hot, empty river bed of night, smoke rising, silent.

"Then," Mr. Villanazul shot back, lifting his shoulders, tightening his mouth, "it must be one of *us!*"

Again the night wind blew, stirring the people in awe.

"This is no time for selfishness!" declared Villanazul. "One of us must *do* this thing! That, or roast in hell another night!"

Now the people on the porch separated away from him, blinking. *"You* will do it, of course, Mr. Villanazul?" they wished to know.

He stiffened. The cigarette almost fell from his fingers. "Oh, but I——" he objected.

"You," they said. "Yes?"

He waved his hands feverishly. "I have a wife and five children, one in arms!"

"But *none* of us are single, and it is your idea and you must have the courage of your convictions, Mr. Villanazul!" everyone said.

He was very frightened and silent. He glanced with startled flashes of his eyes at his wife.

She stood wearily weaving on the night air, trying to see him.

"I'm so *tired,*" she grieved.

"Tina," he said.

"I will die if I do not sleep," she said.

"Oh, but, Tina," he said.

"I will die and there will be many flowers and I will be buried if I do not get some rest," she murmured.

"She looks very bad," said everyone.

Mr. Villanazul hesitated only a moment longer. He touched his wife's slack hot fingers. He touched her hot cheek with his lips.

Without a word he walked from the porch.

They could hear his feet climbing the unlit stairs of the house, up and around to the third floor where Mrs. Navarrez wailed and screamed.

They waited on the porch.

The men lit new cigarettes and flicked away the matches, talking like the wind, the women wandering around among them, all of them coming and talking to Mrs. Villanazul, who stood, lines under her tired eyes, leaning against the porch rail.

"Now," whispered one of the men quietly. "Mr. Villanazul is at the top of the house!"

Everybody quieted.

"Now," hissed the man in a stage whisper. "Mr. Villanazul taps at her door! Tap, tap."

Everyone listened, holding his breath.

Far away there was a gentle tapping sound.

"Now, Mrs. Navarrez, at this intrusion, breaks out anew with crying!"

At the top of the house came a scream.

"Now," the man imagined, crouched, his hand delicately weaving on the air, "Mr. Villanazul pleads and pleads, softly, quietly, to the locked door."

The people on the porch lifted their chins tentatively, trying to see through three flights of wood and plaster to the third floor, waiting.

The screaming faded.

"Now, Mr. Villanazul talks quickly, he pleads, he whispers, he promises," cried the man softly.

The screaming settled to a sobbing, the sobbing to a moan, and finally all died away into breathing and the pounding of hearts and listening.

After about two minutes of standing, sweating, waiting, everyone on the porch heard the door far away upstairs rattle its lock, open, and, a second later, with a whisper, close.

The house was silent.

Silence lived in every room like a light turned off. Silence flowed like a cool wine in the tunnel halls. Silence came through the open casements like a cool breath from the cellar. They all stood breathing the coolness of it.

"Ah," they sighed.

Men flicked away cigarettes and moved on tiptoe into the silent tenement. Women followed. Soon the porch was empty. They drifted in cool halls of quietness.

Mrs. Villanazul, in a drugged stupor, unlocked her door.

"We must give Mr. Villanazul a banquet," a voice whispered.

"Light a candle for him tomorrow."

The doors shut.

In her fresh bed Mrs. Villanazul lay. He is a thoughtful man, she dreamed, eyes closed. For such things, I love him.

The silence was like a cool hand, stroking her to sleep.

"Light a candle for him tomorrow."

The door shut.

In her fresh bed, Mrs. Villanazul lay. He has thoughtful men, she dreamed, eyes closed. For such things, I love him.

The silence was like a cool hand stroking her to sleep.

17

SUN AND SHADOW

The camera clicked like an insect. It was blue and metallic, like a great fat beetle held in the man's precious and tenderly exploiting hands. It winked in the flashing sunlight.

"Hsst, Ricardo, come away!"

"You down there!" cried Ricardo out the window.

"Ricardo, stop!"

He turned to his wife. "Don't tell me to stop, tell them to stop. Go down and tell them, or are you afraid?"

"They aren't hurting anything," said his wife patiently.

He shook her off and leaned out the window and looked down into the alley. "You there!" he cried.

The man with the black camera in the alley glanced up, then went on focusing his machine at the lady in the salt-white beach pants, the white bra, and the green checkered scarf. She leaned against the cracked plaster of the building. Behind her a dark boy smiled, his hand to his mouth.

"Tomás!" yelled Ricardo. He turned to his wife. "Oh, Jesus the Blessed, Tomás is in the street, my own son laughing there." Ricardo started out the door.

"Don't do anything!" said his wife.

"I'll cut off their heads!" said Ricardo, and was gone.

In the street the lazy woman was lounging now against the peeling blue paint of a banister. Ricardo emerged in time to see her doing this. "That's my banister!" he said.

The cameraman hurried up. "No, no, we're taking pictures. Everything's all right. We'll be moving on."

"Everything's not all right," said Ricardo, his brown eyes flashing. He waved a wrinkled hand. "She's on my house."

"We're taking fashion pictures," smiled the photographer.

"*Now* what am I to do?" said Ricardo to the blue sky. "Go mad with this news? Dance around like an epileptic saint?"

"If it's money, well, here's a five-peso bill," smiled the photographer.

Ricardo pushed the hand away. "I *work* for my money. You don't understand. Please go."

The photographer was bewildered. "Wait . . ."

"Tomás, get in the house!"

"But, Papa . . ."

"Gahh!" bellowed Ricardo.

The boy vanished.

"This has *never* happened before," said the photographer.

"It is long past time! What *are* we? Cowards?" Ricardo asked the world.

A crowd was gathering. They murmured and smiled and nudged each other's elbows. The photographer with irritable good will snapped his camera shut, said over his shoulder to the model, "All right, we'll use that other street. I saw a nice cracked wall there and some nice deep shadows. If we hurry . . ."

The girl, who had stood during this exchange nervously twisting her scarf, now seized her make-up kit and darted by Ricardo, but not before he touched at her arm. "Do not misunderstand," he said quickly. She stopped, blinked at him. He went on. "It is not you I am mad at. Or you." He addressed the photographer.

"Then why——" said the photographer.

Ricardo waved his hand. "You are employed; I am employed. We are all people employed. We must understand each other.

But when you come to my house with your camera that looks like the complex eye of a black horsefly, then the understanding is over. I will not have my alley used because of its pretty shadows, or my sky used because of its sun, or my house used because there is an interesting crack in the wall, here! You *see!* Ah, how beautiful! Lean here! Stand there! Sit here! Crouch there! Hold it! Oh, I *heard* you. Do you think I am stupid? I have books up in my room. You see that window? Maria!"

His wife's head popped out. "Show them my books!" he cried.

She fussed and muttered, but a moment later she held out one, then two, then half a dozen books, eyes shut, head turned away, as if they were old fish.

"And two dozen more like them upstairs!" cried Ricardo. "You're not talking to some cow in the forest, you're talking to a man!"

"Look," said the photographer, packing his plates swiftly. "We're going. Thanks for nothing."

"Before you go, you must see what I am getting at," said Ricardo. "I am not a mean man. But I *can* be a very angry man. Do I look like a cardboard cutout?"

"Nobody said anybody looked like anything." The photographer hefted his case and started off.

"There is a photographer two blocks over," said Ricardo, pacing him. "They have cutouts. You stand in front of them. It says 'GRAND HOTEL.' They take a picture of you and it looks like you are in the Grand Hotel. Do you see what I mean? My alley is my alley, my life is my life, my son is my son. My son is not cardboard! I saw you putting my son against the wall, so, and thus, in the background. What do you call it—for the correct air? To make the whole attractive, and the lovely lady in front of him?"

"It's getting late," said the photographer, sweating. The model trotted along on the other side of him.

"We are poor people," said Ricardo. "Our doors peel paint, our walls are chipped and cracked, our gutters fume in the street, the alleys are all cobbles. But it fills me with a terrible rage when I see you make over these things as if I had *planned* it this way,

as if I had years ago induced the wall to crack. Did you think I knew you were coming and aged the paint? Or that I knew you were coming and put my boy in his dirtiest clothes? We are *not* a studio! We are people and must be given attention as people. Have I made it clear?"

"With abundant detail," said the photographer, not looking at him, hurrying.

"Now that you know my wishes and my reasoning, you will do the friendly thing and go home?"

"You are a hilarious man," said the photographer. "Hey!" They had joined a group of five other models and a second photographer at the base of a vast stone stairway which in layers, like a bridal cake, led up to the white town square. "How you doing, Joe?"

"We got some beautiful shots near the Church of the Virgin, some statuary without any noses, lovely stuff," said Joe. "What's the commotion?"

"Pancho here got in an uproar. Seems we leaned against his house and knocked it down."

"My name is Ricardo. My house is completely intact."

"We'll shoot it *here,* dear," said the first photographer. "Stand by the archway of that store. There's a nice antique wall going up there." He peered into the mysteries of his camera.

"So!" A dreadful quiet came upon Ricardo. He watched them prepare. When they were ready to take the picture he hurried forward, calling to a man in a doorway "Jorge! What are you *doing?*"

"I'm standing here," said the man.

"Well," said Ricardo, "isn't that *your* archway? Are you going to let them *use* it?"

"I'm not bothered," said Jorge.

Ricardo shook his arm. "They're treating your property like a movie actor's place. Aren't you insulted?"

"I haven't thought about it." Jorge picked his nose.

"Jesus upon earth, man, *think!*"

"I can't see any harm," said Jorge.

"Am I the *only* one in the world with a tongue in my mouth?" said Ricardo to his empty hands. "And taste on my tongue? Is this a town of backdrops and picture sets? Won't *anyone* do something about this except me?"

The crowd had followed them down the street, gathering others to it as it came; now it was of a fair size and more were coming, drawn by Ricardo's bullish shouts. He stomped his feet. He made fists. He spat. The cameraman and the models watched him nervously. "Do you want a *quaint* man in the background?" he said wildly to the cameraman. "I'll pose back here. Do you want me near this wall, my hat *so,* my feet *so,* the light so and thus on my sandals which I made myself? Do you want me to rip this hole in my shirt a bit larger, eh, like *this? So!* Is my face smeared with enough perspiration? Is my hair long enough, kind sir?"

"Stand there if you want," said the photographer.

"I won't look in the camera," Ricardo assured him.

The photographer smiled and lifted his machine. "Over to your left one step, dear." The model moved. "Now turn your right leg. That's fine. Fine, fine. *Hold* it!"

The model froze, chin tilted up.

Ricardo dropped his pants.

"Oh, my God!" said the photographer.

Some of the models squealed. The crowd laughed and pummeled each other a bit. Ricardo quietly raised his pants and leaned against the wall.

"Was that quaint enough?" he said.

"Oh, my God!" muttered the photographer.

"Let's go down to the docks," said his assistant.

"I think *I'll* go there too." Ricardo smiled.

"Good God, what can we do with the idiot?" whispered the photographer.

"Buy him off!"

"I *tried* that!"

"You didn't go high enough."

"Listen, you run get a policeman. I'll put a stop to this."

The assistant ran. Everyone stood around smoking cigarettes nervously, eying Ricardo. A dog came by and briefly made water against the wall.

"Look at that!" cried Ricardo. "What art! What a pattern! Quick, before the sun dries it!"

The cameraman turned his back and looked out to sea.

The assistant came rushing along the street. Behind him, a native policeman strolled quietly. The assistant had to stop and run back to urge the policeman to hurry. The policeman assured him with a gesture, at a distance, that the day was not yet over and in time they would arrive at the scene of whatever disaster lay ahead.

The policeman took up a position behind the two cameramen. "What seems to be the trouble?"

"That man up there. We want him removed."

"That man up there seems only to be leaning against a wall," said the officer.

"No, no, it's not the leaning, he—— Oh hell," said the cameraman. "The only way to explain is to show you. Take your pose dear."

The girl posed. Ricardo posed, smiling casually.

"Hold it!"

The girl froze.

Ricardo dropped his pants.

Click went the camera.

"Ah," said the policeman.

"Got the evidence right in this old camera if you need it!" said the cameraman.

"Ah," said the policeman, not moving, hand to chin. "So." He surveyed the scene like an amateur photographer himself. He saw the model with the flushed, nervous marble face, the cobbles, the wall, and Ricardo. Ricardo magnificently smoking a cigarette there in the noon sunlight under the blue sky, his pants where a man's pants rarely are.

"Well, officer?" said the cameraman, waiting.

"Just what," said the policeman, taking off his cap and wiping his dark brow, "do you want me to do?"

"Arrest that man! Indecent exposure!"

"Ah," said the policeman.

"Well?" said the cameraman.

The crowd murmured. All the nice lady models were looking out at the sea gulls and the ocean.

"That man up there against the wall," said the officer, "I know him. His name is Ricardo Reyes."

"Hello, Esteban!" called Ricardo.

The officer called back at him, "Hello, Ricardo."

They waved at each other.

"He's not doing anything *I* can see," said the officer.

"What do you mean?" asked the cameraman. "He's as naked as a rock. It's immoral!"

"That man is doing nothing immoral. He's just standing there," said the policeman. "Now if he were *doing* something with his hands or body, something terrible to view, I would act upon the instant. However, since he is simply leaning against the wall, not moving a single limb or muscle, there is nothing wrong."

"He's naked, *naked!*" screamed the cameraman.

"I don't understand." The officer blinked.

"You just don't go around naked, that's all!"

"There are naked people and naked people," said the officer. "Good and bad. Sober and with drink in them. I judge this one to be a man with no drink in him, a good man by reputation; naked, yes, but doing nothing with this nakedness in any way to offend the community."

"What *are* you, his *brother?* What are you, his confederate?" said the cameraman. It seemed that at any moment he might snap and bite and bark and woof and race around in circles under the blazing sun. "Where's the justice? What's going *on* here? Come on, girls, we'll go somewhere else!"

"France," said Ricardo.

"What!" The photographer whirled.

"I said France, or Spain," suggested Ricardo. "Or Sweden. I

have seen some nice pictures of walls in Sweden. But not many cracks in them. Forgive my suggestion."

"We'll get pictures in spite of you!" The cameraman shook his camera, his fist.

"I will be there," said Ricardo. "Tomorrow, the next day, at the bullfights, at the market, anywhere, everywhere you go I go, quietly, with grace. With dignity, to perform my necessary task."

Looking at him, they knew it was true.

"Who are you—who in hell do you think you are?" cried the photographer.

"I have been waiting for you to ask me," said Ricardo. "Consider me. Go home and think of me. As long as there is one man like me in a town of ten thousand, the world will go on. Without me, all would be chaos."

"Good night, nurse," said the photographer, and the entire swarm of ladies, hatboxes, cameras, and make-up kits retreated down the street toward the docks. "Time out for lunch, dears. We'll figure something later!"

Ricardo watched them go, quietly. He had not moved from his position. The crowd still looked upon him and smiled.

Now, Ricardo thought, I will walk up the street to my house, which has paint peeling from the door where I have brushed it a thousand times in passing, and I shall walk over the stones I have worn down in forty-six years of walking, and I shall run my hand over the crack in the wall of my own house, which is the crack made by the earthquake in 1930. I remember well the night, us all in bed, Tomás as yet unborn, and Maria and I much in love, and thinking it was our love which moved the house, warm and great in the night; but it was the earth trembling, and in the morning, that crack in the wall. And I shall climb the steps to the lacework-grille balcony of my father's house, which grillwork he made with his own hands, and I shall eat the food my wife serves me on the balcony, with the books near at hand. And my son Tomás, whom I created out of whole cloth, yes, bed sheets, let us admit it, with my good wife. And we shall sit eating and talking,

not photographs, not backdrops, not paintings, not stage furniture, any of us. But actors, all of us, very fine actors indeed.

As if to second this last thought, a sound startled his ear. He was in the midst of solemnly, with great dignity and grace, lifting his pants to belt them around his waist, when he heard this lovely sound. It was like the winging of soft doves in the air. It was applause.

The small crowd, looking up at him, enacting the final scene of the play before the intermission for lunch, saw with what beauty and gentlemanly decorum he was elevating his trousers. The applause broke like a brief wave upon the shore of the nearby sea.

Ricardo gestured and smiled to them all.

On his way home up the hill he shook hands with the dog that had watered the wall.

18

THE MEADOW

A wall collapses, followed by another and another; with dull thunder, a city falls into ruin.

The night wind blows.

The world lies silent.

London was torn down during the day. Port Said was destroyed. The nails were pulled out of San Francisco. Glasgow is no more.

They are gone, forever.

Boards clatter softly in the wind; sand whines and trickles in small storms upon the still air.

Along the road toward the colorless ruins comes the old night watchman to unlock the gate in the high barbed-wire fence and stand looking in.

There in the moonlight lie Alexandria and Moscow and New York. There in the moonlight lie Johannesburg and Dublin and Stockholm. And Clearwater, Kansas, and Provincetown, and Rio de Janeiro.

Just this afternoon the old man saw it happen, saw the car roaring outside the barbed-wire fence, saw the lean, sun-tanned men in that car, the men with their luxurious charcoal-flannel

suits, and winking gold-mask cuff links, and their burning-gold wrist watches, and eye-blinding rings, lighting their cork-tipped cigarettes with engraved lighters. . . .

"There it is, gentlemen. What a mess. Look what the weather's done to it."

"Yes, sir, it's bad, Mr. Douglas!"

"We just *might* save Paris."

"Yes, *sir!*"

"But, hell! The rain's warped it. That's Hollywood for you! Tear it down! Clear it out! We can use that land. Send a wrecking crew in today!"

"Yes, *sir,* Mr. Douglas!"

The car roaring off and gone away.

And now it is night. And the old night watchman stands inside the gate.

He remembers what happened this same still afternoon when the wreckers came.

A hammering, ripping, clattering; a collapse and a roar. Dust and thunder, thunder and dust!

And the whole of the entire world shook loose its nails and lath and plaster and sill and celluloid window as town after town following town banged over flat and lay still.

A shuddering, a thunder fading away, and then, once more, only the quiet wind.

The night watchman now walks slowly forward along the empty streets.

And one moment he is in Baghdad, and beggers loll in wondrous filth, and women with clear sapphire eyes give veiled smiles from high thin windows.

The wind blows sand and confetti.

The women and beggars vanish.

And it is all strutworks again, it is all papier-mâché and oil-painted canvas and props lettered with the name of this studio, and there is nothing behind any of the building fronts but night and space and stars.

The old man pulls a hammer and a few long nails from his tool chest; he peers around in the junk until he finds a dozen good strong boards and some untorn canvas. And he takes the bright steel nails in his blunt fingers, and they are single-headed nails.

And he begins to put London back together again, hammering and hammering, board by board, wall by wall, window by window, hammering, hammering, louder, louder, steel on steel, steel in wood, wood against sky, working the hours toward midnight, with no end to his striking and fixing and striking again.

"Hey there, *you!*"

The old man pauses.

"You, night *watchman!*"

Out of the shadows hurries a stranger in overalls, calling: "Hey, what's-your-name!"

The old man turns. "The name's Smith."

"Okay, Smith, what in hell's the idea!"

The watchman eyes the stranger quietly. "Who are *you?*"

"Kelly, foreman of the wrecking gang."

The old man nods. "Ah. The ones who tear everything down. You've done plenty today. Why aren't you home bragging about it?"

Kelly hawks and spits. "There was some machinery over on the Singapore set I had to check." He wipes his mouth. . . . "Now, Smith, what in Christ's name you think you're doing? Drop that hammer. You're building it all up again! We tear it down and you put it up. You *crazy?*"

The old man nods. "Maybe I am. But somebody has to put it up again."

"Look, Smith. I do *my* work, you do yours, everyone's happy. But I can't have you messing, see? I'm turning you in to Mr. Douglas."

The old man goes on with his hammering. "Call him up. Send him around. I want to talk to him. *He's* the crazy one."

Kelly laughs. "You kidding? Douglas don't see nobody." He jerks his hand, then bends to examine Smith's newly finished work. "Hey, wait a minute! What *kind* of nails you using? Sin-

gleheads! Now, *cut that!* It'll be hell to pay tomorrow, trying to pull 'em out!"

Smith turns his head and looks for a moment at the other man swaying there. "Well, it stands to reason you can't put the world together with double-headed nails. They're too easy to yank out. You got to use single-headed nails and hammer 'em way in. Like *this!"*

He gives a steel nail one tremendous blow that buries it completely in the wood.

Kelly works his hands on his hips. "I'll give you one more chance. Quit putting things back together and I'll play ball with you."

"Young man," says the night watchman, and keeps on hammering while he talks, and thinks about it, and talks some more, "I was here long before you were born. I was here when all *this* was only a meadow. And there was a wind set the meadow running in waves. For more than thirty years I watched it grow, until it was all of the world together. I lived here *with* it. I lived nice. This is the *real* world to me now. That world out there, beyond the fence, is where I spend time sleeping. I got a little room on a little street, and I see headlines and read about wars and strange, bad people. But here? Here I have the whole world together and it's all peace. I been walking through the cities of *this* world since 1920. Any night I feel like it, I have a one o'clock snack at a bar on the Champs Elysées! I can get me some fine amontillado sherry at a sidewalk café in Madrid, if I want. Or else me and the stone gargoyles, high up there—you *see* them, on top Notra Dame?—we can turn over great state matters and reach big political decisions!"

"Yeah, Pop, sure." Kelly waves impatiently.

"And now you come and kick it down and leave only that world out there which hasn't learned the *first thing* about peace that I know from seeing this land here inside the barbed wire. And so you come and rip it up and there's no peace any more, anywhere. You and your wreckers so proud of your wrecking. Pulling down towns and cities and whole lands!"

"A guy's got to live," says Kelly. "I got a wife and kids."

"That's what they all say. They got wives and kids. And they go on, pulling apart, tearing down, killing. They had *orders!* Somebody *told* them! They *had* to do it!"

"Shut up and gimme that hammer!"

"Don't come any closer!"

"Why, you crazy old——"

"This hammer's good for more than nails!" The old man whistles the hammer through the air; the wrecker jumps back.

"Hell," says Kelly, "you're insane! I'm putting a call through to the main studio; we'll get some cops here quick. My God, one minute you're building things up and talking crazy, but how do I know two minutes from now you won't run wild and start pouring kerosene and lighting matches!"

"I wouldn't harm the smallest piece of kindling in this place, and you know it," says the old man.

"Might burn the whole goddam place down, hell," says Kelly. "Listen, old man, you just wait right *there!*"

The wrecker spins about and runs off into the villages and the ruined cities and the sleeping two-dimensional towns of this night world, and after his footsteps fade there is a music that the wind plays on the long silver barbed wires of the fence, and the old man hammering and hammering and selecting long boards and rearing walls until a time finally comes when his mouth is gasping, his heart is exploding; the hammer drops from his open fingers, steel nails tinkle like coins on the pavement, and the old man cries out to himself alone:

"It's no use, no use. I can't put it all back up before they come. I need so very much help I don't know what to do."

The old man leaves his hammer lying on the road and begins to walk with no direction, with no purpose, it seems, save that he is thinking to make one last round and take one last look at everything and say good-by to whatever there is or was in this world to say good-by to. And so he walks with the shadows all around and the shadows all through this land where time has grown late indeed and the shadows are of all kinds and types and

sizes, shadows of buildings, and shadows of people. And he doesn't look straight *at* them, no, because if he looked at them straight, they would all blow away. No, he just walks, down the middle of Piccadilly Circus . . . the echo of his steps . . . or the Rue de la Paix . . . the sound of him clearing his throat . . . or Fifth Avenue . . . and he doesn't look right or left. And all around him, in dark doorways and empty windows, are his many friends, his good friends, his *very* good friends. Far away there are the hiss and steam and soft whispering of a *caffè espresso* machine, all silver and chrome, and soft Italian singing . . . the flutter of hands in darkness over the open mouths of balalaikas, the rustle of palm trees, a touching of drums with the chimes chiming and small bells belling, and a sound of summer apples dropped in soft night grass which are not apples at all but the motion of women's bared feet slowly dancing a circle to the chimes' faint chiming and the belling of the tiny golden bells. There is the munch of maize kernels crushed on black volcanic stone, the sizzle of tortillas drowned in hot fat, the whisk of charcoals tossing up a thousand fireflies of spark at the blowing of a mouth and the wave of a papaya frond; everywhere faces and forms, everywhere stirs and gestures and ghost fires which float the magical torch-colored faces of Spanish gypsies in air as on a fiery water, the mouths crying out the songs that tell of the oddness and the strangeness and the sadness of living. Everywhere shadows and people, everywhere people and shadows and singing to music.

Just that very trite thing—the wind?

No. The people are all here. They have been here for many years. And tomorrow?

The old man stops, presses his hands to his chest.

They will not be here any more.

A horn blows!

Outside the barbed-wire gate—the enemy! Outside the gate a small black police car and a large black limousine from the studio itself, three miles away.

The horn blares!

The old man seizes the rungs of a ladder and climbs, the sound of the horn pushing him higher and higher. The gate crashes wide; the enemy roars in.

"There he goes!"

The glaring lights of the police shine in upon the cities of the meadow; the lights reveal the stark canvas set-pieces of Manhattan, Chicago, and Chungking! The light glitters on the imitation stone towers of Notre Dame Cathedral, fixes on a tiny figure balancing on the catwalks of Notre Dame, climbing and climbing up where the night and the stars are turning slowly by.

"There he is, Mr. Douglas, at the top!"

"Good God. It's getting so a man can't spend an evening at a quiet party without—"

"He's striking a match! Call the fire department!"

On top of Notre Dame, the night watchman, looking down, shielding the match from the softly blowing wind, sees the police, the workmen, and the producer in a dark suit, a big man, gazing up at him. Then the night watchman slowly turns the match, cupping it, applies it to the tip of his cigar. He lights the cigar in slow puffs.

He calls: "Is Mr. Douglas down there?"

A voice calls back: "What do you want with me?"

The old man smiles. "Come up, alone! Bring a gun if you want! I just want a little talk!"

The voices echo in the vast churchyard:

"Don't *do* it, Mr. Douglas!"

"Give me your gun. Let's get this *over* with so I can get back to the party. Keep me covered, I'll play it safe. I don't want these sets burned. There's two million dollars in lumber alone here. *Ready?* I'm on my way."

The producer climbs high on the night ladders, up through the half shell of Notre Dame to where the old man leans against a plaster gargoyle, quietly smoking a cigar. The producer stops, gun pointed, half through an open trap door.

"All right, Smith. Stay where you are."

Smith removes the cigar from his mouth quietly. "Don't you be afraid of me. I'm all right."

"I wouldn't bet money on that."

"Mr. Douglas," says the night watchman, "did you ever read that story about the man who traveled to the future and found everyone there insane? *Everyone.* But since they were all insane they didn't *know* they were insane. They all acted alike and so they thought themselves normal. And since our hero was the only sane one among them, he was abnormal; therefore, *he* was the insane one. To *them,* at least. Yes, Mr. Douglas, insanity is relative. It all depends on who has who locked in what cage."

The producer swears under his breath. "I didn't climb up here to talk all night. What do you want?"

"I want to talk with the Creator. That's you, Mr. Douglas. You created all this. You came here one day and struck the earth with a magical checkbook and cried, 'Let there be Paris!' And there *was* Paris: streets, bistros, flowers, wine, outdoor bookshops and all. And you clapped your hands again: 'Let there be Constantinople!' And there *it* was! You clapped your hands a thousand times, and each time made something new, and now you think just by clapping your hands one *last* time you can drop it all down in ruins. But, Mr. Douglas, it's not as easy as that!"

"I own fifty-one per cent of the stock in this studio!"

"But did the studio ever *belong* to you, really? Did you ever think to drive here late some night and climb up on this cathedral and see what a *wonderful* world you created? Did you ever wonder if it might not be a good idea for you to sit up here with me and my friends and have a cup of amontillado sherry with us? All right—so the amontillado smells and looks and tastes like coffee. Imagination, Mr. Creator, imagination. But no, you never came around, you never climbed up, you never looked or listened or cared. There was always a party somewhere else. And now, very late, without asking us, you want to destroy it all. You may own fifty-one per cent of the studio stock, but you don't own *them.*"

"Them!" cries the producer. "What's all this business about 'them'?"

"It's hard to put in words. The people who *live* here." The night watchman moves his hand in the empty air toward the half cities and the night. "So many films were made here in all the long years. Extras moved in the streets in costumes, they talked a thousand tongues, they smoked cigarettes and meerschaums and Persian hookahs, even. Dancing girl danced. They *glittered*, oh, how they glittered! Women with veils smiled down from high balconies. Soldiers marched. Children played. Knights in silver armor fought. There were orange-tea shops. People sipped tea in them and dropped their *h*'s. Gongs were beaten. Viking ships sailed the inland seas."

The producer lifts himself up through the trap door and sits on the plankings, the gun cradled more easily in his hand. He seems to be looking at the old man first with one eye, then the other, listening to him with one ear, then the other, shaking his head a little to himself.

The night watchman continues:

"And somehow, after the extras and the men with the cameras and microphones and all the equipment walked away and the gates were shut and they drove off in big cars, somehow something of all those thousands of different people remained. The things they had been, or *pretended* to be, stayed on. The foreign languages, the costumes, the things they did, the things they thought about, their religions and their music, all those little things and big things stayed on. The sights of far places. The smells. The salt wind. The sea. It's all here tonight—if you *listen*."

The producer listens and the old man listens in the drafty strutworks of the cathedral, with the moonlight blinding the eyes of the plaster gargoyles and the wind making the false stone mouths to whisper, and the sound of a thousand lands within a land below blowing and dusting and leaning in that wind, a thousand yellow minarets and milk-white towers and green avenues yet untouched among the hundred new ruins, and all of it murmuring its wires and lathings like a great steel-and-wooden harp

touched in the night, and the wind bringing that self-made sound high up here in the sky to these two men who stand listening and apart.

The producer laughs shortly and shakes his head.

"You *heard*," says the night watchman. "You *did* hear, didn't you? I see it in your face."

Douglas shoves the gun in his coat pocket. "Anything you listen for you can hear. I made the mistake of listening. You should have been a writer. You could throw six of my best ones out of work. Well, what about it—are you ready to come down out of here now?"

"You sound almost polite," says the night watchman.

"Don't know why I should. You ruined a good evening for me."

"Did I? It hasn't been that bad, has it? A bit different, I should say. Stimulating, maybe."

Douglas laughs quietly. "You're not dangerous at all. You just need company. It's your job and everything going to hell and you're lonely. I can't quite figure you, though."

"Don't tell me I've got you thinking?" asks the old man.

Douglas snorts. "After you've lived in Hollywood long enough, you meet all kinds. Besides, I've never been up here before. It's a real view, like you say. But I'll be damned if I can figure why you should worry about all this junk. What's it to you?"

The night watchman gets down on one knee and taps one hand into the palm of the other, illustrating his points. "Look. As I said before, you came here years ago, clapped your hands, and three hundred cities jumped up! Then you added a half thousand other nations and states and peoples and religions and political setups inside the barbed-wire fence. And there was trouble! Oh, nothing you could *see*. It was all in the wind and the spaces between. But it was the same kind of trouble the world out there beyond the fence has—squabbles and riots and invisible wars. But at last the trouble died out. You want to know why?"

"If I didn't, I wouldn't be sitting up here freezing."

A little night music, please, thinks the old man, and moves his

hand on the air like someone playing the proper and beautiful music to background all that he has to tell. . . .

"Because you got Boston joined to Trinidad," he says softly, "part of Trinidad poking out of Lisbon, part of Lisbon leaning on Alexandria, Alexandria tacked onto Shanghai, and a lot of little pegs and nails between, like Chattanooga, Oshkosh, Oslo, Sweet Water, Soissons, Beirut, Bombay, and Port Arthur. You shoot a man in New York and he stumbles forward and drops dead in Athens. You take a political bribe in Chicago and somebody in London goes to jail. You hang a Negro man in Alabama and the people of Hungary have to bury him. The dead Jews of Poland clutter the streets of Sydney, Portland, and Tokyo. You push a knife into a man's stomach in Berlin and it comes out the back of a farmer in Memphis. It's all so *close,* so very *close.* That's why we have peace here. We're all so crowded there *has got to be peace,* or nothing would be left! One fire would destroy all of us, no matter who started it, for what reason. So all of the people, the memories, whatever you want to call them, that are here, have settled down, and this is their world, a good world, a fine world."

The old man stops and licks his lips slowly and takes a breath. "And tomorrow," he says, "you're going to stomp it down."

The old man crouches there a moment longer, then gets to his feet and gazes out at the cities and the thousand shadows in those cities. The great plaster cathedral whines and sways in the night air, back and forth, rocking on the summer tides.

"Well," says Douglas at last, "shall—shall we go down now?"

Smith nods. "I've had my say."

Douglas vanishes, and the watchman listens to the younger man going down and down through the ladders and catwalks of the night. Then, after a reasonable hesitation, the old man takes hold of the ladder, breathes something to himself, and begins the long descent in shadow.

The studio police and the few workers and some minor executives all drive away. Only one large dark car waits outside the

barbed-wire gate as the two men stand talking in the cities of the meadow.

"What are you going to do now?" asks Smith.

"Go back to my party, I suppose," says the producer.

"Will it be fun?"

"Yes." The producer hesitates. "Sure, it'll be fun!" He glances at the night watchman's right hand. "Don't tell me you've found that hammer Kelly told me you were using? You going to start building again? You don't give up, do you?"

"Would you, if you were the last builder and everybody else was a wrecker?"

Douglas starts to walk with the old man. "Well, maybe I'll see you again, Smith."

"No," says Smith, "I won't be here. This all won't be here. If you come back again, it'll be too late."

Douglas stops. "Hell, hell! What do you want me to *do?*"

"A simple thing. Leave all this standing. Leave these cities up."

"I can't do that! Damn it. Business reasons. It has to go."

"A man with a real nose for business and *some* imagination could think up a profitable reason for it to stay," says Smith.

"My car's waiting! How do I get out of here?"

The producer strikes off over a patch of rubble, cuts through half of a tumbled ruin, kicking boards aside, leaning for a moment on plaster façades and strutworks. Dust rains from the sky.

"Watch out!"

The producer stumbles in a thunder of dust and avalanching brick; he gropes, he topples, he is seized upon by the old man and yanked forward.

"Jump!"

They jump, and half the building slides to ruin, crashes into hills and mountains of old paper and lathing. A great bloom of dust strikes out upon the air.

"You all right?"

"Yes. Thanks. Thanks." The producer looks at the fallen building. The dust clears. "You probably saved my life."

"Hardly that. Most of those are papier-mâché bricks. You might have been cut and bruised a little."

"Nevertheless, thanks. What building was that that fell?"

"Norman village tower, built in 1925. Don't get near the rest of it; it might go down."

"I'll be careful." The producer moves carefully in to stand by the set-piece. "Why—I could push this whole damn building over with one hand." He demonstrates; the building leans and quivers and groans. The producer steps quickly back. "I could knock it down in a second."

"But you wouldn't want to do that," says the watchman.

"Oh, wouldn't I? What's one French house more or less, this late in the day?"

The old man takes his arm. "Walk around here to the other side of the house."

They walk to the other side.

"Read that sign," says Smith.

The producer flicks his cigarette lighter, holds the fire up to help him squint, and reads:

"'THE FIRST NATIONAL BANK, MELLIN TOWN.'" He pauses. "'ILLINOIS,'" he says, very slowly.

The building stands there in the sharp light of the stars and the bland light of the moon.

"On one side"—Douglas balances his hand like a scales—"a French tower. On the other side——" He walks seven steps to the right, seven steps to the left, peering. "'THE FIRST NATIONAL BANK.' Bank. Tower. Tower. Bank. Well, I'll be *damned*."

Smith smiles and says, "Still want to push the French tower down, Mr. Douglas?"

"Wait a minute, wait a minute, hold on, hold on," says Douglas, and suddenly begins to *see* the buildings that stand before him. He turns in a slow circle; his eyes move up and down and across and over; his eyes flick here, flick there, see this, see that, examine, file, put away, and re-examine. He begins to walk in silence. They move in the cities of the meadow, over grasses and wild flowers, up to and into and through ruins and half ruins and

up to and into and through complete avenues and villages and towns.

They begin a recital which goes on and on as they walk, Douglas asking, the night watchman answering, Douglas asking, the night watchman answering.

"What's this over here?"

"A Buddhist temple."

"And on the other side of it?"

"The log cabin where Lincoln was born."

"And here?"

"St. Patrick's church, New York."

"And on the reverse?"

"A Russian Orthodox church in Rostov!"

"What's *this?*"

"The door of a castle on the Rhine!"

"And *inside?*"

"A Kansas City soda fountain!"

"And here? And here? And over *there?* And what's *that?*" asks Douglas. "What's this! What about that one! And over *there!*"

It seems as if they are running and rushing and yelling all through the cities, here, there, everywhere, up, down, in, out, climbing, descending, poking, stirring, opening-shutting doors.

"And this, and this, and this, and *this!*"

The night watchman tells all there is to tell.

Their shadows run ahead in narrow alleys, and avenues as broad as rivers made of stone and sand.

They make a great talking circle; they hurry all around and back to where they started.

They are quiet again. The old man is quiet from having said what there was to say, and the producer is quiet from listening and remembering and fitting it all together in his mind. He stands, absent-mindedly fumbling for his cigarette case. It takes him a full minute to open it, examining every action, thinking about it, and to offer the case to the watchman.

"Thanks."

They light up thoughtfully. They puff on their cigarettes and watch the smoke blow away.

Douglas says, "Where's that damned hammer of yours?"

"Here," says Smith.

"You got your nails with you?"

"Yes, sir."

Douglas takes a deep drag on his cigarette and exhales. "Okay, Smith, get to work."

"What?"

"You heard me. Nail what you can back up, on your own time. Most of the stuff that's already torn down is a complete loss. But any bits and pieces that fit and will look decent, put 'em together. Thank God there's a lot still standing. It took me a long time to get it through my head. A man with a nose for business and *some* imagination, you said. This *is* the world, you said. I should have seen it years ago. Here it all is inside the fence, and me too blind to see what could be done with it. The World Federation in my own back yard and me kicking it over. So help me God, we need more crazy people and night watchmen."

"You know," says the night watchman, "I'm getting old and I'm getting strange. You wouldn't be fooling an old and a strange man, would you?"

"I'll make no promises I can't keep," says the producer. "I'll only promise to try. There's a good chance we can go ahead. It would make a beautiful film, there's no doubt of that. We could make it all here, inside the fence, photograph it ten ways from Christmas. There's no doubt about a story, either. You provided it. It's yours. It wouldn't be hard to put some writers to work on it. Good writers. Perhaps only a short subject, twenty minutes, but we could show all the cities and countries here, leaning on and holding each other up. I *like* the idea. I like it very much, believe me. We could show a film like that to anyone anywhere in the world and they'd like it. They couldn't pass it up, it would be too important."

"It's good to hear you talk this way."

"I hope I keep on talking this way," says the producer. "I can't

be trusted. I don't trust myself. Hell, I get excited, up one day, down the next. Maybe you'll have to hit me on the head with that hammer to keep me going."

"I'd be pleased," says Smith.

"And *if* we do the film," says the younger man, "I suppose you could help. You know the sets, probably better than anyone. Any suggestions you might want to make, we'd be glad to have. Then, after we do the film, I suppose you won't mind letting us tear the rest of the world down, right?"

"I'd give my permission," says the watchman.

"Well, I'll call off the hounds for a few days and see what happens. Send out a camera crew tomorrow to see what we can line up for shots. Send out some writers. Maybe you can *all* gab. Hell, hell. We'll work it out." Douglas turns toward the gate. "In the meantime, use your hammer all you want. I'll be seeing you. My God, I'm *freezing!*"

They hurry toward the gate. On the way, the old man finds his lunch box where he abandoned it some hours ago. He picks it up, takes out the thermos, and shakes it. "How about a drink before you go?"

"What've you got? Some of that amontillado you were yelling about?"

"1876."

"Let's have some of that, sure."

The thermos is opened and the liquid poured steaming from it into the cup.

"There you are," says the old man.

"Thanks. Here's to you." The producer drinks. "That's good. Ah, that's damned good!"

"It might taste like coffee, but I tell you it's the finest amontillado ever put under a cork."

"You can say *that* again."

The two of them stand among the cities of the world in the moonlight, drinking the hot drink, and the old man remembers something: "There's an old song fits here, a drinking song, I think, a song that all of us who live inside the fence sing, when

we're of a mind, when I listen right, and the wind's just right in the telephone wires. It goes like this:

> *"We all go the same way home,*
> *All the same collection, in the same direction,*
> *All go the same way home.*
> *So there's no need to part at all,*
> *And we'll all cling together like the ivy on the*
>   *old garden wall . . ."*

They finish drinking the coffee in the middle of Port-au-Prince.

"Hey!" says the producer suddenly. "Take it easy with that cigarette! You want to burn down the whole darn *world?*"

They both look at the cigarette and smile.

"I'll be careful," says Smith.

"So long," says the producer. "I'm *really* late for that party."

"So long, Mr. Douglas."

The gate hasp clicks open and shut, the footsteps die away, the limousine starts up and drives off in the moonlight, leaving behind the cities of the world and an old man standing in the middle of these cities of the world, raising his hand to wave.

"So long," says the night watchman.

And then there is only the wind.

THE GARBAGE COLLECTOR

This is how his work was: he got up at five in the cold dark morning and washed his face with warm water if the heater was working and cold water if the heater was not working. He shaved carefully, talking out to his wife in the kitchen, who was fixing ham and eggs or pancakes or whatever it was that morning. By six o'clock he was driving on his way to work alone, and parking his car in the big yard where all the other men parked their cars as the sun was coming up. The colors of the sky that time of morning were orange and blue and violet and sometimes very red and sometimes yellow or a clear color like water on white rock. Some mornings he could see his breath on the air and some mornings he could not. But as the sun was still rising he knocked his fist on the side of the green truck, and his driver, smiling and saying hello, would climb in the other side of the truck and they would drive out into the great city and go down all the streets until they came to the place where they started work. Sometimes, on the way, they stopped for black coffee and then went on, the warmness in them. And they began the work which meant that he jumped off in front of each house and picked up the garbage cans and brought them back and took off their lids and knocked them against the bin edge, which made the orange peels and can-

taloupe rinds and coffee grounds fall out and thump down and begin to fill the empty truck. There were always steak bones and the heads of fish and pieces of green onion and stale celery. If the garbage was new it wasn't so bad, but if it was very old it was bad. He was not sure if he liked the job or not, but it was a job and he did it well, talking about it a lot at some times and sometimes not thinking of it in any way at all. Some days the job was wonderful, for you were out early and the air was cool and fresh until you had worked too long and the sun got hot and the garbage steamed early. But mostly it was a job significant enough to keep him busy and calm and looking at the houses and cut lawns he passed by and seeing how everybody lived. And once or twice a month he was surprised to find that he loved the job and that it was the finest job in the world.

It went on just that way for many years. And then suddenly the job changed for him. It changed in a single day. Later he often wondered how a job could change so much in such a few short hours.

He walked into the apartment and did not see his wife or hear her voice, but she was there, and he walked to a chair and let her stand away from him, watching him as he touched the chair and sat down in it without saying a word. He sat there for a long time.

"What's wrong?" At last her voice came through to him. She must have said it three or four times.

"Wrong?" He looked at this woman and yes, it was his wife all right, it was someone he knew, and this was their apartment with the tall ceilings and the worn carpeting.

"Something happened at work today," he said.

She waited for him.

"On my garbage truck, something happened." His tongue moved dryly on his lips and his eyes shut over his seeing until there was all blackness and no light of any sort and it was like standing alone in a room when you got out of bed in the middle of a dark night. "I think I'm going to quit my job. Try to understand."

"Understand!" she cried.

"It can't be helped. This is all the strangest damned thing that ever happened to me in my life." He opened his eyes and sat there, his hands feeling cold when he rubbed his thumb and fore-fingers together. "The thing that happened was strange."

"Well, don't just *sit* there!"

He took part of a newspaper from the pocket of his leather jacket. "This is today's paper," he said. "December 10, 1951. Los Angeles *Times*. Civil Defense Bulletin. It says they're buying radios for our garbage trucks."

"Well, what's so bad about a little music?"

"No music. You don't understand. No music."

He opened his rough hand and drew with one clean fingernail, slowly, trying to put everything there where he could see it and she could see it. "In this article the mayor says they'll put sending and receiving apparatus on every garbage truck in town." He squinted at his hand. "After the atom bombs hit our city, those radios will talk to us. And then our garbage trucks will go pick up the bodies."

"Well, that seems practical. When——"

"The garbage trucks," he said, "go out and pick up all the bodies."

"You can't just leave bodies around, can you? You've got to take them and——" His wife shut her mouth very slowly. She blinked, one time only, and she did this very slowly also. He watched that one slow blink of her eyes. Then, with a turn of her body, as if someone else had turned it for her, she walked to a chair, paused, thought how to do it, and sat down, very straight and stiff. She said nothing.

He listened to his wrist watch ticking, but with only a small part of his attention.

At last she laughed. "They were joking!"

He shook his head. He felt his head moving from left to right and from right to left, as slowly as everything else had happened. "No. They put a receiver on my truck today. They said, at the

alert, if you're working, dump your garbage anywhere. When we radio you, get *in* there and haul out the dead."

Some water in the kitchen boiled over loudly. She let it boil for five seconds and then held the arm of the chair with one hand and got up and found the door and went out. The boiling sound stopped. She stood in the door and then walked back to where he still sat, not moving, his head in one position only.

"It's all blueprinted out. They have squads, sergeants, captains, corporals, everything," he said. "We even know where to *bring* the bodies."

"So you've been thinking about it all day," she said.

"All day since this morning. I thought: Maybe now I don't want to be a garbage collector any more. It used to be Tom and me had fun with a kind of game. You got to do that. Garbage is bad. But if you work at it you can make a game. Tom and me did that. We watched people's garbage. We saw what kind they had. Steak bones in rich houses, lettuce and orange peel in poor ones. Sure it's silly, but a guy's got to make his work as good as he can and worth while or why in hell do it? And you're your own boss, in a way, on a truck. You get out early in the morning and it's an outdoor job, anyway; you see the sun come up and you see the town get up, and that's not bad at all. But now, today, all of a sudden it's not the kind of job for me any more."

His wife started to talk swiftly. She named a lot of things and she talked about a lot more, but before she got very far he cut gently across her talking. "I know, I know, the kids and school, our car, I know," he said. "And bills and money and credit. But what about that farm Dad left us? Why can't we move there, away from cities? I know a little about farming. We could stock up, hole in, have enough to live on for months if anything happened."

She said nothing.

"Sure, all of our friends are here in town," he went on reasonably. "And movies and shows and the kids' friends, and . . ."

She took a deep breath. "Can't we think it over a few more days?"

"I don't know. I'm afraid of that. I'm afraid if I think it over, about my truck and my new work, I'll get used to it. And, oh Christ, it just doesn't seem right a man, a human being, should ever let himself get used to any idea like that."

She shook her head slowly, looking at the windows, the gray walls, the dark pictures on the walls. She tightened her hands. She started to open her mouth.

"I'll think tonight," he said. "I'll stay up awhile. By morning I'll know what to do."

"Be careful with the children. It wouldn't be good, their knowing all this."

"I'll be careful."

"Let's not talk any more, then. I'll finish dinner!" She jumped up and put her hands to her face and then looked at her hands and at the sunlight in the windows. "Why, the kids'll be home any minute."

"I'm not very hungry."

"You got to eat, you just got to keep on going." She hurried off, leaving him alone in the middle of a room where not a breeze stirred the curtains, and only the gray ceiling hung over him with a lonely bulb unlit in it, like an old moon in a sky. He was quiet. He massaged his face with both hands. He got up and stood alone in the dining-room door and walked forward and felt himself sit down and remain seated in a dining-room chair. He saw his hands spread on the white tablecloth, open and empty.

"All afternoon," he said, "I've thought."

She moved through the kitchen, rattling silverware, crashing pans against the silence that was everywhere.

"Wondering," he said, "if you put the bodies in the trucks lengthwise or endwise, with the heads on the right, or the *feet* on the right. Men and women together, or separated? Children in one truck, or mixed with men and women? Dogs in special trucks, or just let them lay? Wondering how *many* bodies one garbage truck can hold. And wondering if you stack them on top of each other and finally knowing you must just have to. I can't figure it. I can't work it out. I try, but there's no guessing,

no guessing at all how many you could stack in one single truck."

He sat thinking of how it was late in the day at his work, with the truck full and the canvas pulled over the great bulk of garbage so the bulk shaped the canvas in an uneven mound. And how it was if you suddenly pulled the canvas back and looked in. And for a few seconds you saw the white things like macaroni or noodles, only the white things were alive and boiling up, millions of them. And when the white things felt the hot sun on them they simmered down and burrowed and were gone in the lettuce and the old ground beef and the coffee grounds and the heads of white fish. After ten seconds of sunlight the white things that looked like noodles or macaroni were gone and the great bulk of garbage silent and not moving, and you drew the canvas over the bulk and looked at how the canvas folded unevenly over the hidden collection, and underneath you knew it was dark again, and things beginning to move as they must always move when things got dark again.

He was still sitting there in the empty room when the front door of the apartment burst wide. His son and daughter rushed in, laughing, and saw him sitting there, and stopped.

Their mother ran to the kitchen door, held to the edge of it quickly, and stared at her family. They saw her face and they heard her voice:

"Sit down, children, sit down!" She lifted one hand and pushed it toward them. "You're just in time."

20

THE GREAT FIRE

The morning the great fire started, nobody in the house could put it out. It was Mother's niece, Marianne, living with us while her parents were in Europe, who was all aflame. So nobody could smash the little window in the red box at the corner and pull the trigger to bring the gushing hoses and the hatted firemen. Blazing like so much ignited cellophane, Marianne came downstairs, plumped herself with a loud cry or moan at the breakfast table, and refused to eat enough to fill a tooth cavity.

Mother and Father moved away, the warmth in the room being excessive.

"Good morning, Marianne."

"What?" Marianne looked beyond people and spoke vaguely. "Oh, good morning."

"Did you sleep well last night, Marianne?"

But they knew she hadn't slept. Mother gave Marianne a glass of water to drink, and everyone wondered if it would evaporate in her hand. Grandma, from her table chair, surveyed Marianne's fevered eyes. "You're sick, but it's no microbe," she said. "They couldn't find it under a microscope."

"What?" said Marianne.

"Love is godmother to stupidity," said Father detachedly.

"She'll be all right," Mother said to Father. "Girls only seem stupid because when they're in love they can't hear."

"It affects the semicircular canals," said Father. "Making many girls fall right into a fellow's arms. I *know*. I was almost crushed to death once by a falling woman, and let me tell you——"

"Hush." Mother frowned, looking at Marianne.

"She can't hear what we're saying; she's cataleptic right now."

"He's coming to pick her up this morning," whispered Mother to Father, as if Marianne wasn't even in the room. "They're going riding in his jalopy."

Father patted his mouth with a napkin. "Was our daughter like this, Mama?" he wanted to know. "She's been married and gone so long, I've forgotten. I don't recall she was so foolish. One would never know a girl had an ounce of sense at a time like this. That's what fools a man. He says, Oh, what a lovely brainless girl, she loves me, I think I'll marry her. He marries her and wakes up one morning and all the dreaminess is gone out of her and her intellect has returned, unpacked, and is hanging up undies all about the house. The man begins running into ropes and lines. He finds himself on a little desert isle, a little living room alone in the midst of a universe, with a honeycomb that has turned into a bear trap, with a butterfly metamorphosed into a wasp. He then immediately takes up a hobby: stamp collecting, lodge meetings, or——"

"How you *do* run on," cried Mother. "Marianne, tell us about this young man. What was his name again? Was it Isak Van Pelt?"

"What? Oh—Isak, yes." Marianne had been roving about her bed all night, sometimes flipping poetry books and reading incredible lines, sometimes lying flat on her back, sometimes on her tummy looking out at dreaming moonlit country. The smell of jasmine had touched the room all night and the excessive warmth of early spring (the thermometer read fifty-five degrees) had kept her awake. She looked like a dying moth, if anyone had peeked through the keyhole.

This morning she had clapped her hands over her head in the mirror and come to breakfast, remembering just in time to put on a dress.

Grandma laughed quietly all during breakfast. Finally she said, "You must eat, child, you *must*." So Marianne played with her toast and got half a piece down. Just then there was a loud honk outside. That was Isak! In his jalopy!

"Whoop!" cried Marianne, and ran upstairs quickly.

The young Isak Van Pelt was brought in and introduced around.

When Marianne was finally gone, Father sat down, wiping his forehead. "I don't know. This is too much."

"You were the one who suggested she start going out," said Mother.

"And I'm sorry I suggested it," he said. "But she's been visiting us for six months now, and six more months to go. I thought if she met some nice young man——"

"And they were married," husked Grandma darkly, "why, Marianne might move out almost immediately—is *that* it?"

"Well," said Father.

"Well," said Grandma.

"But now it's worse than before," said Father. "She floats around singing with her eyes shut, playing those infernal love records and talking to herself. A man can stand so much. She's getting so she laughs all the time, too. Do eighteen-year-old girls often wind up in the booby hatch?"

"He seems a nice young man," said Mother.

"Yes, we can always pray for that," said Father, taking out a little shot glass. "Here's to an early marriage."

The second morning Marianne was out of the house like a fireball when first she heard the jalopy horn. There was no time for the young man even to come to the door. Only Grandma saw them roar off together, from the parlor window.

"She almost knocked me down." Father brushed his mustache. "What's *that*? Brained eggs? Well."

In the afternoon, Marianne, home again, drifted about the

living room to the phonograph records. The needle hiss filled the house. She played "That Old Black Magic" twenty-one times, going "la la la" as she swam with her eyes closed in the room.

"I'm afraid to go in my own parlor," said Father. "I retired from business to smoke cigars and enjoy living, not to have a limp relative humming about under the parlor chandelier."

"Hush," said Mother.

"This is a crisis," announced Father, "in my life. After all, she's just visiting."

"You know how visiting girls are. Away from home they think they're in Paris, France. She'll be gone in October. It's not so dreadful."

"Let's see," figured Father slowly. "I'll have been buried just about one hundred and thirty days out at Green Lawn Cemetery by then." He got up and threw his paper down into a little white tent on the floor. "By George, Mother, I'm talking to her right *now!*"

He went and stood in the parlor door, peering through it at the waltzing Marianne. "La," she sang to the music.

Clearing his throat, he stepped through.

"Marianne," he said.

"'That old black magic . . .'" sang Marianne. "Yes?"

He watched her hands swinging in the air. She gave him a sudden fiery looked as she danced by.

"I want to talk to you." He straightened his tie.

"Dah dum dee dum dum dee dum dee dum dum," she sang.

"Did you *hear* me?" he demanded.

"He's *so* nice," she said.

"Evidently."

"Do you know, he bows and opens doors like a doorman and plays a trumpet like Harry James and brought me daisies this morning?"

"I wouldn't doubt."

"His eyes are blue." She looked at the ceiling.

He could find nothing at all on the ceiling to look at.

She kept looking, as she danced, at the ceiling as he came over

and stood near her, looking up, but there wasn't a rain spot or a
settling crack there, and he sighed, "Marianne."

"And we ate lobster at that river café."

"Lobster. I know, but we don't want you breaking down, getting weak. One day, tomorrow, you must stay home and help
your aunt Math make her doilies——"

"Yes, sir." She dreamed around the room with her wings out.

"Did you *hear* me?" he demanded.

"Yes," she whispered. "Yes." Her eyes shut. "Oh yes, yes." Her
skirts whished around. "Uncle," she said, her head back, lolling.

"You'll help your aunt with her doilies?" he cried.

"—with her doilies," she murmured.

"There!" He sat down in the kitchen, plucking up the paper.
"I guess *I* told her!"

But next morning he was on the edge of his bed when he heard
the hot-rod's thunderous muffler and heard Marianne fall downstairs, linger two seconds in the dining room for breakfast, hesitate by the bathroom long enough to consider whether she would
be sick, and then the slam of the front door, the sound of the
jalopy banging down the street, two people singing off key in it.

Father put his head in his hands. "Doilies," he said.

"What?" said Mother.

"Dooley's," said Father. "I'm going down to Dooley's for a
morning visit."

"But Dooley's isn't open until ten."

"I'll wait," decided Father, eyes shut.

That night and seven other wild nights the porch swing sang
a little creaking song, back and forth, back and forth. Father,
hiding in the living room, could be seen in fierce relief whenever
he drafted his ten-cent cigar and the cherry light illumined his
immensely tragic face. The porch swing creaked. He waited for
another creak. He heard little butterfly-soft sounds from outside,
little palpitations of laughter and sweet nothings in small ears.
"My porch," said Father. "My swing," he whispered to his cigar,
looking at it. "My house." He listened for another creak. "My
God," he said.

He went to the tool shed and appeared on the dark porch with a shiny oil can. "No, don't get up. Don't bother. There, and there." He oiled the swing joints. It was dark. He couldn't see Marianne; he could smell her. The perfume almost knocked him off into the rosebush. He couldn't see her gentleman friend, either. "Good night," he said. He went in and sat down and there was no more creaking. Now all he could hear was something that sounded like the mothlike flutter of Marianne's heart.

"He must be very nice," said Mother in the kitchen door, wiping a dinner dish.

"That's what I'm hoping," whispered Father. "That's why I let them have the porch every night!"

"So many days in a row," said Mother. "A girl doesn't go with a nice young man that many times unless he's serious."

"Maybe he'll propose tonight!" was Father's happy thought.

"Hardly so soon. And she is so young."

"Still," he ruminated, "it might happen. It's *got* to happen, by the Lord Harry."

Grandma chuckled from her corner easy chair. It sounded like someone turning the pages of an ancient book.

"What's so funny?" said Father.

"Wait and see," said Grandma. "Tomorrow."

Father stared at the dark, but Grandma would say no more.

"Well, well," said Father at breakfast. He surveyed his eggs with a kindly, paternal eye. "Well, well, by gosh, last night, on the porch, there was *more whispering*. What's his name? Isak? Well, now, if I'm any judge at all, I think he proposed to Marianne last night; yes, I'm positive of it!"

"It would be nice," said Mother. "A spring marriage. But it's so *soon*."

"Look," said Father with full-mouthed logic. "Marianne's the kind of girl who marries quick and young. We can't stand in her way, can we?"

"For once I think you're right," said Mother. "A marriage

would be fine. Spring flowers, and Marianne looking nice in that gown I saw at Haydecker's last week."

They all peered anxiously at the stairs, waiting for Marianne to appear.

"Pardon me," rasped Grandma, sighting up from her morning toast. "But I wouldn't talk of getting rid of Marianne just yet if I were you."

"And why not?"

"Because."

"Because why?"

"I hate to spoil your plans," rustled Grandma, chuckling. She gestured with her little vinegary head. "But while you people were worrying about getting Marianne married, I've been keeping tab on her. Seven days now I've been watching this young fellow each day he came in his car and honked his horn outside. He must be an actor or a quick-change artist or something."

"What?" asked Father.

"Yep," said Grandma. "Because one day he was a young blond fellow, and next day he was a tall dark fellow, and Wednesday he was a chap with a brown mustache, and Thursday he had wavy red hair, and Friday he was shorter, with a Chevrolet stripped down instead of a Ford."

Mother and Father sat for a minute as if hit with hammers right behind the left ear.

At last Father, his face exploding with color, shouted, "Do you mean to *say!* You *sat* there, woman, you say; all those men, and you——"

"You were always hiding," snapped Grandma. "So you wouldn't spoil things. If you'd come out in the open you'd have seen the same as I. I never said a word. She'll simmer down. It's just her time of life. Every woman goes through it. It's hard, but they can survive. A new man every day does wonders for a girl's ego!"

"You, you, you, you, *you!*" Father choked on it, eyes wild, throat gorged too big for his collar. He fell back in his chair, exhausted. Mother sat, stunned.

"Good morning, everyone!" Marianne raced downstairs and popped into a chair. Father stared at her.

"You, you, you, you, you," he accused Grandma.

I shall run down the street shouting, thought Father wildly, and break the fire-alarm window and pull the lever and bring the fire engines and the hoses. Or perhaps there will be a late snowstorm and I shall set Marianne out in it to cool.

He did neither. The heat in the room being excessive, according to the wall calendar, everyone moved out onto the cool porch while Marianne sat looking at her orange juice.

HAIL AND FAREWELL

But of course he was going away, there was nothing else to do, the time was up, the clock had run out, and he was going very far away indeed. His suitcase was packed, his shoes were shined, his hair was brushed, he had expressly washed behind his ears, and it remained only for him to go down the stairs, out the front door, and up the street to the small-town station where the train would make a stop for him alone. Then Fox Hill, Illinois, would be left far off in his past. And he would go on, perhaps to Iowa, perhaps to Kansas, perhaps even to California; a small boy, twelve years old, with a birth certificate in his valise to show he had been born forty-three years ago.

"Willie!" called a voice belowstairs.

"Yes!" He hoisted his suitcase. In his bureau mirror he saw a face made of June dandelions and July apples and warm summer-morning milk. There, as always, was his look of the angel and the innocent, which might never, in the years of his life, change.

"Almost time," called the woman's voice.

"All right!" And he went down the stairs, grunting and smiling. In the living room sat Anna and Steve, their clothes painfully neat.

"Here I am!" cried Willie in the parlor door.

Anna looked like she was going to cry. "Oh, good Lord, you can't really be leaving us, can you, Willie?"

"People are beginning to talk," said Willie quietly. "I've been here three years now. But when people begin to talk, I know it's time to put on my shoes and buy a railway ticket."

"It's all so strange. I don't understand. It's so sudden," Anna said. "Willie, we'll miss you."

"I'll write you every Christmas, so help me. Don't you write me."

"It's been a great pleasure and satisfaction," said Steve, sitting there, his words the wrong size in his mouth. "It's a shame it had to stop. It's a shame you had to tell us about yourself. It's an awful shame you can't stay on."

"You're the nicest folks I ever had," said Willie, four feet high, in no need of a shave, the sunlight on his face.

And then Anna *did* cry. "Willie, Willie." And she sat down and looked as if she wanted to hold him but was afraid to hold him now; she looked at him with shock and amazement and her hands empty, not knowing what to do with him now.

"It's not easy to go," said Willie. "You get used to things. You want to stay. But it doesn't work. I tried to stay on once after people began to suspect. 'How horrible!' people said. 'All these years, playing with our innocent children,' they said, 'and us not guessing! Awful!' they said. And finally I had to just leave town one night. It's not easy. You know darned well how much I love both of you. Thanks for three swell years."

They all went to the front door. "Willie, where're you going?"

"I don't know. I just start traveling. When I see a town that looks green and nice, I settle in."

"Will you ever come back?"

"Yes," he said earnestly with his high voice. "In about twenty years it should begin to show in my face. When it does, I'm going to make a grand tour of all the mothers and fathers I've ever had."

They stood on the cool summer porch, reluctant to say the last

words. Steve was looking steadily at an elm tree. "How many other folks've you stayed with, Willie? How many adoptions?"

Willie figured it, pleasantly enough. "I guess it's about five towns and five couples and over twenty years gone by since I started my tour."

"Well, we can't holler," said Steve. "Better to've had a son thirty-six months than none whatever."

"Well," said Willie, and kissed Anna quickly, seized at his luggage, and was gone up the street in the green noon light, under the trees, a very young boy indeed, not looking back, running steadily.

The boys were playing on the green park diamond when he came by. He stood a little while among the oak-tree shadows, watching them hurl the white, snowy baseball into the warm summer air, saw the baseball shadow fly like a dark bird over the grass, saw their hands open in mouths to catch this swift piece of summer that now seemed most especially important to hold onto. The boys' voices yelled. The ball lit on the grass near Willie.

Carrying the ball forward from under the shade trees, he thought of the last three years now spent to the penny, and the five years before that, and so on down the line to the year when he was really eleven and twelve and fourteen and the voices saying: "What's wrong with Willie, missus?" "Mrs. B., is Willie late a-growin'?" "Willie, you smokin' *cigars* lately?" The echoes died in summer light and color. His mother's voice: "Willie's twenty-one today!" And a thousand voices saying: "Come back, son, when you're fifteen; *then* maybe we'll give you a job."

He stared at the baseball in his trembling hand, as if it were his life, an interminable ball of years strung around and around and around, but always leading back to his twelfth birthday. He heard the kids walking toward him; he felt them blot out the sun, and they were older, standing around him.

"Willie! Where you goin'?" They kicked his suitcase.

How tall they stood to the sun. In the last few months it

seemed the sun had passed a hand above their heads, beckoned, and they were warm metal drawn melting upward; they were golden taffy pulled by an immense gravity to the sky, thirteen, fourteen years old, looking down upon Willie, smiling, but already beginning to neglect him. It had started four months ago:

"Choose up sides! Who wants Willie?"

"Aw, Willie's too little; we don't play with 'kids.'"

And they raced ahead of him, drawn by the moon and the sun and the turning seasons of leaf and wind, and he was twelve years old and not of them any more. And the other voices beginning again on the old, the dreadfully familiar, the cool refrain: "Better feed that boy vitamins, Steve." "Anna, does shortness *run* in your family?" And the cold fist kneading at your heart again and knowing that the roots would have to be pulled up again after so many good years with the "folks."

"Willie, where you goin'?"

He jerked his head. He was back among the towering, shadowing boys who milled around him like giants at a drinking fountain bending down.

"Goin' a few days visitin' a cousin of mine."

"Oh." There was a day, a year ago, when they would have cared very much indeed. But now there was only curiosity for his luggage, their enchantment with trains and trips and far places.

"How about a coupla fast ones?" said Willie.

They looked doubtful, but, considering the circumstances, nodded. He dropped his bag and ran out; the white baseball was up in the sun, away to their burning white figures in the far meadow, up in the sun again, rushing, life coming and going in a pattern. Here, *there!* Mr. and Mrs. Robert Hanlon, Creek Bend, Wisconsin, 1932, the first couple, the first year! Here, there! Henry and Alice Boltz, Limeville, Iowa, 1935! The baseball flying. The Smiths, the Eatons, the Robinsons! 1939! 1945! Husband and wife, husband and wife, husband and wife, no children, no children, no children! A knock on this door, a knock on that

"Pardon me. My name is William. I wonder if——"

"A sandwich? Come in, sit down. Where you *from,* son?"

The sandwich, a tall glass of cold milk, the smiling, the nodding, the comfortable, leisurely talking.

"Son, you look like you been traveling. You run *off* from somewhere?"

"No."

"Boy, are you an orphan?"

Another glass of milk.

"We always wanted kids. It never worked out. Never knew why. One of those things. Well, well. It's getting late, son. Don't you think you better hit for home?"

"Got no home."

"A boy like you? Not dry behind the ears? Your mother'll be worried."

"Got no home and no folks anywhere in the world. I wonder if—I wonder—could I sleep here tonight?"

"Well, now, son, I don't just *know.* We never considered taking in——" said the husband.

"We got chicken for supper tonight," said the wife, "enough for extras, enough for company. . . ."

And the years turning and flying away, the voices, and the faces, and the people, and always the same first conversations. The voice of Emily Robinson, in her rocking chair, in summer-night darkness, the last night he stayed with her, the night she discovered his secret, her voice saying:

"I look at all the little children's faces going by. And I sometimes think, What a shame, what a shame, that all these flowers have to be cut, all these bright fires have to be put out. What a shame these, all of these you see in schools or running by, have to get tall and unsightly and wrinkle and turn gray or get bald, and finally, all bone and wheeze, be dead and buried off away. When I hear them laugh I can't believe they'll ever go the road I'm going. Yet here they *come!* I still remember Wordsworth's poem: 'When all at once I saw a crowd, A host of golden daffodils; Beside the lake, beneath the trees, Fluttering and dancing

in the breeze.' That's how I think of children, cruel as they sometimes are, mean as I know they can be, but not yet showing the
meanness around their eyes or *in* their eyes, not yet full of tired-
ness. They're so eager for everything! I guess that's what I miss
most in older folks, the eagerness gone nine times out of ten, the
freshness gone, so much of the drive and life down the drain. I
like to watch school let out each day. It's like someone threw a
bunch of flowers out the school front doors. How does it feel,
Willie? How does it feel to be young forever? To look like a silver
dime new from the mint? Are you happy? Are you as fine as you
seem?"

The baseball whizzed from the blue sky, stung his hand like a
great pale insect. Nursing it, he hears his memory say:
"I worked with what I had. After my folks died, after I found
I couldn't get man's work anywhere, I tried carnivals, but they
only laughed. 'Son,' they said, 'you're not a midget, and even if
you are, you look like a *boy!* We want midgets with midgets'
faces! Sorry, son, sorry.' So I left home, started out, thinking:
What *was* I? A boy. I looked like a boy, sounded like a boy, so I
might as well go on being a boy. No use fighting it. No use
screaming. So what could I do? What job was handy? And then
one day I saw this man in a restaurant looking at another man's
pictures of his children. 'Sure wish I had kids,' he said. 'Sure
wish I had kids.' He kept shaking his head. And me sitting a few
seats away from him, a hamburger in my hands. I sat there, *frozen!* At that very instant I knew what my job would be for all of
the rest of my life. There *was* work for me, after all. Making
lonely people happy. Keeping myself busy. Playing forever. I
knew I had to play forever. Deliver a few papers, run a few er-
rands, mow a few lawns, maybe. But *hard* work? No. All I had
to do was be a mother's son and a father's pride. I turned to the
man down the counter from me. 'I beg your pardon,' I said. I
smiled at him. . . ."
"But, Willie," said Mrs. Emily long ago, "didn't you ever get
lonely? Didn't you ever want—*things*—that grownups wanted?"

"I fought that out alone," said Willie. "I'm a boy, I told my-self, I'll have to live in a boy's world, read boys' books, play boys' games, cut myself off from everything else. I can't be both. I got to be only one thing—young. And so I played that way. Oh, it wasn't easy. There were times——" He lapsed into silence.

"And the family you lived with, they never knew?"

"No. Telling them would have spoiled everything. I told them I was a runaway; I let them check through official channels, po-lice. Then, when there was no record, let them put in to adopt me. That was best of all; as long as they never guessed. But then, after three years, or five years, they guessed, or a traveling man came through, or a carnival man saw me, and it was over. It al-ways had to end."

"And you're *very* happy and it's *nice* being a child for over forty years?"

"It's a living, as they say. And when you make other people happy, then you're almost happy too. I got my job to do and I do it. And anyway, in a few years now I'll be in my second child-hood. All the fevers will be out of me and all the unfulfilled things and most of the dreams. Then I can relax, maybe, and play the role all the way."

He threw the baseball one last time and broke the reverie. Then he was running to seize his luggage. Tom, Bill, Jamie, Bob, Sam—their names moved on his lips. They were embarrassed at his shaking hands.

"After all, Willie, it ain't as if you're going to China or Tim-buktu."

"That's right, isn't it?" Willie did not move.

"So long, Willie. See you next week!"

"So long, so long!"

And he was walking off with his suitcase again, looking at the trees, going away from the boys and the street where he had lived, and as he turned the corner a train whistle screamed, and he be-gan to run.

The last thing he saw and heard was a white ball tossed at a high roof, back and forth, back and forth, and two voices crying

out as the ball pitched now up, down, and back through the sky, "Annie, annie, over! Annie, annie, over!" like the crying of birds flying off to the far south.

In the early morning, with the smell of the mist and the cold metal, with the iron smell of the train around him and a full night of traveling shaking his bones and his body, and a smell of the sun beyond the horizon, he awoke and looked out upon a small town just arising from sleep. Lights were coming on, soft voices muttered, a red signal bobbed back and forth, back and forth in the cold air. There was that sleeping hush in which echoes are dignified by clarity, in which echoes stand nakedly alone and sharp. A porter moved by, a shadow in shadows.

"Sir," said Willie.

The porter stopped.

"What town's this?" whispered the boy in the dark.

"Valleyville."

"How many people?"

"Ten thousand. Why? This your stop?"

"It looks green." Willie gazed out at the cold morning town for a long time. "It looks nice and quiet," said Willie.

"Son," said the porter, "you know where you *going?*"

"Here," said Willie, and got up quietly in the still, cool, iron-smelling morning, in the train dark, with a rustling and stir.

"I hope you know what you're doing, boy," said the porter.

"Yes, sir," said Willie. "I know what I'm doing." And he was down the dark aisle, luggage lifted after him by the porter, and out in the smoking, steaming-cold, beginning-to-lighten morning. He stood looking up at the porter and the black metal train against the few remaining stars. The train gave a great wailing blast of whistle, the porters cried out all along the line, the cars jolted, and his special porter waved and smiled down at the boy there, the small boy there with the big luggage who shouted up to him, even as the whistle screamed again.

"What?" shouted the porter, hand cupped to ear.

"Wish me luck!" cried Willie.

"Best of luck, son," called the porter, waving, smiling. "Best of luck, boy!"

"Thanks!" said Willie, in the great sound of the train, in the steam and roar.

He watched the black train until it was completely gone away and out of sight. He did not move all the time it was going. He stood quietly, a small boy twelve years old, on the worn wooden platform, and only after three entire minutes did he turn at last to face the empty streets below.

Then, as the sun was rising, he began to walk very fast, so as to keep warm, down into the new town.

THE GOLDEN APPLES OF THE SUN

"South," said the captain.

"But," said his crew, "there simply *aren't* any directions out here in space."

"When you travel on down toward the sun," replied the captain, "and everything gets yellow and warm and lazy, then you're going in one direction only." He shut his eyes and thought about the smoldering, warm, faraway land, his breath moving gently in his mouth. "South." He nodded slowly to himself. "South."

Their rocket was the *Copa de Oro,* also named the *Prometheus* and the *Icarus,* and their destination in all reality was the blazing noonday sun. In high good spirits they had packed along two thousand sour lemonades and a thousand white-capped beers for this journey to the wide Sahara. And now as the sun boiled up at them they remembered a score of verses and quotations:

" 'The golden apples of the sun'?"

"Yeats."

" 'Fear no more the heat of the sun'?"

"Shakespeare, of course!"

" 'Cup of Gold'? Steinbeck. 'The Crock of Gold'? Stephens. And what about the pot of gold at the rainbow's end? *There's* a name for our trajectory, by God. Rainbow!"

"Temperature?"

"One thousand degrees Fahrenheit!"

The captain stared from the huge dark-lensed port, and there indeed was the sun, and to go to that sun and touch it and steal part of it forever away was his quiet and single idea. In this ship were combined the coolly delicate and the coldly practical. Through corridors of ice and milk-frost, ammoniated winter and storming snowflakes blew. Any spark from that vast hearth burning out there beyond the callous hull of this ship, any small fire-breath that might seep through would find winter, slumbering here like all the coldest hours of February.

The audio-thermometer murmured in the arctic silence: "Temperature: two thousand degrees!"

Falling, thought the captain, like a snowflake into the lap of June, warm July, and the sweltering dog-mad days of August.

"Three thousand degrees Fahrenheit!"

Under the snow fields engines raced, refrigerants pumped ten thousand miles per hour in rimed boa-constrictor coils.

"Four thousand degrees Fahrenheit."

Noon. Summer. July.

"Five thousand Fahrenheit!"

And at last the captain spoke with all the quietness of the journey in his voice:

"Now, we are touching the sun."

Their eyes, thinking it, were melted gold.

"Seven thousand degrees!"

Strange how a mechanical thermometer could sound excited, though it possessed only an emotionless steel voice.

"What *time* is it?" asked someone.

Everyone had to smile.

For now there was only the sun and the sun and the sun. It was every horizon, it was every direction. It burned the minutes, the seconds, the hourglasses, the clocks; it burned all time and eternity away. It burned the eyelids and the serum of the dark world behind the lids, the retina, the hidden brain; and it burned sleep and the sweet memories of sleep and cool nightfall.

"Watch it!"

"Captain!"

Bretton, the first mate, fell flat to the winter deck. His protective suit whistled where, burst open, his warmness, his oxygen, and his life bloomed out in a frosted steam.

"Quick!"

Inside Bretton's plastic face-mask, milk crystals had already gathered in blind patterns. They bent to see.

"A structural defect in his suit, Captain. Dead."

"Frozen."

They stared at that other thermometer which showed how winter lived in this snowing ship. One thousand degrees below zero. The captain gazed down upon the frosted statue and the twinkling crystals that iced over it as he watched. Irony of the coolest sort, he thought; a man afraid of fire and killed by frost.

The captain turned away. "No time. No time. Let him lie." He felt his tongue move. "Temperature?"

The dials jumped four thousand degrees.

"Look. Will you look? Look."

Their icicle was melting.

The captain jerked his head to look at the ceiling.

As if a motion-picture projector had jammed a single clear memory frame in his head, he found his mind focused ridiculously on a scene whipped out of childhood.

Spring mornings as a boy he had leaned from his bedroom window into the snow-smelling air to see the sun sparkle the last icicle of winter. A dripping of white wine, the blood of cool but warming April fell from that clear crystal blade. Minute by minute, December's weapon grew less dangerous. And then at last the icicle fell with the sound of a single chime to the graveled walk below.

"Auxiliary pump's broken, sir. Refrigeration. We're losing our ice!"

A shower of warm rain shivered down upon them. The captain jerked his head right and left. "Can you see the trouble? Christ, don't stand there, we haven't time!"

The men rushed; the captain bent in the warm rain, cursing, felt his hands run over the cold machine, felt them burrow and search, and while he worked he saw a future which was removed from them by the merest breath. He saw the skin peel from the rocket beehive, men, thus revealed, running, running, mouths shrieking, soundless. Space was a black mossed well where life drowned its roars and terrors. Scream a big scream, but space snuffed it out before it was half up your throat. Men scurried, ants in a flaming matchbox; the ship was dripping lava, gushing steam, nothing!

"Captain?"

The nightmare flicked away.

"Here." He worked in the soft warm rain that fell from the upper decks. He fumbled at the auxiliary pump. "Damn it!" He jerked the feed line. When it came, it'd be the quickest death in the history of dying. One moment, yelling; a warm flash later only the billion billion tons of space-fire would whisper, unheard, in space. Popped like strawberries in a furnace, while their thoughts lingered on the scorched air a long breath after their bodies were charred roast and fluorescent gas.

"Damn!" He stabbed the auxiliary pump with a screw driver. "Jesus!" He shuddered. The complete annihilation of it. He clamped his eyes tight, teeth tight. God, he thought, we're used to more leisurely dyings, measured in minutes and hours. Even twenty seconds now would be a slow death compared to this hungry idiot thing waiting to eat us!

"Captain, do we pull out or stay?"

"Get the Cup ready. Take over, finish this. Now!"

He turned and put his hand to the working mechanism of the huge Cup; shoved his fingers into the robot Glove. A twitch of his hand here moved a gigantic hand, with gigantic metal fingers, from the bowels of the ship. Now, now, the great metal hand slid out holding the huge *Copa de Oro,* breathless, into the iron furnace, the bodiless body and the fleshless flesh of the sun.

A million years ago, thought the captain, quickly, quickly, as he moved the hand and the Cup, a million years ago a naked man on a lonely northern trail saw lightning strike a tree. And

while his clan fled, with bare hands he plucked a limb of fire, broiling the flesh of his fingers, to carry it, running in triumph, shielding it from the rain with his body, to his cave, where he shrieked out a laugh and tossed it full on a mound of leaves and gave his people summer. And the tribe crept at last, trembling, near the fire, and they put out their flinching hands and felt the new season in their cave, this small yellow spot of changing weather, and they, too, at last, nervously, smiled. And the gift of fire was theirs.

"Captain!"

It took all of four seconds for the huge hand to push the empty Cup to the fire. So here we are again, today, on another trail, he thought, reaching for a cup of precious gas and vacuum, a handful of different fire with which to run back up cold space, lighting our way, and take to Earth a gift of fire that might burn forever. Why?

He knew the answer before the question.

Because the atoms we work with our hands, on Earth, are pitiful; the atomic bomb is pitiful and small and our knowledge is pitiful and small, and only the sun really knows what we want to know, and only the sun has the secret. And besides, it's fun, it's a chance, it's a great thing coming here, playing tag, hitting and running. There is no reason, really, except the pride and vanity of little insect men hoping to sting the lion and escape the maw. My God, we'll say, we *did* it! And here is our cup of energy, fire, vibration, call it what you will, that may well power our cities and sail our ships and light our libraries and tan our children and bake our daily breads and simmer the knowledge of our universe for us for a thousand years until it is well done. Here, from this cup, all good men of science and religion: drink! Warm yourselves against the night of ignorance, the long snows of superstition, the cold winds of disbelief, and from the great fear of darkness in each man. So: we stretch out our hand with the beggar's cup . . .

"Ah."

The Cup dipped into the sun. It scooped up a bit of the flesh of God, the blood of the universe, the blazing thought, the blind-

ing philosophy that set out and mothered a galaxy, that idled and swept planets in their fields and summoned or laid to rest lives and livelihoods.

"Now, *slow,*" whispered the captain.

"What'll happen when we pull it inside? That extra heat now, at this time, Captain?"

"God knows."

"Auxiliary pump all repaired, sir."

"Start it!"

The pump leaped on.

"Close the lid of the Cup and inside now, slow, slow."

The beautiful hand outside the ship trembled, a tremendous image of his own gesture, sank with oiled silence into the ship body. The Cup, lid shut, dripped yellow flowers and white stars, slid deep. The audio-thermometer screamed. The refrigerator system kicked; ammoniated fluids banged the walls like blood in the head of a shrieking idiot.

He shut the outer air-lock door.

"Now."

They waited. The ship's pulse ran. The heart of the ship rushed, beat, rushed, the Cup of gold in it. The cold blood raced around about down through, around about down through.

The captain exhaled slowly.

The ice stopped dripping from the ceiling. It froze again.

"Let's get out of here."

The ship turned and ran.

"Listen!"

The heart of the ship was slowing, slowing. The dials spun on down through the thousands; the needles whirred, invisible. The thermometer voice chanted the change of seasons. They were all thinking now, together: Pull away and away from the fire and the flame, the heat and the melting, the yellow and the white. Go on out now to cool and dark. In twenty hours perhaps they might even dismantle some refrigerators, let winter die. Soon they would move in night so cold it might be necessary to use the ship's new furnace, draw heat from the shielded fire they carried now like an unborn child.

They were going home.

They were going home and there was some little time, even as he tended to the body of Bretton lying in a bank of white winter snow, for the captain to remember a poem he had written many years before:

> Sometimes I see the sun a burning Tree,
> Its golden fruit swung bright in airless air,
> Its apples wormed with man and gravity,
> Their worship breathing from them everywhere,
> As man sees Sun as burning Tree . . .

The captain sat for a long while by the body, feeling many separate things. I feel sad, he thought, and I feel good, and I feel like a boy coming home from school with a handful of dandelions.

"Well," said the captain, sitting, eyes shut, sighing. "Well, where do we go now, eh, where are we going?" He felt his men sitting or standing all about him, the terror dead in them, their breathing quiet. "When you've gone a long, long way down to the sun and touched it and lingered and jumped around and streaked away from it, where are you going then? When you go away from the heat and the noonday light and the laziness, where do you go?"

His men waited for him to say it out. They waited for him to gather all of the coolness and the whiteness and the welcome and refreshing climate of the word in his mind, and they saw him settle the word, like a bit of ice cream, in his mouth, rolling it gently.

"There's only one direction in space from here on out," he said at last.

They waited. They waited as the ship moved swiftly into cold darkness away from the light.

"North," murmured the captain. "North."

And they all smiled, as if a wind had come up suddenly in the middle of a hot afternoon.

A Medicine
for Melancholy

For Dad,
whose love, very late in life, surprised his son.

And for Bernard Berenson and Nicky Mariano,
who gave me a new world.

1

IN A SEASON OF CALM WEATHER

George and Alice Smith detrained at Biarritz one summer noon and in an hour had run through their hotel onto the beach into the ocean and back out to bake upon the sand.

To see George Smith sprawled burning there, you'd think him only a tourist flown fresh as iced lettuce to Europe and soon to be transshipped home. But here was a man who loved art more than life itself.

"There . . ." George Smith sighed. Another ounce of perspiration trickled down his chest. Boil out the Ohio tap water, he thought, then drink down the best Bordeaux. Silt your blood with rich French sediment so you'll see with native eyes!

Why? Why eat, breathe, drink everything French? So that, given time, he might really begin to understand the genius of one man.

His mouth moved, forming a name.

"George?" His wife loomed over him. "I know what you've been thinking. I can read your lips."

He lay perfectly still, waiting.

"And?"

Originally published in *Playboy*. Copyright © 1956 by HMH Publishing Co., Inc.

"Picasso," she said.

He winced. Someday she would learn to pronounce that name.

"Please," she said. "Relax. I know you heard the rumor this morning, but you should see your eyes—your tic is back. All right, Picasso's here, down the coast a few miles away, visiting friends in some small fishing town. But you must forget it or our vacation's ruined."

"I wish I'd never heard the rumor," he said honestly.

"If only," she said, "you liked other painters."

Others? Yes, there were others. He could breakfast most congenially on Caravaggio still lifes of autumn pears and midnight plums. For lunch: those fire-squirting, thick-wormed Van Gogh sunflowers, those blooms a blind man might read with one rush of scorched fingers down fiery canvas. But the great feast? The paintings he saved his palate for? There, filling the horizon like Neptune risen, crowned with limeweed, alabaster, coral, paintbrushes clenched like tridents in horn-nailed fists, and with fish-tail vast enough to fluke summer showers out over all Gibraltar—who else but the creator of *Girl Before a Mirror* and *Guernica?*

"Alice," he said patiently, "how can I explain? Coming down on the train, I thought, Good lord, it's *all* Picasso country!"

But was it really? he wondered. The sky, the land, the people, the flushed pink bricks here, scrolled electric-blue ironwork balconies there, a mandolin ripe as a fruit in some man's thousand fingerprinting hands, billboard tatters blowing like confetti in night winds—how much was Picasso, how much George Smith staring round the world with wild Picasso eyes? He despaired of answering. That old man had distilled turpentines and linseed oil so thoroughly through George Smith that they shaped his being, all Blue Period at twilight, all Rose Period at dawn.

"I keep thinking," he said aloud, "if we saved our money . . ."

"We'll never have five thousand dollars."

"I know," he said quietly. "But it's nice thinking we might bring it off someday. Wouldn't it be great to just step up to him,

say 'Pablo, here's five thousand! Give us the sea, the sand, that
sky, or any old thing you want, we'll be happy . . .'"

After a moment his wife touched his arm.

"I think you'd better go in the water now," she said.

"Yes," he said. "I'd better do just that."

White fire showered up when he cut the water.

During the afternoon George Smith came out and went into
the ocean with the vast spilling motions of now warm, now cool
people who at last, with the sun's decline, their bodies all lobster
colors and colors of broiled squab and guinea hen, trudged for
their wedding-cake hotels.

The beach lay deserted for endless mile on mile save for two
people. One was George Smith, towel over shoulder, out for a
last devotional.

Far along the shore another shorter, square-cut man walked
alone in the tranquil weather. He was deeper-tanned, his close-
shaven head dyed almost mahogany by the sun, and his eyes
were clear and bright as water in his face.

So the shore-line stage was set, and in a few minutes the two
men would meet. And once again Fate fixed the scales for shocks
and surprises, arrivals and departures. And all the while these
two solitary strollers did not for a moment think on coincidence,
that unswum stream which lingers at man's elbow with every
crowd in every town. Nor did they ponder the fact that if man
dares dip into that stream he grabs a wonder in each hand. Like
most, they shrugged at such folly and stayed well up the bank
lest Fate should shove them in.

The stranger stood alone. Glancing about, he saw his aloneness, saw the waters of the lovely bay, saw the sun sliding down
the late colors of the day, and then, half turning, spied a small
wooden object on the sand. It was no more than the slender stick
from a lime ice cream delicacy long since melted away. Smiling,
he picked the stick up. With another glance around to reinsure
his solitude, the man stooped again and, holding the stick gently, with light sweeps of his hand began to do the one thing in
all the world he knew best how to do.

He began to draw incredible figures along the sand.

He sketched one figure and then moved over and, still looking down, completely focused on his work now, drew a second and a third figure, and after that a fourth and a fifth and a sixth.

George Smith, printing the shore line with his feet, gazed here, gazed there, and then saw the man ahead. George Smith, drawing nearer, saw that the man, deeply tanned, was bending down. Nearer yet, and it was obvious what the man was up to. George Smith chuckled. Of course, of course . . . Alone on the beach this man—how old? Sixty-five? Seventy?—was scribbling and doodling away. How the sand flew! How the wild portraits flung themselves out there on the shore! How . . .

George Smith took one more step and stopped, very still.

The stranger was drawing and drawing and did not seem to sense that anyone stood immediately behind him and the world of his drawings in the sand. By now he was so deeply enchanted with his solitudinous creation that depth bombs set off in the bay might not have stopped his flying hand nor turned him round.

George Smith looked down at the sand. And after a long while, looking, he began to tremble.

For there on the flat shore were pictures of Grecian lions and Mediterranean goats and maidens with flesh of sand like powdered gold and satyrs piping on hand-carved horns and children dancing, strewing flowers along and along the beach with lambs gamboling after, and musicians skipping to their harps and lyres and unicorns racing youths toward distant meadows, woodlands, ruined temples, and volcanoes. Along the shore in a never-broken line, the hand, the wooden stylus of this man, bent down in fever and raining perspiration, scribbled, ribboned, looped around over and up, across, in, out, stitched, whispered, stayed, then hurried on as if this traveling bacchanal must flourish to its end before the sun was put out by the sea. Twenty, thirty yards or more the nymphs and dryads and summer founts sprang up in unraveled hieroglyphs. And the sand in the dying light was the color of molten copper on which was now slashed a message that any man in any time might read and savor down

the years. Everything whirled and poised in its own wind and gravity. Now wine was being crushed from under the grape-blooded feet of dancing vintners' daughters, now steaming seas gave birth to coin-sheathed monsters while flowered kites strewed scent on blowing clouds . . . now . . . now . . . now . . .

The artist stopped.

George Smith drew back and stood away.

The artist glanced up, surprised to find someone so near. Then he simply stood there, looking from George Smith to his own creations flung like idle footprints down the way. He smiled at last and shrugged as if to say, Look what I've done; see what a child? You will forgive me, won't you? One day or another we are all fools . . . You too, perhaps? So allow an old fool this, eh? Good! Good!

But George Smith could only look at the little man with the sun-dark skin and the clear sharp eyes and say the man's name once, in a whisper, to himself.

They stood thus for perhaps another five seconds. George Smith staring at the sand-frieze, and the artist watching George Smith with amused curiosity. George Smith opened his mouth, closed it, put out his hand, took it back. He stepped toward the pictures, stepped away. Then he moved along the line of figures, like a man viewing a precious series of marbles cast up from some ancient ruin on the shore. His eyes did not blink, his hand wanted to touch but did not dare to touch. He wanted to run but did not run.

He looked suddenly at the hotel. Run, yes! Run! What? Grab a shovel, dig, excavate, save a chunk of this all-too-crumbling sand? Find a repairman, race him back here with plaster of Paris to cast a mold of some small fragile part of these? No, no. Silly, silly. Or . . . ? His eyes flicked to his hotel window. The camera! Run, get it, get back, and hurry along the shore, clicking, changing film, clicking, until . . .

George Smith whirled to face the sun. It burned faintly on his face; his eyes were two small fires from it. The sun was half un-

derwater, and as he watched it sank the rest of the way in a matter of seconds.

The artist had drawn nearer and now was gazing into George Smith's face with great friendliness, as if he were guessing every thought. Now he was nodding his head in a little bow. Now the ice cream stick had fallen casually from his fingers. Now he was saying good night, good night. Now he was gone, walking back down the beach toward the south.

George Smith stood looking after him. After a full minute he did the only thing he could possibly do. He started at the beginning of the fantastic frieze of satyrs and fauns and wine-dipped maidens and prancing unicorns and piping youths and he walked slowly along the shore. He walked a long way, looking down at the free-running bacchanal. And when he came to the end of the animals and men he turned around and started back in the other direction, just staring down as if he had lost something and did not quite know where to find it. He kept on doing this until there was no more light in the sky or on the sand to see by.

He sat down at the supper table.

"You're late," said his wife. "I just had to come down alone. I'm ravenous."

"That's all right," he said.

"Anything interesting happen on your walk?" she asked.

"No," he said.

"You look funny; George, you didn't swim out too far, did you, and almost drown? I can tell by your face. You *did* swim out too far, didn't you?"

"Yes," he said.

"Well," she said, watching him closely. "Don't ever do that again. Now—what'll you have?"

He picked up the menu and started to read it and stopped suddenly.

"What's wrong?" asked his wife.

He turned his head and shut his eyes for a moment.

"Listen."

She listened.

"I don't hear anything," she said.

"Don't you?"

"No. What is it?"

"Just the tide," he said after a while, sitting there, his eyes still shut. "Just the tide coming in."

2
THE DRAGON

The night blew in the short grass on the moor; there was no other motion. It had been years since a single bird had flown by in the great blind shell of sky. Long ago a few small stones had simulated life when they crumbled and fell into dust. Now only the night moved in the souls of the two men bent by their lonely fire in the wilderness; darkness pumped quietly in their veins and ticked silently in their temples and their wrists.

Firelight fled up and down their wild faces and welled in their eyes in orange tatters. They listened to each other's faint, cool breathing and the lizard blink of their eyelids. At last, one man poked the fire with his sword.

"Don't, idiot; you'll give us away!"

"No matter," said the second man. "The dragon can smell us miles off anyway. God's breath, it's cold. I wish I was back at the castle."

"It's death, not sleep, we're after. . . ."

"Why? Why? The dragon never sets foot in the town!"

"Quiet, fool! He eats men traveling alone from our town to the next!"

"Let them be eaten and let us get home!"

"Wait now; listen!"

The two men froze.

They waited a long time, but there was only the shake of their horses' nervous skin like black velvet tambourines jingling the silver stirrup buckles, softly, softly.

"Ah." The second man sighed. "What a land of nightmares. Everything happens here. Someone blows out the sun; it's night. And then, and *then,* oh, God, listen! This dragon, they say his eyes are fire. His breath a white gas; you can see him burn across the dark lands. He runs with sulfur and thunder and kindles the grass. Sheep panic and die insane. Women deliver forth monsters. The dragon's fury is such that tower walls shake back to dust. His victims, at sunrise, are strewn hither thither on the hills. How many knights, I ask, have gone for this monster and failed, even as we shall fail?"

"Enough of that!"

"More than enough! Out here in this desolation I cannot tell what year this is!"

"Nine hundred years since the Nativity."

"No, no," whispered the second man, eyes shut. "On this moor is no Time, is only Forever. I feel if I ran back on the road the town would be gone, the people yet unborn, things changed, the castles unquarried from the rocks, the timbers still uncut from the forests; don't ask how I know; the moor knows and tells me. And here we sit alone in the land of the fire dragon, God save us!"

"Be you afraid, then gird on your armor!"

"What use? The dragon runs from nowhere; we cannot guess its home. It vanishes in fog; we know not where it goes. Aye, on with our armor, we'll die well dressed."

Half into his silver corselet, the second man stopped again and turned his head.

Across the dim country, full of night and nothingness from the heart of the moor itself, the wind sprang full of dust from clocks that used dust for telling time. There were black suns burning in the heart of this new wind and a million burnt leaves shaken from some autumn tree beyond the horizon. This wind

melted landscapes, lengthened bones like white wax, made the blood roil and thicken to a muddy deposit in the brain. The wind was a thousand souls dying and all time confused and in transit. It was a fog inside of a mist inside of a darkness, and this place was no man's place and there was no year or hour at all, but only these men in a faceless emptiness of sudden frost, storm and white thunder which moved behind the great falling pane of green glass that was the lightning. A squall of rain drenched the turf; all faded away until there was unbreathing hush and the two men waiting alone with their warmth in a cool season.

"There," whispered the first man. "Oh, *there* . . ."

Miles off, rushing with a great chant and a roar—the dragon.

In silence the men buckled on their armor and mounted their horses. The midnight wilderness was split by a monstrous gushing as the dragon roared nearer, nearer; its flashing yellow glare spurted above a hill and then, fold on fold of dark body, distantly seen, therefore indistinct, flowed over that hill and plunged vanishing into a valley.

"Quick!"

They spurred their horses forward to a small hollow.

"This is where it passes!"

They seized their lances with mailed fists and blinded their horses by flipping the visors down over their eyes.

"Lord!"

"Yes, let us use His name."

On the instant, the dragon rounded a hill. Its monstrous amber eye fed on them, fired their armor in red glints and glitters. With a terrible wailing cry and a grinding rush it flung itself forward.

"Mercy, God!"

The lance struck under the unlidded yellow eye, buckled, tossed the man through the air. The dragon hit, spilled him over, down, ground him under. Passing, the black brunt of its shoulder smashed the remaining horse and rider a hundred feet against the side of a boulder, wailing, wailing, the dragon

shrieking, the fire all about, around, under it, a pink, yellow, orange sun-fire with great soft plumes of blinding smoke.

"Did you *see* it?" cried a voice. "Just like I told you!"

"The same! The same! A knight in armor, by the Lord Harry! We *hit* him!"

"You goin' to stop?"

"Did once; found nothing. Don't like to stop on this moor. I get the willies. Got a *feel*, it has."

"But we hit *something!*"

"Gave him plenty of whistle; chap wouldn't budge!"

A steaming blast cut the mist aside.

"We'll make Stokely on time. More coal, eh, Fred?"

Another whistle shook dew from the empty sky. The night train, in fire and fury, shot through a gully, up a rise, and vanished away over cold earth toward the north, leaving black smoke and steam to dissolve in the numbed air minutes after it had passed and gone forever.

A MEDICINE FOR MELANCHOLY

(or: *The Sovereign Remedy Revealed!*)

"Send for some leeches; bleed her," said Doctor Gimp.

"She has no blood left!" cried Mrs. Wilkes. "Oh, Doctor, what ails our Camillia?"

"She's not right."

"Yes, yes?"

"She's poorly." The good doctor scowled.

"Go on, go on!"

"She's a fluttering candle flame, no doubt."

"Ah, Doctor Gimp," protested Mr. Wilkes. "You but tell us as you go out what we told you when you came in!"

"No, more! Give her these pills at dawn, high noon, and sunset. A sovereign remedy!"

"Damn, she's *stuffed* with sovereign remedies now!"

"Tut-tut! That's a shilling as I pass downstairs, sir."

"Go down and send the Devil up!" Mr. Wilkes shoved a coin in the good doctor's hand.

Whereupon the physician, wheezing, taking snuff, sneezing, stamped down into the swarming streets of London on a sloppy morn in the spring of 1762.

Mr. and Mrs. Wilkes turned to the bed where their sweet Camillia lay pale, thin, yes, but far from unlovely, with large wet lilac eyes, her hair a creek of gold upon her pillow.

"Oh," she almost wept. "What's to become of me? Since the start of spring, three weeks, I've been a ghost in my mirror; I frighten me. To think I'll die without seeing my twentieth birthday."

"Child," said the mother. "Where do you hurt?"

"My arms. My legs. My bosom. My head. How many doctors —six?—have turned me like a beef on a spit. No more. Please, let me pass away untouched."

"What a ghastly, what a mysterious illness," said the mother. "Oh, do something, Mr. Wilkes!"

"What?" asked Mr. Wilkes angrily. "She won't have the physician, the apothecary, or the priest!—and Amen to that!— they've wrung me dry! Shall I run in the street then and bring the Dustman up?"

"Yes," said a voice.

"What!" All three turned to stare.

They had quite forgotten her younger brother, Jamie, who stood picking his teeth at a far window, gazing serenely down into the drizzle and the loud rumbling of the town.

"Four hundred years ago," he said serenely, "it was tried, it worked. Don't bring the Dustman up, no, no. But let us hoist Camillia, cot and all, maneuver her downstairs, and set her up outside our door."

"Why? What for?"

"In a single hour"—Jamie's eyes jumped, counting—"a thousand folk rush by our gate. In one day, twenty thousand people run, hobble, or ride by. Each might eye my swooning sister, each count her teeth, pull her ear lobes, and all, all, mind you, would have a sovereign remedy to offer! One of them would just have to be right!"

"Ah," said Mr. Wilkes, stunned.

"Father!" said Jamie breathlessly. "Have you ever known one single man who didn't think he personally wrote *Materia Med-*

ica? This green ointment for sour throat, that ox-salve for miasma or bloat? Right now, ten thousand self-appointed apothecaries sneak off down there, their wisdom lost to us!"

"Jamie boy, you're incredible!"

"Cease!" said Mrs. Wilkes. "No daughter of mine will be put on display in this or any street——"

"Fie, woman!" said Mr. Wilkes. "Camillia melts like snow and you hesitate to move her from this hot room? Come, Jamie, lift the bed!"

"Camillia?" Mrs. Wilkes turned to her daughter.

"I may as well die in the open," said Camillia, "where a cool breeze might stir my locks as I . . ."

"Bosh!" said the father. "You'll not die. Jamie, heave! Ha! There! Out of the way, wife! Up, boy, *higher!*"

"Oh," cried Camillia faintly. "I fly, I *fly* . . . *!*"

Quite suddenly a blue sky opened over London. The population, surprised by the weather, hurried out into the streets, panicking for something to see, to do, to buy. Blind men sang, dogs jigged, clowns shuffled and tumbled, children chalked games and threw balls as if it were carnival time.

Down into all this, tottering, their veins bursting from their brows, Jamie and Mr. Wilkes carried Camillia like a lady Pope sailing high in her sedan-chair cot, eyes clenched shut, praying.

"Careful!" screamed Mrs. Wilkes. "Ah, she's dead! No. There. Put her down. Easy . . ."

And at last the bed was tilted against the house front so that the River of Humanity surging by could see Camillia, a large pale Bartolemy Doll put out like a prize in the sun.

"Fetch a quill, ink, paper, lad," said the father. "I'll make notes as to symptoms spoken of and remedies offered this day. Tonight we'll average them out. Now——"

But already a man in the passing crowd had fixed Camillia with a sharp eye.

"She's sick!" he said.

"Ah," said Mr. Wilkes, gleefully. "It begins. The quill, boy. There. Go on, sir!"

"She's not well." The man scowled. "She does poorly."

"Does poorly——" Mr. Wilkes wrote, then froze. "Sir?" He looked up suspiciously. "Are you a physician?"

"I am, sir."

"I *thought* I knew the words! Jamie, take my cane, drive him off! Go, sir, be gone!"

But the man hastened off, cursing, mightily exasperated.

"She's not well, she does poorly . . . pah!" mimicked Mr. Wilkes, but stopped. For now a woman, tall and gaunt as a specter fresh risen from the tomb, was pointing a finger at Camillia Wilkes.

"Vapors," she intoned.

"Vapors," wrote Mr. Wilkes, pleased.

"Lung-flux," chanted the woman.

"Lung-flux!" Mr. Wilkes wrote, beaming. "Now, that's more *like* it!"

"A medicine for melancholy is needed," said the woman palely. "Be there mummy ground to medicine in your house? The best mummies are: Egyptian, Arabian, Hirasphatos, Libyan, all of great use in magnetic disorders. Ask for me, the Gypsy, at the Flodden Road. I sell stone parsley, male frankincense——"

"Flodden Road, stone parsley—slower, woman!"

"Opobalsam, pontic valerian——"

"Wait, woman! Opobalsam, yes! Jamie, stop her!"

But the woman, naming medicines, glided on.

A girl, no more than seventeen, walked up now and stared at Camillia Wilkes.

"She——"

"One moment!" Mr. Wilkes scribbled feverishly. "—magnetic disorders—pontic valerian—drat! Well, young girl, now. What do you see in my daughter's face? You fix her with your gaze, you hardly breathe. So?"

"She——" The strange girl searched deep into Camillia's eyes, flushed, and stammered. "She suffers from . . . from . . ."

"Spit it out!"

"She . . . she . . . oh!"

And the girl, with a last look of deepest sympathy, darted off through the crowd.

"Silly girl!"

"No, Papa," murmured Camillia, eyes wide. "Not silly. She *saw*. She *knew*. Oh, Jamie, run fetch her, make her tell!"

"No, she offered nothing! Whereas, the Gypsy, see her list!"

"I know it, Papa." Camillia, paler, shut her eyes.

Someone cleared his throat.

A butcher, his apron a scarlet battleground, stood bristling his fierce mustaches there.

"I have seen cows with this look," he said. "I have saved them with brandy and three new eggs. In winter I have saved myself with the same elixir——"

"My daughter is no cow, sir!" Mr. Wilkes threw down his quill. "Nor is she a butcher, nor is it January! Step back, sir, others wait!"

And indeed, now a vast crowd clamored, drawn by the others, aching to advise their favorite swig, recommend some country site where it rained less and shone more sun than in all England or your South of France. Old men and women, especial doctors as all the aged are, clashed by each other in bristles of canes, in phalanxes of crutches and hobble sticks.

"Back!" cried Mrs. Wilkes, alarmed. "They'll crush my daughter like a spring berry!"

"Stand off!" Jamie seized canes and crutches and threw them over the mob, which turned on itself to go seek their missing members.

"Father, I fail, I fail," gasped Camillia.

"Father!" cried Jamie. "There's but one way to stop this riot! Charge them! Make them pay to give us their mind on this ailment!"

"Jamie, you are my son! Quick, boy, paint a sign! Listen, people! Tuppence! Queue up please, a line! Tuppence to speak

your piece! Get your money out, yes! That's it. You, sir. You, madame. And you, sir. Now, my quill! Begin!"

The mob boiled in like a dark sea.

Camillia opened one eye and swooned again.

Sundown, the streets almost empty, only a few strollers now. Camillia moth-fluttered her eyelids at a familiar clinking jingle.

"Three hundred and ninety-nine, four hundred pennies!" Mr. Wilkes counted the last money into a bag held by his grinning son. "There!"

"It will buy me a fine black funeral coach," said the pale girl.

"Hush! Did you imagine, family, so many people, two hundred, would pay to give us their opinion?"

"Yes," said Mrs. Wilkes. "Wives, husbands, children, are deaf to each other. So people gladly pay to have someone listen. Poor things, each today thought he and he alone knew quinsy, dropsy, glanders, could tell the slaver from the hives. So tonight we are rich and two hundred people are happy, having unloaded their full medical kit at our door."

"Gods, instead of quelling the riot, we had to drive them off snapping like pups."

"Read us the list, Father," said Jamie, "of two hundred remedies. Which one is true?"

"I care not," whispered Camillia, sighing. "It grows dark. My stomach is queasy from listening to the names! May I be taken upstairs?"

"Yes, dear. Jamie, lift!"

"Please," said a voice.

Half-bent, the men looked up.

There stood a Dustman of no particular size or shape, his face masked with soot from which shone water-blue eyes and a white slot of an ivory smile. Dust sifted from his sleeves and his pants as he moved, as he talked quietly, nodding.

"I couldn't get through the mob earlier," he said, holding his dirty cap in his hands. "Now, going home, here I am. Must I pay?"

"No, Dustman, you need not," said Camillia gently.

"Hold on——" protested Mr. Wilkes.

But Camillia gave him a soft look and he grew silent.

"Thank you, ma'am." The Dustman's smile flashed like warm sunlight in the growing dusk. "I have but one advice."

He gazed at Camillia. She gazed at him.

"Be this Saint Bosco's Eve, sir, ma'am?"

"Who knows? Not *me*, sir!" said Mr. Wilkes.

"I think it *is* Saint Bosco's Eve, sir. Also, it is the night of the Full Moon. So," said the Dustman humbly, unable to take his eyes from the lovely haunted girl, "you must leave your daughter out in the light of that rising moon."

"Out under the moon!" said Mrs. Wilkes.

"Doesn't that make the lunatic?" asked Jamie.

"Beg pardon, sir." The Dustman bowed. "But the full moon soothes all sick animal, be they human or plain field beast. There is a serenity of color, a quietude of touch, a sweet sculpturing of mind and body in full moonlight."

"It may rain——" said the mother uneasily.

"I swear," said the Dustman quickly. "My sister suffered this same swooning paleness. We set her like a potted lily out one spring night with the moon. She lives today in Sussex, the soul of reconstituted health!"

"Reconstituted! Moonlight! And will cost us not one penny of the four hundred we collected this day, Mother, Jamie, Camillia."

"No!" said Mrs. Wilkes. "I won't have it!"

"Mother," said Camillia.

She looked earnestly at the Dustman.

From his grimed face the Dustman gazed back, his smile like a little scimitar in the dark.

"Mother," said Camillia. "I feel it. The moon will cure me, it will, it will. . . ."

The mother sighed. "This is not my day, nor night. Let me kiss you for the last time, then. There."

And the mother went upstairs.

Now the Dustman backed off, bowing courteously to all.

"All night, now, remember, beneath the moon, not the slightest disturbance until dawn. Sleep well, young lady. Dream, and dream the best. Good night."

Soot was lost in soot; the man was gone.

Mr. Wilkes and Jamie kissed Camillia's brow.

"Father, Jamie," she said. "Don't worry."

And she was left alone to stare off where at a great distance she thought she saw a smile hung by itself in the dark blink off and on, then go round a corner, vanishing.

She waited for the rising of the moon.

Night in London, the voices growing drowsier in the inns, the slamming of doors, drunken farewells, clocks chiming. Camillia saw a cat like a woman stroll by in her furs, saw a woman like a cat stroll by, both wise, both Egyptian, both smelling of spice. Every quarter hour or so a voice drifted down from above:

"You all right, child?"

"Yes, Father."

"Camillia?"

"Mother, Jamie, I'm fine."

And at last. "Good night."

"Good night."

The last lights out. London asleep.

The moon rose.

And the higher the moon, the larger grew Camillia's eyes as she watched the alleys, the courts, the streets, until at last, at midnight, the moon moved over her to show her like a marble figure atop an ancient tomb.

A motion in darkness.

Camillia pricked her ears.

A faint melody sprang out on the air.

A man stood in the shadows of the court.

Camillia gasped.

The man stepped forth into moonlight, carrying a lute which

he strummed softly. He was a man well-dressed, whose face was handsome and, now anyway, solemn.

"A troubadour," said Camillia aloud.

The man, his finger on his lips, moved slowly forward and soon stood by her cot.

"What are you doing out so late?" asked the girl, unafraid but not knowing why.

"A friend sent me to make you well." He touched the lute strings. They hummed sweetly. He was indeed handsome there in the silver light.

"That cannot be," she said, "for it was told me, the *moon* is my cure."

"And so it will be, maiden."

"What songs do you sing?"

"Songs of spring nights, aches and ailments without name. Shall I name your fever, maiden?"

"If you know it, yes."

"First, the symptoms: raging temperatures, sudden cold, heart fast then slow, storms of temper, then sweet calms, drunkenness from having sipped only well water, dizziness from being touched only *thus——*"

He touched her wrist, saw her melt toward delicious oblivion, drew back.

"Depressions, elations," he went on. "Dreams——"

"Stop!" she cried, enthralled. "You know me to the letter. Now, name my ailment!"

"I will." He pressed his lips to the palm of her hand so she quaked suddenly. "The name of the ailment is Camillia Wilkes."

"How strange." She shivered, her eyes glinting lilac fires. "Am I then my own affliction? How sick I make myself! Even now, feel my heart!"

"I feel it, so."

"My limbs, they burn with summer heat!"

"Yes. They scorch my fingers."

"But now, the night wind, see how I shudder, cold! I die, I swear it, I die!"

"I will not let you," he said quietly.

"Are you a doctor, then?"

"No, just your plain, your ordinary physician, like another who guessed your trouble this day. The girl who would have named it but ran off in the crowd."

"Yes, I saw in her eyes she knew what had seized me. But, now, my teeth chatter. And no extra blanket!"

"Give room, please. There. Let me see: two arms, two legs, head and body. I'm all here!"

"What, sir!"

"To warm you from the night, of course."

"How like a hearth! Oh, sir, sir, do I *know* you? Your name?"

Swiftly above her, his head shadowed hers. From it his merry clear-water eyes glowed as did his white ivory slot of a smile.

"Why, Bosco, of course," he said.

"Is there not a saint by that name?"

"Given an hour, you will call me so, yes."

His head bent closer. Thus sooted in shadow, she cried with joyous recognition to welcome her Dustman back.

"The world spins! I pass away! The cure, sweet Doctor, or all is lost!"

"The cure," he said. "And the cure is *this* . . ."

Somewhere, cats sang. A shoe, shot from a window, tipped them off a fence. Then all was silence and the moon . . .

"Shh . . ."

Dawn. Tiptoeing downstairs, Mr. and Mrs. Wilkes peered into their courtyard.

"Frozen stone dead from the terrible night, I *know* it!"

"No, wife, look! Alive! Roses in her cheeks! No, more! Peaches, persimmons! She glows all rosy-milky! Sweet Camillia, alive and well, made whole again!"

They bent by the slumbering girl.

"She smiles, she dreams; what's that she says?"

"The sovereign," sighed the girl, "remedy."

"What, what?"

The girl smiled again, a white smile, in her sleep.

"A medicine," she murmured, "for melancholy."

She opened her eyes.

"Oh, Mother, Father!"

"Daughter! Child! Come upstairs!"

"No." She took their hands, tenderly. "Mother? Father?"

"Yes?"

"No one will see. The sun but rises. Please. Dance with me."

They did not want to dance.

But, celebrating they knew not what, they did.

4

THE END OF THE BEGINNING

He stopped the lawn mower in the middle of the yard, because he felt that the sun at just that moment had gone down and the stars come out. The fresh-cut grass that had showered his face and body died softly away. Yes, the stars were there, faint at first, but brightening in the clear desert sky. He heard the porch screen door tap shut and felt his wife watching him as he watched the night.

"Almost time," she said.

He nodded; he did not have to check his watch. In the passing moments he felt very old, then very young, very cold, then very warm, now this, now that. Suddenly he was miles away. He was his own son talking steadily, moving briskly to cover his pounding heart and the resurgent panics as he felt himself slip into fresh uniform, check food supplies, oxygen flasks, pressure helmet, space-suiting, and turn as every man on earth tonight turned, to gaze at the swiftly filling sky.

Then, quickly, he was back, once more the father of the son, hands gripped to the lawn-mower handle. His wife called, "Come sit on the porch."

"I've got to keep busy!"

Originally published in *Maclean's Magazine* as "Next Stop: The Stars."

She came down the steps and across the lawn. "Don't worry about Robert; he'll be all right."

"But it's all so new," he heard himself say. "It's never been done before. Think of it—a manned rocket going up tonight to build the first space station. Good lord, it can't be done, it doesn't exist, there's no rocket, no proving ground, no take-off time, no technicians. For that matter, I don't even have a son named Bob. The whole thing's too much for me!"

"Then what are you doing out here, staring?"

He shook his head. "Well, late this morning, walking to the office, I heard someone laugh out loud. It shocked me, so I froze in the middle of the street. It was *me,* laughing! Why? Because finally I really *knew* what Bob was going to do tonight; at last I *believed* it. Holy is a word I never use, but that's how I felt stranded in all that traffic. Then, middle of the afternoon I caught myself humming. You know the song. 'A wheel in a wheel. Way in the middle of the air.' I laughed again. The space station, of course, I thought. The big wheel with hollow spokes where Bob'll live six or eight months, then get along to the moon. Walking home, I remembered more of the song. 'Little wheel run by faith, Big wheel run by the grace of God.' I wanted to jump, yell, and flame-out myself!"

His wife touched his arm. "If we stay out here, let's at least be comfortable."

They placed two wicker rockers in the center of the lawn and sat quietly as the stars dissolved out of darkness in pale crushings of rock salt strewn from horizon to horizon.

"Why," said his wife, at last, "it's like waiting for the fireworks at Sisley Field every year."

"Bigger crowd tonight . . ."

"I keep thinking—a billion people watching the sky right now, their mouths all open at the same time."

They waited, feeling the earth move under their chairs.

"What time is it now?"

"Eleven minutes to eight."

"You're always right; there must be a clock in your head."

"I can't be wrong, tonight. I'll be able to tell you one second before they blast off. Look! The ten-minute warning!"

On the western sky they saw four crimson flares open out, float shimmering down the wind above the desert, then sink silently to the extinguishing earth.

In the new darkness the husband and wife did not rock in their chairs.

After a while he said, "Eight minutes." A pause. "Seven minutes." What seemed a much longer pause. "Six . . ."

His wife, her head back, studied the stars immediately above her and murmured, "Why?" She closed her eyes. "Why the rockets, why tonight? Why all this? I'd like to know."

He examined her face, pale in the vast powdering light of the Milky Way. He felt the stirring of an answer, but let his wife continue.

"I mean it's not that old thing again, is it, when people asked why men climbed Mt. Everest and they said, 'Because it's there'? I never understood. That was no answer to me."

Five minutes, he thought. Time ticking . . . his wrist watch . . . a wheel in a wheel . . . little wheel run by . . . big wheel run by . . . way in the middle of . . . four minutes! . . . The men snug in the rocket by now, the hive, the control board flickering with light. . . .

His lips moved.

"All I know is it's really the end of the beginning. The Stone Age, Bronze Age, Iron Age; from now on we'll lump all those together under one big name for when we walked on Earth and heard the birds at morning and cried with envy. Maybe we'll call it the Earth Age, or maybe the Age of Gravity. Millions of years we fought gravity. When we were amoebas and fish we struggled to get out of the sea without gravity crushing us. Once safe on the shore we fought to stand upright without gravity breaking our new invention, the spine, tried to walk without stumbling, run without falling. A billion years Gravity kept us home, mocked us with wind and clouds, cabbage moths and locusts. That's what's so god-awful big about tonight . . . it's the end of

old man Gravity and the age we'll remember him by, for once and all. I don't know where they'll divide the ages, at the Persians, who dreamt of flying carpets, or the Chinese, who all unknowing celebrated birthdays and New Years with strung ladyfingers and high skyrockets, or some minute, some incredible second in the next hour. But we're in at the end of a billion years trying, the end of something long and to us humans, anyway, honorable."

Three minutes . . . two minutes fifty-nine seconds . . . two minutes fifty-eight seconds . . .

"But," said his wife, "I still don't know why."

Two minutes, he thought. *Ready? Ready? Ready?* The far radio voice calling. *Ready! Ready! Ready!* The quick, faint replies from the humming rocket. *Check! Check! Check!*

Tonight, he thought, even if we fail with this first, we'll send a second and a third ship and move on out to all the planets and later, all the stars. We'll just keep going until the big words like immortal and forever take on meaning. Big words, yes, that's what we want. Continuity. Since our tongues first moved in our mouths we've asked, What does it all mean? No other question made sense, with death breathing down our necks. But just let us settle in on ten thousand worlds spinning around ten thousand alien suns and the question will fade away. Man will be endless and infinite, even as space is endless and infinite. Man will go on, as space goes on, forever. Individuals will die as always, but our history will reach as far as we'll ever need to see into the future, and with the knowledge of our survival for all time to come, we'll know security and thus the answer we've always searched for. Gifted with life, the least we can do is preserve and pass on the gift to infinity. That's a goal worth shooting for.

The wicker chairs whispered ever so softly on the grass.

One minute.

"One minute," he said aloud.

"Oh!" His wife moved suddenly to seize his hands. "I hope that Bob . . ."

"He'll be all right!"

"Oh, God, take care . . ."

Thirty seconds.

"Watch now."

Fifteen, ten, five . . .

"Watch!"

Four, three, two, one.

"There! There! Oh, there, there!"

They both cried out. They both stood. The chairs toppled back, fell flat on the lawn. The man and his wife swayed, their hands struggled to find each other, grip, hold. They saw the brightening color in the sky and, ten seconds later, the great uprising comet burn the air, put out the stars, and rush away in fire flight to become another star in the returning profusion of the Milky Way. The man and wife held each other as if they had stumbled on the rim of an incredible cliff that faced an abyss so deep and dark there seemed no end to it. Staring up, they heard themselves sobbing and crying. Only after a long time were they able to speak.

"It got away, it did, *didn't* it?"

"Yes . . ."

"It's all right, isn't it?"

"Yes . . . yes . . ."

"It didn't fall back . . . ?"

"No, no, it's all right, Bob's all right, it's all right."

They stood away from each other at last.

He touched his face with his hand and looked at his wet fingers. "I'll be damned," he said, "I'll be damned."

They waited another five and then ten minutes until the darkness in their heads, the retina, ached with a million specks of fiery salt. Then they had to close their eyes.

"Well," she said, "now let's go in."

He could not move. Only his hand reached a long way out by itself to find the lawn-mower handle. He saw what his hand had done and said, "There's just a little more to do. . . ."

"But you can't see."

"Well enough," he said. "I must finish this. Then we'll sit on the porch awhile before we turn in."

He helped her put the chairs on the porch and sat her down and then walked back out to put his hands on the guide bar of the lawn mower. The lawn mower. A wheel in a wheel. A simple machine which you held in your hands, which you sent on ahead with a rush and a clatter while you walked behind with your quiet philosophy. Racket, followed by warm silence. Whirling wheel, then soft footfall of thought.

I'm a billion years old, he told himself; I'm one minute old. I'm one inch, no, ten thousand *miles,* tall. I look down and can't see my feet they're so far off and gone away below.

He moved the lawn mower. The grass showering up fell softly around him; he relished and savored it and felt that he was all mankind bathing at last in the fresh waters of the fountain of youth.

Thus bathed, he remembered the song again about the wheels and the faith and the grace of God being way up there in the middle of the sky where that single star, among a million motionless stars, dared to move and keep on moving.

Then he finished cutting the grass.

5

THE WONDERFUL ICE CREAM SUIT

It was summer twilight in the city, and out front of the quiet-clicking pool hall three young Mexican-American men breathed the warm air and looked around at the world. Sometimes they talked and sometimes they said nothing at all but watched the cars glide by like black panthers on the hot asphalt or saw trolleys loom up like thunderstorms, scatter lightning, and rumble away into silence.

"Hey," sighed Martínez at last. He was the youngest, the most sweetly sad of the three. "It's a swell night, huh? Swell."

As he observed the world it moved very close and then drifted away and then came close again. People, brushing by, were suddenly across the street. Buildings five miles away suddenly leaned over him. But most of the time everything—people, cars, and buildings—stayed way out on the edge of the world and could not be touched. On this quiet warm summer evening Martínez's face was cold.

"Nights like this you wish . . . lots of things."

"Wishing," said the second man, Villanazul, a man who shouted books out loud in his room but spoke only in whispers

Originally published in *The Saturday Evening Post* as "The Magic White Suit."
Copyright © 1958 by The Curtis Publishing Company.

on the street. "Wishing is the useless pastime of the unemployed."

"Unemployed?" cried Vamenos, the unshaven. "Listen to him! We got no jobs, no money!"

"So," said Martínez, "we got no friends."

"True." Villanazul gazed off toward the green plaza where the palm trees swayed in the soft night wind. "Do you know what I wish? I wish to go into that plaza and speak among the businessmen who gather there nights to talk big talk. But dressed as I am, poor as I am, who would listen? So, Martínez, we have each other. The friendship of the poor is real friendship. We——"

But now a handsome young Mexican with a fine thin mustache strolled by. And on each of his careless arms hung a laughing woman.

"*Madre mía!*" Martínez slapped his own brow. "How does that one rate *two* friends?"

"It's his nice new white summer suit." Vamenos chewed a black thumbnail. "He looks sharp."

Martínez leaned out to watch the three people moving away, and then at the tenement across the street, in one fourth-floor window of which, far above, a beautiful girl leaned out, her dark hair faintly stirred by the wind. She had been there forever, which was to say for six weeks. He had nodded, he had raised a hand, he had smiled, he had blinked rapidly, he had even bowed to her, on the street, in the hall when visiting friends, in the park, downtown. Even now, he put his hand up from his waist and moved his fingers. But all the lovely girl did was let the summer wind stir her dark hair. He did not exist. He was nothing.

"*Madre mía!*" He looked away and down the street where the man walked his two friends around a corner. "Oh, if just I had one suit, one! I wouldn't need money if I *looked* okay."

"I hesitate to suggest," said Villanazul, "that you see Gómez. But he's been talking some crazy talk for a month now about clothes. I keep on saying I'll be in on it to make him go away. That Gómez."

"Friend," said a quiet voice.

"Gómez!" Everyone turned to stare.

Smiling strangely, Gómez pulled forth an endless thin yellow ribbon which fluttered and swirled on the summer air.

"Gómez," said Martínez, "what you doing with that tape measure?"

Gómez beamed. "Measuring people's skeletons."

"Skeletons!"

"Hold on." Gómez squinted at Martínez. "*Caramba!* Where you *been* all my life! Let's try *you!*"

Martínez saw his arm seized and taped, his leg measured, his chest encircled.

"Hold still!" cried Gómez. "Arm—perfect. Leg—chest—*perfecto!* Now quick, the height! There! Yes! Five foot five! You're in! Shake!" Pumping Martínez's hand, he stopped suddenly. "Wait. You got . . . ten bucks?"

"I have!" Vamenos waved some grimy bills. "Gómez, measure me!"

"All I got left in the world is nine dollars and ninety-two cents." Martínez searched his pockets. "That's enough for a new suit? Why?"

"Why? Because you got the right skeleton, that's why!"

"Señor Gómez, I don't hardly know you——"

"Know me? You're going to live with me! Come on!"

Gómez vanished into the poolroom. Martínez, escorted by the polite Villanazul, pushed by an eager Vamenos, found himself inside.

"Domínguez!" said Gómez.

Domínguez, at a wall telephone, winked at them. A woman's voice squeaked on the receiver.

"Manulo!" said Gómez.

Manulo, a wine bottle tilted bubbling to his mouth, turned.

Gómez pointed at Martínez.

"At last we found our fifth volunteer!"

Domínguez said, "I got a date, don't bother me——" and stopped. The receiver slipped from his fingers. His little black telephone book full of fine names and numbers went quickly back into his pocket. "Gómez, you——?"

"Yes, yes! Your money, now! *Ándale!*"

The woman's voice sizzled on the dangling phone.

Domínguez glanced at it uneasily.

Manulo considered the empty wine bottle in his hand and the liquor-store sign across the street.

Then very reluctantly both men laid ten dollars each on the green velvet pool table.

Villanazul, amazed, did likewise, as did Gómez, nudging Martínez. Martínez counted out his wrinkled bills and change. Gómez flourished the money like a royal flush.

"Fifty bucks! The suit costs sixty! All we need is ten bucks!"

"Wait," said Martínez. "Gómez, are we talking about *one* suit? *Uno?*"

"*Uno!*" Gómez raised a finger. "One wonderful white ice cream summer suit! White, white as the August moon!"

"But who will own this one suit?"

"Me!" said Manulo.

"Me!" said Domínguez.

"Me!" said Villanazul.

"Me!" cried Gómez. "*And* you, Martínez. Men, let's show him. Line up!"

Villanazul, Manulo, Domínguez, and Gómez rushed to plant their backs against the poolroom wall.

"Martínez, you too, the other end, line up! Now, Vamenos, lay that billiard cue across our heads!"

"Sure, Gómez, sure!"

Martínez, in line, felt the cue tap his head and leaned out to see what was happening. "Ah!" he gasped.

The cue lay flat on all their heads, with no rise or fall, as Vamenos slid it along, grinning.

"We're all the same height!" said Martínez.

"The same!" Everyone laughed.

Gómez ran down the line, rustling the yellow tape measure here and there on the men so they laughed even more wildly.

"Sure!" he said. "It took a month, four weeks, mind you, to find four guys the same size and shape as me, a month of running

around measuring. Sometimes I found guys with five-foot-five skeletons, sure, but all the meat on their bones was too much or not enough. Sometimes their bones were too long in the legs or too short in the arms. Boy, all the bones! I tell you! But now, five of us, same shoulders, chests, waists, arms, and as for weight? Men!"

Manulo, Domínguez, Villanazul, Gómez, and at last Martínez stepped onto the scales which flipped ink-stamped cards at them as Vamenos, still smiling wildly, fed pennies. Heart pounding, Martínez read the cards.

"One hundred thirty-five pounds . . . one thirty-six . . . one thirty-three . . . one thirty-four . . . one thirty-seven . . . a miracle!"

"No," said Villanazul simply, "Gómez."

They all smiled upon that genius who now circled them with his arms.

"Are we not fine?" he wondered. "All the same size, all the same dream—the suit. So each of us will look beautiful at least one night each week, eh?"

"I haven't looked beautiful in years," said Martínez. "The girls run away."

"They will run no more, they will freeze," said Gómez, "when they see you in the cool white summer ice cream suit."

"Gómez," said Villanazul, "just let me ask one thing."

"Of course, *compadre*."

"When we get this nice new white ice cream summer suit, some night you're not going to put it on and walk down to the Greyhound bus in it and go live in El Paso for a year in it, are you?"

"Villanazul, Villanazul, how can you say that?"

"My eye sees and my tongue moves," said Villanazul. "How about the *Everybody Wins!* Punchboard Lotteries you ran and you kept running when nobody won? How about the United Chili Con Carne and Frijole Company you were going to organize and all that ever happened was the rent ran out on a two-by-four office?"

"The errors of a child now grown," said Gómez. "Enough! In

this hot weather someone may buy the special suit that is made just for us that stands waiting in the window of SHUMWAY'S SUNSHINE SUITS! We have fifty dollars. Now we need just one more skeleton!"

Martínez saw the men peer around the pool hall. He looked where they looked. He felt his eyes hurry past Vamenos, then come reluctantly back to examine his dirty shirt, his huge nicotined fingers.

"Me!" Vamenos burst out at last. "My skeleton, measure it, it's great! Sure, my hands are big, and my arms, from digging ditches! But——"

Just then Martínez heard passing on the sidewalk outside that same terrible man with his two girls, all laughing together.

He saw anguish move like the shadow of a summer cloud on the faces of the other men in this poolroom.

Slowly Vamenos stepped onto the scales and dropped his penny. Eyes closed, he breathed a prayer.

"*Madre mía,* please . . ."

The machinery whirred; the card fell out. Vamenos opened his eyes.

"Look! One thirty-five pounds! Another miracle!"

The men stared at his right hand and the card, at his left hand and a soiled ten-dollar bill.

Gómez swayed. Sweating, he licked his lips. Then his hand shot out, seized the money.

"The clothing store! The suit! *Vamos!*"

Yelling, everyone ran from the poolroom.

The woman's voice was still squeaking on the abandoned telephone. Martínez, left behind, reached out and hung the voice up. In the silence he shook his head. "*Santos,* what a dream! Six men," he said, "one suit. What will come of this? Madness? Debauchery? Murder? But I go with God. Gómez, wait for me!"

Martínez was young. He ran fast.

Mr. Shumway, of SHUMWAY'S SUNSHINE SUITS, paused while adjusting a tie rack, aware of some subtle atmospheric change outside his establishment.

"Leo," he whispered to his assistant. "Look . . ."

Outside, one man, Gómez, strolled by, looking in. Two men, Manulo and Domínguez, hurried by, staring in. Three men, Villanazul, Martínez, and Vamenos, jostling shoulders, did the same.

"Leo." Mr. Shumway swallowed. "Call the police!"

Suddenly six men filled the doorway.

Martínez, crushed among them, his stomach slightly upset, his face feeling feverish, smiled so wildly at Leo that Leo let go the telephone.

"Hey," breathed Martínez, eyes wide. "There's a great suit over there!"

"No." Manulo touched a lapel. *"This* one!"

"There is only one suit in all the world!" said Gómez coldly. "Mr. Shumway, the ice cream white, size thirty-four, was in your window just an hour ago! It's gone! You didn't——"

"Sell it?" Mr. Shumway exhaled. "No, no. In the dressing room. It's still on the dummy."

Martínez did not know if he moved and moved the crowd or if the crowd moved and moved him. Suddenly they were all in motion. Mr. Shumway, running, tried to keep ahead of them.

"This way, gents. Now which of you . . . ?"

"All for one, one for all!" Martínez heard himself say, and laughed. "We'll all try it on!"

"All?" Mr. Shumway clutched at the booth curtain as if his shop were a steamship that had suddenly tilted in a great swell. He stared.

That's it, thought Martínez, look at our smiles. Now, look at the skeletons behind our smiles! Measure here, there, up, down, yes, do you *see?*

Mr. Shumway saw. He nodded. He shrugged.

"All!" He jerked the curtain. "There! Buy it, and I'll throw in the dummy free!"

Martínez peered quietly into the booth, his motion drawing the others to peer too.

The suit was there.

And it was white.

Martínez could not breathe. He did not want to. He did not need to. He was afraid his breath would melt the suit. It was enough, just looking.

But at last he took a great trembling breath and exhaled, whispering, *"Ay. Ay, caramba!"*

"It puts out my eyes," murmured Gómez.

"Mr. Shumway," Martínez heard Leo hissing. "Ain't it dangerous precedent, to sell it? I mean, what if everybody bought *one* suit for *six* people?"

"Leo," said Mr. Shumway, "you ever hear one single fifty-nine-dollar suit make so many people happy at the same time before?"

"Angels' wings," murmured Martínez. "The wings of white angels."

Martínez felt Mr. Shumway peering over his shoulder into the booth. The pale glow filled his eyes.

"You know something, Leo?" he said in awe. "That's a *suit!*"

Gómez, shouting, whistling, ran up to the third-floor landing and turned to wave to the others, who staggered, laughed, stopped, and had to sit down on the steps below.

"Tonight!" cried Gómez. "Tonight you move in with me, eh? Save rent as well as clothes, eh? Sure! Martínez, you got the suit?"

"Have I?" Martínez lifted the white gift-wrapped box high. "From us to us! *Ay-hah!*"

"Vamenos, you got the dummy?"

"Here!"

Vamenos, chewing an old cigar, scattering sparks, slipped. The dummy, falling, toppled, turned over twice, and banged down the stairs.

"Vamenos! Dumb! Clumsy!"

They seized the dummy from him. Stricken, Vamenos looked about as if he'd lost something.

Manulo snapped his fingers. "Hey, Vamenos, we got to celebrate! Go borrow some wine!"

Vamenos plunged downstairs in a whirl of sparks.

The others moved into the room with the suit, leaving Martínez in the hall to study Gómez's face.

"Gómez, you look sick."

"I am," said Gómez. "For what have I done?" He nodded to the shadows in the room working about the dummy. "I pick Domínguez, a devil with the women. All right. I pick Manulo, who drinks, yes, but who sings as sweet as a girl, eh? Okay. Villanazul reads books. You, you wash behind your ears. But then what do I do? Can I wait? No! I got to buy that suit! So the last guy I pick is a clumsy slob who has the right to wear *my* suit——" He stopped, confused. "Who gets to wear *our* suit one night a week, fall down in it, or not come in out of the rain in it! Why, why, why did I *do* it!"

"Gómez," whispered Villanazul from the room. "The suit is ready. Come see if it looks as good using *your* light bulb."

Gómez and Martínez entered.

And there on the dummy in the center of the room was the phosphorescent, the miraculously white-fired ghost with the incredible lapels, the precise stitching, the neat buttonholes. Standing with the white illumination of the suit upon his cheeks, Martínez suddenly felt he was in church. White! White! It was white as the whitest vanilla ice cream, as the bottled milk in tenement halls at dawn. White as a winter cloud all alone in the moonlit sky late at night. Seeing it here in the warm summer-night room made their breath almost show on the air. Shutting his eyes, he could see it printed on his lids. He knew what color his dreams would be this night.

"White . . ." murmured Villanazul. "White as the snow on that mountain near our town in Mexico, which is called the Sleeping Woman."

"Say that again," said Gómez.

Villanazul, proud yet humble, was glad to repeat his tribute. ". . . white as the snow on the mountain called——"

"I'm back!"

Shocked, the men whirled to see Vamenos in the door, wine bottles in each hand.

"A party! Here! Now tell us, who wears the suit first tonight? Me?"

"It's too late!" said Gómez.

"Late! It's only nine-fifteen!"

"Late?" said everyone, bristling. "Late?"

Gómez edged away from these men who glared from him to the suit to the open window.

Outside and below it was, after all, thought Martínez, a fine Saturday night in a summer month and through the calm warm darkness the women drifted like flowers on a quiet stream. The men made a mournful sound.

"Gómez, a suggestion." Villanazul licked his pencil and drew a chart on a pad. "You wear the suit from nine-thirty to ten, Manulo till ten-thirty, Domínguez till eleven, myself till eleven-thirty, Martínez till midnight, and——"

"Why me *last?*" demanded Vamenos, scowling.

Martínez thought quickly and smiled. "After midnight is the *best* time, friend."

"Hey," said Vamenos, "that's right. I never thought of that. Okay."

Gómez sighed. "All right. A half hour each. But from now on, remember, we each wear the suit just one night a week. Sundays we draw straws for who wears the suit the extra night."

"Me!" laughed Vamenos. "I'm lucky!"

Gómez held onto Martínez, tight.

"Gómez," urged Martínez, "you first. Dress."

Gómez could not tear his eyes from that disreputable Vamenos. At last, impulsively, he yanked his shirt off over his head. "Ay-yeah!" he howled. "Ay-*yeee!*"

Whisper rustle . . . the clean shirt.

"Ah . . . !"

How clean the new clothes feel, thought Martínez, holding the coat ready. How clean they sound, how clean they smell!

Whisper . . . the pants . . . the tie, rustle . . . the suspend-

ers. Whisper . . . now Martínez let loose the coat, which fell in place on flexing shoulders.

"*Ole!*"

Gómez turned like a matador in his wondrous suit-of-lights.

"*Ole,* Gómez, *ole!*"

Gómez bowed and went out the door.

Martínez fixed his eyes to his watch. At ten sharp he heard someone wandering about in the hall as if they had forgotten where to go. Martínez pulled the door open and looked out.

Gómez was there, heading for nowhere.

He looks sick, thought Martínez. No, stunned, shook up, surprised, many things.

"Gómez! This is the place!"

Gómez turned around and found his way through the door.

"Oh, friends, friends," he said. "Friends, what an experience! This suit! This suit!"

"Tell us, Gómez!" said Martínez.

"I can't, how can I say it!" He gazed at the heavens, arms spread, palms up.

"*Tell* us, Gómez!"

"I have no words, no words. You must see, yourself! Yes, you must see——" And here he lapsed into silence, shaking his head until at last he remembered they all stood watching him. "Who's next? Manulo?"

Manulo, stripped to his shorts, leapt forward.

"Ready!"

All laughed, shouted, whistled.

Manulo, ready, went out the door. He was gone twenty-nine minutes and thirty seconds. He came back holding to doorknobs, touching the wall, feeling his own elbows, putting the flat of his hand to his face.

"Oh, let me tell you," he said. "*Compadres,* I went to the bar, eh, to have a drink? But no, I did not go in the bar, do you hear? I did not drink. For as I walked I began to laugh and sing. Why, why? I listened to myself and asked this. Because. The suit made me feel better than wine ever did. The suit made me drunk,

drunk! So I went to the *Guadalajara Refritería* instead and played the guitar and sang four songs, very high! The suit, ah, the suit!"

Domínguez, next to be dressed, moved out through the world, came back from the world.

The black telephone book! thought Martínez. He had it in his hands when he left! Now, he returns, hands empty! What? What?

"On the street," said Domínguez, seeing it all again, eyes wide, "on the street I walked, a woman cried, 'Domínguez, is that *you?*' Another said, 'Domínguez? No, Quetzalcoatl, the Great White God come from the East,' do you hear? And suddenly I didn't want to go with six women or eight, no. One, I thought. One! And to this one, who knows *what* I would say? 'Be mine!' Or 'Marry me!' *Caramba!* This suit is dangerous! But I did not care! I live, I live! Gómez, did it happen this way with you?"

Gómez, still dazed by the events of the evening, shook his head. "No, no talk. It's too much. Later. Villanazul . . . ?"

Villanazul moved shyly forward.

Villanazul went shyly out.

Villanazul came shyly home.

"Picture it," he said, not looking at them, looking at the floor, talking to the floor. "The Green Plaza, a group of elderly businessmen gathered under the stars and they are talking, nodding, talking. Now one of them whispers. All turn to stare. They move aside, they make a channel through which a white-hot light burns its way as through ice. At the center of the great light is this person. I take a deep breath. My stomach is jelly. My voice is very small, but it grows louder. And what do I say? I say, 'Friends. Do you know Carlyle's *Sartor Resartus?* In that book we find *his* Philosophy of Suits. . . .'"

And at last it was time for Martínez to let the suit float him out to haunt the darkness.

Four times he walked around the block. Four times he paused beneath the tenement porches, looking up at the window where the light was lit; a shadow moved, the beautiful girl was there, not there, away and gone, and on the fifth time there she was on

the porch above, driven out by the summer heat, taking the cooler air. She glanced down. She made a gesture.

At first he thought she was waving to him. He felt like a white explosion that had riveted her attention. But she was not waving. Her hand gestured and the next moment a pair of dark-framed glasses sat upon her nose. She gazed at him.

Ah, ah, he thought, so that's it. So! Even the blind may see this suit! He smiled up at her. He did not have to wave. And at last she smiled back. She did not have to wave either. Then, because he did not know what else to do and he could not get rid of this smile that had fastened itself to his cheeks, he hurried, almost ran, around the corner, feeling her stare after him. When he looked back she had taken off her glasses and gazed now with the look of the nearsighted at what, at most, must be a moving blob of light in the great darkness here. Then for good measure he went around the block again, through a city so suddenly beautiful he wanted to yell, then laugh, then yell again.

Returning, he drifted, oblivious, eyes half closed, and seeing him in the door, the others saw not Martínez but themselves come home. In that moment, they sensed that something had happened to them all.

"You're late!" cried Vamenos, but stopped. The spell could not be broken.

"Somebody tell me," said Martínez. "Who am I?"

He moved in a slow circle through the room.

Yes, he thought, yes, it's the suit, yes, it had to do with the suit and them all together in that store on this fine Saturday night and then here, laughing and feeling more drunk without drinking as Manulo said himself, as the night ran and each slipped on the pants and held, toppling, to the others and, balanced, let the feeling get bigger and warmer and finer as each man departed and the next took his place in the suit until now here stood Martínez all splendid and white as one who gives orders and the world grows quiet and moves aside.

"Martínez, we borrowed three mirrors while you were gone. Look!"

The mirrors, set up as in the store, angled to reflect three Martínezes and the echoes and memories of those who had occupied this suit with him and known the bright world inside this thread and cloth. Now, in the shimmering mirror, Martínez saw the enormity of this thing they were living together and his eyes grew wet. The others blinked. Martínez touched the mirrors. They shifted. He saw a thousand, a million white-armored Martínezes march off into eternity, reflected, re-reflected, forever, indomitable, and unending.

He held the white coat out on the air. In a trance, the others did not at first recognize the dirty hand that reached to take the coat. Then:

"Vamenos!"

"Pig!"

"You didn't wash!" cried Gómez. "Or even shave, while you waited! *Compadres,* the bath!"

"The bath!" said everyone.

"No!" Vamenos flailed. "The night air! I'm dead!"

They hustled him yelling out and down the hall.

Now here stood Vamenos, unbelievable in white suit, beard shaved, hair combed, nails scrubbed.

His friends scowled darkly at him.

For was it not true, thought Martínez, that when Vamenos passed by, avalanches itched on mountaintops? If he walked under windows, people spat, dumped garbage, or worse. Tonight now, this night, he would stroll beneath ten thousand wide-opened windows, near balconies, past alleys. Suddenly the world absolutely sizzled with flies. And here was Vamenos, a fresh-frosted cake.

"You sure look keen in that suit, Vamenos," said Manulo sadly.

"Thanks." Vamenos twitched, trying to make his skeleton comfortable where all their skeletons had so recently been. In a small voice Vamenos said, "Can I go now?"

"Villanazul!" said Gómez. "Copy down these rules."

Villanazul licked his pencil.

"First," said Gómez, "don't fall down in that suit, Vamenos!"

"I won't."

"Don't lean against buildings in that suit."

"No buildings."

"Don't walk under trees with birds in them in that suit. Don't smoke. Don't drink——"

"Please," said Vamenos, "can I *sit down* in this suit?"

"When in doubt, take the pants off, fold them over a chair."

"Wish me luck," said Vamenos.

"Go with God, Vamenos."

He went out. He shut the door.

There was a ripping sound.

"Vamenos!" cried Martínez.

He whipped the door open.

Vamenos stood with two halves of a handkerchief torn in his hands, laughing.

"Rrrip! Look at your faces! Rrrip!" He tore the cloth again. "Oh, oh, your faces, your faces! Ha!"

Roaring, Vamenos slammed the door, leaving them stunned and alone.

Gómez put both hands on top of his head and turned away. "Stone me. Kill me. I have sold our souls to a demon!"

Villanazul dug in his pockets, took out a silver coin, and studied it for a long while.

"Here is my last fifty cents. Who else will help me buy back Vamenos' share of the suit?"

"It's no use." Manulo showed them ten cents. "We got only enough to buy the lapels and the buttonholes."

Gómez, at the open window, suddenly leaned out and yelled. "Vamenos! No!"

Below on the street, Vamenos, shocked, blew out a match and threw away an old cigar butt he had found somewhere. He made a strange gesture to all the men in the window above, then waved airily and sauntered on.

Somehow, the five men could not move away from the window. They were crushed together there.

"I bet he eats a hamburger in that suit," mused Villanazul. "I'm thinking of the mustard."

"Don't!" cried Gómez. "No, no!"

Manulo was suddenly at the door.

"I need a drink, bad."

"Manulo, there's wine here, that bottle on the floor——"

Manulo went out and shut the door.

A moment later Villanazul stretched with great exaggeration and strolled about the room.

"I think I'll walk down to the plaza, friends."

He was not gone a minute when Domínguez, waving his black book at the others, winked and turned the doorknob.

"Domínguez," said Gómez.

"Yes?"

"If you see Vamenos, by accident," said Gómez, "warn him away from Mickey Murrillo's Red Rooster Café. They got fights not only *on* TV but *out front* of the TV too."

"He wouldn't go into Murrillo's," said Domínguez. "That suit means too much to Vamenos. He wouldn't do anything to hurt it."

"He'd shoot his mother first," said Martínez.

"Sure he would."

Martínez and Gómez, alone, listened to Domínguez's footsteps hurry away down the stairs. They circled the undressed window dummy.

For a long while, biting his lips, Gómez stood at the window, looking out. He touched his shirt pocket twice, pulled his hand away, and then at last pulled something from the pocket. Without looking at it, he handed it to Martínez.

"Martínez, take this."

"What is it?"

Martínez looked at the piece of folded pink paper with print on it, with names and numbers. His eyes widened.

"A ticket on the bus to El Paso three weeks from now!"

Gómez nodded. He couldn't look at Martínez. He stared out into the summer night.

"Turn it in. Get the money," he said. "Buy us a nice white panama hat and a pale blue tie to go with the white ice cream suit, Martínez. Do that."

"Gómez——"

"Shut up. Boy, is it hot in here! I need air."

"Gómez. I am touched. Gómez——"

But the door stood open. Gómez was gone.

Mickey Murrillo's Red Rooster Café and Cocktail Lounge was squashed between two big brick buildings and, being narrow, had to be deep. Outside, serpents of red and sulphur-green neon fizzed and snapped. Inside, dim shapes loomed and swam away to lose themselves in a swarming night sea.

Martínez, on tiptoe, peeked through a flaked place on the red-painted front window.

He felt a presence on his left, heard breathing on his right. He glanced in both directions.

"Manulo! Villanazul!"

"I decided I wasn't thirsty," said Manulo. "So I took a walk."

"I was just on my way to the plaza," said Villanazul, "and decided to go the long way around."

As if by agreement, the three men shut up now and turned together to peer on tiptoe through various flaked spots on the window.

A moment later, all three felt a new very warm presence behind them and heard still faster breathing.

"Is our white suit in there?" asked Gómez's voice.

"Gómez!" said everybody, surprised. "Hi!"

"Yes!" cried Domínguez, having just arrived to find his own peephole. "There's the suit! And, praise God, Vamenos is still *in* it!"

"I can't see!" Gómez squinted, shielding his eyes. "What's he *doing?*"

Martínez peered. Yes! There, way back in the shadows, was a

big chunk of snow and the idiot smile of Vamenos winking above it, wreathed in smoke.

"He's smoking!" said Martínez.

"He's drinking!" said Domínguez.

"He's eating a taco!" reported Villanazul.

"A *juicy* taco," added Manulo.

"No," said Gómez. "No, no, no. . . ."

"Ruby Escuadrillo's with him!"

"Let me see that!" Gómez pushed Martínez aside.

Yes, there was Ruby! Two hundred pounds of glittering sequins and tight black satin on the hoof, her scarlet fingernails clutching Vamenos' shoulder. Her cowlike face, floured with powder, greasy with lipstick, hung over him!

"That hippo!" said Domínguez. "She's crushing the shoulder pads. Look, she's going to sit on his lap!"

"No, no, not with all that powder and lipstick!" said Gómez. "Manulo, inside! Grab that drink! Villanazul, the cigar, the taco! Domínguez, date Ruby Escuadrillo, get her away. *Ándale*, men!"

The three vanished, leaving Gómez and Martínez to stare, gasping, through the peephole.

"Manulo, he's got the drink, he's *drinking* it!"

"*Ay!* There's Villanazul, he's got the cigar, he's eating the taco!"

"Hey, Domínguez, he's got Ruby! What a *brave* one!"

A shadow bulked through Murrillo's front door, traveling fast.

"Gómez!" Martínez clutched Gómez's arm. "That was Ruby Escuadrillo's boy friend, Toro Ruíz. If he finds her with Vamenos, the ice cream suit will be covered with blood, *covered* with blood——"

"Don't make me nervous," said Gómez. "Quickly!"

Both ran. Inside they reached Vamenos just as Toro Ruíz grabbed about two feet of the lapels of that wonderful ice cream suit.

"Let go of Vamenos!" said Martínez.

"Let go that *suit!*" corrected Gómez.

Toro Ruíz, tap-dancing Vamenos, leered at these intruders.

Villanazul stepped up shyly.

Villanazul smiled. "Don't hit him. Hit me."

Toro Ruíz hit Villanazul smack on the nose.

Villanazul, holding his nose, tears stinging his eyes, wandered off.

Gómez grabbed one of Toro Ruíz's arms, Martínez the other.

"Drop him, let go, *cabrón, coyote, vaca!*"

Toro Ruíz twisted the ice cream suit material until all six men screamed in mortal agony. Grunting, sweating, Toro Ruíz dislodged as many as climbed on. He was winding up to hit Vamenos when Villanazul wandered back, eyes streaming.

"Don't hit him. Hit me!"

As Toro Ruíz hit Villanazul on the nose, a chair crashed on Toro's head.

"*Ai!*" said Gómez.

Toro Ruíz swayed, blinking, debating whether to fall. He began to drag Vamenos with him.

"Let go!" cried Gómez. "Let go!"

One by one, with great care, Toro Ruíz's banana-like fingers let loose of the suit. A moment later he was ruins at their feet.

"*Compadres,* this way!"

They ran Vamenos outside and set him down where he freed himself of their hands with injured dignity.

"Okay, okay. My time ain't up. I still got two minutes and, let's see—ten seconds."

"What!" said everybody.

"Vamenos," said Gómez, "you let a Guadalajara cow climb on you, you pick fights, you smoke, you drink, you eat tacos, and *now* you have the nerve to say your time ain't up?"

"I got two minutes and one second left!"

"Hey, Vamenos, you sure look sharp!" Distantly, a woman's voice called from across the street.

Vamenos smiled and buttoned the coat.

"It's Ramona Álvarez! Ramona, wait!" Vamenos stepped off the curb.

"Vamenos," pleaded Gómez. "What can you do in one minute and"—he checked his watch—"forty seconds!"

"Watch! Hey, Ramona!"

Vamenos loped.

"Vamenos, look out!"

Vamenos, surprised, whirled, saw a car, heard the shriek of brakes.

"No," said all five men on the sidewalk.

Martínez heard the impact and flinched. His head moved up. It looks like white laundry, he thought, flying through the air. His head came down.

Now he heard himself and each of the men make a different sound. Some swallowed too much air. Some let it out. Some choked. Some groaned. Some cried aloud for justice. Some covered their faces. Martínez felt his own fist pounding his heart in agony. He could not move his feet.

"I don't want to live," said Gómez quietly. "Kill me, someone."

Then, shuffling, Martínez looked down and told his feet to walk, stagger, follow one after the other. He collided with other men. Now they were trying to run. They ran at last and somehow crossed a street like a deep river through which they could only wade, to look down at Vamenos.

"Vamenos!" said Martínez. "You're alive!"

Strewn on his back, mouth open, eyes squeezed tight, tight, Vamenos motioned his head back and forth, back and forth, moaning.

"Tell me, tell me, oh, tell me, tell me."

"Tell you what, Vamenos?"

Vamenos clenched his fists, ground his teeth.

"The suit, what have I done to the suit, the suit, the suit!"

The men crouched lower.

"Vamenos, it's . . . why, it's *okay!*"

"You lie!" said Vamenos. "It's torn, it must be, it must be, it's torn, all around, *underneath?*"

"No." Martínez knelt and touched here and there. "Vamenos, all around, underneath even, it's okay!"

Vamenos opened his eyes to let the tears run free at last. "A miracle," he sobbed. "Praise the saints!" He quieted at last. "The car?"

"Hit and run." Gómez suddenly remembered and glared at the empty street. "It's good he didn't stop. We'd have——"

Everyone listened.

Distantly a siren wailed.

"Someone phoned for an ambulance."

"Quick!" said Vamenos, eyes rolling. "Set me up! Take off our coat!"

"Vamenos——"

"Shut up, idiots!" cried Vamenos. "The coat, that's it! Now, the pants, the pants, quick, quick, *peónes!* Those doctors! You seen movies? They rip the pants with razors to get them off! They don't *care!* They're maniacs! Ah, God, quick, quick!"

The siren screamed.

The men, panicking, all handled Vamenos at once.

"Right leg, *easy,* hurry, cows! Good! Left leg, now, left, you hear, there, easy, *easy!* Ow, God! Quick! Martínez, your pants, take them off!"

"What?" Martínez froze.

The siren shrieked.

"Fool!" wailed Vamenos. "All is lost! Your pants! Give me!"

Martínez jerked at his belt buckle.

"Close in, make a circle!"

Dark pants, light pants flourished on the air.

"Quick, here come the maniacs with the razors! Right leg on, left leg, *there!*"

"The zipper, cows, zip my zipper!" babbled Vamenos.

The siren died.

"*Madre mía,* yes, just in time! They arrive." Vamenos lay back down and shut his eyes. "*Gracias.*"

Martínez turned, nonchalantly buckling on the white pants as the interns brushed past.

"Broken leg," said one intern as they moved Vamenos onto a stretcher.

"*Compadres,*" said Vamenos, "don't be mad with me."

Gómez snorted. "Who's mad?"

In the ambulance, head tilted back, looking out at them upside down, Vamenos faltered.

"*Compadres,* when . . . when I come from the hospital . . . am I still in the bunch? You won't kick me out? Look, I'll give up smoking, keep away from Murrillo's, swear off women——"

"Vamenos," said Martínez gently, "don't promise nothing."

Vamenos, upside down, eyes brimming wet, saw Martínez there, all white now against the stars.

"Oh, Martínez, you sure look great in that suit. *Compadres,* don't he look *beautiful?*"

Villanazul climbed in beside Vamenos. The door slammed. The four remaining men watched the ambulance drive away.

Then, surrounded by his friends, inside the white suit, Martínez was carefully escorted back to the curb.

In the tenement, Martínez got out the cleaning fluid and the others stood around, telling him how to clean the suit and, later, how not to have the iron too hot and how to work the lapels and the crease and all. When the suit was cleaned and pressed so it looked like a fresh gardenia just opened, they fitted it to the dummy.

"Two o'clock," murmured Villanazul. "I hope Vamenos sleeps well. When I left him at the hospital, he looked good."

Manulo cleared his throat. "Nobody else is going out with that suit tonight, huh?"

The others glared at him.

Manulo flushed. "I mean . . . it's late. We're tired. Maybe no one will use the suit for forty-eight hours, huh? Give it a rest. Sure. Well. Where do we sleep?"

The night being still hot and the room unbearable, they carried the suit on its dummy out and down the hall. They brought with them also some pillows and blankets. They climbed the stairs toward the roof of the tenement. There, thought Martínez, is the cooler wind, and sleep.

On the way, they passed a dozen doors that stood open, peo-

ple still perspiring and awake, playing cards, drinking pop, fanning themselves with movie magazines.

I wonder, thought Martínez. I wonder if— Yes!

On the fourth floor, a certain door stood open.

The beautiful girl looked up as the men passed. She wore glasses and when she saw Martínez she snatched them off and hid them under her book.

The others went on, not knowing they had lost Martínez, who seemed stuck fast in the open door.

For a long moment he could say nothing. Then he said:

"José Martínez."

And she said:

"Celia Obregón."

And then both said nothing.

He heard the men moving up on the tenement roof. He moved to follow.

She said quickly, "I saw you tonight!"

He came back.

"The suit," he said.

"The suit," she said, and paused. "But not the suit."

"Eh?" he said.

She lifted the book to show the glasses lying in her lap. She touched the glasses.

"I do not see well. You would think I would wear my glasses, but no. I walk around for years now, hiding them, seeing nothing. But tonight, even without the glasses, I see. A great whiteness passes below in the dark. So white! And I put on my glasses quickly!"

"The suit, as I said," said Martínez.

"The suit for a little moment, yes, but there is another whiteness above the suit."

"Another?"

"Your teeth! Oh, such white teeth, and so many!"

Martínez put his hand over his mouth.

"So happy, Mr. Martínez," she said. "I have not often seen such a happy face and such a smile."

"Ah," he said, not able to look at her, his face flushing now.

"So, you see," she said quietly, "the suit caught my eye, yes, the whiteness filled the night below. But the teeth were much whiter. Now, I have forgotten the suit."

Martínez flushed again. She, too, was overcome with what she had said. She put her glasses on her nose, and then took them off, nervously, and hid them again. She looked at her hands and at the door above his head.

"May I——" he said, at last.

"May you——"

"May I call for you," he asked, "when next the suit is mine to wear?"

"Why must you wait for the suit?" she said.

"I thought——"

"You do not need the suit," she said.

"But——"

"If it were just the suit," she said, "anyone would be fine in it. But no, I watched. I saw many men in that suit, all different, this night. So again I say, you do not need to wait for the suit."

"*Madre mía, madre mía!*" he cried happily. And then, quieter, "I will need the suit for a little while. A month, six months, a year. I am uncertain. I am fearful of many things. I am young."

"That is as it should be," she said.

"Good night, Miss——"

"Celia Obregón."

"Celia Obregón," he said, and was gone from the door.

The others were waiting on the roof of the tenement. Coming up through the trapdoor, Martínez saw they had placed the dummy and the suit in the center of the roof and put their blankets and pillows in a circle around it. Now they were lying down. Now a cooler night wind was blowing here, up in the sky.

Martínez stood alone by the white suit, smoothing the lapels, talking half to himself.

"Ay, *caramba*, what a night! Seems ten years since seven o'clock, when it all started and I had no friends. Two in the morning, I got all *kinds* of friends. . . ." He paused and thought,

Celia Obregón, Celia Obregón. ". . . all kinds of friends," he went on. "I got a room, I got clothes. You tell *me*. You know what?" He looked around at the men lying on the rooftop, surrounding the dummy and himself. "It's funny. When I wear this suit, I know I will win at pool, like Gómez. A woman will look at me like Domínguez. I will be able to sing like Manulo, sweetly. I will talk fine politics like Villanazul. I'm strong as Vamenos. So? So, tonight, I am more than Martínez. I am Gómez, Manulo, Domínguez, Villanazul, Vamenos. I am everyone. Ay . . . ay . . ."

He stood a moment longer by this suit which could save all the ways they sat or stood or walked. This suit which could move fast and nervous like Gómez or slow and thoughtfully like Villanazul or drift like Domínguez, who never touched ground, who always found a wind to take him somewhere. This suit which belonged to them but which also owned them all. This suit that was—what? A parade.

"Martínez," said Gómez. "You going to sleep?"

"Sure. I'm just thinking."

"What?"

"If we ever get rich," said Martínez softly, "it'll be kind of sad. Then we'll all have suits. And there won't be no more nights like tonight. It'll break up the old gang. It'll never be the same after that."

The men lay thinking of what had just been said.

Gómez nodded gently.

"Yeah . . . it'll never be the same . . . after that."

Martínez lay down on his blanket. In darkness, with the others, he faced the middle of the roof and the dummy, which was the center of their lives.

And their eyes were bright, shining, and good to see in the dark as the neon lights from nearby buildings flicked on, flicked off, flicked on, flicked off, revealing and then vanishing, revealing and then vanishing, their wonderful white vanilla ice cream summer suit.

6

FEVER DREAM

They put him between fresh, clean, laundered sheets and there was always a newly squeezed glass of thick orange juice on the table under the dim pink lamp. All Charles had to do was call and Mom or Dad would stick their heads into his room to see how sick he was. The acoustics of the room were fine; you could hear the toilet gargling its porcelain throat of mornings, you could hear rain tap the roof or sly mice run in the secret walls or the canary singing in its cage downstairs. If you were very alert, sickness wasn't too bad.

He was thirteen, Charles was. It was mid-September, with the land beginning to burn with autumn. He lay in the bed for three days before the terror overcame him.

His hand began to change. His right hand. He looked at it and it was hot and sweating there on the counterpane alone. It fluttered, it moved a bit. Then it lay there, changing color.

That afternoon the doctor came again and tapped his thin chest like a little drum. "How are you?" asked the doctor, smiling. "I know, don't tell me: 'My *cold* is fine, Doctor, but *I* feel awful!' Ha!" He laughed at his own oft-repeated joke.

Charles lay there and for him that terrible and ancient jest

was becoming a reality. The joke fixed itself in his mind. His mind touched and drew away from it in a pale terror. The doctor did not know how cruel he was with his jokes! "Doctor," whispered Charles, lying flat and colorless. "My *hand*, it doesn't *belong* to me any more. This morning it *changed* into something else. I want you to change it back, Doctor, Doctor!"

The doctor showed his teeth and patted his hand. "It looks fine to me, son. You just had a little fever dream."

"But it changed, Doctor, oh, Doctor," cried Charles, pitifully holding up his pale wild hand. "It *did!*"

The doctor winked. "I'll give you a pink pill for that." He popped a tablet onto Charles' tongue. "Swallow!"

"Will it make my hand change back and become *me*, again?"

"Yes, yes."

The house was silent when the doctor drove off down the road in his car under the quiet, blue September sky. A clock ticked far below in the kitchen world. Charles lay looking at his hand.

It did not change back. It was still something else.

The wind blew outside. Leaves fell against the cool window.

At four o'clock his other hand changed. It seemed almost to become a fever. It pulsed and shifted, cell by cell. It beat like a warm heart. The fingernails turned blue and then red. It took about an hour for it to change and when it was finished, it looked just like any ordinary hand. But it was not ordinary. It no longer was him any more. He lay in a fascinated horror and then fell into an exhausted sleep.

Mother brought the soup up at six. He wouldn't touch it. "I haven't any hands," he said, eyes shut.

"Your hands are perfectly good," said mother.

"No," he wailed. "My hands are gone. I feel like I have stumps. Oh, Mama, Mama, hold me, hold me, I'm scared!"

She had to feed him herself.

"Mama," he said, "get the doctor, please, again. I'm so sick."

"The doctor'll be here tonight at eight," she said, and went out.

At seven, with night dark and close around the house, Charles was sitting up in bed when he felt the thing happening to first

one leg and then the other. "Mama! Come quick!" he screamed. But when mama came the thing was no longer happening.

When she went downstairs, he simply lay without fighting as his legs beat and beat, grew warm, red-hot, and the room filled with the warmth of his feverish change. The glow crept up from his toes to his ankles and then to his knees.

"May I come in?" The doctor smiled in the doorway.

"Doctor!" cried Charles. "Hurry, take off my blankets!"

The doctor lifted the blankets tolerantly. "There you are. Whole and healthy. Sweating, though. A little fever. I told you not to move around, bad boy." He pinched the moist pink cheek. "Did the pills help? Did your hand change back?"

"No, no, now it's my other hand and my legs!"

"Well, well, I'll have to give you three more pills, one for each limb, eh, my little peach?" laughed the doctor.

"Will they help me? Please, please. What've I *got?*"

"A mild case of scarlet fever, complicated by a slight cold."

"Is it a germ that lives and has more little germs in me?"

"Yes."

"Are you *sure* it's scarlet fever? You haven't taken any tests!"

"I guess I know a certain fever when I see one," said the doctor, checking the boy's pulse with cool authority.

Charles lay there, not speaking until the doctor was crisply packing his black kit. Then in the silent room, the boy's voice made a small, weak pattern, his eyes alight with remembrance. "I read a book once. About petrified trees, wood turning to stone. About how trees fell and rotted and minerals got in and built up and they look just like trees, but they're not, they're stone." He stopped. In the quiet warm room his breathing sounded.

"Well?" asked the doctor.

"I've been thinking," said Charles after a time. "Do germs ever get big? I mean, in biology class they told us about one-celled animals, amoebas and things, and how millions of years ago they got together until there was a bunch and they made the first body. And more and more cells got together and got bigger and then finally maybe there was a fish and finally here *we* are, and

all we are is a bunch of cells that decided to get together, to help each other out. Isn't that right?" Charles wet his feverish lips.

"What's all this about?" the doctor bent over him.

"I've got to tell you this. Doctor, oh, I've got to!" he cried. "What would happen, oh just pretend, please pretend, that just like in the old days, a lot of microbes got together and wanted to make a bunch, and reproduced and made *more*——"

His white hands were on his chest now, crawling toward his throat.

"And they decided to *take over* a person!" cried Charles.

"Take over a person?"

"Yes, *become* a person. *Me,* my hands, my feet! What if a disease somehow knew how to kill a person and yet live after him?"

He screamed.

The hands were on his neck.

The doctor moved forward, shouting.

At nine o'clock the doctor was escorted out to his car by the mother and father, who handed him his bag. They conversed in the cool night wind for a few minutes. "Just be sure his hands are kept strapped to his legs," said the doctor. "I don't want him hurting himself."

"Will he be all right, Doctor?" The mother held to his arm a moment.

He patted her shoulder. "Haven't I been your family physician for thirty years? It's the fever. He imagines things."

"But those bruises on his throat, he almost choked himself."

"Just you keep him strapped; he'll be all right in the morning."

The car moved off down the dark September road.

At three in the morning, Charles was still awake in his small black room. The bed was damp under his head and his back. He was very warm. Now he no longer had any arms or legs, and his body was beginning to change. He did not move on the bed, but looked at the vast blank ceiling space with insane concentration. For a while he had screamed and thrashed, but now he was weak

and hoarse from it, and his mother had gotten up a number of times to soothe his brow with a wet towel. Now he was silent, his hands strapped to his legs.

He felt the walls of his body change, the organs shift, the lungs catch fire like burning bellows of pink alcohol. The room was lighted up as with the flickerings of a hearth.

Now he had no body. It was all gone. It was under him, but it was filled with a vast pulse of some burning, lethargic drug. It was as if a guillotine had neatly lopped off his head, and his head lay shining on a midnight pillow while the body, below, still alive, belonged to somebody else. The disease had eaten his body and from the eating had reproduced itself in feverish duplicate. There were the little hand hairs and the fingernails and the scars and the toenails and the tiny mole on his right hip, all done again in perfect fashion.

I am dead, he thought. I've been killed, and yet I live. My body is dead, it is all disease and nobody will know. I will walk around and it will not be me, it will be something else. It will be something all bad, all evil, so big and so evil it's hard to understand or think about. Something that will buy shoes and drink water and get married some day maybe and do more evil in the world than has ever been done.

Now the warmth was stealing up his neck, into his cheeks, like a hot wine. His lips burned, his eyelids, like leaves, caught fire. His nostrils breathed out blue flame, faintly, faintly.

This will be all, he thought. It'll take my head and my brain and fix each eye and every tooth and all the marks in my brain, and every hair and every wrinkle in my ears, and there'll be nothing left of me.

He felt his brain fill with a boiling mercury. He felt his left eye clench in upon itself and, like a snail, withdraw, shift. He was blind in his left eye. It no longer belonged to him. It was enemy territory. His tongue was gone, cut out. His left cheek was numbed, lost. His left ear stopped hearing. It belonged to someone else now. This thing that was being born, this mineral thing

replacing the wooden log, this disease replacing healthy animal cell.

He tried to scream and he was able to scream loud and high and sharply in the room, just as his brain flooded down, his right eye and right ear were cut out, he was blind and deaf, all fire, all terror, all panic, all death.

His scream stopped before his mother ran through the door to his side.

It was a good, clear morning, with a brisk wind that helped carry the doctor up the path before the house. In the window above, the boy stood, fully dressed. He did not wave when the doctor waved and called, "What's this? Up? My God!"

The doctor almost ran upstairs. He came gasping into the bedroom.

"What are you doing out of bed?" he demanded of the boy. He tapped his thin chest, took his pulse and temperature. "Absolutely amazing! Normal. Normal, by God!"

"I shall never be sick again in my life," declared the boy, quietly, standing there, looking out the wide window. "Never."

"I hope not. Why, you're looking fine, Charles."

"Doctor?"

"Yes, Charles?"

"Can I go to school *now?*" asked Charles.

"Tomorrow will be time enough. You sound positively eager."

"I am. I like school. All the kids. I want to play with them and wrestle with them, and spit on them and play with the girls' pigtails and shake the teacher's hand, and rub my hands on all the cloaks in the cloakroom, and I want to grow up and travel and shake hands with people all over the world, and be married and have lots of children, and go to libraries and handle books and—*all* of that I want to!" said the boy, looking off into the September morning. "What's the name you called me?"

"What?" The doctor puzzled. "I called you nothing but Charles."

"It's better than no name at all, I guess." The boy shrugged.

"I'm glad you want to go back to school," said the doctor.

"I really anticipate it," smiled the boy. "Thank you for your help, Doctor. Shake hands."

"Glad to."

They shook hands gravely, and the clear wind blew through the open window. They shook hands for almost a minute, the boy smiling up at the old man and thanking him.

Then, laughing, the boy raced the doctor downstairs and out to his car. His mother and father followed for the happy farewell.

"Fit as a fiddle!" said the doctor. "Incredible!"

"And strong," said the father. "He got out of his straps himself during the night. Didn't you, Charles?"

"Did I?" said the boy.

"You did! How?"

"Oh," the boy said, "that was a long time ago."

"A long time ago!"

They all laughed, and while they were laughing, the quiet boy moved his bare foot on the sidewalk and merely touched, brushed against a number of red ants that were scurrying about on the sidewalk. Secretly, his eyes shining, while his parents chatted with the old man, he saw the ants hesitate, quiver, and lie still on the cement. He sensed they were cold now.

"Good-by!"

The doctor drove away, waving.

The boy walked ahead of his parents. As he walked he looked away toward the town and began to hum "School Days" under his breath.

"It's good to have him well again," said the father.

"Listen to him. He's so looking forward to school!"

The boy turned quietly. He gave each of his parents a crushing hug. He kissed them both several times.

Then without a word he bounded up the steps into the house.

In the parlor, before the others entered, he quickly opened the bird cage, thrust his hand in, and petted the yellow canary, *once*.

Then he shut the cage door, stood back, and waited.

7

THE MARRIAGE MENDER

In the sun the headboard was like a fountain, tossing up plumes of clear light. It was carved with lions and gargoyles and bearded goats. It was an awe-inspiring object even at midnight, as Antonio sat on the bed and unlaced his shoes and put his large calloused hand out to touch its shimmering harp. Then he rolled over into this fabulous machine for dreaming, and he lay breathing heavily, his eyes beginning to close.

"Every night," his wife's voice said, "we sleep in the mouth of a calliope."

Her complaint shocked him. He lay a long while before daring to reach up his hard-tipped fingers to stroke the cold metal of the intricate headboard, the threads of this lyre that had sung many wild and beautiful songs down the years.

"This is no calliope," he said.

"It cries like one," Maria said. "A billion people on this world tonight have beds. Why, I ask the saints, not us?"

"This," said Antonio gently, "is a bed." He plucked a little tune on the imitation brass harp behind his head. To his ears it was "Santa Lucia."

"This bed has humps like a herd of camels was under it."

"Now, Mama," Antonio said. He called her Mama when she

was mad, though they had no children. "You were never this way," he went on, "until five months ago when Mrs. Brancozzi downstairs bought her new bed."

Maria said wistfully, "Mrs. Brancozzi's bed. It's like snow. It's all flat and white and smooth."

"I don't want any damn snow, all flat and white and smooth! These springs—feel them!" he cried angrily. "They know me. They recognize that this hour of night I lie *thus,* at two o'clock, *so!* Three o'clock *this* way, four o'clock *that.* We are like a tumbling act, we've worked together for years and know all the holds and falls."

Maria sighed, and said, "Sometimes I dream we're in the taffy machine at Bartole's candy store."

"This bed," he announced to the darkness, "served our family before Garibaldi! From this wellspring alone came precincts of honest voters, a squad of clean-saluting Army men, two confectioners, a barber, four second leads for *Il Trovatore* and *Rigoletto,* and two geniuses so complex they never *could* decide what to do in their lifetime! Not to forget enough beautiful women to provide ballrooms with their finest decoration. A cornucopia of plenty, this bed! A veritable harvesting machine!"

"We have been married two years," she said with dreadful control over her voice. "Where are *our* second leads for *Rigoletto,* our geniuses, our ballroom decorations?"

"Patience, Mama."

"Don't call me Mama! While this bed is busy favoring you all night, never once has it done for me. Not even so much as a baby *girl!*"

He sat up. "You've let these women in this tenement ruin you with their dollar-down, dollar-a-week talk. Has Mrs. Brancozzi children? Her and her new bed that she's had for five months?"

"No! But *soon!* Mrs. Brancozzi says . . . and her bed, so beautiful."

He slammed himself down and yanked the covers over him. The bed screamed like all the Furies rushing through the night sky, fading away toward the dawn.

The moon changed the shape of the window pattern on the floor. Antonio awoke. Maria was not beside him.

He got up and went to peer through the half-open door of the bathroom. His wife stood at the mirror looking at her tired face.

"I don't feel well," she said.

"We argued." He put out his hand to pat her. "I'm sorry. We'll think it over. About the bed, I mean. We'll see how the money goes. And if you're not well tomorrow, see the doctor, eh? Now, come back to bed."

At noon the next day, Antonio walked from the lumberyard to a window where stood fine new beds with their covers invitingly turned back.

"I," he whispered to himself, "am a beast."

He checked his watch. Maria, at this time, would be going to the doctor's. She had been like cold milk this morning; he had told her to go. He walked on to the candy-store window and watched the taffy machine folding and threading and pulling. Does taffy scream? he wondered. Perhaps, but so high we cannot hear it. He laughed. Then, in the stretched taffy, he saw Maria. Frowning, he turned and walked back to the furniture store. No. Yes. No. Yes! He pressed his nose to the icy window. Bed, he thought, you in there, new bed, do you *know* me? Will you be kind to my back, nights?

He took out his wallet slowly, and peered at the money. He sighed, gazed for a long time at that flat marbletop, that unfamiliar enemy, that new bed. Then, shoulders sagging, he walked into the store, his money held loosely in his hand.

"Maria!" He ran up the steps two at a time. It was nine o'clock at night and he had managed to beg off in the middle of his overtime at the lumberyard to rush home. He rushed through the open doorway, smiling.

The apartment was empty.

"Ah," he said disappointedly. He laid the receipt for the new bed on top of the bureau where Maria might see it when she entered. On those few evenings when he worked late she visited with any one of several neighbors downstairs.

I'll go find her, he thought, and stopped. No. I want to tell her alone. I'll wait. He sat on the bed. "Old bed," he said, "good-by to you. I am very sorry." He patted the brass lions nervously. He paced the floor. *Come on,* Maria. He imagined her smile.

He listened for her quick running on the stair, but he heard only a slow, measured tread. He thought: That's not my Maria, slow like that, no.

The doorknob turned.

"Maria!"

"You're early!" She smiled happily at him. Did she guess? Was it written on his face? "I've been downstairs," she cried, "telling everyone!"

"Telling everyone?"

"The doctor! I saw the doctor!"

"The doctor?" He looked bewildered. "And?"

"And, Papa, *and*——"

"Do you mean—Papa?"

"Papa, Papa, Papa, Papa!"

"Oh," he said, gently, "you walked so carefully on the stairs."

He took hold of her, but not too tight, and he kissed her cheeks, and he shut his eyes, and he yelled. Then he had to wake a few neighbors and tell them, shake them, tell them again. There had to be a little wine and a careful waltz around, an embracing, a trembling, a kissing of brow, eyelids, nose, lips, temples, ears, hair, chin—and then it was past midnight.

"A miracle," he sighed.

They were alone in their room again, the air warm from the people who had been here a minute before, laughing, talking. But now they were alone again.

Turning out the light, he saw the receipt on the bureau.

Stunned, he tried to decide in what subtle and delicious way to break this additional news to her.

Maria sat upon her side of the bed in the dark, hypnotized with wonder. She moved her hands as if her body was a strange doll, taken apart, and now to be put back together again, limb by limb, her motions as slow as if she lived beneath a warm sea at midnight. Now, at last, careful not to break herself, she lay back upon the pillow.

"Maria, I have something to tell you."

"Yes?" she said faintly.

"Now that you are as you are." He squeezed her hand. "You deserve the comfort, the rest, the beauty of a new bed."

She did not cry out happily or turn to him or seize him. Her silence was a thinking silence.

He was forced to continue. "This bed is nothing but a pipe organ, a calliope."

"It is a bed," she said.

"A herd of camels sleep under it."

"No," she said quietly, "from it will come precincts of honest voters, captains enough for *three* armies, two ballerinas, a famous lawyer, a very tall policeman, and seven basso profundos, altos, and sopranos."

He squinted across the dimly lighted room at the receipt upon the bureau. He touched the worn mattress under him. The springs moved softly to recognize each limb, each tired muscle, each aching bone.

He sighed. "I never argue with you, little one."

"Mama," she said.

"Mama," he said.

And then as he closed his eyes and drew the covers to his chest and lay in the darkness by the great fountain, in the sight of a jury of fierce metal lions and amber goats and smiling gargoyles, he listened. And he heard it. It was very far away at first, very tentative, but it came clearer as he listened.

Softly, her arm back over her head, Maria's finger tips began to tap a little dance on the gleaming harp strings, on the shim-

mering brass pipes of the ancient bed. The music was—yes, of course: "Santa Lucia!" His lips moved to it in a warm whisper. Santa Lucia! Santa Lucia.

It was very beautiful.

8

THE TOWN WHERE NO ONE GOT OFF

Crossing the continental United States by night, by day, on the train, you flash past town after wilderness town where nobody ever gets off. Or rather, no person who doesn't *belong,* no person who hasn't roots in these country graveyards ever bothers to visit their lonely stations or attend their lonely views.

I spoke of this to a fellow passenger, another salesman like myself, on the Chicago–Los Angeles train as we crossed Iowa.

"True," he said. "People get off in Chicago; everyone gets off there. People get off in New York, get off in Boston, get off in L.A. People who don't live there go there to see and come back to tell. But what tourist ever just got off at Fox Hill, Nebraska, to *look* at it? You? Me? No! I don't know anyone, got no business there, it's no health resort, so why bother?"

"Wouldn't it be a fascinating change," I said, "some year to plan a really different vacation? Pick some village lost on the plains where you don't know a soul and go there for the hell of it?"

"You'd be bored stiff."

Originally published in Ellery Queen's *Mystery Magazine.* Copyright © 1958 by Davis Publications, Inc.

"I'm not bored thinking of it!" I peered out the window. "What's the next town coming up on this line?"

"Rampart Junction."

I smiled. "Sounds good. I might get off there."

"You're a liar and a fool. What you want? Adventure? Romance? Go ahead, jump off the train. Ten seconds later you'll call yourself an idiot, grab a taxi, and race us to the next town."

"Maybe."

I watched telephone poles flick by, flick by, flick by. Far ahead I could see the first faint outlines of a town.

"But I don't think so," I heard myself say.

The salesman across from me looked faintly surprised.

For slowly, very slowly, I was rising to stand. I reached for my hat. I saw my hand fumble for my one suitcase. I was surprised myself.

"Hold on!" said the salesman. "What're you doing?"

The train rounded a curve suddenly. I swayed. Far ahead I saw one church spire, a deep forest, a field of summer wheat.

"It looks like I'm getting off the train," I said.

"Sit down," he said.

"No," I said. "There's something about that town up ahead. I've got to go see. I've got the time. I don't have to be in L.A., really, until next Monday. If I don't get off the train now, I'll always wonder what I missed, what I let slip by when I had the chance to see it."

"We were just talking. There's nothing there."

"You're wrong," I said. "There is."

I put my hat on my head and lifted the suitcase in my hand.

"By God," said the salesman, "I think you're really going to do it."

My heart beat quickly. My face was flushed.

The train whistled. The train rushed down the track. The town was near!

"Wish me luck," I said.

"Luck!" he cried.

I ran for the porter, yelling.

There was an ancient flake-painted chair tilted back against the station-platform wall. In this chair, completely relaxed so he sank into his clothes, was a man of some seventy years whose timbers looked as if he'd been nailed there since the station was built. The sun had burned his face dark and tracked his cheek with lizard folds and stitches that held his eyes in a perpetual squint. His hair smoked ash-white in the summer wind. His blue shirt, open at the neck to show white clock springs, was bleached like the staring late afternoon sky. His shoes were blistered as if he had held them, uncaring, in the mouth of a stove, motionless, forever. His shadow under him was stenciled a permanent black.

As I stepped down the old man's eyes flicked every door on the train and stopped, surprised, at me.

I thought he might wave.

But there was only a sudden coloring of his secret eyes; a chemical change that was recognition. Yet he had not twitched so much as his mouth, an eyelid, a finger. An invisible bulk had shifted inside him.

The moving train gave me an excuse to follow it with my eyes. There was no one else on the platform. No autos waited by the cobwebbed, nailed-shut office. I alone had departed the iron thunder to set foot on the choppy waves of platform lumber.

The train whistled over the hill.

Fool! I thought. My fellow passenger had been right. I would panic at the boredom I already sensed in this place. All right, I thought, fool, yes, but run, no!

I walked my suitcase down the platform, not looking at the old man. As I passed, I heard his thin bulk shift again, this time so I could hear it. His feet were coming down to touch and tap the mushy boards.

I kept walking.

"Afternoon," a voice said faintly.

I knew he did not look at me but only at that great cloudless spread of shimmering sky.

"Afternoon," I said.

I started up the dirt road toward the town. One hundred yards away, I glanced back.

.The old man, still seated there, stared at the sun, as if posing a question.

I hurried on.

I moved through the dreaming late afternoon town, utterly anonymous and alone, a trout going upstream, not touching the banks of a clear-running river of life that drifted all about me.

My suspicions were confirmed: it was a town where nothing happened, where occurred only the following events:

At four o'clock sharp, the Honneger Hardware door slammed as a dog came out to dust himself in the road. Four-thirty, a straw sucked emptily at the bottom of a soda glass, making a sound like a great cataract in the drugstore silence. Five o'clock, boys and pebbles plunged in the town river. Five-fifteen, ants paraded in the slanting light under some elm trees.

And yet—I turned in a slow circle—somewhere in this town there must be something worth seeing. I knew it was there. I knew I had to keep walking and looking. I knew I would find it.

I walked. I looked.

All through the afternoon there was only one constant and unchanging factor: the old man in the bleached blue pants and shirt was never far away. When I sat in the drugstore he was out front spitting tobacco that rolled itself into tumblebugs in the dust. When I stood by the river he was crouched downstream making a great thing of washing his hands.

Along about seven-thirty in the evening, I was walking for the seventh or eighth time through the quiet streets when I heard footsteps beside me.

I looked over, and the old man was pacing me, looking straight ahead, a piece of dried grass in his stained teeth.

"It's been a long time," he said quietly.

We walked along in the twilight.

"A long time," he said, "waitin' on that station platform."

"You?" I said.

"Me." He nodded in the tree shadows.

"Were you waiting for someone at the station?"

"Yes," he said. "You."

"Me?" The surprise must have shown in my voice. "But why . . . ? You never saw me before in your life."

"Did I say I did? I just said I was waitin'."

We were on the edge of town now. He had turned and I had turned with him along the darkening riverbank toward the trestle where the night trains ran over going east, going west, but stopping rare few times.

"You want to know anything about me?" I asked, suddenly. "You the sheriff?"

"No, not the sheriff. And no, I don't want to know nothing about you." He put his hands in his pockets. The sun was set now. The air was suddenly cool. "I'm just surprised you're here at last, is all."

"Surprised?"

"Surprised," he said, "and . . . pleased."

I stopped abruptly and looked straight at him.

"How long have you been sitting on that station platform?"

"Twenty years, give or take a few."

I knew he was telling the truth; his voice was as easy and quiet as the river.

"Waiting for me?" I said.

"Or someone like you," he said.

We walked on in the growing dark.

"How you like our town?"

"Nice, quiet," I said.

"Nice, quiet." He nodded. "Like the people?"

"People look nice and quiet."

"They are," he said. "Nice, quiet."

I was ready to turn back but the old man kept talking and in order to listen and be polite I had to walk with him in the vaster darkness, the tides of field and meadow beyond town.

"Yes," said the old man, "the day I retired, twenty years ago, I sat down on that station platform and there I been, sittin', doin' nothin', waitin' for something to happen, I didn't know what, I

didn't know, I couldn't say. But when it finally happened, I'd
know it, I'd look at it and say, yes, sir, that's what I was waitin'
for. Train wreck? No. Old woman friend come back to town after
fifty years? No. No. It's hard to say. Someone. Something. And
it seems to have something to do with you. I wish I could say——"

"Why don't you try?" I said.

The stars were coming out. We walked on.

"Well," he said slowly, "you know much about your own in-
sides?"

"You mean my stomach or you mean psychologically?"

"That's the word. I mean your head, your brain, you know
much about *that?*"

The grass whispered under my feet. "A little."

"You hate many people in your time?"

"Some."

"We all do. It's normal enough to hate, ain't it, and not only
hate but, while we don't talk about it, don't we sometimes want
to hit people who hurt us, even *kill* them?"

"Hardly a week passes we don't get that feeling," I said, "and
put it away."

"We put away all our lives," he said. "The town says thus and
so, Mom and Dad say this and that, the law says such and such.
So you put away one killing and another and two more after that.
By the time you're my age, you got lots of that kind of stuff between your ears. And unless you went to war, nothin' ever happened to get rid of it."

"Some men trapshoot or hunt ducks," I said. "Some men box
or wrestle."

"And some don't. I'm talkin' about them that don't. Me. All
my life I've been saltin' down those bodies, puttin' 'em away on
ice in my head. Sometimes you get mad at a town and the people
in it for makin' you put things aside like that. You like the old
cave men who just gave a hell of a yell and whanged someone on
the head with a club."

"Which all leads up to . . . ?"

"Which all leads up to: everybody'd like to do one killin' in

his life, to sort of work off that big load of stuff, all those killin's in his mind he never did have the guts to do. And once in a while a man has a chance. Someone runs in front of his car and he forgets the brakes and keeps goin'. Nobody can prove nothin' with that sort of thing. The man don't even tell himself he did it. He just didn't get his foot on the brake in time. But you know and I know what really happened, don't we?"

"Yes," I said.

The town was far away now. We moved over a small stream on a wooden bridge, just near the railway embankment.

"Now," said the old man, looking at the water, "the only kind of killin' worth doin' is the one where nobody can guess who did it or why they did it or who they did it to, right? Well, I got this idea maybe twenty years ago. I don't think about it every day or every week. Sometimes months go by, but the idea's this: only one train stops here each day, sometimes not even that. Now, if you wanted to kill someone you'd have to wait, wouldn't you, for years and years, until a complete and actual stranger came to your town, a stranger who got off the train for no reason, a man nobody knows and who don't know nobody in the town. Then, and only then, I thought, sittin' there on the station chair, you could just go up and when nobody's around, kill him and throw him in the river. He'd be found miles downstream. Maybe he'd never be found. Nobody would ever think to come to Rampart Junction to find him. He wasn't goin' there. He was on his way someplace else. There, that's my whole idea. And I'd know that man the minute he got off the train. Know him, just as clear . . ."

I had stopped walking. It was dark. The moon would not be up for an hour.

"Would you?" I said.

"Yes," he said. I saw the motion of his head looking at the stars. "Well, I've talked enough." He sidled close and touched my elbow. His hand was feverish, as if he had held it to a stove before touching me. His other hand, his right hand, was hidden, tight and bunched, in his pocket. "I've talked enough."

Something screamed.

I jerked my head.

Above, a fast flying night express razored along the unseen tracks, flourished light on hill, forest, farm, town dwellings, field, ditch, meadow, plowed earth and water, then, raving high, cut off away, shrieking, gone. The rails trembled for a little while after that. Then, silence.

The old man and I stood looking at each other in the dark. His left hand was still holding my elbow. His other hand was still hidden.

"May I say something?" I said at last.

The old man nodded.

"About myself," I said. I had to stop. I could hardly breathe. I forced myself to go on. "It's funny. I've often thought the same way as you. Sure, just today, going cross-country, I thought, How perfect, how perfect, how really perfect it could be. Business has been bad for me, lately. Wife sick. Good friend died last week. War in the world. Full of boils, myself. It would do me a world of good——"

"What?" the old man said, his hand on my arm.

"To get off this train in a small town," I said, "where nobody knows me, with this gun under my arm, and find someone and kill them and bury them and go back down to the station and get on and go home and nobody the wiser and nobody ever to know who did it, ever. Perfect, I thought, a perfect crime. And I got off the train."

We stood there in the dark for another minute, staring at each other. Perhaps we were listening to each other's hearts beating very fast, very fast indeed.

The world turned under me. I clenched my fists. I wanted to fall. I wanted to scream like the train.

For suddenly I saw that all the things I had just said were not lies put forth to save my life.

All the things I had just said to this man were true.

And now I knew why I had stepped from the train and walked up through this town. I knew what I had been looking for.

I heard the old man breathing hard and fast. His hand was

tight on my arm as if he might fall. His teeth were clenched. He leaned toward me as I leaned toward him. There was a terrible silent moment of immense strain as before an explosion.

He forced himself to speak at last. It was the voice of a man crushed by a monstrous burden.

"How do I know you got a gun under your arm?"

"You don't know." My voice was blurred. "You can't be sure."

He waited. I thought he was going to faint.

"That's how it is?" he said.

"That's how it is," I said.

He shut his eyes tight. He shut his mouth tight.

After another five seconds, very slowly, heavily, he managed to take his hand away from my own immensely heavy arm. He looked down at his right hand then, and took it, empty, out of his pocket.

Slowly, with great weight, we turned away from each other and started walking blind, completely blind, in the dark.

The midnight Passenger-to-be-picked-up flare sputtered on the tracks. Only when the train was pulling out of the station did I lean from the open Pullman door and look back.

The old man was seated there with his chair tilted against the station wall, with his faded blue pants and shirt and his sun-baked face and his sun-bleached eyes. He did not glance at me as the train slid past. He was gazing east along the empty rails where tomorrow or the next day or the day after the day after that, a train, some train, any train, might fly by here, might slow, might stop. His face was fixed, his eyes were blindly frozen, toward the east. He looked a hundred years old.

The train wailed.

Suddenly old myself, I leaned out, squinting.

Now the darkness that had brought us together stood between. The old man, the station, the town, the forest, were lost in the night.

For an hour I stood in the roaring blast staring back at all that darkness.

9

A SCENT OF SARSAPARILLA

Mr. William Finch stood quietly in the dark and blowing attic all morning and afternoon for three days. For three days in late November, he stood alone, feeling the soft white flakes of Time falling out of the infinite cold steel sky, silently, softly, feathering the roof and powdering the eaves. He stood, eyes shut. The attic, wallowed in seas of wind in the long sunless days, creaked every bone and shook down ancient dusts from its beams and warped timbers and lathings. It was a mass of sighs and torments that ached all about him where he stood sniffing its elegant dry perfumes and feeling of its ancient heritages. Ah. Ah.

Listening, downstairs, his wife Cora could not hear him walk or shift or twitch. She imagined she could only hear him breathe, slowly out and in, like a dusty bellows, alone up there in the attic, high in the windy house.

"Ridiculous," she muttered.

When he hurried down for lunch the third afternoon, he smiled at the bleak walls, the chipped plates, the scratched silverware, and even at his wife!

"What's all the excitement?" she demanded.

Originally published in *Star Science Fiction Stories #1,* published by Ballantine Books, Inc.

"Good spirits is all. Wonderful spirits!" he laughed. He seemed almost hysterical with joy. He was seething in a great warm ferment which, obviously, he had trouble concealing. His wife frowned.

"What's that *smell?*"

"Smell, smell, smell?"

"Sarsaparilla." She sniffed suspiciously. "That's what it is!"

"Oh, it couldn't be!" His hysterical happiness stopped as quickly as if she'd switched him off. He seemed stunned, ill at ease, and suddenly very careful.

"Where did you go this morning?" she asked.

"You *know* I was cleaning the attic."

"Mooning over a lot of trash. I didn't hear a sound. Thought maybe you weren't in the attic at all. What's that?" She pointed.

"Well, now how did *those* get there?" he asked the world.

He peered down at the pair of black spring-metal bicycle clips that bound his thin pants cuffs to his bony ankles.

"Found them in the attic," he answered himself. "Remember when we got out on the gravel road in the early morning on our tandem bike, Cora, forty years ago, everything fresh and new?"

"If you don't finish that attic today, I'll come up and toss everything out myself."

"Oh, no," he cried. "I have everything the way I want it!"

She looked at him coldly.

"Cora," he said, eating his lunch, relaxing, beginning to enthuse again, "you know what attics are? They're Time Machines, in which old, dim-witted men like me can travel back forty years to a time when it was summer all year round and children raided ice wagons. Remember how it tasted? You held the ice in your handkerchief. It was like sucking the flavor of linen and snow at the same time."

Cora fidgeted.

It's not impossible, he thought, half closing his eyes, trying to see it and build it. Consider an attic. Its very atmosphere is Time. It deals in other years, the cocoons and chrysalises of another age. All the bureau drawers are little coffins where a thousand

yesterdays lie in state. Oh, the attic's a dark, friendly place, full of Time, and if you stand in the very center of it, straight and tall, squinting your eyes, and thinking and thinking, and smelling the Past, and putting out your hands to feel of Long Ago, why, it . . .

He stopped, realizing he had spoken some of this aloud. Cora was eating rapidly.

"Well, wouldn't it be interesting," he asked the part in her hair, "if Time Travel *could* occur? And what more logical, proper place for it to happen than in an attic like *ours,* eh?"

"It's not always summer back in the old days," she said. "It's just your crazy memory. You remember all the good things and forget the bad. It wasn't always summer."

"Figuratively speaking, Cora, it was."

"Wasn't."

"What I mean is this," he said, whispering excitedly, bending forward to see the image he was tracing on the blank dining-room wall. "If you rode your unicycle carefully between the years, balancing, hands out, careful, careful, if you rode from year to year, spent a week in 1909, a day in 1900, a month or a fortnight somewhere else, 1905, 1898, you could stay with summer the rest of your life."

"Unicycle?"

"You know, one of those tall chromium one-wheeled bikes, single-seater, the performers ride in vaudeville shows, juggling. Balance, true balance, it takes, not to fall off, to keep the bright objects flying in the air, beautiful, up and up, a light, a flash, a sparkle, a bomb of brilliant colors, red, yellow, blue, green, white, gold; all the Junes and Julys and Augusts that ever were, in the air, about you, at once, hardly touching your hands, flying, suspended, and you, smiling, among them. Balance, Cora, *balance.*"

"Blah," she said, "blah, blah." And added, "blah!"

He climbed the long cold stairs to the attic, shivering.

There were nights in winter when he woke with porcelain in

his bones, with cool chimes blowing in his ears, with frost piercing his nerves in a raw illumination like white-cold fireworks exploding and showering down in flaming snows upon a silent land deep in his subconscious. He was cold, cold, cold, and it would take a score of endless summers, with their green torches and bronze suns to thaw him free of his wintry sheath. He was a great tasteless chunk of brittle ice, a snowman put to bed each night, full of confetti dreams, tumbles of crystal and flurry. And there lay winter outside forever, a great leaden wine press smashing down its colorless lid of sky, squashing them all like so many grapes, mashing color and sense and being from everyone, save the children who fled on skis and toboggans down mirrored hills which reflected the crushing iron shield that hung lower above town each day and every eternal night.

Mr. Finch lifted the attic trap door. But here, *here*. A dust of summer sprang up about him. The attic dust simmered with heat left over from other seasons. Quietly, he shut the trap door down.

He began to smile.

The attic was quiet as a thundercloud before a storm. On occasion, Cora Finch heard her husband murmuring, murmuring, high up there.

At five in the afternoon, singing *My Isle of Golden Dreams,* Mr. Finch flipped a crisp new straw hat in the kitchen door. "Boo!"

"Did you sleep all afternoon?" snapped his wife. "I called up at you four times and no answer."

"Sleep?" He considered this and laughed, then put his hand quickly over his mouth. "Well, I guess I did."

Suddenly she saw him. "My God!" she cried, "where'd you get that coat?"

He wore a red candy-striped coat, a high white, choking collar and ice cream pants. You could smell the straw hat like a handful of fresh hay fanned in the air.

"Found 'em in an old trunk."

She sniffed. "Don't smell of moth balls. Looks brand-new."

"Oh, no!" he said hastily. He looked stiff and uncomfortable as she eyed his costume.

"This isn't a summer-stock company," she said.

"Can't a fellow have a little fun?"

"That's all you've ever had." She slammed the oven door. "While I've stayed home and knitted, lord knows, you've been down at the store helping ladies' elbows in and out doors."

He refused to be bothered. "Cora." He looked deep into the crackling straw hat. "Wouldn't it be nice to take a Sunday walk the way we used to do, with your silk parasol and your long dress whishing along, and sit on those wire-legged chairs at the soda parlor and smell the drugstore the way they used to smell? Why don't drugstores smell that way any more? And order two sarsaparillas for us, Cora, and then ride out in our 1910 Ford to Hannahan's Pier for a box supper and listen to the brass band. How about it?"

"Supper's ready. Take that dreadful uniform off."

"If you could make a wish and take a ride on those oak-laned country roads like they had before cars started rushing, would you *do* it?" he insisted, watching her.

"Those old roads were dirty. We came home looking like Africans. Anyway," she picked up a sugar jar and shook it, "this morning I had forty dollars here. Now it's gone! Don't tell me you ordered those clothes from a costume house. They're brandnew; they didn't come from any trunk!"

"I'm——" he said.

She raved for half an hour, but he could not bring himself to say anything. The November wind shook the house and as she talked, the snows of winter began to fall again in the cold steel sky.

"Answer me!" she cried. "Are you crazy, spending our money that way, on clothes you can't wear?"

"The attic," he started to say.

She walked off and sat in the living room.

The snow was falling fast now and it was a cold dark November evening. She heard him climb up the stepladder, slowly, into

the attic, into that dusty place of other years, into that black place of costumes and props and Time, into a world separate from this world below.

He closed the trap door down. The flashlight, snapped on, was company enough. Yes, here was all of Time compressed in a Japanese paper flower. At the touch of memory, everything would unfold into the clear water of the mind, in beautiful blooms, in spring breezes, larger than life. Each of the bureau drawers slid forth, might contain aunts and cousins and grand-mamas, ermined in dust. Yes, Time was here. You could feel it breathing, an atmospheric instead of a mechanical clock.

Now the house below was as remote as another day in the past. He half shut his eyes and looked and looked on every side of the waiting attic.

Here, in prismed chandelier, were rainbows and mornings and noons as bright as new rivers flowing endlessly back through time. His flashlight caught and flickered them alive, the rainbows leapt up to curve the shadows back with colors, with colors like plums and strawberries and Concord grapes, with colors like cut lemons and the sky where the clouds drew off after storming and the blue was there. And the dust of the attic was incense burning and all of time burning, and all you need do was peer into the flames. It was indeed a great machine of Time, this attic, he knew, he felt, he was sure, and if you touched prisms here, door-knobs there, plucked tassels, chimed crystals, swirled dust, punched trunk hasps and gusted the vox humana of the old hearth bellows until it puffed the soot of a thousand ancient fires into your eyes, if, indeed, you played this instrument, this warm machine of parts, if you fondled all of its bits and pieces, its le-vers and changers and movers, then, then, *then!*

He thrust out his hands to orchestrate, to conduct, to flourish. There was music in his head, in his mouth shut tight, and he played the great machine, the thunderously silent organ, bass, tenor, soprano, low, high, and at last, at last, a chord that shud-dered him so that he had to shut his eyes.

About nine o'clock that night she heard him calling, "Cora!"
She went upstairs. His head peered down at her from above,
smiling at her. He waved his hat. "Good-by, Cora."

"What do you mean?" she cried.

"I've thought it over for three days and I'm saying good-by."

"Come down out of there, you fool!"

"I drew five hundred dollars from the bank yesterday. I've
been thinking about this. And then when *it* happened, well . . .
Cora . . ." He shoved his eager hand down. "For the last time,
will you come along with me?"

"In the attic? Hand down that stepladder, William Finch. I'll
climb up there and run you out of that filthy place!"

"I'm going to Hannahan's Pier for a bowl of clam chowder,"
he said. "And I'm requesting the brass band to play 'Moonlight
Bay.' Oh, come on, Cora . . ." He motioned his extended hand.

She simply stared at his gentle, questioning face.

"Good-by," he said.

He waved gently, gently. Then his face was gone, the straw
hat was gone.

"William!" she screamed.

The attic was dark and silent.

Shrieking, she ran and got a chair and used it to groan her
way up into the musty darkness. She flourished a flashlight. "William! William!"

The dark spaces were empty. A winter wind shook the house.

Then she saw the far west attic window, ajar.

She fumbled over to it. She hesitated, held her breath. Then,
slowly, she opened it. The ladder was placed outside the window,
leading down onto a porch roof.

She pulled back from the window.

Outside the opened frame the apple trees shone bright green,
it was twilight of a summer day in July. Faintly, she heard explosions, firecrackers going off. She heard laughter and distant
voices. Rockets burst in the warm air, softly, red, white, and
blue, fading.

She slammed the window and stood reeling. "William!"

Wintry November light glowed up through the trap in the attic floor behind her. Bent to it, she saw the snow whispering against the cold clear panes down in that November world where she would spend the next thirty years.

She did not go near the window again. She sat alone in the black attic, smelling the one smell that did not seem to fade. It lingered like a sigh of satisfaction, on the air. She took a deep, long breath.

The old, the familiar, the unforgettable scent of drugstore sarsaparilla.

10

ICARUS MONTGOLFIER WRIGHT

He lay on his bed and the wind blew through the window over his ears and over his half-opened mouth so it whispered to him in his dream. It was like the wind of time hollowing the Delphic caves to say what must be said of yesterday, today, tomorrow. Sometimes one voice gave a shout far off away, sometimes two, a dozen, an entire race of men cried out through his mouth, but their words were always the same:

"Look, look, we've done it!"

For suddenly he, they, one or many, were flung in the dream, and flew. The air spread in a soft warm sea where he swam, disbelieving.

"Look, look! It's done!"

But he didn't ask the world to watch; he was only shocking his senses wide to see, taste, smell, touch the air, the wind, the rising moon. He swam alone in the sky. The heavy earth was gone.

But wait, he thought, wait now!

Tonight—what night is this?

The night before, of course. The night before the first flight of a rocket to the Moon. Beyond this room on the baked desert floor one hundred yards away the rocket waits for me.

Originally published in *Fantasy & Science Fiction Magazine*.

Well, does it now? Is there *really* a rocket?

Hold on! he thought, and twisted, turned, sweating, eyes tight, to the wall, the fierce whisper in his teeth. Be certain-sure! You, now, who *are* you?

Me? he thought. *My* name?

Jedediah Prentiss, born 1938, college graduate 1959, licensed rocket pilot, 1965. Jedediah Prentiss . . . Jedediah Prentiss. . . .

The wind whistled his name away! He grabbed for it, yelling.

Then, gone quiet, he waited for the wind to bring his name back. He waited a long while, and there was only silence, and then after a thousand heartbeats he felt motion.

The sky opened out like a soft blue flower. The Aegean Sea stirred soft white fans through a distant wine-colored surf.

In the wash of the waves on the shore, he heard his name.

Icarus.

And again in a breathing whisper.

Icarus.

Someone shook his arm and it was his father saying his name and shaking away the night. And he himself lay small, half-turned to the window and the shore below and the deep sky, feeling the first wind of morning ruffle the golden feathers bedded in amber wax lying by the side of his cot. Golden wings stirred half-alive in his father's arms, and the faint down on his own shoulders quilled trembling as he looked at these wings and beyond them to the cliff.

"Father, how's the wind?"

"Enough for me, but never enough for you. . . ."

"Father, don't worry. The wings seem clumsy now, but my bones in the feathers will make them strong, my blood in the wax will make it live!"

"My blood, my bones too, remember; each man lends his flesh to his children, asking that they tend it well. Promise you'll not go high, Icarus. *The* sun or *my* son, the heat of one, the fever of the other, could melt these wings. Take care!"

And they carried the splendid golden wings into the morning

and heard them whisper in their arms, whisper his name or a name or some name that blew, spun, and settled like a feather on the soft air.

Montgolfier.

His hands touched fiery rope, bright linen, stitched thread gone hot as summer. His hands fed wool and straw to a breathing flame.

Montgolfier.

And his eye soared up along the swell and sway, the oceanic tug and pull, the immensely wafted silver pear still filling with the shimmering tidal airs channeled up from the blaze. Silent as a god tilted slumbering above French countryside, this delicate linen envelope, this swelling sack of oven-baked air would soon pluck itself free. Draughting upward to blue worlds of silence, his mind and his brother's mind would sail with it, muted, serene among island clouds where uncivilized lightnings slept. Into that uncharted gulf and abyss where no birdsong or shout of man could follow, the balloon would hush itself. So cast adrift, he, Montgolfier, and all men, might hear the unmeasured breathing of God and the cathedral tread of eternity.

"Ah . . ." He moved, the crowd moved, shadowed by the warm balloon. "Everything's ready, everything's right. . . ."

Right. His lips twitched in his dream. Right. Hiss, whisper, flutter, rush. Right.

From his father's hands a toy jumped to the ceiling, whirled in its own wind, suspended, while he and his brother stared to see it flicker, rustle, whistle, heard it murmuring their names.

Wright.

Whispering: wind, sky, cloud, space, wing, fly . . .

"Wilbur, Orville? Look, how's *that?*"

Ah. In his sleep, his mouth sighed.

The toy helicopter hummed, bumped the ceiling, murmured eagle, raven, sparrow, robin, hawk; murmured eagle, raven, sparrow, robin, hawk. Whispered eagle, whispered raven, and at last, fluttering to their hands with a susurration, a wash of blow-

ing weather from summers yet to come, with a last whir and exhalation, whispered hawk.

Dreaming, he smiled.

He saw the clouds rush down the Aegean sky.

He felt the balloon sway drunkenly, its great bulk ready for the clear running wind.

He felt the sand hiss up the Atlantic shelves from the soft dunes that might save him if he, a fledgling bird, should fall. The framework struts hummed and chorded like a harp, and himself caught up in its music.

Beyond this room he felt the primed rocket glide on the desert field, its fire-wings folded, its fire-breath kept, held ready to speak for three billion men. In a moment he would wake and walk slowly out to that rocket.

And stand on the rim of the cliff.

Stand cool in the shadow of the warm balloon.

Stand whipped by tidal sands drummed over Kitty Hawk.

And sheathe his boy's wrists, arms, hands, fingers with golden wings in golden wax.

And touch for a final time the captured breath of man, the warm gasp of awe and wonder siphoned and sewn to lift their dreams.

And spark the gasoline engine.

And take his father's hand and wish him well with his own wings, flexed and ready, here on the precipice.

Then whirl and jump.

Then cut the cords to free the great balloon.

Then rev the motor, prop the plane on air.

And crack the switch, to fire the rocket fuse.

And together in a single leap, swim, rush, flail, jump, sail, and glide, upturned to sun, moon, stars, they would go above Atlantic, Mediterranean; over country, wilderness, city, town; in gaseous silence, riffling feather, rattle-drum frame, in volcanic eruption, in timid, sputtering roar; in start, jar, hesitation, then steady ascension, beautifully held, wondrously transported, they would laugh and cry each his own name to himself. Or shout the

names of others unborn or others long-dead and blown away by the wine wind or the salt wind or the silent hush of balloon wind or the wind of chemical fire. Each feeling the bright feathers stir and bud deep-buried and thrusting to burst from their riven shoulder blades! Each leaving behind the echo of their flying, a sound to encircle, recircle the earth in the winds and speak again in other years to the sons of the sons of their sons, asleep but hearing the restless midnight sky.

Up, yet further up, higher, higher! A spring tide, a summer flood, an unending river of wings!

A bell rang softly.

No, he whispered, I'll wake in a moment. Wait . . .

The Aegean slid away below the window, gone; the Atlantic dunes, the French countryside, dissolved down to New Mexico desert. In his room near his cot stirred no plumes in golden wax. Outside, no wind-sculpted pear, no trap-drum butterfly machine. Outside only a rocket, a combustible dream, waiting for the friction of his hand to set it off.

In the last moment of sleep someone asked his name.

Quietly, he gave the answer as he had heard it during the hours from midnight on.

"Icarus Montgolfier Wright."

He repeated it slowly so the questioner might remember the order and spelling down to the last incredible letter.

"Icarus Montgolfier Wright.

"Born: nine hundred years before Christ. Grammar school: Paris, 1783. High school, college: Kitty Hawk, 1903. Graduation from Earth to Moon: this day, God willing, August 1, 1970. Death and burial, with luck, on Mars, summer 1999 in the Year of Our Lord."

Then he let himself drift awake.

Moments later, crossing the desert Tarmac, he heard someone shouting again and again and again.

And if no one was there or if someone was there behind him, he could not tell. And whether it was one voice or many, young

or old, near or very far away, rising or falling, whispering or shouting to him all three of his brave new names, he could not tell, either. He did not turn to see.

For the wind was slowly rising and he let it take hold and blow him all the rest of the way across the desert to the rocket which stood waiting there.

11

THE HEADPIECE

The parcel arrived in the late afternoon mail. Mr. Andrew Lemon knew what was inside by shaking it. It whispered in there like a large hairy tarantula.

It took him some time to get up his courage, tremble the wrappings open, and remove the lid from the white cardboard box.

There the bristly thing lay on its snowy tissue bed, as impersonal as the black horsehair clock springs stuffed in an old sofa. Andrew Lemon chuckled.

"Indians come and gone, left this piece of a massacre behind as a sign, a warning. Well. *There!*"

And he fitted the new patent-leather black shining toupee to his naked scalp. He tugged at it like someone touching his cap to passers-by.

The toupee fit perfectly, covering the neat coin-round hole which marred the top of his brow. Andrew Lemon gazed at the strange man in the mirror and yelled with delight.

"Hey there, who're you? Face's familiar, but, by gosh now, pass you on the street without looking twice! Why? Because, *it's* gone! Darn hole's covered, nobody'd guess it was ever there. Happy New Year, man, that's what it is, Happy New Year!"

Originally published in *Lilliput*, London.

He walked around and around his little apartment, smiling, needing to do something, but not yet ready to open the door and surprise the world. He walked by the mirror, glancing sidewise at someone going past there and each time laughed and shook his head. Then he sat down in the rocker and rocked, grinning, and tried to look at a couple of copies of *Wild West Weekly* and then *Thrilling Movie Magazine*. But he couldn't keep his right hand from crawling up along his face, tremulously, to feel at the rim of that crisp new sedge above his ears.

"Let me buy you a drink, young fellow!"

He opened the fly-specked medicine cabinet and took three gulps from a bottle. Eyes watering, he was on the verge of cutting himself a chew of tobacco when he stopped, listening.

Outside in the dark hallway there was a sound like a field mouse moving softly, daintily on the threadbare carpeting.

"Miss Fremwell!" he said to the mirror.

Suddenly the toupee was off his head and into the box as if, frightened, it had scuttled back there of itself. He clapped the lid down, sweating cold, afraid of even the sound that woman made moving by like a summer breeze.

He tiptoed to a door that was nailed shut in one wall and bent his raw and now furiously blushing head. He heard Miss Fremwell unlock her door and shut it and move delicately about her room with little tinkles of chinaware and chimes of cutlery, turning in a merry-go-round to make her dinner. He backed away from that door that was bolted, locked, latched, and driven shut with its four-inch hard steel nails. He thought of the nights he had flinched in bed, thinking he heard her quietly pulling out the nails, pulling out the nails, touching at the bolts and slithering the latch . . . And how it always took him an hour to turn away toward sleep after that.

Now she would rustle about her room for an hour or so. It would grow dark. The stars would be out and shining when he tapped on her door and asked if she'd sit on the porch or walk in the park. Then the only way she could possibly know of this third blind and staring eye in his head would be to run her hand

in a Braille-like motion there. But her small white fingers had never moved within a thousand miles of that scar which was no more to her than, well, one of those pockmarks off on the full moon tonight. His toe brushed a copy of *Wonder Science Tales*. He snorted. Perhaps if she thought at all of his damaged head—she wrote songs and poems, didn't she, once in a while?—she figured that a long time back a meteor had run and hit him and vanished up there where there were no shrubs or trees, where it was just white, above his eyes. He snorted again and shook his head. Perhaps, perhaps. But however she thought, he would see her only when the sun had set.

He waited another hour, from time to time spitting out the window into the warm summer night.

"Eight-thirty. Here goes."

He opened the hall door and stood for a moment looking back at that nice new toupee hidden in its box. No, he still could not bring himself to wear it.

He stepped along the hall to Miss Naomi Fremwell's door, a door so thinly made it seemed to beat with the sound of her small heart there behind it.

"Miss Fremwell," he whispered.

He wanted to cup her like a small white bird in his great bowled hands, speak soft to her quietness. But then, in wiping the sudden perspiration from his brow, he found again the pit and only at the last quick moment saved himself from falling over, in, and screaming, down! He clapped his hand to that place to cover that emptiness. After he had held his hand tight to the hole for a long moment he was then afraid to pull his hand away. It had changed. Instead of being afraid he might fall in there, he was afraid something terrible, something secret, something private, might gush out and drown him.

He brushed his free hand across her door, disturbing little more than dust.

"Miss Fremwell?"

He looked to see if there were too many lamps lit under her doorsill, the light of which might strike out at him when she

swung the door wide. The very thrust of lamplight alone might knock his hand away, and reveal that sunken wound. Then mightn't she peer through it, like a keyhole, into his life?

The light was dim under the doorsill.

He made a fist of one hand and brought it down gently, three times, on Miss Fremwell's door.

The door opened and moved slowly back.

Later, on the front porch, feverishly adjusting and readjusting his senseless legs, perspiring, he tried to work around to asking her to marry him. When the moon rose high, the hole in his brow looked like a leaf shadow fallen there. If he kept one profile to her, the crater did not show; it was hidden away over on the other side of his world. It seemed that when he did this, though, he only had half as many words and felt only half a man.

"Miss Fremwell," he managed to say at last.

"Yes?" She looked at him as if she didn't quite see him.

"Miss Naomi, I don't suppose you ever really noticed me lately."

She waited. He went on.

"I've been noticing you. Fact is, well, I might as well put it right out on the line and get it over with. We been sitting out here on the porch for quite a few months. I mean we've known each other a long time. Sure, you're a good fifteen years younger than me, but would there be anything wrong with our getting engaged, do you think?"

"Thank you very much, Mr. Lemon," she said quickly. She was very polite. "But I——"

"Oh, I know," he said, edging forward with the words. "I know! It's my head, it's always this darn thing up here on my head!"

She looked at his turned-away profile in the uncertain light.

"Why, no, Mr. Lemon, I don't think I would say that, I don't think that's it at all. I have wondered a bit about it, certainly, but I don't think it's an interference in any way. A friend of mine, a very dear friend, married a man once, I recall, who had

a wooden leg. She told me she didn't even know he had it after a while."

"It's always this darn hole," cried Mr. Lemon bitterly. He took out his plug of tobacco, looked at it as if he might bite it, decided not to, and put it away. He formed a couple of fists and stared at them bleakly as if they were big rocks. "Well, I'll tell you all about it, Miss Naomi. I'll tell you how it happened."

"You don't have to if you don't want."

"I was married once, Miss Naomi. Yes, I was, darn it. And one day my wife she just took hold of a hammer and hit me right on the head!"

Miss Fremwell gasped. It was as if she had been struck herself.

Mr. Lemon brought one clenching fist down through the warm air.

"Yes, ma'am, she hit me straight on with that hammer, she did. I tell you, the world blew up on me. Everything fell down on me. It was like the house coming down in one heap. That one little hammer buried me, *buried* me! The pain? I can't tell you!"

Miss Fremwell turned in on herself. She shut her eyes and thought, biting her lips. Then she said, "Oh, poor Mr. Lemon."

"She did it so calm," said Mr. Lemon, puzzled. "She just stood over me where I lay on the couch and it was a Tuesday afternoon about two o'clock and she said, 'Andrew, wake up!' and I opened my eyes and looked at her is all and then she hit me with that hammer. Oh, Lord."

"But why?" asked Miss Fremwell.

"For no reason, no reason at all. Oh, what an ornery woman."

"But why should she do a thing like that?" said Miss Fremwell.

"I told you: for no reason."

"Was she crazy?"

"Must of been. Oh, yes, she *must* of been."

"Did you prosecute her?"

"Well, no, I didn't. After all, she didn't know what she was doing."

"Did it knock you out?"

Mr. Lemon paused and there it was again, so clear, so tall, in his mind, the old thought of it. Seeing it there, he put it in words.

"No, I remember just standing up. I stood up and I said to her, 'What'd you do?' and I stumbled toward her. There was a mirror. I saw the hole in my head, deep, and blood coming out. It made an Indian of me. She just stood there, my wife did. And at last she screamed three kinds of horror and dropped that hammer on the floor and ran out the door."

"Did you faint then?"

"No. I didn't faint. I got out on the street some way and I mumbled to somebody I needed a doctor. I got on a bus, mind you, a bus! And paid my fare! And said to leave me by some doctor's house downtown. Everybody screamed, I tell you. I got sort of weak then, and next thing I knew the doctor was working on my head, had it cleaned out like a new thimble, like a bunghole in a barrel. . . ."

He reached up and touched that spot now, fingers hovering over it as a delicate tongue hovers over the vacated area where once grew a fine tooth.

"A neat job. The doctor kept staring at me too, as if he expected me to fall down dead any minute."

"How long did you stay in the hospital?"

"Two days. Then I was up and around, feeling no better, no worse. By that time my wife had picked up and skedaddled."

"Oh, my goodness, my goodness," said Miss Fremwell, recovering her breath. "My heart's going like an egg beater. I can hear and feel and see it all, Mr. Lemon. Why, why, oh, *why* did she do it?"

"I already told you, for no reason I could see. She was just took with a notion, I guess."

"But there must have been an argument——?"

Blood drummed in Mr. Lemon's cheeks. He felt that place up there on his head glow like a fiery crater. "There wasn't no argument. I was just sitting, peaceful as you please. I like to sit, my shoes off, my shirt unbuttoned, afternoons."

"Did you—did you know any other women?"

"No, never, none!"

"You didn't—drink?"

"Just a nip once in a while, you know how it is."

"Did you gamble?"

"No, no, no!"

"But a hole punched in your head like that, Mr. Lemon, my land, my land! All over nothing?"

"You women are all alike. You see something and right off you expect the worst. I tell you there was no reason. She just fancied hammers."

"What did she say before she hit you?"

"Just 'Wake up, Andrew.'"

"No, before that."

"Nothing. Not for half an hour or an hour, anyway. Oh, she said something about wanting to go shopping for something or other, but I said it was too hot. I'd better lie down, I didn't feel so good. She didn't appreciate how I felt. She must have got mad and thought about it for an hour and grabbed that hammer and come in and gone kersmash. I think the weather got her too."

Miss Fremwell sat back thoughtfully in the lattice shadow, her brows moving slowly up and then slowly down.

"How long were you married to her?"

"A year. I remember we got married in July and in July it was I got sick."

"Sick?"

"I wasn't a well man. I worked in a garage. Then I got these backaches so I couldn't work and had to lie down afternoons. Ellie, she worked in the First National Bank."

"I see," said Miss Fremwell.

"What?"

"Nothing," she said.

"I'm an easy man to get on with. I don't talk too much. I'm easygoing and relaxed. I don't waste money. I'm economical. Even Ellie had to admit that. I don't argue. Why, sometimes Ellie would jaw at me and jaw at me, like bouncing a ball hard

on a house, but me not bouncing back. I just sat. I took it easy. What's the use of always stirring around and talking, right?"

Miss Fremwell looked over at Mr. Lemon's brow in the moonlight. Her lips moved, but he could not hear what she said.

Suddenly she straightened up and took a deep breath and blinked around surprised to see the world out beyond the porch lattice. The sounds of traffic came in to the porch now, as if they had been tuned up; they had been so quiet for a time. Miss Fremwell took a deep breath and let it out.

"As you yourself say, Mr. Lemon, nobody ever got anywhere arguing."

"Right!" he said. "I'm easygoing, I tell you——"

But Miss Fremwell's eyes were lidded now and her mouth was strange. He sensed this and tapered off.

A night wind blew fluttering her light summer dress and the sleeves of his shirt.

"It's late," said Miss Fremwell.

"Only nine o'clock!"

"I have to get up early tomorrow."

"But you haven't answered my question yet, Miss Fremwell."

"Question?" She blinked. "Oh, the question. Yes." She rose from the wicker seat. She hunted around in the dark for the screen-door knob. "Oh now, Mr. Lemon, let me think it over."

"That's fair enough," he said. "No use arguing, is there?"

The screen door closed. He heard her find her way down the dark warm hall. He breathed shallowly, feeling of the third eye in his head, the eye that saw nothing.

He felt a vague unhappiness shift around inside his chest like an illness brought on by too much talking. And then he thought of the fresh white gift box waiting with its lid on in his room. He quickened. Opening the screen door, he walked down the silent hall and went into his room. Inside he slipped and almost fell on a slick copy of *True Romance Tales*. He switched on the light excitedly, smiling, fumbled the box open, and lifted the toupee from the tissues. He stood before the bright mirror and followed directions with the spirit gum and tapes and tucked it here and

stuck it there and shifted it again and combed it neat. Then he opened the door and walked along the hall to knock for Miss Fremwell.

"Miss Naomi?" he called, smiling.

The light under her door clicked out at the sound of his voice. He stared at the dark keyhole with disbelief.

"Oh, Miss Naomi?" he said again, quickly.

Nothing happened in the room. It was dark. After a moment he tried the knob experimentally. The knob rattled. He heard Miss Fremwell sigh. He heard her say something. Again the words were lost. Her small feet tapped to the door. The light came on.

"Yes?" she said, behind the panel.

"Look, Miss Naomi," he entreated. "Open the door. Look."

The bolt of the door snapped back. She jerked the door open about an inch. One of her eyes looked at him sharply.

"Look," he announced proudly, adjusting the toupee so it very definitely covered the sunken crater. He imagined he saw himself in her bureau mirror and was pleased. "Look here, Miss Fremwell!"

She opened the door a bit wider and looked. Then she slammed the door and locked it. From behind the thin paneling her voice was toneless.

"I can still see the hole, Mr. Lemon," she said.

12
DARK THEY WERE, AND GOLDEN-EYED

The rocket metal cooled in the meadow winds. Its lid gave a bulging *pop*. From its clock interior stepped a man, a woman, and three children. The other passengers whispered away across the Martian meadow, leaving the man alone among his family.

The man felt his hair flutter and the tissues of his body draw tight as if he were standing at the center of a vacuum. His wife, before him, seemed almost to whirl away in smoke. The children, small seeds, might at any instant be sown to all the Martian climes.

The children looked up at him, as people look to the sun to tell what time of their life it is. His face was cold.

"What's wrong?" asked his wife.

"Let's get back on the rocket."

"Go back to Earth?"

"Yes! Listen!"

The wind blew as if to flake away their identities. At any moment the Martian air might draw his soul from him, as marrow comes from a white bone. He felt submerged in a chemical that could dissolve his intellect and burn away his past.

They looked at Martian hills that time had worn with a crushing pressure of years. They saw the old cities, lost in their meadows, lying like children's delicate bones among the blowing lakes of grass.

"Chin up, Harry," said his wife. "It's too late. We've come over sixty million miles."

The children with their yellow hair hollered at the deep dome of Martian sky. There was no answer but the racing hiss of wind through the stiff grass.

He picked up the luggage in his cold hands. "Here we go," he said—a man standing on the edge of a sea, ready to wade in and be drowned.

They walked into town.

Their name was Bittering. Harry and his wife Cora; Dan, Laura, and David. They built a small white cottage and ate good breakfasts there, but the fear was never gone. It lay with Mr. Bittering and Mrs. Bittering, a third unbidden partner at every midnight talk, at every dawn awakening.

"I feel like a salt crystal," he said, "in a mountain stream, being washed away. We don't belong here. We're Earth people. This is Mars. It was meant for Martians. For heaven's sake, Cora, let's buy tickets for home!"

But she only shook her head. "One day the atom bomb will fix Earth. Then we'll be safe here."

"Safe and insane!"

Tick-tock, seven o'clock sang the voice-clock; *time to get up*. And they did.

Something made him check everything each morning—warm hearth, potted blood-geraniums—precisely as if he expected something to be amiss. The morning paper was toast-warm from the 6 A.M. Earth rocket. He broke its seal and tilted it at his breakfast place. He forced himself to be convivial.

"Colonial days all over again," he declared. "Why, in ten years there'll be a million Earthmen on Mars. Big cities, everything! They said we'd fail. Said the Martians would resent our inva-

sion. But did we find any Martians? Not a living soul! Oh, we found their empty cities, but no one in them. Right?"

A river of wind submerged the house. When the windows ceased rattling Mr. Bittering swallowed and looked at the children.

"I don't know," said David. "Maybe there're Martians around we don't see. Sometimes nights I think I hear 'em. I hear the wind. The sand hits my window. I get scared. And I see those towns way up in the mountains where the Martians lived a long time ago. And I think I see things moving around those towns, Papa. And I wonder if those Martians *mind* us living here. I wonder if they won't do something to us for coming here."

"Nonsense!" Mr. Bittering looked out the windows. "We're clean, decent people." He looked at his children. "All dead cities have some kind of ghosts in them. Memories, I mean." He stared at the hills. "You see a staircase and you wonder what Martians looked like climbing it. You see Martian paintings and you wonder what the painter was like. You make a little ghost in your mind, a memory. It's quite natural. Imagination." He stopped. "You haven't been prowling up in those ruins, have you?"

"No, Papa." David looked at his shoes.

"See that you stay away from them. Pass the jam."

"Just the same," said little David, "I bet something happens."

Something happened that afternoon.

Laura stumbled through the settlement, crying. She dashed blindly onto the porch.

"Mother, Father—the war, Earth!" she sobbed. "A radio flash just came. Atom bombs hit New York! All the space rockets blown up. No more rockets to Mars, ever!"

"Oh, Harry!" The mother held onto her husband and daughter.

"Are you sure, Laura?" asked the father quietly.

Laura wept. "We're stranded on Mars, forever and ever!"

For a long time there was only the sound of the wind in the late afternoon.

Alone, thought Bittering. Only a thousand of us here. No way

back. No way. No way. Sweat poured from his face and his hands and his body; he was drenched in the hotness of his fear. He wanted to strike Laura, cry, "No, you're lying! The rockets will come back!" Instead, he stroked Laura's head against him and said, "The rockets will get through someday."

"Father, what will we do?"

"Go about our business, of course. Raise crops and children. Wait. Keep things going until the war ends and the rockets come again."

The two boys stepped out onto the porch.

"Children," he said, sitting there, looking beyond them, "I've something to tell you."

"We know," they said.

In the following days, Bittering wandered often through the garden to stand alone in his fear. As long as the rockets had spun a silver web across space, he had been able to accept Mars. For he had always told himself: Tomorrow, if I want, I can buy a ticket and go back to Earth.

But now: The web gone, the rockets lying in jigsaw heaps of molten girder and unsnaked wire. Earth people left to the strangeness of Mars, the cinnamon dusts and wine airs, to be baked like gingerbread shapes in Martian summers, put into harvested storage by Martian winters. What would happen to him, the others? This was the moment Mars had waited for. Now it would eat them.

He got down on his knees in the flower bed, a spade in his nervous hands. Work, he thought, work and forget.

He glanced up from the garden to the Martian mountains. He thought of the proud old Martian names that had once been on those peaks. Earthmen, dropping from the sky, had gazed upon hills, rivers, Martian seas left nameless in spite of names. Once Martians had built cities, named cities; climbed mountains, named mountains; sailed seas, named seas. Mountains melted, seas drained, cities tumbled. In spite of this, the Earthmen had

felt a silent guilt at putting new names to these ancient hills and valleys.

Nevertheless, man lives by symbol and label. The names were given.

Mr. Bittering felt very alone in his garden under the Martian sun, anachronism bent here, planting Earth flowers in a wild soil.

Think. Keep thinking. Different things. Keep your mind free of Earth, the atom war, the lost rockets.

He perspired. He glanced about. No one watching. He removed his tie. Pretty bold, he thought. First your coat off, now your tie. He hung it neatly on a peach tree he had imported as a sapling from Massachusetts.

He returned to his philosophy of names and mountains. The Earthmen had changed names. Now there were Hormel Valleys, Roosevelt Seas, Ford Hills, Vanderbilt Plateaus, Rockefeller Rivers, on Mars. It wasn't right. The American settlers had shown wisdom, using old Indian prairie names: Wisconsin, Minnesota, Idaho, Ohio, Utah, Milwaukee, Waukegan, Osseo. The old names, the old meanings.

Staring at the mountains wildly, he thought: Are you up there? All the dead ones, you Martians? Well, here we are, alone, cut off! Come down, move us out! We're helpless!

The wind blew a shower of peach blossoms.

He put out his sun-browned hand, gave a small cry. He touched the blossoms, picked them up. He turned them, he touched them again and again. Then he shouted for his wife.

"Cora!"

She appeared at a window. He ran to her.

"Cora, these blossoms!"

She handled them.

"Do you see? They're different. They've changed! They're not peach blossoms any more!"

"Look all right to me," she said.

"They're not. They're *wrong!* I can't tell how. An extra petal, a leaf, something, the color, the smell!"

The children ran out in time to see their father hurrying about

the garden, pulling up radishes, onions, and carrots from their beds.

"Cora, come look!"

They handled the onions, the radishes, the carrots among them.

"Do they look like carrots?"

"Yes . . . no." She hesitated. "I don't know."

"They're changed."

"Perhaps."

"You know they have! Onions but not onions, carrots but not carrots. Taste: the same but different. Smell: not like it used to be." He felt his heart pounding, and he was afraid. He dug his fingers into the earth. "Cora, what's happening? What is it? We've got to get away from this." He ran across the garden. Each tree felt his touch. "The roses. The roses. They're turning green!"

And they stood looking at the green roses.

And two days later Dan came running. "Come see the cow. I was milking her and I saw it. Come on!"

They stood in the shed and looked at their one cow.

It was growing a third horn.

And the lawn in front of their house very quietly and slowly was coloring itself like spring violets. Seed from Earth but growing up a soft purple.

"We must get away," said Bittering. "We'll eat this stuff and then we'll change—who knows to what? I can't let it happen. There's only one thing to do. Burn this food!"

"It's not poisoned."

"But it is. Subtly, very subtly. A little bit. A very little bit. We mustn't touch it."

He looked with dismay at their house. "Even the house. The wind's done something to it. The air's burned it. The fog at night. The boards, all warped out of shape. It's not an Earthman's house any more."

"Oh, your imagination!"

He put on his coat and tie. "I'm going into town. We've got to do something now. I'll be back."

"Wait, Harry!" his wife cried.

But he was gone.

In town, on the shadowy step of the grocery store, the men sat with their hands on their knees, conversing with great leisure and ease.

Mr. Bittering wanted to fire a pistol in the air.

What are you doing, you fools! he thought. Sitting here! You've heard the news—we're stranded on this planet. Well, move! Aren't you frightened? Aren't you afraid? What are you going to do?

"Hello, Harry," said everyone.

"Look," he said to them. "You did hear the news, the other day, didn't you?"

They nodded and laughed. "Sure. Sure, Harry."

"What are you going to do about it?"

"Do, Harry, do? What *can* we do?"

"Build a rocket, that's what!"

"A rocket, Harry? To go back to all that trouble? Oh, Harry!"

"But you *must* want to go back. Have you noticed the peach blossoms, the onions, the grass?"

"Why, yes, Harry, seems we did," said one of the men.

"Doesn't it scare you?"

"Can't recall that it did much, Harry."

"Idiots!"

"Now, Harry."

Bittering wanted to cry. "You've got to work with me. If we stay here, we'll all change. The air. Don't you smell it? Something in the air. A Martian virus, maybe; some seed, or a pollen. Listen to me!"

They stared at him.

"Sam," he said to one of them.

"Yes, Harry?"

"Will you help me build a rocket?"

"Harry, I got a whole load of metal and some blueprints. You want to work in my metal shop on a rocket, you're welcome. I'll sell you that metal for five hundred dollars. You should be able to

construct a right pretty rocket, if you work alone, in about thirty years."

Everyone laughed.

"Don't laugh."

Sam looked at him with quiet good humor.

"Sam," Bittering said. "Your eyes——"

"What about them, Harry?"

"Didn't they used to be grey?"

"Well now, I don't remember."

"They were, weren't they?"

"Why do you ask, Harry?"

"Because now they're kind of yellow-colored."

"Is that so, Harry?" Sam said, casually.

"And you're taller and thinner——"

"You might be right, Harry."

"Sam, you shouldn't have yellow eyes."

"Harry, what color eyes have *you* got?" Sam said.

"My eyes? They're blue, of course."

"Here you are, Harry." Sam handed him a pocket mirror. "Take a look at yourself."

Mr. Bittering hesitated, and then raised the mirror to his face.

There were little, very dim flecks of new gold captured in the blue of his eyes.

"Now look what you've done," said Sam a moment later. "You've broken my mirror."

Harry Bittering moved into the metal shop and began to build the rocket. Men stood in the open door and talked and joked without raising their voices. Once in a while they gave him a hand on lifting something. But mostly they just idled and watched him with their yellowing eyes.

"It's suppertime, Harry," they said.

His wife appeared with his supper in a wicker basket.

"I won't touch it," he said. "I'll eat only food from our Deepfreeze. Food that came from Earth. Nothing from our garden."

His wife stood watching him. "You can't build a rocket."

"I worked in a shop once, when I was twenty. I know metal. Once I get it started, the others will help," he said, not looking at her, laying out the blueprints.

"Harry, Harry," she said, helplessly.

"We've got to get away, Cora. We've *got* to!"

The nights were full of wind that blew down the empty moon-lit sea meadows past the little white chess cities lying for their twelve-thousandth year in the shallows. In the Earthmen's settlement, the Bittering house shook with a feeling of change.

Lying abed, Mr. Bittering felt his bones shifted, shaped, melted like gold. His wife, lying beside him, was dark from many sunny afternoons. Dark she was, and golden-eyed, burnt almost black by the sun, sleeping, and the children metallic in their beds, and the wind roaring forlorn and changing through the old peach trees, the violet grass, shaking out green rose petals.

The fear would not be stopped. It had his throat and heart. It dripped in a wetness of the arm and the temple and the trembling palm.

A green star rose in the east.

A strange word emerged from Mr. Bittering's lips.

"*Iorrt. Iorrt.*" He repeated it.

It was a Martian word. He knew no Martian.

In the middle of the night he arose and dialed a call through to Simpson, the archeologist.

"Simpson, what does the word *Iorrt* mean?"

"Why that's the old Martian word for our planet Earth. Why?"

"No special reason."

The telephone slipped from his hand.

"Hello, hello, hello, hello," it kept saying while he sat gazing out at the green star. "Bittering? Harry, are you there?"

The days were full of metal sound. He laid the frame of the rocket with the reluctant help of three indifferent men. He grew very tired in an hour or so and had to sit down.

"The altitude," laughed a man.

"Are you *eating*, Harry?" asked another.

"I'm eating," he said, angrily.

"From your Deepfreeze?"

"Yes!"

"You're getting thinner, Harry."

"I'm not!"

"And taller."

"Liar!"

His wife took him aside a few days later. "Harry, I've used up all the food in the Deepfreeze. There's nothing left. I'll have to make sandwiches using food grown on Mars."

He sat down heavily.

"You must eat," she said. "You're weak."

"Yes," he said.

He took a sandwich, opened it, looked at it, and began to nibble at it.

"And take the rest of the day off," she said. "It's hot. The children want to swim in the canals and hike. Please come along."

"I can't waste time. This is a crisis!"

"Just for an hour," she urged. "A swim'll do you good."

He rose, sweating. "All right, all right. Leave me alone. I'll come."

"Good for you, Harry."

The sun was hot, the day quiet. There was only an immense staring burn upon the land. They moved along the canal, the father, the mother, the racing children in their swim suits. They stopped and ate meat sandwiches. He saw their skin baking brown. And he saw the yellow eyes of his wife and his children, their eyes that were never yellow before. A few tremblings shook him, but were carried off in waves of pleasant heat as he lay in the sun. He was too tired to be afraid.

"Cora, how long have your eyes been yellow?"

She was bewildered. "Always, I guess."

"They didn't change from brown in the last three months?"

She bit her lips. "No. Why do you ask?"

"Never mind."

They sat there.

"The children's eyes," he said. "They're yellow, too."

"Sometimes growing children's eyes change color."

"Maybe *we're* children, too. At least to Mars. That's a thought." He laughed. "Think I'll swim."

They leaped into the canal water, and he let himself sink down and down to the bottom like a golden statue and lie there in green silence. All was water-quiet and deep, all was peace. He felt the steady, slow current drift him easily.

If I lie here long enough, he thought, the water will work and eat away my flesh until the bones show like coral. Just my skeleton left. And then the water can build on that skeleton—green things, deep water things, red things, yellow things. Change. Change. Slow, deep, silent change. And isn't that what it is up *there?*

He saw the sky submerged above him, the sun made Martian by atmosphere and time and space.

Up there, a big river, he thought, a Martian river, all of us lying deep in it, in our pebble houses, in our sunken boulder houses, like crayfish hidden, and the water washing away our old bodies and lengthening the bones and——

He let himself drift up through the soft light.

Dan sat on the edge of the canal, regarding his father seriously. "*Utha,*" he said.

"What?" asked his father.

The boy smiled. "You know. *Utha's* the Martian word for 'father.'"

"Where did you learn it?"

"I don't know. Around. *Utha!*"

"What do you want?"

The boy hesitated. "I—I want to change my name."

"Change it?"

"Yes."

His mother swam over. "What's wrong with Dan for a name?"

Dan fidgeted. "The other day you called Dan, Dan, Dan. I

didn't even hear. I said to myself, That's not my name. I've a new name I want to use."

Mr. Bittering held to the side of the canal, his body cold and his heart pounding slowly. "What is this new name?"

"Linnl. Isn't that a good name? Can I use it? Can't I, please?"

Mr. Bittering put his hand to his head. He thought of the silly rocket, himself working alone, himself alone even among his family, so alone.

He heard his wife say, "Why not?"

He heard himself say, "Yes, you can use it."

"Yaaa!" screamed the boy. "I'm Linnl, Linnl!"

Racing down the meadowlands, he danced and shouted.

Mr. Bittering looked at his wife. "Why did we do that?"

"I don't know," she said. "It just seemed like a good idea."

They walked into the hills. They strolled on old mosaic paths, beside still pumping fountains. The paths were covered with a thin film of cool water all summer long. You kept your bare feet cool all the day, splashing as in a creek, wading.

They came to a small deserted Martian villa with a good view of the valley. It was on top of a hill. Blue marble halls, large murals, a swimming pool. It was refreshing in this hot summertime. The Martians hadn't believed in large cities.

"How nice," said Mrs. Bittering, "if we could move up here to this villa for the summer."

"Come on," he said. "We're going back to town. There's work to be done on the rocket."

But as he worked that night, the thought of the cool blue marble villa entered his mind. As the hours passed, the rocket seemed less important.

In the flow of days and weeks, the rocket receded and dwindled. The old fever was gone. It frightened him to think he had let it slip this way. But somehow the heat, the air, the working conditions——

He heard the men murmuring on the porch of his metal shop.

"Everyone's going. You heard?"

"All going. That's right."

Bittering came out. "Going where?" He saw a couple of trucks, loaded with children and furniture, drive down the dusty street.

"Up to the villas," said the man.

"Yeah, Harry. I'm going. So is Sam. Aren't you, Sam?"

"That's right, Harry. What about you?"

"I've got work to do here."

"Work! You can finish that rocket in the autumn, when it's cooler."

He took a breath. "I got the frame all set up."

"In the autumn is better." Their voices were lazy in the heat.

"Got to work," he said.

"Autumn," they reasoned. And they sounded so sensible, so right.

"Autumn would be best," he thought. "Plenty of time, then."

No! cried part of himself, deep down, put away, locked tight, suffocating. No! No!

"In the autumn," he said.

"Come on, Harry," they all said.

"Yes," he said, feeling his flesh melt in the hot liquid air. "Yes, in the autumn. I'll begin work again then."

"I got a villa near the Tirra Canal," said someone.

"You mean the Roosevelt Canal, don't you?"

"Tirra. The old Martian name."

"But on the map——"

"Forget the map. It's Tirra now. Now I found a place in the Pillan mountains——"

"You mean the Rockefeller range," said Bittering.

"I mean the Pillan mountains," said Sam.

"Yes," said Bittering, buried in the hot, swarming air. "The Pillan mountains."

Everyone worked at loading the truck in the hot, still afternoon of the next day.

Laura, Dan, and David carried packages. Or, as they preferred to be known, Ttil, Linnl, and Werr carried packages.

The furniture was abandoned in the little white cottage.

"It looked just fine in Boston," said the mother. "And here in the cottage. But up at the villa? No. We'll get it when we come back in the autumn."

Bittering himself was quiet.

"I've some ideas on furniture for the villa," he said after a time. "Big, lazy furniture."

"What about your encyclopedia? You're taking it along, surely?"

Mr. Bittering glanced away. "I'll come and get it next week."

They turned to their daughter. "What about your New York dresses?"

The bewildered girl stared. "Why, I don't want them any more."

They shut off the gas, the water, they locked the doors and walked away. Father peered into the truck.

"Gosh, we're not taking much," he said. "Considering all we brought to Mars, this is only a handful!"

He started the truck.

Looking at the small white cottage for a long moment, he was filled with a desire to rush to it, touch it, say good-by to it, for he felt as if he were going away on a long journey, leaving something to which he could never quite return, never understand again.

Just then Sam and his family drove by in another truck.

"Hi, Bittering! Here we go!"

The truck swung down the ancient highway out of town. There were sixty others traveling the same direction. The town filled with a silent, heavy dust from their passage. The canal waters lay blue in the sun, and a quiet wind moved in the strange trees.

"Good-by, town!" said Mr. Bittering.

"Good-by, good-by," said the family, waving to it.

They did not look back again.

Summer burned the canals dry. Summer moved like flame upon the meadows. In the empty Earth settlement, the painted houses flaked and peeled. Rubber tires upon which children had

swung in back yards hung suspended like stopped clock pendulums in the blazing air.

At the metal shop, the rocket frame began to rust.

In the quiet autumn Mr. Bittering stood, very dark now, very golden-eyed, upon the slope above his villa, looking at the valley.

"It's time to go back," said Cora.

"Yes, but we're not going," he said quietly. "There's nothing there any more."

"Your books," she said. "Your fine clothes.

"Your *llles* and your fine *ior uele rre,*" she said.

"The town's empty. No one's going back," he said. "There's no reason to, none at all."

The daughter wove tapestries and the sons played songs on ancient flutes and pipes, their laughter echoing in the marble villa.

Mr. Bittering gazed at the Earth settlement far away in the low valley. "Such odd, such ridiculous houses the Earth people built."

"They didn't know any better," his wife mused. "Such ugly people. I'm glad they've gone."

They both looked at each other, startled by all they had just finished saying. They laughed.

"Where did they go?" he wondered. He glanced at his wife. She was golden and slender as his daughter. She looked at him, and he seemed almost as young as their eldest son.

"I don't know," she said.

"We'll go back to town maybe next year, or the year after, or the year after that," he said, calmly. "Now—I'm warm. How about taking a swim?"

They turned their backs to the valley. Arm in arm they walked silently down a path of clear-running spring water.

Five years later a rocket fell out of the sky. It lay steaming in the valley. Men leaped out of it, shouting.

"We won the war on Earth! We're here to rescue you! Hey!"

But the American-built town of cottages, peach trees, and the-

aters was silent. They found a flimsy rocket frame rusting in an empty shop.

The rocket men searched the hills. The captain established headquarters in an abandoned bar. His lieutenant came back to report.

"The town's empty, but we found native life in the hills, sir. Dark people. Yellow eyes. Martians. Very friendly. We talked a bit, not much. They learn English fast. I'm sure our relations will be most friendly with them, sir."

"Dark, eh?" mused the captain. "How many?"

"Six, eight hundred, I'd say, living in those marble ruins in the hills, sir. Tall, healthy. Beautiful women."

"Did they tell you what became of the men and women who built this Earth-settlement, Lieutenant?"

"They hadn't the foggiest notion of what happened to this town or its people."

"Strange. You think those Martians killed them?"

"They look surprisingly peaceful. Chances are a plague did this town in, sir."

"Perhaps. I suppose this is one of those mysteries we'll never solve. One of those mysteries you read about."

The captain looked at the room, the dusty windows, the blue mountains rising beyond, the canals moving in the light, and he heard the soft wind in the air. He shivered. Then, recovering, he tapped a large fresh map he had thumbtacked to the top of an empty table.

"Lots to be done, Lieutenant." His voice droned on and quietly on as the sun sank behind the blue hills. "New settlements. Mining sites, minerals to be looked for. Bacteriological specimens taken. The work, all the work. And the old records were lost. We'll have a job of remapping to do, renaming the mountains and rivers and such. Calls for a little imagination.

"What do you think of naming those mountains the Lincoln Mountains, this canal the Washington Canal, those hills—we can name those hills for you, Lieutenant. Diplomacy. And you, for a favor, might name a town for me. Polishing the apple. And

why not make this the Einstein Valley, and further over . . .
are you *listening,* Lieutenant?"

The lieutenant snapped his gaze from the blue color and the
quiet mist of the hills far beyond the town.

"What? Oh, *yes,* sir!"

why not make this the Lincoln Valley and further over
as you assume, Lieutenant?"

The lieutenant snapped his gaze from the blue color and the
quiet mist of the hills far beyond the town.

"What . . . Oh, yes, sir.

13

THE SMILE

In the town square the queue had formed at five in the morning while cocks were crowing far out in the rimed country and there were no fires. All about, among the ruined buildings, bits of mist had clung at first, but now with the new light of seven o'clock it was beginning to disperse. Down the road, in twos and threes, more people were gathering in for the day of marketing, the day of festival.

The small boy stood immediately behind two men who had been talking loudly in the clear air, and all of the sounds they made seemed twice as loud because of the cold. The small boy stomped his feet and blew on his red, chapped hands, and looked up at the soiled gunny-sack clothing of the men and down the long line of men and women ahead.

"Here, boy, what're you doing out so early?" said the man behind him.

"Got my place in line, I have," said the boy.

"Whyn't you run off, give your place to someone who appreciates?"

"Leave the boy alone," said the man ahead, suddenly turning.

"I was joking." The man behind put his hand on the boy's

Originally published in *Fantastic Magazine*.

head. The boy shook it away coldly. "I just thought it strange, a boy out of bed so early."

"This boy's an appreciator of arts, I'll have you know," said the boy's defender, a man named Grigsby. "What's your name, lad?"

"Tom."

"Tom here is going to spit clean and true, right, Tom?"

"I sure am!"

Laughter passed down the line.

A man was selling cracked cups of hot coffee up ahead. Tom looked and saw the little hot fire and the brew bubbling in a rusty pan. It wasn't really coffee. It was made from some berry that grew on the meadowlands beyond town, and it sold a penny a cup to warm their stomachs; but not many were buying, not many had the wealth.

Tom stared ahead to the place where the line ended, beyond a bombed-out stone wall.

"They say she *smiles*," said the boy.

"Aye, she does," said Grigsby.

"They say she's made of oil and canvas."

"True. And that's what makes me think she's not the original one. The original, now, I've heard, was painted on wood a long time ago."

"They say she's four centuries old."

"Maybe more. No one knows what year this is, to be sure."

"It's 2061!"

"That's what they say, boy, yes. Liars. Could be 3000 or 5000, for all we know. Things were in a fearful mess there for a while. All we got now is bits and pieces."

They shuffled along the cold stones of the street.

"How much longer before we see her?" asked Tom uneasily.

"Just a few more minutes. They got her set up with four brass poles and velvet rope, all fancy, to keep folks back. Now mind, no rocks, Tom; they don't allow rocks thrown at her."

"Yes, sir."

The sun rose higher in the heavens, bringing heat which made the men shed their grimy coats and greasy hats.

"Why're we all here in line?" asked Tom at last. "Why're we all here to spit?"

Grigsby did not glance down at him, but judged the sun. "Well, Tom, there's lots of reasons." He reached absently for a pocket that was long gone, for a cigarette that wasn't there. Tom had seen the gesture a million times. "Tom, it has to do with hate. Hate for everything in the Past. I ask you, Tom, how did we get in such a state, cities all junk, roads like jigsaws from bombs, and half the cornfields glowing with radioactivity at night? Ain't that a lousy stew, I ask you?"

"Yes, sir, I guess so."

"It's this way, Tom. You hate whatever it was that got you all knocked down and ruined. That's human nature. Unthinking, maybe, but human nature anyway."

"There's hardly nobody or nothing we don't hate," said Tom.

"Right! The whole blooming kaboodle of them people in the Past who run the world. So here we are on a Thursday morning with our guts plastered to our spines, cold, live in caves and such, don't smoke, don't drink, don't nothing except have our festivals, Tom, our festivals."

And Tom thought of the festivals in the past few years. The year they tore up all the books in the square and burned them and everyone was drunk and laughing. And the festival of science a month ago when they dragged in the last motorcar and picked lots and each lucky man who won was allowed one smash of a sledge hammer at the car.

"Do I remember *that,* Tom? Do I *remember?* Why, I got to smash the front window, the window, you hear? My God, it made a lovely sound! *Crash!*"

Tom could hear the glass fall in glittering heaps.

"And Bill Henderson, he got to bash the engine. Oh, he did a smart job of it, with great efficiency. Wham!"

"But best of all," recalled Grigsby, "there was the time they smashed a factory that was still trying to turn out airplanes.

"Lord, did we feel good blowing it up!" said Grigsby. "And then we found that newspaper plant and the munitions depot and exploded them together. Do you understand, Tom?"

Tom puzzled over it. "I guess."

It was high noon. Now the odors of the ruined city stank on the hot air and things crawled among the tumbled buildings.

"Won't it ever come back, mister?"

"What, civilization? Nobody wants it. Not me!"

"I could stand a bit of it," said the man behind another man. "There were a few spots of beauty in it."

"Don't worry your heads," shouted Grigsby. "There's no room for that, either."

"Ah," said the man behind the man. "Someone'll come along someday with imagination and patch it up. Mark my words. Someone with a heart."

"No," said Grigsby.

"I say yes. Someone with a soul for pretty things. Might give us back a kind of *limited* sort of civilization, the kind we could live in in peace."

"First thing you know there's war!"

"But maybe next time it'd be different."

At last they stood in the main square. A man on horseback was riding from the distance into the town. He had a piece of paper in his hand. In the center of the square was the roped-off area. Tom, Grigsby, and the others were collecting their spittle and moving forward—moving forward prepared and ready, eyes wide. Tom felt his heart beating very strongly and excitedly, and the earth was hot under his bare feet.

"Here we go, Tom, let fly!"

Four policemen stood at the corners of the roped area, four men with bits of yellow twine on their wrists to show their authority over other men. They were there to prevent rocks being hurled.

"This way," said Grigsby at the last moment, "everyone feels he's had his chance at her, you see, Tom? Go on, now!"

Tom stood before the painting and looked at it for a long time.

"Tom, spit!"

His mouth was dry.

"Get on, Tom! Move!"

"But," said Tom, slowly, "she's *beautiful!*"

"Here, I'll spit for you!" Grigsby spat and the missile flew in the sunlight. The woman in the portrait smiled serenely, secretly, at Tom, and he looked back at her, his heart beating, a kind of music in his ears.

"She's beautiful," he said.

"Now get on, before the police——"

"Attention!"

The line fell silent. One moment they were berating Tom for not moving forward, now they were turning to the man on horseback.

"What do they call it, sir?" asked Tom, quietly.

"The picture? *Mona Lisa,* Tom, I think. Yes, the *Mona Lisa.*"

"I have an announcement," said the man on horseback. "The authorities have decreed that as of high noon today the portrait in the square is to be given over into the hands of the populace there, so they may participate in the destruction of——"

Tom hadn't even time to scream before the crowd bore him, shouting and pummeling about, stampeding toward the portrait. There was a sharp ripping sound. The police ran to escape. The crowd was in full cry, their hands like so many hungry birds pecking away at the portrait. Tom felt himself thrust almost through the broken thing. Reaching out in blind imitation of the others, he snatched a scrap of oily canvas, yanked, felt the canvas give, then fell, was kicked, sent rolling to the outer rim of the mob. Bloody, his clothing torn, he watched old women chew pieces of canvas, men break the frame, kick the ragged cloth, and rip it into confetti.

Only Tom stood apart, silent in the moving square. He looked down at his hand. It clutched the piece of canvas close to his chest, hidden.

"Hey there, Tom!" cried Grigsby.

Without a word, sobbing, Tom ran. He ran out and down the

bomb-pitted road, into a field, across a shallow stream, not looking back, his hand clenched tightly, tucked under his coat.

At sunset he reached the small village and passed on through. By nine o'clock he came to the ruined farm dwelling. Around back, in the half silo, in the part that still remained upright, tented over, he heard the sounds of sleeping, the family—his mother, father, and brother. He slipped quickly, silently, through the small door and lay down, panting.

"Tom?" called his mother in the dark.

"Yes."

"Where've you been?" snapped his father. "I'll beat you in the morning."

Someone kicked him. His brother, who had been left behind to work their little patch of ground.

"Go to sleep," cried his mother, faintly.

Another kick.

Tom lay getting his breath. All was quiet. His hand was pushed to his chest, tight, tight. He lay for half an hour this way, eyes closed.

Then he felt something, and it was a cold white light. The moon rose very high and the little square of light moved in the silo and crept slowly over Tom's body. Then, and only then, did his hand relax. Slowly, carefully, listening to those who slept about him, Tom drew his hand forth. He hesitated, sucked in his breath, and then, waiting, opened his hand and uncrumpled the tiny fragment of painted canvas.

All the world was asleep in the moonlight.

And there on his hand was the Smile.

He looked at it in the white illumination from the midnight sky. And he thought, over and over to himself, quietly, *the Smile, the lovely Smile*.

An hour later he could still see it, even after he had folded it carefully and hidden it. He shut his eyes and the Smile was there in the darkness. And it was still there, warm and gentle, when he went to sleep and the world was silent and the moon sailed up and then down the cold sky toward morning.

14

THE FIRST NIGHT OF LENT

So you want to know all the whys and wherefores of the Irish? What shapes them to their Dooms and runs them on their way? you ask. Well, listen, then. For though I've known but a single Irishman in all my life, I knew him, without pause, for one hundred and forty-four consecutive nights. Stand close; perhaps in him you'll see that entire race which marches out of the rains but to vanish through the mists; hold on, here they come! Look out, there they go!

This Irishman, his name was Nick.

During the autumn of 1953, I began a screenplay in Dublin, and each afternoon a hired cab drove me thirty miles out from the River Liffey to the huge grey Georgian country house where my producer-director rode to hounds. There, we discussed my eight pages of daily script through the long fall, winter, and early spring evenings. Then, each midnight, ready to turn back to the Irish Sea and the Royal Hibernian Hotel, I'd wake the operator in the Kilcock village exchange and have her put me through to the warmest, if totally unheated, spot in town.

Originally published in *Playboy*. Copyright © 1956 by HMH Publishing Co., Inc.

"Heber Finn's pub?" I'd shout, once connected. "Is Nick there? Could you send him along here, please?"

My mind's eye saw them, the local boys, lined up, peering over the barricade at that freckled mirror so like a frozen winter pond and themselves discovered all drowned and deep under that lovely ice. Amid all their jostlings and their now-here's-a-secret-in-a-stage-whisper-commotion stood Nick, my village driver, his quietness abounding. I heard Heber Finn sing out from the phone. I heard Nick start up and reply:

"Just look at me, headin' for the door!"

Early on, I learned that "headin' for the door" was no nerve-shattering process that might affront dignity or destroy the fine filigree of any argument being woven with great and breathless beauty at Heber Finn's. It was, rather, a gradual disengagement, a leaning of the bulk so one's gravity was diplomatically shifted toward that far empty side of the public room where the door, shunned by all, stood neglected. Meantime, a dozen conversational warps and woofs must be ticked, tied, and labeled so next morn, with hoarse cries of recognition, patterns might be seized and the shuttle thrown with no pause for breath or thought.

Timing it, I figured the long part of Nick's midnight journey —the length of Heber Finn's—took half an hour. The short part —from Finn's to the house where I waited—took but five minutes.

So it was on the night before the first night of Lent. I called. I waited.

And at last, down through the night forest, thrashed the 1931 Chevrolet, peat-turf colored on top like Nick. Car and driver gasped, sighed, wheezed softly, easily, gently, as they nudged into the courtyard and I groped down the front steps under a moonless but brightly starred sky.

I peered through the car window at unstirred dark; the dashboard had been dead these many years.

"Nick . . . ?"

"None other," he whispered secretly. "And ain't it a fine warm evenin'?"

The temperature was fifty. But, Nick'd been no nearer Rome than the Tipperary shore line; so weather was relative.

"A fine warm evening." I climbed up front and gave the squealing door its absolutely compulsory, rust-splintering slam. "Nick, how've you been since?"

"Ah." He let the car bulk and grind itself down the forest path. "I got me health. Ain't that all-and-everything with Lent comin' on tomorra?"

"Lent," I mused. "What will you give up for Lent, Nick?"

"I been turnin' it over." Nick sucked his cigarette suddenly; the pink, lined mask of his face blinked off the smoke. "And why not these terrible things ya see in me mouth? Dear as gold-fillin's, and a dread congestor of the lungs they be. Put it all down, add 'em up, and ya got a sick loss by the year's turnin', ya know. So ya'll not find these filthy creatures in me face again the whole time of Lent, and, who knows, after!"

"Bravo!" said I, a non-smoker.

"Bravo, says I to meself," wheezed Nick, one eye flinched with smoke.

"Good luck," I said.

"I'll need it," whispered Nick, "with the Sin's own habit to be broke."

And we moved with firm control, with thoughtful shift of weight, down and around a turfy hollow and through a mist and into Dublin at thirty-one easy miles an hour.

Bear with me while I stress it: Nick was the most careful driver in all God's world, including any sane, small, quiet, butter-and-milk producing country you name.

Above all, Nick stands innocent and sainted when compared to those motorists who key that small switch marked paranoia each time they fuse themselves to their bucket seats in Los Angeles, Mexico City, or Paris. Also, to those blind men who, forsaking tin cups and canes, but still wearing their Hollywood dark-glasses, laugh insanely down the Via Veneto, shaking brake-drum lining like carnival serpentine out their race-car

windows. Consider the Roman ruins; surely they are the wreckage strewn and left by those motor-biking otters who, all night beneath your hotel window, shriek down dark Roman alleys, Christians hell-bent for the Colosseum lion pits.

Nick, now. See his easy hands loving the wheel in a slow clocklike turning as soft and silent as winter constellations snow down the sky. Listen to his mist-breathing voice all night-quiet as he charms the road, his foot a tenderly benevolent pat on the whispering accelerator, never a mile under thirty, never two miles over. Nick, Nick, and his steady boat gentling a mild sweet lake where all Time slumbers. Look, compare. And bind such a man to you with summer grasses, gift him with silver, shake his hand warmly at each journey's end.

"Good night, Nick," I said at the hotel. "See you tomorrow."

"God willing," whispered Nick.

And he drove softly away.

Let twenty-three hours of sleep, breakfast, lunch, supper, late night-cap pass. Let hours of writing bad script into fair script fade to peat mist and rain, and there I come again, another midnight, out of that Georgian mansion, its door throwing a warm hearth of color before me as I tread down the steps to feel Braillewise in fog for the car I know hulks there; I hear its enlarged and asthmatic heart gasping in the blind air, and Nick coughing his "gold by the ounce is not more precious" cough.

"Ah, there you are, sir!" said Nick.

And I climbed in the sociable front seat and gave the door its slam. "Nick," I said, smiling.

And then the impossible happened. The car jerked as if shot from the blazing mouth of a cannon, roared, took off, bounced, skidded, then cast itself in full, stoning ricochet down the path among shattered bushes and writhing shadows. I snatched my knees as my head hit the car top four times.

Nick! I almost shouted. Nick!

Visions of Los Angeles, Mexico City, Paris, jumped through my mind. I gazed in frank dismay at the speedometer. Eighty,

ninety, one hundred kilometers; we shot out a great blast of gravel behind and hit the main road, rocked over a bridge and slid down in the midnight streets of Kilcock. No sooner in than out of town at one hundred ten kilometers, I felt all Ireland's grass put down its ears when we, with a yell, jumped over a rise.

Nick! I thought, and turned, and there he sat, only one thing the same. On his lips a cigarette burned, blinding first one eye, then the other.

But the rest of Nick, behind the cigarette, was changed as if the Adversary himself had squeezed and molded and fired him with a dark hand. There he was, whirling the wheel round-about, over-around; here we frenzied under trestles, out of tunnels, here knocked crossroad signs spinning like weather-cocks in whirlwinds.

Nick's face; the wisdom was drained from it, the eyes neither gentle nor philosophical, the mouth neither tolerant, nor at peace. It was a face washed raw, a scalded, peeled potato, a face more like a blinding searchlight raking its steady and meaning-less glare ahead while his quick hands snaked and bit and bit the wheel again to lean us round curves and jump us off cliff after cliff of night.

It's not Nick, I thought, it's his brother. Or a dire thing's come in his life, some destroying affliction or blow, a family sorrow or sickness, yes, that's the answer.

And then Nick spoke, and his voice, it was changed too. Gone was the mellow peat bog, the moist sod, the warm fire in out of the cold rain, gone the gentle grass. Now the voice fairly cracked at me, a clarion, a trumpet, all iron and tin.

"Well, how ya been since!" Nick shouted. "How is it with ya!" he cried.

And the car, it too had suffered violence. It protested the change, yes, for it was an old and much-beaten thing that had done its time and now only wished to stroll along, like a crusty beggar toward sea and sky, careful of its breath and bones. But Nick would have none of that, and cadged the wreck on as if thundering toward Hell, there to warm his cold hands at some

special blaze. Nick leaned, the car leaned; great livid gases blew out in fireworks from the exhaust. Nick's frame, my frame, the car's frame, all together, were wracked and shuddered and ticked wildly.

My sanity was saved from being torn clean off the bone by a simple act. My eyes, seeking the cause of our plaguing flight, ran over the man blazing here like a sheet of ignited vapor from the Abyss, and laid hands to the answering clue.

"Nick," I gasped, "it's the first night of Lent!"

"So?" Nick said, surprised.

"So," I said, "remembering your Lenten promise, why's that cigarette in your mouth?"

Nick did not know what I meant for a moment. Then he cast his eyes down, saw the jiggling smoke, and shrugged.

"Ah," he said, "I give up the *other.*"

And suddenly it all came clear.

The other one hundred forty odd nights, at the door of the old Georgian house I had accepted from my employer a fiery douse of scotch or bourbon or some-such drink "against the chill." Then, breathing summer wheat or barley or oats or whatever from my scorched and charcoaled mouth, I had walked out to a cab where sat a man who, during all the long evenings' wait for me to phone for his services, had *lived* in Heber Finn's pub.

Fool! I thought, how could you have forgotten this!

And there in Heber Finn's, during the long hours of lacy talk that was like planting and bringing to crop a garden among busy men, each contributing his seed or flower, and wielding the implements, their tongues, and the raised, foam-hived glasses, their own hands softly curled about the dear drinks, there Nick had taken into himself a mellowness.

And that mellowness had distilled itself down in a slow rain that damped his smoldering nerves and put the wilderness fires in every limb of him out. Those same showers laved his face to leave the tidal marks of wisdom, the lines of Plato and Aeschylus there. The harvest mellowness colored his cheeks,

warmed his eyes soft, lowered his voice to a husking mist, and spread in his chest to slow his heart to a gentle jog trot. It rained out his arms to loosen his hard-mouthed hands on the shuddering wheel and sit him with grace and ease in his horsehair saddle as he gentled us through the fogs that kept us and Dublin apart.

And with the malt on my own tongue, fluming up my sinus with burning vapors, I had never detected the scent of any spirits on my old friend here.

"Ah," said Nick again. "Yes; I give up the *other*."

The last bit of jigsaw fell in place.

Tonight, the first night of Lent.

Tonight, for the first time in all the nights I had driven with him, Nick was sober.

All those other one hundred and forty-odd nights, Nick hadn't been driving careful and easy just for my safety, no, but because of the gentle weight of mellowness sloping now on this side, now on that side of him as we took the long, scything curves.

Oh, who really knows the Irish, say I, and which half of them is which? Nick?—who is Nick?—and what in the world is he? Which Nick's the real Nick, the one that everyone knows?

I will not think on it!

There is only *one* Nick for me. The one that Ireland shaped herself with her weathers and waters, her seedings and harvestings, her brans and mashes, her brews, bottlings, and ladlings-out, her summer-grain-colored pubs astir and adance with the wind in the wheat and barley by night, you may hear the good whisper way out in forest, on bog, as you roll by. That's Nick to the teeth, eye, and heart, to his easygoing hands. If you ask what makes the Irish what they are, I'd point on down the road and tell where you turn to Heber Finn's.

The first night of Lent, and before you count nine, we're in Dublin! I'm out of the cab and it's puttering there at the curb and I lean in to put my money in the hands of my driver. Earnestly, pleadingly, warmly, with all the friendly urging in the world, I look into that fine man's raw, strange, torchlike face.

"Nick," I said.

"Sir!" he shouted.

"Do me a favor," I said.

"Anything!" he shouted.

"Take this extra money," I said, "and buy the biggest bottle of Irish moss you can find. And just before you pick me up tomorrow night, Nick, drink it down, drink it all. Will you do that, Nick? Will you promise me, cross your heart and hope to die, to do that?"

He thought on it, and the very thought damped down the ruinous blaze in his face.

"Ya make it terrible hard on me," he said.

I forced his fingers shut on the money. At last he put it in his pocket and faced silently ahead.

"Good night, Nick," I said. "See you tomorrow."

"God willing," said Nick.

And he drove away.

15

THE TIME OF GOING AWAY

The thought was three days and three nights growing. During the days he carried it like a ripening peach in his head. During the nights he let it take flesh and sustenance, hung out on the silent air, colored by country moon and country stars. He walked around and around the thought in the silence before dawn. On the fourth morning he reached up an invisible hand, picked it, and swallowed it whole.

He arose as swiftly as possible and burned all his old letters, packed a few clothes in a very small case, and put on his midnight suit and a tie the shiny color of ravens' feathers, as if he were in mourning. He sensed his wife in the door behind him watching his little play with the eyes of a critic who may leap on stage any moment and stop the show. When he brushed past her, he murmured, "Excuse me."

"Excuse me!" she cried. "Is that all you say? Creeping around here, planning a trip!"

"I didn't plan it; it happened," he said. "Three days ago I got this premonition. I knew I was going to die."

"Stop that kind of talk," she said. "It makes me nervous."

The horizon was mirrored softly in his eyes. "I hear my blood

running slow. Listening to my bones is like standing in an attic hearing the beams shift and the dust settle."

"You're only seventy-five," said his wife. "You stand on your own two legs, see, hear, eat, and sleep good, don't you? What's all this talk?"

"It's the natural tongue of existence speaking to me," said the old man. "Civilization's got us too far away from our natural selves. Now you take the pagan islanders——"

"I won't!"

"Everyone knows the pagan islanders got a feel for when it's time to die. They walk around shaking hands with friends and give away all their earthly goods——"

"Don't their wives have a say?"

"They give some of their earthly goods to their wives."

"I should think so!"

"And some to their friends——"

"I'll argue that!"

"And some to their friends. Then they paddle their canoes off into the sunset and never return."

His wife looked high up along him as if he were timber ripe for cutting. "Desertion!" she said.

"No, no, Mildred; death, pure and simple. The Time of Going Away, they call it."

"Did anyone ever charter a canoe and follow to see what those fools were up to?"

"Of course not," said the old man, mildly irritated. "That would spoil everything."

"You mean they had other wives and pretty friends off on another island?"

"No, no, it's just a man needs aloneness, serenity, when his juices turn cold."

"If you could prove those fools really died, I'd shut up." His wife squinted one eye. "Anyone ever *find* their bones on those far islands?"

"The fact is that they just sail on into the sunset, like ani-

mals who sense the Great Time at hand. Beyond that, I don't
wish to know."

"Well, *I* know," said the old woman. "You been reading more
articles in the *National Geographic* about the Elephants' Boneyard."

"Graveyard, not Boneyard!" he shouted.

"Graveyard, Boneyard. I thought I burned those magazines;
you got some hid?"

"Look here, Mildred," he said severely, seizing the suitcase
again. "My mind points north; nothing you say can head me
south. I'm tuned to the infinite secret wellsprings of the primi-
tive soul."

"You're tuned to whatever you read last in that bog-trotters'
gazette!" She pointed a finger at him. "You think I got no memory?"

His shoulders fell. "Let's not go through the list again, please."

"What about the hairy mammoth episode?" she asked. "When
they found that frozen elephant in the Russian tundra thirty
years back? You and Sam Hertz, that old fool, with your fine
idea of running off to Siberia to corner the world market in
canned edible hairy mammoth? You think I don't still hear you
saying, 'Imagine the prices members of the National Geographic
Society will pay to have the tender meat of the Siberian hairy
mammoth, ten thousand years old, ten thousand years extinct,
right in their homes!' You think my scars have healed from
that?"

"I see them clearly," he said.

"You think I've forgotten the time you went out to find the
Lost Tribe of the Osseos, or whatever, in Wisconsin some place
where you could dogtrot to town Saturday nights and tank up,
and fell in that quarry and broke your leg and laid there three
nights?"

"Your recall," he said, "is total."

"Then what's this about pagan natives and the Time of Going
Away? I'll tell you what it is—it's the Time of Staying at Home!
It's the time when fruit don't fall off the trees into your hand,

you got to walk to the store for it. And why do we *walk* to the store for it? Someone in this house, I'll name no names, took the car apart like a clock some years back and left it strewn all down the yard. I've raised auto parts in my garden ten years come Thursday. Ten more years and all that's left of our car is little heaps of rust. Look out that window! It's leaf-raking-and-burning time. It's chopping-trees-and-sawing-wood-for-the-fire time. It's clean-out-stoves-and-hang-stormdoors-and-windows time. It's shingle-the-roof time, *that's* what it is, and if you think you're out to escape it, think again!"

He placed his hand to his chest. "It pains me you have so little trust in my natural sensitivity to oncoming Doom."

"It pains *me* that *National Geographics* fall in the hands of crazy old men. I see you read those pages then fall into those dreams I always have to sweep up after. Those *Geographic* and *Popular Mechanics* publishers should be forced to see all the half-finished rowboats, helicopters, and one-man batwing gliders in our attic, garage, and cellar. Not only *see,* but cart them home!"

"Chatter on," he said. "I stand before you, a white stone sinking in the tides of Oblivion. For God's sake, woman, can't I drag myself off to die in peace?"

"Plenty of time for Oblivion when I find you stone cold across the kindling pile."

"Jesting Pilate!" he said. "Is recognition of one's own mortality nothing but vanity?"

"You're chewing it like a plug of tobacco."

"Enough!" he said. "My earthly goods are stacked on the back porch. Give them to the Salvation Army."

"The *Geographics* too?"

"Yes, damn it, the *Geographics!* Now stand aside!"

"If you're going to die, you won't need that suitcase full of clothing," she said.

"Hands off, woman! It may take some few hours. Am I to be stripped of my last creature comforts? This should be a tender

scene of parting. Instead—bitter recriminations, sarcasm, doubt strewn to every wind."

"All right," she said. "Go spend a cold night in the woods."

"I'm not necessarily going to the woods."

"Where else is there for a man in Illinois to go to die?"

"Well," he said and paused. "Well, there's always the open highway."

"And be run down, of course; I'd forgotten that."

"No, no!" He squeezed his eyes shut, then opened them again. "The empty side roads leading nowhere, everywhere, through night forests, wilderness, to distant lakes. . . ."

"Now, you're not going to go rent a canoe, are you, and paddle off? Remember the time you tipped over and almost drowned at Fireman's Pier?"

"Who said anything about canoes?"

"You did! Pagan islanders, you said, paddling off into the great unknown."

"That's the South Seas! Here a man has to strike off on foot to find his natural source, seek his natural end. I might walk north along the Lake Michigan shore, the dunes, the wind, the big breakers there."

"Willie, Willie," she said softly, shaking her head. "Oh, Willie, Willie, what will I do with you?"

He lowered his voice. "Just let me have my head," he said.

"Yes," she said, quietly. "Yes." And tears came to her eyes.

"Now, now," he said.

"Oh, Willie . . ." She looked a long while at him. "Do you really think with all your heart you're not going to live?"

He saw himself reflected, small but perfect, in her eye, and looked away uneasily. "I thought all night about the universal tide that brings man in and takes him out. Now it's morning and good-by."

"Good-by?" She looked as if she'd never heard the word before.

His voice was unsteady. "Of course, if you absolutely insist I stay, Mildred——"

"No!" She braced herself and blew her nose. "You feel what you feel; I can't fight that!"

"You *sure?*" he said.

"You're the one that's sure, Willie," she said. "Get on along now. Take your heavy coat; the nights are cold."

"But——" he said.

She ran and brought his coat and kissed his cheek and drew back quickly before he could enclose her in his bear hug. He stood there working his mouth, gazing at the big armchair by the fire. She threw open the front door. "You got food?"

"I won't need . . ." He paused. "I got a boiled ham sandwich and some pickles in my case. Just one. That's all I figured I'd . . ."

And then he was out the door and down the steps and along the path toward the woods. He turned and was going to say something but thought better of it, waved, and went on.

"Now, Will," she called. "Don't overdo. Don't make too much distance the first hour! You get tired, sit down! You get hungry, eat! And . . ."

But here she had to stop and turn away and get out her handkerchief.

A moment later she looked up the path and it looked as though nobody had passed there in the last ten thousand years. It was so empty she had to go in and shut the door.

Nighttime, nine o'clock, nine-fifteen, stars out, moon round, house lights strawberry-colored through the curtains, the chimney blowing long comet tails of fireworks, sighing warm. Down the chimney, sounds of pots and pans and cutlery, fire on the hearth, like a great orange cat. In the kitchen, the big iron cookstove full of jumping flames, pans boiling, bubbling, frying, vapors and steams in the air. From time to time the old woman turned and her eyes listened and her mouth listened, wide, to the world outside this house, this fire, and this food.

Nine-thirty and, from a great distance away from the house, a solid whacking, chunking sound.

The old woman straightened up and laid down a spoon.

Outside, the dull solid blows came again and again in the moonlight. The sound went on for three or four minutes, during which she hardly moved except to tighten her mouth or her fists with each solid chunking blow. When the sounds stopped, she threw herself at the stove, the table, stirring, pouring, lifting, carrying, setting down.

She finished just as new sounds came from the dark land outside the windows. Footsteps came slowly up the path, heavy shoes weighed the front porch.

She went to the door and waited for a knock.

None came.

She waited a full minute.

Outside on the porch a great bulk stirred and shifted from side to side uneasily.

Finally she sighed and called sharply at the door. "Will, is that you breathing out there?"

No answer. Only a kind of sheepish silence behind the door.

She snatched the door wide.

The old man stood there, an incredible stack of cordwood in his arm. His voice came from behind the stack.

"Saw smoke in the chimney; figured you might need wood," he said.

She stood aside. He came in and placed the wood carefully by the hearth, not looking at her.

She looked out on the porch and picked up the suitcase and brought it in and shut the door.

She saw him sitting at the dinner table.

She stirred the soup on the stove to a great boiling whirl.

"Roast beef in the oven?" he asked quietly.

She opened the oven door. The steam breathed across the room to wrap him up. He closed his eyes, seated there, bathed.

"What's that other smell, the burning?" he asked a moment later.

She waited, back turned, and finally said, *"National Geographics."*

He nodded slowly, saying nothing.

Then the food was on the table, warm and tremulous, and there was a moment of silence after she sat down and looked at him. She shook her head. She looked at him. Then she shook her head again silently.

"Do you want to ask the blessing?" she said.

"*You,*" he said.

They sat there in the warm room by the bright fire and bowed their heads and closed their eyes. She smiled and began.

"Thank you, Lord . . ."

16
ALL SUMMER IN A DAY

"Ready?"

"Ready."

"Now?"

"Soon."

"Do the scientists really know? Will it happen today, will it?"

"Look, look; see for yourself!"

The children pressed to each other like so many roses, so many weeds, intermixed, peering out for a look at the hidden sun.

It rained.

It had been raining for seven years; thousands upon thousands of days compounded and filled from one end to the other with rain, with the drum and gush of water, with the sweet crystal fall of showers and the concussion of storms so heavy they were tidal waves come over the islands. A thousand forests had been crushed under the rain and grown up a thousand times to be crushed again. And this was the way life was forever on the planet Venus, and this was the schoolroom of the children of the rocket men and women who had come to a raining world to set up civilization and live out their lives.

Originally published in *Fantasy & Science Fiction Magazine*.

"It's stopping, it's stopping!"

"Yes, yes!"

Margot stood apart from them, from these children who could never remember a time when there wasn't rain and rain and rain. They were all nine years old, and if there had been a day, seven years ago, when the sun came out for an hour and showed its face to the stunned world, they could not recall. Sometimes, at night, she heard them stir, in remembrance, and she knew they were dreaming and remembering gold or a yellow crayon or a coin large enough to buy the world with. She knew they thought they remembered a warmness, like a blushing in the face, in the body, in the arms and legs and trembling hands. But then they always awoke to the tatting drum, the endless shaking down of clear bead necklaces upon the roof, the walk, the gardens, the forests, and their dreams were gone.

All day yesterday they had read in class about the sun. About how like a lemon it was, and how hot. And they had written small stories or essays or poems about it:

> *I think the sun is a flower,*
> *That blooms for just one hour.*

That was Margot's poem, read in a quiet voice in the still classroom while the rain was falling outside.

"Aw, you didn't write that!" protested one of the boys.

"I did," said Margot. "I *did*."

"William!" said the teacher.

But that was yesterday. Now the rain was slackening, and the children were crushed in the great thick windows.

"Where's teacher?"

"She'll be back."

"She'd better hurry, we'll miss it!"

They turned on themselves, like a feverish wheel, all tumbling spokes.

Margot stood alone. She was a very frail girl who looked as if she had been lost in the rain for years and the rain had washed out the blue from her eyes and the red from her mouth and

the yellow from her hair. She was an old photograph dusted from an album, whitened away, and if she spoke at all her voice would be a ghost. Now she stood, separate, staring at the rain and the loud wet world beyond the huge glass.

"What're *you* looking at?" said William.

Margot said nothing.

"Speak when you're spoken to." He gave her a shove. But she did not move; rather she let herself be moved only by him and nothing else.

They edged away from her, they would not look at her. She felt them go away. And this was because she would play no games with them in the echoing tunnels of the underground city. If they tagged her and ran, she stood blinking after them and did not follow. When the class sang songs about happiness and life and games her lips barely moved. Only when they sang about the sun and the summer did her lips move as she watched the drenched windows.

And then, of course, the biggest crime of all was that she had come here only five years ago from Earth, and she remembered the sun and the way the sun was and the sky was when she was four in Ohio. And they, they had been on Venus all their lives, and they had been only two years old when last the sun came out and had long since forgotten the color and heat of it and the way it really was. But Margot remembered.

"It's like a penny," she said once, eyes closed.

"No it's not!" the children cried.

"It's like a fire," she said, "in the stove."

"You're lying, you don't remember!" cried the children.

But she remembered and stood quietly apart from all of them and watched the patterning windows. And once, a month ago, she had refused to shower in the school shower rooms, had clutched her hands to her ears and over her head, screaming the water mustn't touch her head. So after that, dimly, dimly, she sensed it, she was different and they knew her difference and kept away.

There was talk that her father and mother were taking her

back to Earth next year; it seemed vital to her that they do so, though it would mean the loss of thousands of dollars to her family. And so, the children hated her for all these reasons of big and little consequence. They hated her pale snow face, her waiting silence, her thinness, and her possible future.

"Get away!" The boy gave her another push. "What're you waiting for?"

Then, for the first time, she turned and looked at him. And what she was waiting for was in her eyes.

"Well, don't wait around here!" cried the boy savagely. "You won't see nothing!"

Her lips moved.

"Nothing!" he cried. "It was all a joke, wasn't it?" He turned to the other children. "Nothing's happening today. *Is* it?"

They all blinked at him and then, understanding, laughed and shook their heads. "Nothing, nothing!"

"Oh, but," Margot whispered, her eyes helpless. "But this is the day, the scientists predict, they say, they *know,* the sun . . ."

"All a joke!" said the boy, and seized her roughly. "Hey, everyone, let's put her in a closet before teacher comes!"

"No," said Margot, falling back.

They surged about her, caught her up and bore her, protesting, and then pleading, and then crying, back into a tunnel, a room, a closet, where they slammed and locked the door. They stood looking at the door and saw it tremble from her beating and throwing herself against it. They heard her muffled cries. Then, smiling, they turned and went out and back down the tunnel, just as the teacher arrived.

"Ready, children?" She glanced at her watch.

"Yes!" said everyone.

"Are we all here?"

"Yes!"

The rain slackened still more.

They crowded to the huge door.

The rain stopped.

It was as if, in the midst of a film concerning an avalanche, a tornado, a hurricane, a volcanic eruption, something had, first, gone wrong with the sound apparatus, thus muffling and finally cutting off all noise, all of the blasts and repercussions and thunders, and then, second, ripped the film from the projector and inserted in its place a peaceful tropical slide which did not move or tremor. The world ground to a standstill. The silence was so immense and unbelievable that you felt your ears had been stuffed or you had lost your hearing altogether. The children put their hands to their ears. They stood apart. The door slid back and the smell of the silent, waiting world came in to them.

The sun came out.

It was the color of flaming bronze and it was very large. And the sky around it was a blazing blue tile color. And the jungle burned with sunlight as the children, released from their spell, rushed out, yelling, into the springtime.

"Now, don't go too far," called the teacher after them. "You've only two hours, you know. You wouldn't want to get caught out!"

But they were running and turning their faces up to the sky and feeling the sun on their cheeks like a warm iron; they were taking off their jackets and letting the sun burn their arms.

"Oh, it's better than the sun lamps, isn't it?"

"Much, much better!"

They stopped running and stood in the great jungle that covered Venus, that grew and never stopped growing, tumultuously, even as you watched it. It was a nest of octopi, clustering up great arms of fleshlike weed, wavering, flowering in this brief spring. It was the color of rubber and ash, this jungle, from the many years without sun. It was the color of stones and white cheeses and ink, and it was the color of the moon.

The children lay out, laughing, on the jungle mattress, and heard it sigh and squeak under them, resilient and alive. They ran among the trees, they slipped and fell, they pushed each other, they played hide-and-seek and tag, but most of all they

squinted at the sun until tears ran down their faces, they put their hands up to that yellowness and that amazing blueness and they breathed of the fresh, fresh air and listened and listened to the silence which suspended them in a blessed sea of no sound and no motion. They looked at everything and savored everything. Then, wildly, like animals escaped from their caves, they ran and ran in shouting circles. They ran for an hour and did not stop running.

And then——

In the midst of their running one of the girls wailed.

Everyone stopped.

The girl, standing in the open, held out her hand.

"Oh, look, look," she said, trembling.

They came slowly to look at her opened palm.

In the center of it, cupped and huge, was a single raindrop.

She began to cry, looking at it.

They glanced quietly at the sky.

"Oh. Oh."

A few cold drops fell on their noses and their cheeks and their mouths. The sun faded behind a stir of mist. A wind blew cool around them. They turned and started to walk back toward the underground house, their hands at their sides, their smiles vanishing away.

A boom of thunder startled them and like leaves before a new hurricane, they tumbled upon each other and ran. Lightning struck ten miles away, five miles away, a mile, a half mile. The sky darkened into midnight in a flash.

They stood in the doorway of the underground for a moment until it was raining hard. Then they closed the door and heard the gigantic sound of the rain falling in tons and avalanches, everywhere and forever.

"Will it be seven more years?"

"Yes. Seven."

Then one of them gave a little cry.

"Margot!"

"What?"

"She's still in the closet where we locked her."

"Margot."

They stood as if someone had driven them, like so many stakes, into the floor. They looked at each other and then looked away. They glanced out at the world that was raining now and raining and raining steadily. They could not meet each other's glances. Their faces were solemn and pale. They looked at their hands and feet, their faces down.

"Margot."

One of the girls said, "Well . . . ?"

No one moved.

"Go on," whispered the girl.

They walked slowly down the hall in the sound of cold rain. They turned through the doorway to the room in the sound of the storm and thunder, lightning on their faces, blue and terrible. They walked over to the closet door slowly and stood by it.

Behind the closet door was only silence.

They unlocked the door, even more slowly, and let Margot out.

17

THE GIFT

Tomorrow would be Christmas, and even while the three of them rode to the rocket port the mother and father were worried. It was the boy's first flight into space, his very first time in a rocket, and they wanted everything to be perfect. So when, at the custom's table, they were forced to leave behind his gift which exceeded the weight limit by no more than a few ounces and the little tree with the lovely white candles, they felt themselves deprived of the season and their love.

The boy was waiting for them in the Terminal room. Walking toward him, after their unsuccessful clash with the Interplanetary officials, the mother and father whispered to each other.

"What shall we do?"

"Nothing, nothing. What *can* we do?"

"Silly rules!"

"And he so wanted the tree!"

The siren gave a great howl and people pressed forward into the Mars Rocket. The mother and father walked at the very last, their small pale son between them, silent.

"I'll think of something," said the father.

"What . . . ?" asked the boy.

And the rocket took off and they were flung headlong into dark space.

The rocket moved and left fire behind and left Earth behind on which the date was December 24, 2052, heading out into a place where there was no time at all, no month, no year, no hour. They slept away the rest of the first "day." Near midnight, by their Earth-time New York watches, the boy awoke and said, "I want to go look out the porthole."

There was only one port, a "window" of immensely thick glass of some size, up on the next deck.

"Not quite yet," said the father. "I'll take you up later."

"I want to see where we are and where we're going."

"I want you to wait for a reason," said the father.

He had been lying awake, turning this way and that, thinking of the abandoned gift, the problem of the season, the lost tree and the white candles. And at last, sitting up, no more than five minutes ago, he believed he had found a plan. He need only carry it out and this journey would be fine and joyous indeed.

"Son," he said, "in exactly one half hour it will be Christmas."

"Oh," said the mother, dismayed that he had mentioned it. Somehow she had rather hoped that the boy would forget.

The boy's face grew feverish and his lips trembled. "I know, I know. Will I get a present, will I? Will I have a tree? You promised——"

"Yes, yes, all that, and more," said the father.

The mother started. "But——"

"I mean it," said the father. "I really mean it. All and more, much more. Excuse me, now. I'll be back."

He left them for about twenty minutes. When he came back he was smiling. "Almost time."

"Can I hold your watch?" asked the boy, and the watch was handed over and he held it ticking in his fingers as the rest of the hour drifted by in fire and silence and unfelt motion.

"It's Christmas *now!* Christmas! Where's my present?"

"Here we go," said the father and took his boy by the shoulder

and led him from the room, down the hall, up a rampway, his wife following.

"I don't understand," she kept saying.

"You will. Here we are," said the father.

They had stopped at the closed door of a large cabin. The father tapped three times and then twice in a code. The door opened and the light in the cabin went out and there was a whisper of voices.

"Go on in, son," said the father.

"It's dark."

"I'll hold your hand. Come on, Mama."

They stepped into the room and the door shut, and the room was very dark indeed. And before them loomed a great glass eye, the porthole, a window four feet high and six feet wide, from which they could look out into space.

The boy gasped.

Behind him, the father and the mother gasped with him, and then in the dark room some people began to sing.

"Merry Christmas, son," said the father.

And the voices in the room sang the old, the familiar carols, and the boy moved forward slowly until his face was pressed against the cool glass of the port. And he stood there for a long long time, just looking and looking out into space and the deep night at the burning and the burning of ten billion billion white and lovely candles. . . .

18

THE GREAT COLLISION OF MONDAY LAST

The man staggered through the flung-wide doors of Heber Finn's pub as if struck by lightning. Reeling, blood on his face, coat, and torn pants, his moan froze every customer at the bar. For a time you heard only the soft foam popping in the lacy mugs, as the customers turned, some faces pale, some pink, some veined and wattle-red. Every eyelid down the line gave a blink.

The stranger swayed in his ruined clothes, eyes wide, lips trembling. The drinkers clenched their fists. Yes! they cried, silently—go on, man! what *happened?*

The stranger leaned far out on the air.

"Collision," he whispered. "Collision on the road."

Then, chopped at the knees, he fell.

"Collision!" A dozen men rushed at the body.

"Kelly!" Heber Finn vaulted the bar. "Get to the road! Mind the victim; easy does it! Joe, run for the Doc!"

"Wait!" said a quiet voice.

From the private stall at the dark end of the pub, the cubby where a philosopher might brood, a dark man blinked out at the crowd.

"Doc!" cried Heber Finn. "It's you!"

Originally published in *Argosy*, London, as "Collision of Monday."

Doctor and men hustled out into the night.

"Collision . . ." The man on the floor twitched his lips.

"Softly, boys." Heber Finn and two others gentled the victim atop the bar. He looked handsome as death on the fine inlaid wood with the prismed mirror making him two dread calamities for the price of one.

Outside on the steps, the crowd halted, shocked as if an ocean had sunk Ireland in the dusk and now bulked all about them. Fog in fifty-foot rollers and breakers put out the moon and stars. Blinking, cursing, the men leapt out to vanish in the deeps.

Behind, in the bright doorframe, a young man stood. He was neither red enough nor pale enough of face, nor dark enough or light enough in spirit to be Irish, and so must be American. He was. That established, it follows he dreaded interfering with what seemed village ritual. Since arriving in Ireland, he could not shake the feeling that at all times he was living stage center of the Abbey Theatre. Now, not knowing his lines, he could only stare after the rushing men.

"But," he protested weakly, "I didn't hear any cars on the road."

"You did not!" said an old man almost pridefully. Arthritis limited him to the top step where he teetered, shouting at the white tides where his friends had submerged. "Try the crossroad, boys! That's where it most often does!"

"The crossroad!" Far and near, footsteps rang.

"Nor," said the American, "did I hear a collision."

The old man snorted with contempt. "Ah, we don't be great ones for commotion, nor great crashing sounds. But collision you'll see if you step on out there. Walk, now, don't run! It's the devil's own night. Running blind you might hit into Kelly, beyond, who's a great one for running just to squash his lungs. Or you might head on with Feeney, too drunk to find any road, never mind what's *on* it! You got a torch, a flash? Blind you'll be, but use it. Walk now, you *hear?*"

The American groped through the fog to his car, found his flashlight, and, immersed in the night beyond Heber Finn's,

made direction by the heavy clubbing of shoes and a rally of voices ahead. A hundred yards off in eternity the men approached, grunting whispers: "Easy now!" "Ah, the shameful blight!" "Hold on, don't jiggle him!"

The American was flung aside by a steaming lump of men who swept suddenly from the fog, bearing atop themselves a crumpled object. He glimpsed a blood-stained and livid face high up there, then someone cracked his flashlight down.

By instinct, sensing the far whiskey-colored light of Heber Finn's, the catafalque surged on toward that fixed and familiar harbor.

Behind came dim shapes and a chilling insect rattle.

"Who's that!" cried the American.

"Us, with the vehicles," someone husked. "You might say—we got the collision."

The flashlight fixed them. The American gasped. A moment later, the battery failed.

But not before he had seen two village lads jogging along with no trouble at all, easily, lightly, toting under their arms two ancient black bicycles minus front and tail lights.

"What . . . ?" said the American.

But the lads trotted off, the accident with them. The fog closed in. The American stood abandoned on an empty road, his flashlight dead in his hand.

By the time he opened the door at Heber Finn's, both "bodies" as they called them, had been stretched on the bar.

"We got the bodies on the bar," said the old man, turning as the American entered.

And there was the crowd lined up not for drinks, but blocking the way so the Doc had to shove sidewise from one to another of these relics of blind driving by night on the misty roads.

"One's Pat Nolan," whispered the old man. "Not working at the moment. The other's Mr. Peevey from Meynooth, in candy and cigarettes mostly." Raising his voice, "Are they dead now, Doc?"

"Ah, be still, won't you?" The Doc resembled a sculptor troubled at finding some way to finish up two full-length marble statues at once. "Here, let's put one victim on the floor!"

"The floor's a tomb," said Heber Finn. "He'll catch his death down there. Best leave him up where the warm air gathers from our talk."

"But," said the American quietly, confused, "I've never heard of an accident like this in all my life. Are you sure there were absolutely no cars? Only these two men on their *bikes?*"

"Only?" the old man shouted. "Great God, man, a fellow working up a drizzling sweat can pump along at sixty kilometers. With a long downhill glide his bike hits ninety or ninety-five! So here they come, these two, no front or tail lights——"

"Isn't there a law against that?"

"To hell with government interference! So here the two come, no lights, flying home from one town to the next. Thrashing like Sin Himself's at their behinds! Both going opposite ways but both on the same side of the road. Always ride the wrong side of the road, it's safer, they say. But look on these lads, fair destroyed by all that official palaver. Why? Don't you see? One remembered it, but the other didn't! Better if the officials kept their mouths shut! For here the two be, dying."

"Dying?" The American stared.

"Well, think on it, man! What stands between two able-bodied hell-bent fellas jumping along the path from Kilcock to Meynooth? Fog! Fog is all! Only fog to keep their skulls from bashing together. Why, look when two chaps hit at a cross like that, it's like a strike in bowling alleys, tenpins flying! Bang! There go your friends, nine feet up, heads together like dear chums met, flailing the air, their bikes clenched like two tomcats. Then they all fall down and just lay there, feeling around for the Dark Angel."

"Surely these men won't——"

"Oh, won't they? Why, last year alone in all the Free State no night passed some soul did not meet in fatal collision with another!"

"You mean to say over three hundred Irish bicyclists die every year, hitting each other?"

"God's truth and a pity."

"I never ride my bike nights." Heber Finn eyed the bodies. "I walk."

"But still then the damn bikes run you down!" said the old man. "Awheel or afoot, some idiot's always panting up Doom the other way. They'd sooner split you down the seam than wave hello. Oh, the brave men I've seen ruined or half-ruined or worse, and headaches their lifetimes after." The old man trembled his eyelids shut. "You might almost think, mightn't you, that human beings was not made to handle such delicate instruments of power."

"Three hundred dead each year." The American seemed dazed.

"And that don't count the 'walking wounded' by the thousands every fortnight who, cursing, throw their bikes in the bog forever and take government pensions to salve their all-but-murdered bodies."

"Should we stand here talking?" The American gestured helplessly toward the victims. "Is there a hospital?"

"On a night with no moon," Heber Finn continued, "best walk out through the middle of fields and be damned to the evil roads! That's how I have survived into this my fifth decade."

"Ah . . ." The men stirred restlessly.

The Doc, sensing he had withheld information too long, feeling his audience drift away, now snatched their attention back by straightening up briskly and exhaling.

"Well!"

The pub quickened into silence.

"This chap here——" The Doc pointed. "Bruises, lacerations, and agonizing backaches for two weeks running. As for the other lad, however——" And here the Doc let himself scowl for a long moment at the paler one there looking rouged, waxed, and ready for final rites. "Concussion."

"Concussion!"

The quiet wind rose and fell in the silence.

"He'll survive if we run him quick now to Meynooth Clinic. So whose car will volunteer?"

The crowd turned as a staring body toward the American. He felt the gentle shift as he was drawn from outside the ritual to its deep and innermost core. He flushed, remembering the front of Heber Finn's pub, where seventeen bicycles and one automobile were parked at this moment. Quickly, he nodded.

"There! A volunteer, lads! Quick now, hustle this boy—gently!—to our good friend's vehicle!"

The men reached out to lift the body, but froze when the American coughed. They saw him circle his hand to all, and tip his cupped fingers to his lips. They gasped in soft surprise. The gesture was not done when drinks foamed down the bar.

"For the road!"

And now even the luckier victim, suddenly revived, face like cheese, found a mug gentled to his hand with whispers.

"Here, lad, here . . . tell us . . ."

". . . what happened, eh? eh?"

Then the body was gone off the bar, the potential wake over, the room empty save for the American, the Doc, the revived lad, and two softly cudgeling friends. Outside you could hear the crowd putting the one serious result of the great collision into the volunteer's car.

The Doc said, "Finish your drink, Mr.——?"

"McGuire," said the American.

"By the saints, he's Irish!"

No, thought the American, far away, looking numbly around at the pub, at the recovered bicyclist seated, waiting for the crowd to come back and mill about him, seeing the blood-spotted floor, the two bicycles tilted near the door like props from a vaudeville turn, the dark night waiting outside with its improbable fog, listening to the roll and cadence and gentle equilibrium of these voices balanced each in its own throat and environment. No, thought the American named McGuire, I'm almost, but certainly not quite, Irish. . . .

"Doctor," he heard himself say as he placed money on the bar, "do you often have auto wrecks, collisions, between people in *cars?*"

"Not in our town!" The Doc nodded scornfully east. "If you like that sort of thing, now, Dublin's the very place for it!"

Crossing the pub together, the Doc took his arm as if to impart some secret which would change his Fates. Thus steered, the American found the stout inside himself a shifting weight he must accommodate from side to side as the Doc breathed soft in his ear.

"Look here now, McGuire, admit it, you've driven but little in Ireland, right? Then, listen! Driving to Meynooth, fog and all, you'd best take it fast! Raise a din! Why? Scare the cyclists and cows off the path, both sides! If you drive slow, why you'll creep up on and do away with dozens before they know what took them off! And another thing: when a car approaches, douse your lights! Pass each other, lights out, in safety. Them devil's own lights have put out more eyes and demolished more innocents than all of seeing's worth. Is it clear, now? Two things: speed, and douse your lights when cars loom up!"

At the door, the American nodded. Behind him he heard the one victim, settled easy in his chair, working the stout around on his tongue, thinking, preparing, beginning his tale:

"Well, I'm on me way home, blithe as you please, asailing downhill near the cross when——"

Outside in the car with the other collision victim moaning softly in the back seat, the Doc offered final advice.

"Always wear a cap, lad. If you want to walk nights ever, on the roads, that is. A cap'll save you the frightful migraines should you meet Kelly or Moran or any other hurtling full-tilt the other way, full of fiery moss and hard-skulled from birth. Even on foot, these men are dangerous. So you see, there's rules for pedestrians too in Ireland, and wear a cap at night is Number One!"

Without thinking, the American fumbled under the seat, brought forth a brown tweed cap purchased in Dublin that day,

and put it on. Adjusting it, he looked out at the dark mist boiling across the night. He listened to the empty highway waiting for him ahead, quiet, quiet, quiet, but not quiet somehow. For hundreds of long strange miles up and down all of Ireland he saw a thousand crossroads covered with a thousand fogs through which one thousand tweed-capped, grey-muffled phantoms wheeled along in mid-air, singing, shouting, and smelling of Guiness Stout.

He blinked. The phantoms shadowed off. The road lay empty and dark and waiting.

Taking a deep breath, shutting his eyes, the American named McGuire turned the key in the switch and stepped on the starter.

THE LITTLE MICE

"They're very odd," I said. "The little Mexican couple."

"How do you mean?" asked my wife.

"Never a sound," I said. "Listen."

Ours was a house deep back in among tenements, to which another half house had been added. When my wife and I purchased the house, we rented the additional quarters which lay walled up against one side of our parlor. Now, listening at this particular wall, we heard our hearts beat.

"I know they're home," I whispered. "But in the three years they've lived here I've never heard a dropped pan, a spoken word, or the sound of a light switch. Good God, what are they *doing* in there?"

"I'd never thought," said my wife. "It *is* peculiar."

"Only one light on, that same dim little blue twenty-five-watt bulb they burn in their parlor. If you walk by and peer in their front door, there *he* is, sitting in his armchair, not saying a word, his hands in his lap. There she is, sitting in the other armchair, looking at him, saying nothing. They don't move."

"At first glance I always think they're not home," said my wife.

Originally published in *Escapade* as "The Mice."

"Their parlor's so dark. But if you stare long enough, your eyes get used to it and you can make them out, sitting there."

"Some day," I said, "I'm going to run in, turn on their lights, and yell! My God, if *I* can't stand their silence, how can they? They can talk, can't they?"

"When he pays the rent each month, he says hello."

"What else?"

"Good-by."

I shook my head. "When we meet in the alley he smiles and runs."

My wife and I sat down for an evening of reading, the radio, and talk. "Do they have a radio?"

"No radio, television, telephone. Not a book, magazine, or paper in their house."

"Ridiculous!"

"Don't get so excited."

"I know, but you can't sit in a dark room two or three years and not speak, not listen to a radio, not read or even eat, can you? I've never smelled a steak or an egg frying. Damn it, I don't believe I've ever heard them go to bed!"

"They're doing it to mystify us, dear."

"They're succeeding!"

I went for a walk around the block. It was a nice summer evening. Returning, I glanced idly in their front door. The dark silence was there, and the heavy shapes, sitting, and the little blue light burning. I stood a long time, finishing my cigarette. It was only in turning to go that I saw him in the doorway, looking out with his bland, plump face. He didn't move. He just stood there, watching me.

"Evening," I said.

Silence. After a moment, he turned, moving away into the dark room.

In the morning, the little Mexican left the house at seven o'clock, alone, hurrying down the alley, observing the same silence he kept in his rooms. She followed at eight o'clock, walk-

ing carefully, all lumpy under her dark coat, a black hat balanced on her frizzy, beauty-parlor hair. They had gone to work this way, remote and silent, for years.

"Where do they work?" I asked at breakfast.

"He's a blast-furnace man at U. S. Steel here. She sews in a dress loft somewhere."

"That's hard work."

I typed a few pages of my novel, read, idled, typed some more. At five in the afternoon I saw the little Mexican woman come home, unlock her door, hurry inside, hook the screen, and lock the door tight.

He arrived at six sharp in a rush. Once on their back porch, however, he became infinitely patient. Quietly, raking his hand over the screen, lightly, like a fat mouse scrabbling, he waited. At last she let him in. I did not see their mouths move.

Not a sound during suppertime. No frying. No rattle of dishes. Nothing.

I saw the small blue lamp go on.

"That's how he is," said my wife, "when he pays the rent. Raps so quietly I don't hear. I just happen to glance out the window and there he is. God knows how long he's waited, standing, sort of 'nibbling' at the door."

Two nights later, on a beautiful July evening, the little Mexican man came out on the back porch and looked at me, working in the garden and said, "You're crazy!" He turned to my wife. "You're crazy too!" He waved his plump hand quietly. "I don't like you. Too much *noise*. I don't like you. You're crazy."

He went back into his little house.

August, September, October, November. The "mice," as we now referred to them, lay quietly in their dark nest. Once my wife gave him some old magazines with his rent receipt. He accepted these politely, with a smile and a bow, but no word. An hour later she saw him put the magazines in the yard incinerator and strike a match.

The next day he paid the rent three months in advance, no

doubt figuring that he would only have to see us up close once every twelve weeks. When I saw him on the street he crossed quickly to the other side to greet an imaginary friend. She, similarly, ran by me, smiling wildly, bewildered, nodding. I never got nearer than twenty yards to her. If there was plumbing to be fixed in their house, they went silently forth on their own, not telling us, and brought back a plumber who worked, it seemed, with a flashlight.

"God damnedest thing," he told me when I saw him in the alley. "Damn fool place there hasn't got any light bulbs in the sockets. When I asked where they all were, damn it, they just *smiled* at me!"

I lay at night thinking about the little mice. Where were they from? Mexico, yes. What part? A farm, a small village, somewhere by a river? Certainly no city or town. But a place where there were stars and the normal lights and darknesses, the goings and comings of the moon and the sun they had known the better part of their lives. Yet here they were, far, far away from home, in an impossible city, he sweating out the hell of blast furnaces all day, she bent to jittering needles in a sewing loft. They came home then to this block, through a loud city, avoided clanging streetcars and saloons that screamed like red parrots along their way. Through a million shriekings they ran back to their parlor, their blue light, their comfortable chairs, and their silence. I often thought of this. Late at night I felt if I put out my hand, in the dark of my own bedroom, I might feel adobe and hear a cricket and a river running by under the moon and someone singing softly to a faint guitar.

Late one December evening the next-door tenement burned. Flames roared at the sky, bricks fell in avalanches, and sparks littered the roof where the quiet mice lived.

I pounded their door.

"Fire!" I cried. "Fire!"

They sat motionless in their blue-lighted room.

I pounded violently. "You *hear?* Fire!"

The fire engines arrived. They gushed water into the tenement. More bricks fell. Four of them smashed holes in the little house. I climbed to the roof, extinguished the small fires there, and scrambled down, my face dirty and my hands cut. The door to the little house opened. The quiet little Mexican and his wife stood in the doorway, solid and unmoved.

"Let me in!" I cried. "There's a hole in your roof; some sparks may have fallen in your bedroom!"

I pulled the door wide, pushed past them.

"No!" the little man grunted.

"Ah!" the little woman ran in a circle like a broken toy.

I was inside with a flashlight. The little man seized my arm. I smelled his breath.

And then my flashlight shot through the rooms of their house. Light sparkled on a hundred wine bottles standing in the hall, two hundred bottles shelved in the kitchen, six dozen along the parlor wallboards, more of the same on bedroom bureaus and in closets. I do not know if I was more impressed with the hole in the bedroom ceiling or the endless glitter of so many bottles. I lost count. It was like an invasion of gigantic shining beetles, struck dead, deposited, and left by some ancient disease.

In the bedroom I felt the little man and woman behind me in the doorway. I heard their loud breathing and I could feel their eyes. I raised the beam of my flashlight away from the glittering bottles, I focused it carefully, and for the rest of my visit, on the hole in the yellow ceiling.

The little woman began to cry. She cried softly. Nobody moved.

The next morning they left.

Before we even knew they were going, they were half down the alley at 6 A.M., carrying their luggage, which was light enough to be entirely empty. I tried to stop them. I talked to them. They were old friends, I said. Nothing had changed, I said. They had nothing to do with the fire, I said, or the roof. They were innocent bystanders, I *insisted!* I would fix the roof myself, no charge, no charge to them! But they did not look at

me. They looked at the house and at the open end of the alley ahead of them while I talked. Then, when I stopped they nodded to the alley as if agreeing that it was time to go, and walked off, and then began to run, it seemed, away from me, toward the street where there were streetcars and buses and automobiles and many loud avenues stretching in a maze. They hurried proudly, though, heads up, not looking back.

It was only by accident I ever met them again. At Christmas time, one evening, I saw the little man running quietly along the twilight street ahead of me. On a personal whim I followed. When he turned, I turned. At last, five blocks away from our old neighborhood, he scratched quietly at the door of a little white house. I saw the door open, shut, and lock him in. As night settled over the tenement city, a small light burned like blue mist in the tiny living room as I passed. I thought I saw, but probably imagined, two silhouettes there, he on his side of the room in his own particular chair, and she on her side of the room, sitting, sitting in the dark, and one or two bottles beginning to collect on the floor behind the chairs, and not a sound, not a sound between them. Only the silence.

I did not go up and knock. I strolled by. I walked on along the avenue, listening to the parrot cafés scream. I bought a newspaper, a magazine, and a quarter-edition book. Then I went home to where all the lights were lit and there was warm food upon the table.

THE SHORE LINE AT SUNSET

Tom, knee-deep in the waves, a piece of driftwood in his hand, listened.

The house, up toward the Coast Highway in the late afternoon, was silent. The sounds of closets being rummaged, suitcase locks snapping, vases being smashed, and of a final door crashing shut, all had faded away.

Chico, standing on the pale sand, flourished his wire strainer to shake out a harvest of lost coins. After a moment, without glancing at Tom, he said, "Let her go."

So it was every year. For a week or a month, their house would have music swelling from the windows, there would be new geraniums potted on the porch rail, new paint on the doors and steps. The clothes on the wire line changed from harlequin pants to sheath dresses to handmade Mexican frocks like white waves breaking behind the house. Inside, the paintings on the walls shifted from imitation Matisse to pseudo-Italian Renaissance. Sometimes, looking up, he would see a woman drying her hair like a bright yellow flag on the wind. Sometimes the flag was black or red. Sometimes the woman was tall, sometimes short, against the sky. But there was never more than one woman at a time. And, at last, a day like today came. . . .

Tom placed his driftwood on the growing pile near where Chico sifted the billion footprints left by people long vanished from their holidays.

"Chico. What are we doing here?"

"Living the life of Reilly, boy!"

"I don't feel like Reilly, Chico."

"Work at it, boy!"

Tom saw the house a month from now, the flowerpots blowing dust, the walls hung with empty squares, only sand carpeting the floors. The rooms would echo like shells in the wind. And all night every night bedded in separate rooms he and Chico would hear a tide falling away and away down a long shore, leaving no trace.

Tom nodded, imperceptibly. Once a year he himself brought a nice girl here, knowing she was right at last and that in no time they would be married. But his women always stole silently away before dawn, feeling they had been mistaken for someone else, not being able to play the part. Chico's friends left like vacuum cleaners, with a terrific drag, roar, rush, leaving no lint unturned, no clam unprized of its pearl, taking their purses with them like toy dogs which Chico had petted as he opened their jaws to count their teeth.

"That's four women so far this year."

"Okay, referee." Chico grinned. "Show me the way to the showers."

"Chico——" Tom bit his lower lip, then went on. "I been thinking. Why don't we split up?"

Chico just looked at him.

"I mean," said Tom, quickly, "maybe we'd have better luck, alone."

"Well, I'll be goddamned," said Chico slowly, gripping the strainer in his big fists before him. "Look here, boy, don't you know the facts? You and me, we'll be here come the year 2000. A couple of crazy dumb old gooney-birds drying their bones in the sun. Nothing's ever going to happen to us now, Tom, it's too late. Get that through your head and shut up."

Tom swallowed and looked steadily at the other man. "I'm thinking of leaving—next week."

"Shut up, shut up, and get to work!"

Chico gave the sand an angry showering rake that tilled him forty-three cents in dimes, pennies, and nickels. He stared blindly at the coins shimmering down the wires like a pinball game all afire.

Tom did not move, holding his breath.

They both seemed to be waiting for something.

The something happened.

"Hey . . . hey . . . hey . . ."

From a long way off down the coast a voice called.

The two men turned slowly.

"Hey . . . hey . . . oh, hey . . . !"

A boy was running, yelling, waving, along the shore two hundred yards away. There was something in his voice that made Tom feel suddenly cold. He held onto his own arms, waiting.

"Hey!"

The boy pulled up, gasping, pointing back along the shore.

"A woman, a funny woman, by the North Rock!"

"A woman!" The words exploded from Chico's mouth and he began to laugh. "Oh, no, no!"

"What you mean, a 'funny' woman?" asked Tom.

"I don't know," cried the boy, his eyes wide. "You got to come see! Awful funny!"

"You mean 'drowned'?"

"Maybe! She came out of the water, she's lying on the shore, you got to see, yourself . . . funny . . ." The boy's voice died. He gazed off north again. "She's got a fish's tail."

Chico laughed. "Not before supper, please."

"Please!" cried the boy, dancing now. "No lie! Oh, hurry!"

He ran off, sensed he was not followed, and looked back in dismay.

Tom felt his lips move. "Boy wouldn't run this far for a joke, would he, Chico?"

"People have run further for less."

Tom started walking. "All right, son."

"Thanks, mister, oh thanks!"

The boy ran. Twenty yards up the coast, Tom looked back. Behind him, Chico squinted, shrugged, dusted his hands wearily, and followed.

They moved north along the twilight beach, their skin weathered in tiny folds about their burnt pale eyes, looking younger for their hair cut close to the skull so you could not see the grey. There was a fair wind and the ocean rose and fell with prolonged concussions.

"What," said Tom, "what if we get to North Rock and it's true? The ocean *has* washed some *thing* up?"

But before Chico could answer, Tom was gone, his mind racing down coasts littered with horseshoe crabs, sand dollars, starfish, kelp, and stone. From all the times he'd talked on what lives in the sea, the names returned with the breathing fall of waves. Argonauts, they whispered, codlings, pollacks, houndfish, tautog, tench, sea elephant, they whispered, gillings, flounders, and beluga, the white whale, and grampus, the sea dog . . . always you thought how these must look from their deep-sounding names. Perhaps you would never in your life see them rise from the salt meadows beyond the safe limits of the shore, but they were there, and their names, with a thousand others, made pictures. And you looked and wished you were a frigate-bird that might fly nine thousand miles around to return some year with the full size of the ocean in your head.

"Oh, quick!" The boy had run back to peer in Tom's face. "It might be gone!"

"Keep your shirt on, boy," said Chico.

They came around the North Rock. A second boy stood there, looking down.

Perhaps from the corner of his eye, Tom saw something on the sand that made him hesitate to look straight at it, but fix instead on the face of the boy standing there. The boy was pale and he seemed not to breathe. On occasion he remembered to take a breath, his eyes focused, but the more they saw there on the sand

the more they took time off from focusing and turned blank and looked stunned. When the ocean came in over his tennis shoes, he did not move or notice.

Tom glanced away from the boy to the sand.

And Tom's face, in the next moment, became the face of the boy. His hands assumed the same curl at his sides and his mouth moved to open and stay half open and his eyes, which were light in color, seemed to bleach still more with so much looking.

The setting sun was ten minutes above the sea.

"A big wave came in and went out," said the first boy, "and here she was."

They looked at the woman lying there.

Her hair was very long and it lay on the beach like the threads of an immense harp. The water stroked along the threads and floated them up and let them down, each time in a different fan and silhouette. The hair must have been five or six feet long and now it was strewn on the hard wet sand and it was the color of limes.

Her face . . .

The men bent half down in wonder.

Her face was white sand sculpture, with a few water drops shimmering on it like summer rain upon a cream-colored rose. Her face was that moon which when seen by day is pale and unbelievable in the blue sky. It was milk-marble veined with faint violet in the temples. The eyelids, closed down upon the eyes, were powdered with a faint water color, as if the eyes beneath gazed through the fragile tissue of the lids and saw them standing there above her, looking down and looking down. The mouth was a pale flushed sea-rose, full and closed upon itself. And her neck was slender and white and her breasts were small and white, now covered, uncovered, covered, uncovered in the flow of water, the ebb of water, the flow, the ebb, the flow. And the breasts were flushed at their tips, and her body was startlingly white, almost an illumination, a white-green lightning against the sand. And as the water shifted her, her skin glinted like the surface of a pearl.

The lower half of her body changed itself from white to very pale blue, from very pale blue to pale green, from pale green to emerald green, to moss and lime green, to scintillas and sequins all dark green, all flowing away in a fount, a curve, a rush of light and dark, to end in a lacy fan, a spread of foam and jewel on the sand. The two halves of this creature were so joined as to reveal no point of fusion where pearl woman, woman of a whiteness made of cream-water and clear sky merged with that half which belonged to the amphibious slide and rush of current that came up on the shore and shelved down the shore, tugging its half toward its proper home. The woman was the sea, the sea was woman. There was no flaw or seam, no wrinkle or stitch; the illusion, if illusion it was, held perfectly together and the blood from one moved into and through and mingled with what must have been the ice waters of the other.

"I wanted to run get help." The first boy seemed not to want to raise his voice. "But Skip said she was dead and there's no help for that. Is she?"

"She was never alive," said Chico. "Sure," he went on, feeling their eyes on him suddenly. "It's something left over from a movie studio. Liquid rubber skinned over a steel frame. A prop, a dummy."

"Oh, no, it's real!"

"We'll find a label somewhere," said Chico. "Here."

"Don't!" cried the first boy.

"Hell." Chico touched the body to turn it, and stopped. He knelt there, his face changing.

"What's the matter?" asked Tom.

Chico took his hand away and looked at it. "I was wrong." His voice faded.

Tom took the woman's wrist. "There's a pulse."

"You're feeling your own heartbeat."

"I just don't know . . . maybe . . . maybe . . ."

The woman was there and her upper body was all moon pearl and tidal cream and her lower body all slithering ancient green-

black coins that slid upon themselves in the shift of wind and water.

"There's a trick somewhere!" cried Chico, suddenly.

"No. No!" Just as suddenly Tom burst out in laughter. "No trick! My God, my God, I feel great! I haven't felt so great since I was a kid!"

They walked slowly around her. A wave touched her white hand so the fingers faintly softly waved. The gesture was that of someone asking for another and another wave to come in and lift the fingers and then the wrist and then the arm and then the head and finally the body and take all of them together back down out to sea.

"Tom." Chico's mouth opened and closed. "Why don't you go get our truck?"

Tom didn't move.

"You hear me?" said Chico.

"Yes, but——"

"But what? We could sell this somewhere, I don't know—the university, that aquarium at Seal Beach or . . . well, hell, why couldn't we just set up a place? Look." He shook Tom's arm. "Drive to the pier. Buy us three hundred pounds of chipped ice. When you take anything out of the water you *need* ice, don't you?"

"I never thought."

"Think about it! Get moving!"

"I don't know, Chico."

"What you mean? She's real, isn't she?" He turned to the boys. "*You* say she's real, don't you? Well, then, what are we waiting for?"

"Chico," said Tom. "You better go get the ice yourself."

"Someone's got to stay and make sure she don't go back out with the tide!"

"Chico," said Tom. "I don't know how to explain. I don't want to get that ice for you."

"I'll go myself, then. Look, boys, build the sand up here to keep the waves back. I'll give you five bucks apiece. Hop to it!"

The sides of the boys' faces were bronze-pink from the sun which was touching the horizon now. Their eyes were a bronze color looking at Chico.

"My God!" said Chico. "This is better than finding ambergris!" He ran to the top of the nearest dune, called, "Get to work!" and was gone.

Now Tom and the two boys were left with the lonely woman by the North Rock and the sun was one-fourth of the way below the western horizon. The sand and the woman were pink-gold.

"Just a little line," whispered the second boy. He drew his fingernail along under his own chin, gently. He nodded to the woman. Tom bent again to see the faint line under either side of her firm white chin, the small, almost invisible line where the gills were or had been and were now almost sealed shut, invisible.

He looked at the face and the great strands of hair spread out in a lyre on the shore.

"She's beautiful," he said.

The boys nodded without knowing it.

Behind them, a gull leaped up quickly from the dunes. The boys gasped and turned to stare.

Tom felt himself trembling. He saw the boys were trembling too. A car horn hooted. Their eyes blinked, suddenly afraid. They looked up toward the highway.

A wave poured about the body, framing it in a clear white pool of water.

Tom nodded the boys to one side.

The wave moved the body an inch in and two inches out toward the sea.

The next wave came and moved the body two inches in and six inches out toward the sea.

"But——" said the first boy.

Tom shook his head.

The third wave lifted the body two feet down toward the sea. The wave after that drifted the body another foot down the shingles and the next three moved it six feet down.

The first boy cried out and ran after it.

Tom reached him and held his arm. The boy looked helpless and afraid and sad.

For a moment there were no more waves. Tom looked at the woman, thinking, she's true, she's real, she's mine . . . but . . . she's dead. Or will be if she stays here.

"We can't let her go," said the first boy. "We can't, we just can't!"

The other boy stepped between the woman and the sea. "What would we do with her?" he wanted to know, looking at Tom, "if we kept her?"

The first boy tried to think. "We could—we could——" He stopped and shook his head. "Oh, my Gosh."

The second boy stepped out of the way and left a path from the woman to the sea.

The next wave was a big one. It came in and went out and the sand was empty. The whiteness was gone and the black diamonds and the great threads of the harp.

They stood by the edge of the sea, looking out, the man and the two boys, until they heard the truck driving up on the dunes behind them.

The last of the sun was gone.

They heard footsteps running on the dunes and someone yelling.

They drove back down the darkening beach in the light truck with the big treaded tires in silence. The two boys sat in the rear on the bags of chipped ice. After a long while, Chico began to swear steadily, half to himself, spitting out the window.

"Three hundred pounds of ice. Three hundred *pounds* of ice! What do I do with it now? And I'm soaked to the skin, soaked! You didn't even move when I jumped in and swam out to look around! Idiot, idiot! You haven't changed! Like every other time, like always, you do nothing, nothing, just stand there, stand there, do nothing, nothing, just stare!"

"And what did you do, I ask, what?" said Tom, in a tired

voice, looking ahead. "The same as you always did, just the same, no different, no different at all. You should've seen yourself."

They dropped the boys off at their beach house. The youngest spoke in a voice you could hardly hear against the wind. "Gosh, nobody'll ever believe . . ."

The two men drove down the coast and parked.

Chico sat for two or three minutes waiting for his fists to relax on his lap, and then he snorted.

"Hell. I guess things turn out for the best." He took a deep breath. "It just came to me. Funny. Twenty, thirty years from now, middle of the night, our phone'll ring. It'll be one of those two boys, grown-up, calling long-distance from a bar somewhere. Middle of the night, them calling to ask one question. It's *true*, isn't it? they'll say. It *did* happen, didn't it? Back in 1958, it really happened to *us?* And we'll sit there on the edge of the bed, middle of the night, saying, Sure, boy, sure, it really happened to us in 1958. And they'll say, Thanks, and we'll say, Don't mention it, any old time. And we'll all say good night. And maybe they won't call again for a couple of years."

The two men sat on their front-porch steps in the dark.

"Tom?"

"What?"

Chico waited a moment.

"Tom, next week—you're not going away."

It was not a question but a quiet statement.

Tom thought about it, his cigarette dead in his fingers. And he knew that now he could never go away. For tomorrow and the day after the day after that he would walk down and go swimming there in all the green and white fires and the dark caverns in the hollows under the strange waves. Tomorrow and tomorrow and tomorrow.

"Yes, Chico. I'm staying here."

Now the silver looking glasses advanced in a crumpling line all along the coast from a thousand miles north to a thousand miles south. The mirrors did not reflect so much as one building or one tree or one highway or one car or even one man himself.

The mirrors reflected only the quiet moon and then shattered into a billion bits of glass that spread out in a glaze on the shore. Then the sea was dark awhile, preparing another line of mirrors to rear up and surprise the two men who sat there for a long time never once blinking their eyes, waiting.

THE STRAWBERRY WINDOW

In his dream he was shutting the front door with its strawberry windows and lemon windows and windows like white clouds and windows like clear water in a country stream. Two dozen panes squared round the one big pane, colored of fruit wines and gelatins and cool water ices. He remembered his father holding him up as a child. "Look!" And through the green glass the world was emerald, moss, and summer mint. "Look!" The lilac pane made livid grapes of all the passersby. And at last the strawberry glass perpetually bathed the town in roseate warmth, carpeted the world in pink sunrise, and made the cut lawn seem imported from some Persian rug bazaar. The strawberry window, best of all, cured people of their paleness, warmed the cold rain, and set the blowing, shifting February snows afire.

"Yes, yes! There——!"

He awoke.

He heard his boys talking before he was fully out of his dream and he lay in the dark now, listening to the sad sound their talk made, like the wind blowing the white sea-bottoms into the blue hills, and then he remembered.

Originally published in *Star Science Fiction Stories #3*, published by Ballantine Books, Inc.

We're on Mars, he thought.

"What?" His wife cried out in her sleep.

He hadn't realized he had spoken; he lay as still as he possibly could. But now, with a strange kind of numb reality, he saw his wife rise to haunt the room, her pale face staring through the small, high windows of their quonset hut at the clear but unfamiliar stars.

"Carrie," he whispered.

She did not hear.

"Carrie," he whispered. "There's something I want to tell you. For a month now I've been wanting to say . . . tomorrow . . . tomorrow morning, there's going to be . . ."

But his wife sat all to herself in the blue starlight and would not look at him.

If only the sun stayed up, he thought, if only there was no night. For during the day he nailed the settlement town together, the boys were in school, and Carrie had cleaning, gardening, cooking to do. But when the sun was gone and their hands were empty of flowers or hammers and nails and arithmetics, their memories, like night birds, came home in the dark.

His wife moved, a slight turn of her head.

"Bob," she said at last, "I want to go home."

"Carrie!"

"This isn't home," she said.

He saw that her eyes were wet and brimming. "Carrie, hold on awhile."

"I've got no fingernails from holding on now!"

As if she still moved in her sleep, she opened her bureau drawers and took out layers of handkerchiefs, shirts, underclothing, and put it all on top of the bureau, not seeing it, letting her fingers touch and bring it out and put it down. The routine was long familiar now. She would talk and put things out and stand quietly awhile, and then later put all the things away and come, dryfaced, back to bed and dreams. He was afraid that some night she would empty every drawer and reach for the few ancient suitcases against the wall.

"Bob . . ." Her voice was not bitter, but soft, featureless, and as uncolored as the moonlight that showed what she was doing. "So many nights for six months I've talked this way; I'm ashamed. You work hard building houses in town. A man who works so hard shouldn't have to listen to a wife gone sad on him. But there's nothing to do but talk it out. It's the little things I miss most of all. I don't know—silly things. Our front-porch swing. The wicker rocking chair, summer nights. Looking at the people walk or ride by those evenings, back in Ohio. Our black upright piano, out of tune. My Swedish cut glass. Our parlor furniture— oh, it was like a herd of elephants, I know, and all of it old. And the Chinese hanging crystals that hit when the wind blew. And talking to neighbors there on the front porch, July nights. All those crazy, silly things . . . they're not important. But it seems those are things that come to mind around three in the morning. I'm sorry."

"Don't be," he said. "Mars is a far place. It smells funny, looks funny, and feels funny. I think to myself nights too. We came from a nice town."

"It was green," she said. "In the spring and summer. And yellow and red in the fall. And ours was a nice house; my, it was old, eighty–ninety years or so. Used to hear the house talking at night, whispering away. All the dry wood, the banisters, the front porch, the sills. Wherever you touched, it talked to you. Every room a different way. And when you had the whole house talking, it was a family around you in the dark, putting you to sleep. No other house, the kind they build nowadays, can be the same. A lot of people have got to go through and live in a house to make it mellow down all over. This place here, now, this hut, it doesn't know I'm in it, doesn't care if I live or die. It makes a noise like tin, and tin's cold. It's got no pores for the years to sink in. It's got no cellar for you to put things away for next year and the year after that. It's got no attic where you keep things from last year and all the other years before you were born. If we only had a little bit up here that was familiar, Bob, then we could make room for all

that's strange. But when everything, *every single thing* is strange, then it takes forever to make things familiar."

He nodded in the dark. "There's nothing you say that I haven't thought."

She was looking at the moonlight where it lay upon the suitcases against the wall. He saw her move her hand down toward them.

"Carrie!"

"What?"

He swung his legs out of bed. "Carrie, I've done a crazy damn-fool thing. All these months I heard you dreaming away, scared, and the boys at night and the wind, and Mars out there, the sea-bottoms and all, and . . ." He stopped and swallowed. "You got to understand what I did and why I did it. All the money we had in the bank a month ago, all the money we saved for ten years, I spent."

"Bob!"

"I threw it away, Carrie, I swear, I threw it away on nothing. It was going to be a surprise. But now, tonight, there you are, and there are those damned suitcases on the floor and . . ."

"Bob," she said, turning around. "You mean we've gone through all *this,* on Mars, putting away extra money every week, only to have you burn it up in a few hours?"

"I don't know," he said. "I'm a crazy fool. Look, it's not long till morning. We'll get up early. I'll take you down to see what I've done. I don't want to tell you, I want you to see. And if it's no go, then, well, there's always those suitcases and the rocket to Earth four times a week."

She did not move. "Bob, Bob," she murmured.

"Don't say any more," he said.

"Bob, Bob . . ." She shook her head slowly, unbelievingly. He turned away and lay back down on his own side of the bed, and she sat on the other side, and for a moment did not lie down, but only sat looking at the bureau where her handkerchiefs and jewelry and clothing lay ready in neat stacks where she had left them.

Outside a wind the color of moonlight stirred up the sleeping dust and powdered the air.

At last she lay back, but said nothing more and was a cold weight in the bed, staring down the long tunnel of night toward the faintest sign of morning.

They got up in the very first light and moved in the small quonset hut without a sound. It was a pantomime prolonged almost to the time when someone might scream at the silence, as the mother and father and the boys washed and dressed and ate a quiet breakfast of toast and fruit juice and coffee, with no one looking directly at anyone and everyone watching someone in the reflective surfaces of toaster, glassware, or cutlery, where all their faces were melted out of shape and made terribly alien in the early hour. Then, at last, they opened the quonset door and let in the air that blew across the cold blue-white Martian seas, where only the sand tides dissolved and shifted and made ghost patterns, and they stepped out under a raw and staring cold sky and began their walk toward a town, which seemed no more than a motion-picture set far on ahead of them on a vast, empty stage.

"What part of town are we going to?" asked Carrie.

"The rocket depot," he said. "But before we get there, I've a lot to say."

The boys slowed down and moved behind their parents, listening. The father gazed ahead, and not once in all the time he was talking did he look at his wife or sons to see how they were taking all that he said.

"I believe in Mars," he began quietly. "I guess I believe some day it'll belong to us. We'll nail it down. We'll settle in. We won't turn tail and run. It came to me one day a year ago, right after we first arrived. Why did we come? I asked myself. Because, I said, because. It's the same thing with the salmon every year. The salmon don't know why they go where they go, but they go, anyway. Up rivers they don't remember, up streams, jumping waterfalls, but finally making it to where they propagate and die, and the

whole thing starts again. Call it racial memory, instinct, call it nothing, but there it is. And here we are."

They walked in the silent morning with the great sky watching them and the strange blue and steam-white sands sifting about their feet on the new highway.

"So here we are. And from Mars where? Jupiter, Neptune, Pluto, and on out? Right. *And on out.* Why? Some day the sun will blow up like a leaky furnace. Boom—there goes Earth. But maybe Mars won't be hurt; or if Mars is hurt maybe Pluto won't be, or if Pluto's hurt, then where'll *we* be, our sons' sons, that is?"

He gazed steadily up into that flawless shell of plum-colored sky.

"Why, we'll be on some world with a number maybe; planet 6 of star system 97, planet 2 of system 99! So damn far off from here you need a nightmare to take it in! We'll be gone, do you see, gone off away and safe! And I thought to myself, ah, ah. So that's the reason we came to Mars, so *that's* the reason men shoot off their rockets."

"Bob——"

"Let me finish; not to make money, no. Not to see the sights, no. Those are the lies men tell, the fancy reasons they give themselves. Get rich, get famous, they say. Have fun, jump around, they say. But all the while, inside, something else is ticking along the way it ticks in salmon or whales, the way it ticks, by God, in the smallest microbe you want to name. And that little clock that ticks in everything living, you know what it says? It says get away, spread out, move along, keep swimming. Run to so many worlds and build so many towns that *nothing* can ever kill man. You *see,* Carrie? It's not just us come to Mars, it's the race, the whole darn human race, depending on how *we* make out in our lifetime. This thing is so big I want to laugh, I'm so scared stiff of it."

He felt the boys walking steadily behind him and he felt Carrie beside him and he wanted to see her face and how she was taking all this, but he didn't look there, either.

"All this is no different than me and Dad walking the fields when I was a boy, casting seed by hand when our seeder broke

down and we'd no money to fix it. It had to be done, somehow, for the later crops. My God, Carrie, my God, you *remember* those Sunday-supplement articles, THE EARTH WILL FREEZE IN A MILLION YEARS! I bawled once, as a boy, reading articles like that. My mother asked why. I'm bawling for all those poor people up ahead, I said. Don't worry about them, Mother said. But, Carrie, that's my whole point; we *are* worrying about them. Or we wouldn't be here. It matters if Man with a capital M keeps going. There's nothing better than Man with a capital M in my books. I'm prejudiced, of course, because I'm one of the breed. But if there's any way to get hold of that immortality men are always talking about, this is the way—spread out—seed the universe. Then you got a harvest against crop failures anywhere down the line. No matter if Earth has famines or the rust comes in. You got the new wheat lifting on Venus or where-in-hell-ever man gets to in the next thousand years, I'm crazy with the idea, Carrie, crazy. When I finally hit on it I got so excited I wanted to grab people, you, the boys, and tell them. But hell, I knew that wasn't necessary. I knew a day or night would come when you'd hear that ticking in yourselves too, and then you'd see, and no one'd have to say anything again about all this. It's big talk, Carrie, I know, and big thoughts for a man just short of five feet five, but by all that's holy, it's true."

They moved through the deserted streets of the town and listened to the echoes of their walking feet.

"And this morning?" said Carrie.

"I'm coming to this morning," he said. "Part of *me* wants to go home too. But the other part says if we go, everything's lost. So I thought, what bothers us most? Some of the things we once had. Some of the boys' things, your things, mine. And I thought, if it takes an old thing to get a new thing started, by God, I'll use the old thing. I remember from history books that a thousand years ago they put charcoals in a hollowed out cow horn, blew on them during the day, so they carried their fire on marches from place to place, to start a fire every night with the sparks left over from morning. Always a new fire, but always something of the old in

it. So I weighed and balanced it off. Is the Old worth all our money? I asked. No! It's only the things we *did* with the Old that have any worth. Well, then, is the New worth *all* our money? I asked. Do you feel like investing in the day after the middle of next week? Yes! I said. If I can fight this thing that makes us want to go back to Earth, I'd dip my money in kerosene and strike a match!"

Carrie and the two boys did not move. They stood on the street, looking at him as if he were a storm that had passed over and around, almost blowing them from the ground, a storm that was now dying away.

"The freight rocket came in this morning," he said, quietly. "Our delivery's on it. Let's go and pick it up."

They walked slowly up the three steps into the rocket depot and across the echoing floor toward the freight room that was just sliding back its doors, opening for the day.

"Tell us again about the salmon," said one of the boys.

In the middle of the warm morning they drove out of town in a rented truck filled with great crates and boxes and parcels and packages, long ones, tall ones, short ones, flat ones, all numbered and neatly addressed to one Robert Prentiss, New Toledo, Mars.

They stopped the truck by the quonset hut and the boys jumped down and helped their mother out. For a moment Bob sat behind the wheel, and then slowly got out himself to walk around and look into the back of the truck at the crates.

And by noon all but one of the boxes were opened and their contents placed on the sea-bottom where the family stood among them.

"Carrie . . ."

And he led her up the old porch steps that now stood uncrated on the edge of town.

"Listen to 'em, Carrie."

The steps squeaked and whispered underfoot.

"What do they say, tell me what they say?"

She stood on the ancient wooden steps, holding to herself, and could not tell him.

He waved his hand. "Front porch here, living room there, dining room, kitchen, three bedrooms. Part we'll build new, part we'll bring. Of course all we got here now is the front porch, some parlor furniture, and the old bed."

"All that money, Bob!"

He turned, smiling. "You're not mad, now, look at me! You're not mad. We'll bring it all up, next year, five years! The cut-glass vases, that Armenian carpet your mother gave us in 1961! Just *let* the sun explode!"

They looked at the other crates, numbered and lettered: Front-porch swing, front-porch wicker rocker, hanging Chinese crystals . . .

"I'll blow them myself to make them ring."

They set the front door, with its little panes of colored glass, on the top of the stairs, and Carrie looked through the strawberry window.

"What do you see?"

But he knew what she saw, for he gazed through the colored glass, too. And there was Mars, with its cold sky warmed and its dead seas fired with color, with its hills like mounds of strawberry ice, and its sand like burning charcoals sifted by wind. The strawberry window, the strawberry window, breathed soft rose colors on the land and filled the mind and the eye with the light of a never-ending dawn. Bent there, looking through, he heard himself say:

"The town'll be out this way in a year. This'll be a shady street, you'll have your porch, and you'll have friends. You won't *need* all this so much, then. But starting right here, with this little bit that's familiar, watch it spread, watch Mars change so you'll know it as if you've known it all your life."

He ran down the steps to the last and as-yet unopened canvas-covered crate. With his pocket knife he cut a hole in the canvas. "Guess!" he said.

"My kitchen stove? My furnace?"

"Not in a million years." He smiled very gently. "Sing me a song," he said.

"Bob, you're clean off your head."

"Sing me a song worth all the money we had in the bank and now don't have, but who gives a blast in hell," he said.

"I don't know anything but 'Genevieve, Sweet Genevieve!' "

"Sing that," he said.

But she could not open her mouth and start the song. He saw her lips move and try, but there was no sound.

He ripped the canvas wider and shoved his hand into the crate and touched around for a quiet moment, and started to sing the words himself until he moved his hand a last time and then a single clear piano chord sprang out on the morning air.

"There," he said. "Let's take it right on to the end. Everyone! Here's the harmony."

22

THE DAY IT RAINED FOREVER

The hotel stood like a hollowed dry bone under the very center of the desert sky where the sun burned the roof all day. All night, the memory of the sun stirred in every room like the ghost of an old forest fire. Long after dusk, since light meant heat, the hotel lights stayed off. The inhabitants of the hotel preferred to feel their way blind through the halls in their never-ending search for cool air.

This one particular evening Mr. Terle, the proprietor, and his only boarders, Mr. Smith and Mr. Fremley, who looked and smelled like two ancient rags of cured tobacco, stayed late on the long veranda. In their creaking glockenspiel rockers they gasped back and forth in the dark, trying to rock up a wind.

"Mr. Terle . . . ? Wouldn't it be *really* nice . . . someday . . . if you could buy . . . air conditioning . . . ?"

Mr. Terle coasted awhile, eyes shut.

"Got no money for such things, Mr. Smith."

The two old boarders flushed; they hadn't paid a bill now in twenty-one years.

Much later Mr. Fremley sighed a grievous sigh. "Why, why don't we all just quit, pick up, get outa here, move to a decent city? Stop this swelterin' and fryin' and sweatin'."

"Who'd buy a dead hotel in a ghost town?" said Mr. Terle quietly. "No. No, we'll just set here and wait, wait for that great day, January 29."

Slowly, all three men stopped rocking.

January 29.

The one day in all the year when it really let go and rained.

"Won't wait long." Mr. Smith tilted his gold railroad watch like the warm summer moon in his palm. "Two hours and nine minutes from now it'll *be* January 29. But I don't see nary a cloud in ten thousand miles."

"It's rained every January 29 since I was born!" Mr. Terle stopped, surprised at his own loud voice. "If it's a day late this year, I won't pull God's shirttail."

Mr. Fremley swallowed hard and looked from east to west across the desert toward the hills. "I wonder . . . will there ever be a gold rush hereabouts again?"

"No gold," said Mr. Smith. "And what's more, I'll make you a bet—no rain. No rain tomorrow or the day after the day after tomorrow. No rain all the rest of this year."

The three old men sat staring at the big sun-yellowed moon that burned a hole in the high stillness.

After a long while, painfully, they began to rock again.

The first hot morning breezes curled the calendar pages like a dried snake skin against the flaking hotel front.

The three men, thumbing their suspenders up over their hat rack shoulders, came barefoot downstairs to blink out at that idiot sky.

"January 29 . . ."

"Not a drop of mercy there."

"Day's young."

"*I'm* not." Mr. Fremley turned and went away.

It took him five minutes to find his way up through the delirious hallways to his hot, freshly baked bed.

At noon, Mr. Terle peered in.

"Mr. Fremley . . . ?"

"Damn desert cactus, that's us!" gasped Mr. Fremley, lying there, his face looking as if at any moment it might fall away in a blazing dust on the raw plank floor. "But even the best damn cactus got to have just a sip of water before it goes back to another year of the same damn furnace. I tell you I won't move again, I'll lie here an' die if I don't hear more than birds pattin' around up on that roof!"

"Keep your prayers simple and your umbrella handy," said Mr. Terle and tiptoed away.

At dusk, on the hollow roof a faint pattering sounded.

Mr. Fremley's voice sang out mournfully from his bed.

"Mr. Terle, that ain't rain! That's you with the garden hose sprinklin' well water on the roof! Thanks for tryin', but cut it out, now."

The pattering sound stopped. There was a sigh from the yard below.

Coming around the side of the hotel a moment later, Mr. Terle saw the calendar fly out and down in the dust.

"Damn January 29!" cried a voice. "Twelve more months! Have to wait twelve more months, now!"

Mr. Smith was standing there in the doorway. He stepped inside and brought out two dilapidated suitcases and thumped them on the porch.

"Mr. Smith!" cried Mr. Terle. "You can't leave after thirty years!"

"They say it rains twenty days a month in Ireland," said Mr. Smith. "I'll get a job there and run around with my hat off and my mouth open."

"You can't go!" Mr. Terle tried frantically to think of something; he snapped his fingers. "You owe me nine thousand dollars rent!"

Mr. Smith recoiled; his eyes got a look of tender and unexpected hurt in them.

"I'm sorry." Mr. Terle looked away. "I didn't mean that. Look now—you just head for Seattle. Pours two inches a week there. Pay me when you can, or never. But do me a favor: wait till mid-

night. It's cooler then, anyhow. Get you a good night's walk toward the city."

"Nothin'll happen between now and midnight."

"You got to have faith. When everything else is gone, you got to believe a thing'll happen. Just stand here with me, you don't have to sit, just stand here and think of rain. That's the last thing I'll ever ask of you."

On the desert sudden little whirlwinds of dust twisted up, sifted down. Mr. Smith's eyes scanned the sunset horizon.

"What do I think? Rain, oh you rain, come along here? Stuff like that?"

"Anything. Anything at all!"

Mr. Smith stood for a long time between his two mangy suitcases and did not move. Five, six minutes ticked by. There was no sound, save the two men's breathing in the dusk.

Then at last, very firmly, Mr. Smith stooped to grasp the luggage handles.

Just then, Mr. Terle blinked. He leaned forward, cupping his hand to his ear.

Mr. Smith froze, his hands still on the luggage.

From away among the hills, a murmur, a soft and tremulous rumble.

"Storm coming!" hissed Mr. Terle.

The sound grew louder; a kind of whitish cloud rose up from the hills.

Mr. Smith stood tall on tiptoe.

Upstairs Mr. Fremley sat up like Lazarus.

Mr. Terle's eyes grew wider and yet wider to take hold of what was coming. He held to the porch rail like the captain of a calm-foundered vessel feeling the first stir of some tropic breeze that smelled of lime and the ice-cool white meat of coconut. The smallest wind stroked over his aching nostrils as over the flues of a white-hot chimney.

"There!" cried Mr. Terle. "There!"

And over the last hill, shaking out feathers of fiery dust, came the cloud, the thunder, the racketing storm.

Over the hill the first car to pass in twenty days flung itself down the valley with a shriek, a thud, and a wail.

Mr. Terle did not dare to look at Mr. Smith.

Mr. Smith looked up, thinking of Mr. Fremley in his room.

Mr. Fremley, at the window, looked down and saw the car expire and die in front of the hotel.

For the sound that the car made was curiously final. It had come a very long way on blazing sulphur roads, across salt flats abandoned ten million years ago by the shingling off of waters. Now, with wire-ravelings like cannibal hair sprung up from seams, with a great eyelid of canvas top thrown back and melted to spearmint gum over the rear seat, the auto, a Kissel car, vintage 1924, gave a final shuddering as if to expel its ghost upon the air.

The old woman in the front seat of the car waited patiently, looking in at the three men and the hotel as if to say, Forgive me, my friend is ill; I've known him a long while, and now I must see him through his final hour. So she just sat in the car waiting for the faint convulsions to cease and for the great relaxation of all the bones which signifies that the final process is over. She must have sat a full half minute longer listening to her car, and there was something so peaceful about her that Mr. Terle and Mr. Smith leaned slowly toward her. At last she looked at them with a grave smile and raised her hand.

Mr. Fremley was surprised to see his hand go out the window, above and wave back to her.

On the porch Mr. Smith murmured, "Strange. It's not a storm. And I'm not disappointed. How come?"

But Mr. Terle was down the path and to the car.

"We thought you were . . . that is . . ." He trailed off. "Terle's my name, Joe Terle."

She took his hand and looked at him with absolutely clear and unclouded light blue eyes like water that has melted from snow a thousand miles off and come a long way, purified by wind and sun.

"Miss Blanche Hillgood," she said, quietly. "Graduate of the Grinnell College, unmarried teacher of music, thirty years high-

school glee club and student orchestra conductor, Green City, Iowa, twenty years private teacher of piano, harp, and voice, one month retired and living on a pension and now, taking my roots with me, on my way to California."

"Miss Hillgood, you don't look to be going anywhere from here."

"I had a feeling about that." She watched the two men circle the car cautiously. She sat like a child on the lap of a rheumatic grandfather, undecided. "Is there nothing we can do?"

"Make a fence of the wheels, dinner gong of the brake drums, the rest'll make a fine rock garden."

Mr. Fremley shouted from the sky. "Dead? I say, is the car dead? I can *feel* it from here! Well—it's way past time for supper!"

Mr. Terle put out his hand. "Miss Hillgood, that there is Joe Terle's Desert Hotel, open twenty-six hours a day. Gila monsters and road runners please register before going upstairs. Get you a night's sleep, free, we'll knock our Ford off its blocks and drive you to the city come morning."

She let herself be helped from the car. The machine groaned as if in protest at her going. She shut the door carefully with a soft click.

"One friend gone, but the other still with me. Mr. Terle, could you please bring her in out of the weather?"

"Her, ma'am?"

"Forgive me, I never think of things but what they're people. The car was a man, I suppose, because it took me places. But a harp, now, don't you agree, is female?"

She nodded to the rear seat of the car. There, tilted against the sky like an ancient scrolled leather ship prow cleaving the wind, stood a case which towered above any driver who might sit up in front and sail the desert calms or the city traffics.

"Mr. Smith," said Mr. Terle, "lend a hand."

They untied the huge case and hoisted it gingerly out between them.

"What you got there?" cried Mr. Fremley from above.

Mr. Smith stumbled. Miss Hillgood gasped. The case shifted in the two men's arms.

From within the case came a faint musical humming.

Mr. Fremley, above, heard. It was all the answer he needed. Mouth open, he watched the lady and the two men and their boxed friend sway and vanish in the cavernous porch below.

"Watch out!" said Mr. Smith. "Some damn fool left his luggage here——" He stopped. "Some damn fool? *Me!*"

The two men looked at each other. They were not perspiring any more. A wind had come up from somewhere, a gentle wind that fanned their shirt collars and flapped the strewn calendar gently in the dust.

"*My* luggage . . ." said Mr. Smith.

Then they all went inside.

"More wine, Miss Hillgood? Ain't had wine on the table in years."

"Just a touch, if you please."

They sat by the light of a single candle which made the room an oven and struck fire from the good silverware and the un-cracked plates as they talked and drank warm wine and ate.

"Miss Hillgood, get on with your life."

"All my life," she said, "I've been so busy running from Bee-thoven to Bach to Brahms, I never noticed I was twenty-nine. Next time I looked up I was forty. Yesterday, seventy-one. Oh, there were men; but they'd given up singing at ten and given up flying when they were twelve. I always figured we were born to fly, one way or other, so I couldn't stand most men shuffling along with all the iron of the earth in their blood. I never met a man who weighed less than nine hundred pounds. In their black busi-ness suits, you could hear them roll by like funeral wagons."

"So you flew away?"

"Just in my mind, Mr. Terle. It's taken sixty years to make the final break. All that time I grabbed onto piccolos and flutes and violins because they make streams in the air, you know, like streams and rivers on the ground. I rode every tributary and tried

every fresh-water wind from Handel on down to a whole slew of
Strausses. It's been the far way around that's brought me here."

"How'd you finally make up your mind to leave?" asked Mr.
Smith.

"I looked around last week and said, 'Why, look, you've been
flying *alone!*' No one in all Green City really cares *if* you fly or
how high you go. It's always, 'Fine, Blanche,' or 'thanks for the
recital at the PTA tea, Miss H.' But no one really listening. And
when I talked a long time ago about Chicago or New York, folks
swatted me and laughed. 'Why be a little frog in a big pond when
you can be the biggest frog in all Green City!' So I stayed on,
while the folks who gave me advice moved away or died or both.
The rest had wax in their ears. Just last week I shook myself and
said, 'Hold on! Since when do *frogs* have wings?' "

"So now you're headin' west?" said Mr. Terle.

"Maybe to play in pictures or in that orchestra under the stars.
But somewhere I just must play at last for someone who'll hear
and really listen. . . ."

They sat there in the warm dark. She was finished, she had said
it all now, foolish or not—and she moved back quietly in her
chair.

Upstairs someone coughed.

Miss Hillgood heard, and rose.

It took Mr. Fremley a moment to ungum his eyelids and make
out the shape of the woman bending down to place the tray by
his rumpled bed.

"What you all talking about down there just now?"

"I'll come back later and tell you word for word," said Miss
Hillgood. "Eat now. The salad's fine." She moved to leave the
room.

He said, quickly, "You goin' to stay?"

She stopped half out the door and tried to trace the expression
on his sweating face in the dark. He, in turn, could not see her
mouth or eyes. She stood a moment longer, silently, then went
on down the stairs.

"She must not've heard me," said Mr. Fremley.

But he knew she had heard.

Miss Hillgood crossed the downstairs lobby to fumble with the locks on the upright leather case.

"I must pay you for my supper."

"On the house," said Mr. Terle.

"I must pay," she said, and opened the case.

There was a sudden flash of gold.

The two men quickened in their chairs. They squinted at the little old woman standing beside the tremendous heart-shaped object which towered above her with its shining columbined pedestal atop which a calm Grecian face with antelope eyes looked serenely at them even as Miss Hillgood looked now.

The two men shot each other the quickest and most startled of glances, as if each had guessed what might happen next. They hurried across the lobby, breathing hard, to sit on the very edge of the hot velvet lounge, wiping their faces with damp handkerchiefs.

Miss Hillgood drew a chair under her, rested the golden harp gently back on her shoulder, and put her hands to the strings.

Mr. Terle took a breath of fiery air and waited.

A desert wind came suddenly along the porch outside, tilting the chairs so they rocked this way and that like boats on a pond at night.

Mr. Fremley's voice protested from above. "What's goin' on down there?"

And then Miss Hillgood moved her hands.

Starting at the arch near her shoulder, she played her fingers out along the simple tapestry of wires toward the blind and beautiful stare of the Greek goddess on her column, and then back. Then for a moment she paused and let the sounds drift up through the baked lobby air and into all the empty rooms.

If Mr. Fremley shouted, above, no one heard. For Mr. Terle and Mr. Smith were so busy jumping up to stand riven in the shadows, they heard nothing save the storming of their own hearts and the shocked rush of all the air in their lungs. Eyes

wide, mouths dropped, in a kind of pure insanity, they stared at
the two women there, the blind Muse proud on her golden pillar, and the seated one, gentle eyes closed, her small hands
stretched forth on the air.

Like a girl, they both thought wildly, like a little girl putting
her hands out a window to feel what? Why, of course, of course!

To feel the rain.

The echo of the first shower vanished down remote causeways
and roof drains, away.

Mr. Fremley, above, rose from his bed as if pulled round by
his ears.

Miss Hillgood played.

She played and it wasn't a tune they knew at all, but it was a
tune they had heard a thousand times in their long lives, words
or not, melody or not. She played and each time her fingers
moved, the rain fell pattering through the dark hotel. The rain
fell cool at the open windows and the rain rinsed down the baked
floor boards of the porch. The rain fell on the roof top and fell
on hissing sand, it fell on rusted car and empty stable and dead
cactus in the yard. It washed the windows and laid the dust and
filled the rain barrels and curtained the doors with beaded
threads that might part and whisper as you walked through. But
more than anything the soft touch and coolness of it fell on Mr.
Smith and Mr. Terle. Its gentle weight and pressure moved
them down and down until it had seated them again. By its continuous budding and prickling on their faces it made them shut
up their eyes and mouths and raise their hands to shield it away.
Seated there, they felt their heads tilt slowly back to let the rain
fall where it would.

The flash flood lasted a minute, then faded away as the fingers
trailed down the loom, let drop a few last bursts and squalls and
then stopped.

The last chord hung in the air like a picture taken when lightning strikes and freezes a billion drops of water on their down-
ward flight. Then the lightning went out. The last drops fell
through darkness in silence.

Miss Hillgood took her hands from the strings, her eyes still shut.

Mr. Terle and Mr. Smith opened their eyes to see those two miraculous women way over there across the lobby somehow come through the storm untouched and dry.

They trembled. They leaned forward as if they wished to speak. They looked helpless, not knowing what to do.

And then a single sound from high above in the hotel corridors drew their attention and told them what to do.

The sound came floating down feebly, fluttering like a tired bird beating its ancient wings.

The two men looked up and listened.

It was the sound of Mr. Fremley.

Mr. Fremley, in his room, applauding.

It took five seconds for Mr. Terle to figure out what it was. Then he nudged Mr. Smith and began, himself, to beat his palms together. The two men struck their hands in mighty explosions. The echoes ricocheted around about in the hotel caverns above and below, striking walls, mirrors, windows, trying to fight free of the rooms.

Miss Hillgood opened her eyes now, as if this new storm had come on her in the open, unprepared.

The men gave their own recital. They smashed their hands together so fervently it seemed they had fistfuls of firecrackers to set off, one on another. Mr. Fremley shouted. Nobody heard. Hands winged out, banged shut again and again until fingers puffed up and the old men's breath came short and they put their hands at last on their knees, a heart pounding inside each one.

Then, very slowly, Mr. Smith got up and still looking at the harp, went outside and carried in the suitcases. He stood at the foot of the lobby stairs looking for a long while at Miss Hillgood. He glanced down at her single piece of luggage resting there by the first tread. He looked from her suitcase to her and raised his eyebrows questioningly.

Miss Hillgood looked at her harp, at her suitcase, at Mr. Terle, and at last back to Mr. Smith.

She nodded once.

Mr. Smith bent down and with his own luggage under one arm and her suitcase in the other, he started the long slow climb up the stairs in the gentle dark. As he moved, Miss Hillgood put the harp back on her shoulder and either played in time to his moving or he moved in time to her playing, neither of them knew which.

Half up the flight, Mr. Smith met Mr. Fremley who, in a faded robe, was testing his slow way down.

Both stood there, looking deep into the lobby at the one man on the far side in the shadows, and the two women further over, no more than a motion and a gleam. Both thought the same thoughts.

The sound of the harp playing, the sound of the cool water falling every night and every night of their lives, after this. No spraying the roof with the garden hose now any more. Only sit on the porch or lie in your night bed and hear the falling . . . the falling . . . the falling . . .

Mr. Smith moved on up the stair; Mr. Fremley moved down.

The harp, the harp. Listen, listen!

The fifty years of drought were over.

The time of the long rains had come.